"What d'ye plan on doing with me?"

He gave her no time to think, to catch her breath, to pull away . . . if she had a mind and the strength to do so.

Caitrina had been kissed a few years back by young John MacKinnon. But she knew, as the captain's beguiling mouth dipped down to hers, that this kiss was going to be very, very different.

There was nothing gentle or curious about it. His mouth covered hers with dominance and scalding heat while he dragged her in against the rigid, flat lines of his body. He kissed her until she began to believe he had every right to do so—until her knees went weak and a slight gasp escaped her lips.

He finally broke away with a slow, seductive smile she wanted to gaze at for years to come.

She slapped him hard across his face.

Tamed by a Highlander

Seduced by a Highlander

"*Seduced by a Highlander* is sparkling, sexy, and seductive! I couldn't put it down! Paula Quinn is a rising star!"
— Karen Hawkins, *New York Times* bestselling author

"Top Pick! An engrossing story brimming with atmosphere and passionate characters...a true keeper."
— *RT Book Reviews*

"Scottish romance at its very best! Deliciously romantic and sensual, Paula Quinn captures the heart of the Highlands in a tender, passionate romance that you won't be able to put down."
— Monica McCarty, *New York Times* bestselling author

Ravished by a Highlander

"Deftly combines historical fact and powerful romance... There's much more than just sizzling sensuality: history buffs will love the attention to period detail and cameos by real-life figures, and the protagonists embody compassion, responsibility, and unrelenting, almost self-sacrificial honor. Quinn's seamless prose and passionate storytelling will leave readers hungry for future installments."
— *Publishers Weekly* (starred review)

"4½ Stars! Top Pick! Quinn once again captures the aura of the Highlands. Here is an amazing love story where characters' deep emotions and sense of honor for their countrymen will enchant readers."
— *RT Book Reviews*

"Incomparable...Paula Quinn expertly interweaves fact and fiction so well that you will come to truly believe every one of her characters can be found in the pages of history...a romantic adventure of the heart, where emotional confrontations leave an unforgettable impact."

—SingleTitles.com

Also by Paula Quinn

The Wicked Ways of Alexander Kidd

PAULA QUINN

FOREVER

NEW YORK   BOSTON

Forever
Hachette Book Group
1290 Avenue of the Americas
New York, NY 10104

www.HachetteBookGroup.com

Printed in the United States of America

First Edition: October 2014
10 9 8 7 6 5 4 3 2 1

OPM

Forever is an imprint of Grand Central Publishing.
The Forever name and logo are trademarks of Hachette Book Group, Inc.

The Hachette Speakers Bureau provides a wide range of authors for speaking events. To find out more, go to www.hachettespeakersbureau.com or call (866) 376-6591.

The publisher is not responsible for websites (or their content) that are not owned by the publisher.

MacGregor/Grant
Family Tree

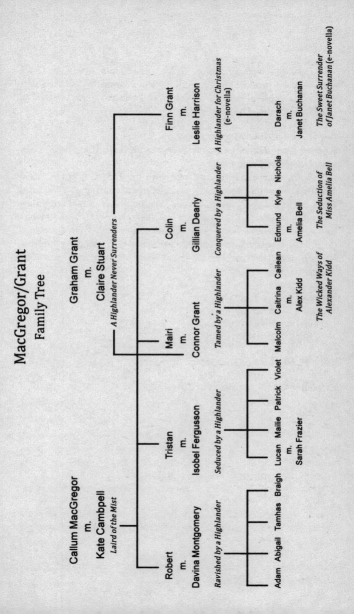

Graham Grant
m.
Claire Stuart
A Highlander Never Surrenders

Callum MacGregor
m.
Kate Campbell
Laird of the Mist

Robert
m.
Davina Montgomery
Ravished by a Highlander

Adam Abigail Tamhas Braigh

Tristan
m.
Isobel Fergusson
Seduced by a Highlander

Lucan Maille Patrick Violet
m.
Sarah Frazier

Mairi
m.
Connor Grant
Tamed by a Highlander

Malcolm Caitrina Cailean
m.
Alex Kidd

The Wicked Ways of Alexander Kidd

Colin
m.
Gillian Dearly
Conquered by a Highlander

Edmund Kyle Nichola
m.
Amelia Bell

The Seduction of Miss Amelia Bell

Finn Grant
m.
Leslie Harrison
A Highlander for Christmas
(e-novella)

Darach
m.
Janet Buchanan
The Sweet Surrender of Janet Buchanan (e-novella)

Cast of Characters

Caitrina Grant

    Connor Grant ~ *her father*
    Mairi MacGregor ~ *her mother*
    Cailean Grant ~ *her brother*
    Malcolm Grant ~ *her eldest brother*
Robert & Davina MacGregor ~ *her uncle and aunt*
    Adam MacGregor ~ *their eldest son*
    Abigail MacGregor ~ *their daughter*
    Tamhas & Braigh MacGregor ~ *their twin sons*
Tristan & Isobel MacGregor ~ *her uncle and aunt*
    Lucan MacGregor ~ *their eldest son*
    Mailie MacGregor ~ *their daughter*
    Patrick MacGregor ~ *their son*
    Violet MacGregor ~ *their daughter*
Colin & Gillian MacGregor ~ *her uncle and aunt*
    Edmund MacGregor ~ *their eldest son*
    Kyle MacGregor ~ *their son*

Captain Alexander Kidd

The ship's crew:
  Samuel Pierce ~ *his quartermaster*
  Mr. Bonnet ~ *his first mate*
  Gustaaf ~ *the boatswain*
  Cooper ~ *the sailing master*
  Robbie Owens ~ *the cook*
  Nicky ~ *Robbie's brother*
  Jack Hanson ~ *the master gunner*
  Harry Hanes ~ *the carpenter/physician*
  Simon ~ *the musician*
  Jacques ~ *a swabbie*
William Kidd ~ *Alex's father*
  Hendrik Andersen ~ *William Kidd's boatswain*

The Wicked Ways of
Alexander Kidd

Chapter One

Captain Alexander Kidd hooked his sapphire-ringed finger into the narrow handle of his jug of rum and brought it to his lips. The woman spread on the table beneath him looked up and moaned while she spread her palms over his sculpted chest. He wiped his mouth and looked at her. The hunger in the slow, salacious smile he lavished on her made her drip around the base of him. He ran his hand up her thigh, withdrew from her hot body, and then drove himself deeper into her, biting down on her pink nipple. Ah, but there was nothing better than warm rum and an even warmer whore. Plundering a ship was a close second, but he'd done that already this morning. He laughed and the wench tightened her legs around his waist. He tipped his jug and drizzled his rum over her breasts and her belly, watching with dark, hungry eyes.

He wasn't sure of her name. He didn't need to know it. He paid her to please him and she did.

He heard the sound of fighting from beyond the door of the candlelit room. Fighting was good, but now was the time for pleasure. He bent forward and drank from her behind his veil of dark hair.

He sank into her, deep and slow, then withdrew almost completely. Teasing her with what she wanted, he spread his palm over her belly and pulled cries from her throat with the gyration of his hips. His smooth thrusts arched her back and brought them both to climax.

Done, he pulled back, fastened his breeches, and took another swig from his jug.

"Will I see you again?" the wench asked when he stood over her, covering his tattoos of Neptune and Poseidon with his shirt.

He looked at her and shook his head. The last thing he wanted in his life was a woman. His father taught him to trust no man, but he'd learned firsthand not to trust a woman. He'd never make that mistake again. He never returned to the same wench's bed twice, providing no hope in forming attachments.

Pity, this one was a lovely thing with eyes as dark as coal and long raven hair. She was likely a native of the Americas and brought here to New York as a slave to work in this backstreet brothel.

He plucked an extra coin from a small pouch tied into his sash and tossed it to her, then stepped out of the room and out of her life, and into a brawl that sent his quartermaster flying across the full length of the front room.

Alex downed what was left in his jug, then smashed the clay vessel over the head of the man who'd done the punching. He watched the culprit go down, then cupped his groin and readjusted. A woman at a table at the other end of the room smiled at him and waved. He returned the salutation but headed to a larger table, preferring, for now, to share drink and laughter with the drunken, rowdy seamen who helped him sail his ship. He tucked in his shirt then slipped into a chair and ordered another jug of rum.

"Cap'n." His tanned, one-eyed first mate turned to him. "Tell this scab-pickin', bottom feeder"—he hooked his thumb over his shoulder, pointing it at another sailor who looked insulted enough to start killing people—"who among us plays the better jig on the pipes?"

"I've already told ya, Mr. Bonnet," Alex answered, giving his attention to his brocade coat and feathered tricorn hat resting where he'd left them on a chair to his right. "I prefer Simon's jigs over yars. That's why he's the ship's musician and ya're me first mate."

Alex paid his one-eyed comrade no mind when Mr. Bonnet cursed him for breathing. He didn't put it past his crew to turn on him if doing so gained them something they wanted bad enough. They were pirates, and just like any pirate, they were loyal to the coin in their pockets and the food on the table. He looked up instead at the man who'd sailed by him a few moments ago.

"I think me tooth came loose that time."

This man was different though. Alex had known his quartermaster, Samuel Pierce, for more than eight years now. Sam was a loyal friend, there with Alex when he learned of his father's arrest, at his side during his father's hanging, with him when Alex's heart was broken, the first and only time, by a woman. They'd plundered many ships together and fought many battles, watching the other's back. Alex trusted him with his very life and loved him like a brother. "The gold one?" he asked, eyebrow raised.

Three of his men who had been deep in conversation stopped talking and turned to eye Sam.

"Not the gold one," the quartermaster growled at them.

"But if any of ya be wantin' to try to pry it loose from me jaw, just stick yer fingers in there if ya have the balls."

Alex laughed and swigged his rum. "Robbie Owens there doesn't have 'em."

It was true, poor Robbie had lost his balls two summers ago when the mother of two of his children caught him in her sister's bed. Fortunate for Robbie the ship's carpenter, Harry Hanes, knew how to stop bleeding and sew a man up good as new. Well, perhaps not like new.

"Captain Kidd?" A stranger appeared at the table, drawing all the men's attention to him. Another man would have taken a step back, or at least reconsidered his decision to make himself known to them as pistols came into view, along with blood-stained daggers.

But not this man. He remained unflinchingly cool in his drab but costly attire, clean hands folded in front of him.

"Who's askin'?" Samuel said, reaching for the cutlass tucked into his boot.

"My name is Hendrik Andersen. I was a friend of the captain's father, William Kidd."

"Me father had no friends," Alex corrected, reclining in his chair and slamming his booted foot on the table. "None who were worth more than bilge rat shit."

"I've been looking for you for several years now," the stranger continued as if Alex hadn't spoken.

It didn't bode well for Alex that he'd been searched for and found.

"What do ya want?" Alex asked him. "Make yar plea convincin' or I'll kill ya where ya stand. I should do it now fer claimin' to be a friend to me father. None of his crew stood by him when he was arrested. None watched him die. All had abandoned him."

"But not you."

Alex slowly removed his leg from the table and sat up in his chair. His movements caused Sam and several others to draw their daggers, others their pistols, and they begged Alex to let them fire.

Aye, him, too. He'd abandoned his father along with the rest of them. Oh, he'd been there in the crowd that day in London to watch his father swing, but Alex had abandoned him long before that. And what made it worse was that he'd done it for a woman.

No one but Sam had known that Alex was present at his father's execution. His father hadn't even known. William Kidd began his career as a privateer, authorized by the government to attack foreign or enemy vessels at sea. He never admitted to being a pirate. But Alex knew the truth and had followed in his footsteps, another fact his father had kept secret to his grave, loyal to his outlaw son upon death.

"What is it ya be wantin' to tell me?" Alex demanded quietly.

Andersen didn't bat an eyelash. "I would speak to you alone."

"Nay," Alex said, not risking a stab in the gut the instant they were alone. Anyone could have sent Andersen to hunt Alex down, the Royal Navy, any number of governors from New York, even the throne. They believed Alex knew where to find the treasure that cost his father his life. Sadly, they were mistaken. "Say what ya would now and say it quickly. Ya're tryin' me patience."

The man cleared his throat and glanced at the others. "Very well, then. May I sit?" When Alex nodded, he pulled out the chair nearest Alex's coat and hat and sat down on it. Alex watched him catch his hat before it hit the floor and then place it, with the due respect a captain's expensive leather hat deserved, back on the chair. "I was your father's boatswain. I was with him when he captured the *Quedagh Merchant*."

Everyone at the table grew silent. They all knew about the rumors of the *Quedagh Merchant*, the infamous Armenian ship said to be loaded with gold and silver, gems of every size and color, not to mention satins, muslin, and priceless East Indian goods, including silks. It was a treasure any pirate worth his weight in salt would kill for... or die for. His father was rumored to have captured it shortly after Alex left him to begin his own life of adventure and piracy. Since Alex didn't remember ever seeing Andersen on his father's ship, he concluded that the Dutchman would have had to have joined his father's crew right after he left.

No proof was ever discovered against William Kidd but Alex didn't doubt that his father had indeed captured the ship. What he didn't believe was that his father had trusted anyone with its whereabouts.

"Are ya tellin' me ya know where the *Quedagh Merchant* is?" Alex wouldn't have believed him if Andersen answered with an aye. The first Captain Kidd had been tried and hanged for piracy and murder rather than give up the location of that ship. Since Alex hadn't been with him when he took it, nor had Alex seen him alive since, he didn't know its whereabouts either.

"I'm telling you nothing of the sort, but..." Andersen paused and looked around. When Alex nodded for him to continue, he obliged. "There is a map."

A map. That sounded quite plausible, Alex decided, trying to keep his heart beating at a steady pace. His father may have denied his true profession, but he wouldn't have gone to his grave without a map to his greatest treasure. What if somehow he had come out of the trial alive? His father would have made certain there was a map. Who would he have given it to for safekeeping? He'd told his son that there was only one other man whom he trusted but not who the man was. Was it his boatswain?

"Where is this map?" he asked his guest casually.

Still reluctant, Andersen looked straight at Mr. Bonnet's patched eye and the scar running down beneath it. "You trust these men?"

"Not always, but I need them, same as they need me. Where is the map? Who has it?" If there really was a map, Alex wanted to know who had it. He wouldn't try to steal it. He didn't deserve it. Whoever had it did.

"Scotland."

"Where in Scotland?"

"I have a condition, Captain Kidd," Andersen was foolish enough to announce.

Half the men at the table readied their daggers and aimed their pistols again. Metal gleamed against the firelight coming from the hearth.

"If yar condition isn't that ya walk out of here alive"— Alex tipped one corner of his mouth up—"then I'm afraid I must refuse."

"I wish to sail with you."

Alex shook his head. "I already have a boatswain. I don't need any more men."

"You need me."

Alex laughed. "Kill him," he told Sam, rising from his chair.

"You need me to find the people who have your map," Andersen exclaimed as Sam's dagger edged along his throat.

Holding up his hand, Alex halted his quartermaster's next move. Not that his friend was truly going to kill Andersen. At least, not while he knew the whereabouts of this alleged map. After that...

"I was born in Scotland. I don't need ya to find me way 'round. Now tell me who has it."

"Will I sail with you?"

Regaining his seat, Alex narrowed his eyes on him. It was obvious that this man who claimed to be a friend to his father wanted the map for himself. But why not just go to Scotland and get the map himself if he knew where it was? Why did he need Alex?

"You will never find them on your own, Captain," Andersen forged ahead, undaunted by Alex's scowl. "And if you do, they will kill you before your feet touch land. They are hidden in the mists in the Highlands."

"They?"

"The MacGregors."

MacGregors. Alex had heard of them. "They are outlawed, are they not?"

Sam nodded. "King William re-enacted the proscription against them when he gained the throne."

"Their reputation of savagery precedes them," Alex said, remembering tales he'd heard about them.

"Your father knew the clan chief," Andersen told him. "He took a few others and me with him as witnesses when he brought the map to them to guard. The chief agreed to surrender the map to you... and to you alone."

"What do ya mean to me?"

"It was your father's map," Andersen said. "He left it to his son."

Alex leaned back in his chair and took in what he was hearing. His father had found the *Quedagh Merchant* and left the map of its whereabouts to him? Had William Kidd forgiven him for leaving? Nay, he couldn't absorb it all now. Perhaps tomorrow...

"So when do we leave?"

Alex smiled at him. "Bring to me mind the reason I need ya again?"

"Because the chief doesn't know you, or whose son you are. If you happen to find them on your own you will have no way to convince them of your identity. They'll kill all of you for finding them. They value their privacy highly."

"So ya intend on provin' me identity?" Alex asked him. "How?" he asked when Andersen nodded his head.

"A letter."

Alex cocked his brow. "A letter?"

"From your father to the chief, stating that you are his son and the map should be handed over to you. I have been made privy to things about you that can prove who you are. And because I traveled with your father and already met them, my word will validate."

Believable and clever on his father's part. Alex would take this Dutchman with him. He wondered how much Andersen knew about him. He hadn't seen his father in a little under a decade and he'd changed much in that time. How could anyone prove his identity?

"And what of these folks who have the map?" he asked. "How do ya know they haven't already looked fer the ship?"

"They are Highlanders, not pirates. Their island is their treasure and they guard it unceasingly."

Alex thought about everything he'd been told so far. He shared a look with Samuel. As his quartermaster, Sam had as much say in what treasures they sought and plundered as the captain. If Sam didn't feel right about Andersen and his claim of a map, Alex wouldn't ask the crew to go with him on his voyage to Scotland.

Sam ran his fingers through the blond waves on his uncovered head and nodded.

"I'll let ya board me ship." Alex turned back to their guest. "But I have a few conditions of me own. First, ya'll take four successive watches fer the first three nights at sea while we travel to Scotland. The crew can use the rest to recuperate from our time ashore. Second, ya'll aid our navigator and cook, Mr. Cooper, in any way he commands to get us to our destination as safely and as quickly as possible. I inherited my father's enemies, from the Royal Navy on up to the throne itself. If word of a map... nay, a whisper of it, reaches their ears, we will have to fly over waves or hoist our flag and kill some soldiers. I'm prepared to do either. Are ya?"

"If you command it."

Alex grinned at him and sank languorously into his chair. "I'm almost certain that at some point in our journey we'll discover if ya speak true." He held up another jewel-encircled finger to quiet him when Andersen would have spoken. "Next, I want the letter me father wrote and would hear of his adventures from ya. We parted long ago." Alex missed his father. Captain William Kidd had been an ornery man, wary of every sailor in his company. He taught Alex everything he knew about ships and sailing.

"He spoke of you often," Andersen told him.

Hell. What would he have told this man? That his son never returned to his father's ship after their brief anchor in Lisbon? That his son never tried to find him? But Alex had tried at first. "Ya will tell me what he said."

Andersen nodded.

"Very good. Then I've one last condition before I allow ya aboard me ship."

"What is it?"

"Pay fer our drinks. Do ya agree to these conditions?"

"Aye, Captain."

Alex grinned at him. "Then welcome to *Poseidon's Adventure*. We sail at dawn." He cut his dark gaze across the room, to the woman who had waved at him earlier. She crooked her finger at him now. He sprang to his feet with the grace of a great cat and smoothed back any stray strands of chestnut hair that had fallen over his forehead. Tonight was a good night. He felt redeemed, released from a weight he'd carried for years. He wanted to celebrate. "Andersen," he said on his way. "Ya're in charge of me coat and hat. Guard them well, or 'twill cost ya a finger."

He grinned, turning fully to address his crew. "I'll meet ya all in an hour to stock the ship. Until then, enjoy yarselves. Who knows when we'll be ashore again?"

He smiled at the woman rising from her chair at his approach. She was eager to be pillaged and he was willing to oblige.

Chapter Two

Caitrina Grant hurried toward her father's solar, her blood thrashing like a storm through her veins. It couldn't be true. It just couldn't. Her father would never have consented to a marriage between her and Hugh MacDonald, and never without telling her!

She paused a moment in her tracks. What if her father was tired of her refusing every offer of marriage that came to her? What in blazes would she do if it was true?

She came to the solar door and heard her parents laughing inside. She knocked and then, without waiting for an invitation, she plunged inside.

Her parents were locked in each other's embrace and came apart slowly upon seeing her. Caitrina was used to seeing them showing their affection for each other. She hated to be the one to ruin their evening but they needed to talk.

"Tell me it isna' true," she pleaded, moving like a rushing wind toward them. "Tell me ye havena' promised me to Hugh MacDonald."

When her father looked away, guilt plaguing his vivid

blue eyes, she knew it was true. "How could ye?" she demanded. "Ye know I dinna' want to wed anyone!"

"Cait, sit doun," her mother offered. "Let us speak of this like—"

"I dinna' wish to sit," she insisted, desperation marring her voice. "Mother, we have spoken of this already. I want more than to be a wife and a mother. I want to know what else is oot there fer me!"

"Daughter," her father tried a bit more soothingly. "Ye don't know what the world is like beyond Skye."

"I wish to find oot."

"There are dangers at every turn," he continued over her. "I cannot . . . I will not take the chance of any calamity befallin' ye. We love ye and we don't want to see ye alone. Ye need a good, strong man to see to yer comfort and yer protection. Ye've turned down everyone who has asked fer yer hand, but 'tis time—"

She shook her head and went to her father. "Papa, please," she begged him, taking hold of his sleeve. "Dinna' sentence me to a life of such tedium. Ye know I dislike sewin'. I canna' cook. I dinna' want to read aboot other peoples' adventures. I want to live them fer myself."

Connor Grant let out a long sigh and turned to her mother. "She's just like ye, Mairi." His wife nodded her head, which did little for Caitrina's cause since, if all the tales she heard were true, Mairi MacGregor had once been an active spy with a group of militia who hunted down those who tried to maintain their doctrine as sole religion in Scotland.

"We're proscribed, Caitrina," her father reminded her. "The instant ye leave Camlochlin yer life would be in danger. I'm sorry, but I cannot allow ye the life ye desire."

Her eyes filled up with tears and she looked toward her

mother for help. None came. No! She loved her parents but she would not obey them in this. Not this.

She ran from the solar and out of the manor house. She would figure something out, think of a way to convince them that she would be safe away from Skye. She had to, or she would go mad.

Sometime later, she stood on the rocky shore of Loch nan Leachd and set her gaze over the water toward Loch Scavaig in the distance. Beneath the late setting sun her eyes matched the tumultuous blue depths swelling and breaking before her. The song of the waves crashing against sheer walls of rock played like a hypnotizing symphony to her ears. She closed her eyes and slowed her breath to rein in her riotous heart. It wouldn't do to begin her night aching for something indefinable and unrealistic.

It wasn't the water that pulled her in but what lay beyond it. Directions. So many of them, it made her head spin thinking of the different paths her life could take. Oh, she couldn't marry Hugh, or anyone else for that matter. She sought adventure, felt curiosity burning through her veins. She wanted to meet new people, learn new customs, live vicariously without the net of home to guard her. But her father would never let her leave.

No one left Camlochlin. Not for good. Nor would she. It was home, a mother's love, a promise of safety in a treacherous world. Caitrina loved it as much as anyone else. But she wanted more. She might even want a little danger.

"Dinna' smile at the water lest ye tempt jealous sirens to swim ashore and kill ye."

She opened her eyes and sighed at her cousin, who wasn't there a moment ago. "Kyle, ye really must learn to announce yerself. Ye're too quiet."

"I thought ye might have heard Goliath and Sage barking up the slope," he answered. When she shook her head and looked over her shoulder at the giant mixed wolfhounds racing up the side of Sgurr na Stri, he offered her a knowing look. "Ye lose yerself too deeply to yer thoughts, Trina."

"Kyle," she said, ignoring his warning, "did ye hear aboot my betrothal to Hugh MacDonald?"

"Aye," he said softly, not pushing her as to whether or not she would go along with it. He knew her, perhaps better than anyone else did.

"Do ye think my faither will allow me to travel to France if I agree to wed Hugh upon my return?" One adventure. Was that asking too much? "To see our grandparents," she added after he began shaking his head.

"What's in France, Trina? And dinna' say our grandparents. Ye'll be seeing them in a month."

She shrugged, turning toward the loch. No sense in lying to Kyle. He could see right through deceit. Besides, she loved him too much to lie to him. "The same thing that's in England, I suppose. Stuffy nobles and feigned smiles. But I dinna' want to spend my last free summer before I'm forced to be someone's wife hunting deer and rabbits, or embroidering, or even reading!"

They looked at each other, Trina expecting the scandalous arch of Kyle's brow. Most of her cousins adored books as much as swords. Not her, unless the books were about adventure—or archery. She loved arrows; the height and the distance they reached on the wind. The precision achieved by dedicated practice.

She quirked her mouth at him. "Come now, Kyle, ye know how I feel aboot living nestled away in the mountains while the world—which I learned aboot from books—goes on withoot me? And now I'm to be saddled doun with babes…"

A veil of mist passed across his cerulean gaze, briefly transforming him into the cool, calculating performer who could sniff out the truth better than a hound on the trail of its prey. "Ye're trouble fer some poor sot oot there, Caitrina Grant, and I dinna' believe 'twill be Hugh Mac-Donald. Ye'll go to France and not return fer a year or two." He wouldn't tell her parents her plans. Kyle would never betray her. Even as children he had protected her, though she had brothers who were more than happy to do so. Kyle had kept all her secrets, even when she practiced swordplay with the boys when she was supposed to be learning to sew.

The veil lifted; his smile on her was soft, indulgent. "Come now, the others are waiting."

She nodded and followed him on the path behind the mountain as the mist began to roll in from the Cuillins to the north.

"Speak to yer faither, Kyle. Please."

"Aboot what?"

"Aboot speaking to my faither aboot me going to France to see our grandparents. I'll return. I promise."

He shook his head as he made his way over the steep rocky incline. His steps were sure and silent enough not to disturb the others waiting for them ... or the deer they meant to hunt. "Yer faither willna' let ye go alone, Trina. No matter who speaks to him."

"Come with me then," she offered, holding back his wrist before they reached their hunting party. "He'll let me go if ye're with me. He knows that ye're clear-headed and confident, and ye could fight us oot of trouble if ye need to."

He laughed, cutting her off. "He also knows that I'm Colin's son, driven as my father was to discover the secrets in men's hearts. I'm the last person yer faither wants traveling with ye to France. Who the hell knows what we would get ourselves into before we even reached Brittany and our grandparents?"

She sighed rather than give voice to the endless possibilities his query stirred. She had no doubt that they would find adventure on their journey together. Kyle was the reason for her sanity. He spoke true about his desire to learn everything there was to learn about everyone in Camlochlin. He did it well, and without truly letting them know everything about him.

But she knew.

She knew he was bored playing his wee games with the same minds. There was nothing left to learn, not here.

"Think of the interesting people we will meet."

He blinked at the gossamer mist descending on them. "If tragedy befell ye I would no longer wish to live. And yer faither would see my wish fulfilled."

"Ye insult me." She brooded instantly and pushed ahead of him. "Ferget my offer. I dinna' want to journey with someone who believes my life is in anyone else's hands but God's and my own."

"Fine," he called out, staring after her. "I didna' want to go with ye in the first place."

She let her mouth fall open since she wasn't facing him. She snapped it back shut before she pivoted around and marched back to him.

"Because ye dinna' want to have to protect me. Is that it?" Before he answered she poked him in the shoulder. "'Twould more likely be me protecting ye, Kyle MacGregor!"

He smiled, either afraid of her or confident enough not to laugh right in her face. No one in Camlochlin fought like Kyle. He'd mastered every weapon he put his hands to and practiced with his father every day without fail. Why? She wanted to ask him many times…especially now. What was his purpose at becoming the best? Who was he planning on fighting on Skye?

"Kyle."

"What?"

"Help me with this endeavor!" she pleaded, knowing no one but him would offer to go with her. "I will go mad if this is all there is to my life! I'll be married by next summer and fat with bairns by the summer after that! Help me, please. I will not allow myself to be injured. I vow it. Dinna' fret over me."

She wasn't certain if he was smiling or not. The mist was thick and the moon was behind them, over the water.

"I'll always fret over ye. But I'll do what I can to help ye."

She squealed and flung her arms around his neck. "Thank ye, cousin."

"Och, Kyle," a voice called out from a few feet away. "What did ye promise her now?"

Caitrina released Kyle and turned to offer her younger brother a smug grin—one that he couldn't see in the dim light. "Mayhap, Cailean, if ye were more willing to assist me in my endeavors, I would not have to rely solely on Kyle."

"If yer endeavors continue to shock no' only our clan but the other four clans we share this island with, then I fear my aid willna' be forthcoming."

"If by shock," she said, pushing him out of her way so she could reach the others, "ye mean my refusal to marry Kevin MacKinnon last winter, I—"

"And Alistair MacDonald the summer before that."

"And dinna' ferget Jamie MacLeod the spring before that."

Caitrina turned around to glare at Kyle for jumping into the fray.

"Should I wed men I dinna' love?"

"Nae, ye should not," Kyle answered her, his smile audible in the fog. "Now quit fretting over it and let us show these lads who the better hunters are."

"We already know, Kyle," said Braigh MacGregor, youngest son of the MacGregor chief. "They are ye and Edmund."

"Nae," Tamhas, Braigh's paternal sixteen-year-old twin, argued. "The best are Malcolm and Cailean. Uncle Connor and Aunt Mairi made certain they practiced weaponry every day."

"And I was there with my brothers at the end of each day," Trina reminded them. "'Twould do well fer ye both not to underestimate any lass in this holding. Fer if ye do, 'twill be doubly difficult to accept the next clan chief." She said nothing more but left them to whatever they thought of her prediction. She stepped through the frail curtain wall and disappeared in the mist.

She knew she was fortunate to live with men who, because of women like her grandmothers, Claire and Kate, and Mairi, her mother, respected women. But there were still restrictions, like not being able to travel off Skye without escort, and having to marry men their fathers chose for them because their fathers thought they needed protecting.

She heard Kyle's footsteps behind her. Even he didn't think she could protect herself. Was that why he always seemed to be tailing her? She clenched her teeth, wanting to prove to him that she was no defenseless maiden in need of a champion. Och, those books about knights in armor, courtly love, and butterflies and unicorns were ruining her life!

She moved left, then backtracked a dozen silent steps, passing her brother and her cousins on their way to the hunt. She'd scouted the braes and glens all day yesterday and tracked deer prints. She knew where to go. She would bring home the biggest prize on her own.

Soon, she heard the call of the sea in the distance, beyond Loch Scavaig. She listened only for the sound of movement in the fog, ignoring everything else. She had a point to prove. She couldn't track prints presently but she'd memorized the path, and raced farther up the craggy slope. The chill of an early spring numbed her face and slapped her dark hair behind her. It wasn't that she didn't love this place. She loved it with her all heart. In its vast, wide-open magnificence she'd learned to run, to fly.

It was only natural to want to fly away, wasn't it?

She slowed, trying to concentrate on her task. She heard a sound and stopped. She remained silent, waiting… waiting. When no other sound came, she continued on. Reaching the crest, she paused again at the odd sound of creaking wood reaching her from what seemed another plane. She turned toward the loch and the mist rolling over it beneath her. She blinked at the sight of something dark drifting across the shallows, its high peaks—were they masts?—piercing the fragile mist.

A ship? What in blazes…? She inched forward. It couldn't be what she thought it was. Ships didn't come to Camlochlin without invitation, and never at night, unless they meant harm.

Whatever it was, it disappeared in the fog. Should she alert the others? To what? A shadow? They would tease her and accuse her of creating a distraction because she hadn't caught anything. She wanted to continue on and win but she should investigate. She began to descend the slope, doing her best to do so as quietly as possible. No reason to frighten away any potential game she could hunt later.

A movement along the shoreline caught her eye. Immediately, she nocked her arrow and raised her bow. Taking aim, she waited with a pounding heart. It could be a deer, or it could be something else. Her heavy breath thundered in her ears and she fought to control it. She kept her eyes on the shoreline and her ear inclined for any sound of her kin returning. She couldn't lie; part of her wished they were there, at her back.

Being afraid caused her no shame. Acting on it would though.

She braced her legs and narrowed her eyes against the brisk wind. A moment passed with the parting of clouds and the full, milky moon spreading its light upon the darkness, and for an instant, on a man prowling along the rocks.

He was dressed in breeches and a long coat; she knew he was no inhabitant of Camlochlin. Neither did the long, curved cutlass dangling from his hand and catching light from the moon prove him a Highlander.

He looked up, but Trina didn't have time to catch sight of his face beneath the wide brim of his hat. Heart pounding, she released her arrow, wishing she could look upon him and either recognize him or kill him.

His tricorn flew off his head, stabbed by her arrow and carried off into the loch. Mist shrouded him when Trina looked again. He disappeared. Her breath came hard and heavy. This was no deer she was hunting. Who was he? What should she do? Did he come by ship? Dear God, her kin could be under attack right now and here she was wasting moments on questions.

She leaped a few feet down the slope and landed on bent knees and legs ready to fly her to where she wanted to go.

"What kind of coward seeks to kill at such a distance?" A deep, downy male voice called up to her. "Meet me on less foggy ground and let us draw swords on more equal footin'."

His challenge was issued with arrogance, as if he feared nothing. Not even MacGregors. Fool.

She moved forward, nocking another arrow in place. "Who are ye?" she called out.

"Ah, a woman," he said, his smile evident behind the silvery curtain that concealed him. She didn't need to see him to feel the effect his rich voice had on her. He wasn't Scottish. English perhaps. His clipped cadence was softened by a slow, deep drawl that coursed through her and down her spine like heat on a sultry summer night.

"A dead man," she countered, ignoring how he sounded, "speaking but saying nothing that will convince me not to shoot him in the face this time."

He laughed and the heat returned for a moment.

"We have a law at sea." His warm breath fell against her lobe, causing her to twist around, stunned to find him right there behind her. She hadn't sensed his movement. Now, he was so close she could see the contours of his face, the shape of his mouth over her as he came in close and took hold of her bow. "If ye're goin' to kill a man, look him in the eyes when ya do it."

Trina tried not to show her fear, but that didn't mean her knees weren't knocking together. She'd never killed a man before and doing so at close range, close enough to look him in the eyes, would be difficult, mayhap impossible. She was thankful for the mist. Getting a good, clear look at this man might slow her reflexes, but she had to do something. She blinked and rammed her knee into his groin, or rather, because of the blinding dimness, his upper thigh. She was about to run when a familiar voice stopped her.

"Back away from her or ye'll suffer a dozen arrows. We never miss!"

Relief flooded through her at Kyle's confident declaration breaking through the fog and the sound of rushing waves. No one *ever* saw Kyle coming.

"I surrender peacefully," the intruder called out with a graceful sweep of his cutlass before him and a gallant bow.

"Who are ye?" Kyle demanded.

"I be Alexander Kidd, captain of *Poseidon's Adventure*, and only son and heir of William Kidd, most infamous pirate to sail the high seas."

A pirate? He was a pirate? Trina didn't know whether to believe him or pick up a rock and smash it over his head. She'd never seen a pirate before. She wanted to take another look at him. He had to be lying. Why would a pirate come here? It was more likely that he was a captain in the Royal Navy come to arrest her uncles and brothers for something they did on one of their excursions to the Lowlands.

"We should shoot him," she called out to her kin. "Set the dogs on him."

She could feel his eyes on her, hard, dark eyes that cut through the moonlight.

"After I've surrendered?" he said in her direction, sounding disappointed.

"Caitrina, step away from him," Cailean commanded, provoking a deep-throated growl from the wolfhounds at his feet.

"What d'ye want?" Kyle demanded, slowly moving closer.

"I want an audience with yar chief," the intruder announced. "He has somethin' that belongs to me."

Trina laughed and began to step away from him. "Kill him and let us run home and warn—"

The remainder of her words was cut off by one arm coiling around her waist and another around her throat. The cool edge of a dagger against her throat set her heart to pounding against his hard angles.

"Ya're beginnin' to tempt me to take more than just me map."

The husky timbre of his voice along her neck sent bolts of charged, fiery energy through her. Caitrina closed her eyes, hating her body for betraying her.

"Now, be a good little lady and call off yar lads or me men will open fire."

She blinked at the mist as shadows began to appear, one after the other. He was telling the truth, at least about having a small army at his back. She opened her mouth to call to Kyle when her captor sank to the ground behind her, hit in the head by a rock from Braigh's sling.

The shadows hurried forward. Hell, Trina had to think quickly! Her small troupe couldn't fight the Royal Navy *or* a shipload of pirates. But there was a way to hold them off. She drew her dagger and reached down, taking the unconscious intruder by the hair.

"Stop!" she called out, holding the dagger to the captain's throat. "Any one of ye takes another step and I'll leave him to the seagulls!"

❊

Chapter Three

The sun rose quickly, spilling light into one of the most cavernous great halls Alex had ever been in. The place had to be big in order to accompany the giants it housed. Even their dogs were huge, six in all. Ugly, scruffy looking beasts that growled under their breath if he all but looked at them. He didn't remember other Highlanders being this tall and broad of shoulder. Even with his entire crew, Alex doubted any kind of victory over these men. Presently, he didn't have his crew. None of his men were allowed entry into the castle save for Samuel and Hendrik Andersen.

Despite the growing knot on his head and the pounding that accompanied it, he managed a smile for a pretty red-haired lass who set a cup down on the table in front of him.

"The chief will see ye shortly," she said, or rather sang.

One of the Highlanders seated at the table tugged on her skirt and she inclined her ear to him. She smiled behind a veil of sunset and fire curls and turned to Alex. She nodded at what the man was whispering to her. Alex didn't need to hear what the lad was saying. When one grew up at sea, sometimes with raging winds snatching voices from the air, one learned to read lips.

When the girl covered her mouth and giggled, Alex's lips cocked to the left, as did his head. He didn't mind folks thinking him a scoundrel, but he wouldn't tolerate them thinking him lily livered. "I assure ya," he corrected the lad at her ear, "I have not shit meself since I was a babe. Even if yer chief sports two heads and a bolt of lightnin' shootin' out of his arse, me streak will remain unblemished."

Beside him, Samuel laughed softly and shoved at Alex's shoulder. "Remember that wench in Tonga who pushed a snake out of her—"

Alex silenced him with a heel to Sam's toe under the table, then softened his smile on the couple. "Pardon me quartermaster."

"How did ye know what I told her?" the lad who'd whispered asked, a glint of steel, reflecting from the drawn dagger in his lap, lighting his blue-green eyes. "Did ye read my lips?"

"I did," Alex confessed, recognizing this one's voice from the hills. "'Tis a skill vital in me profession. Be ya the one who struck me?"

"That was my cousin, Braigh. I'm Kyle. This is Mailie. Mayhap ye could give me a lesson before ye leave?"

"If I get what I came fer then I don't see why not. Only it will take more than one lesson to learn to read a person's lips."

"Well, my uncle Rob might kill ye tonight. One lesson is all I might be afforded."

His uncle, the chief. The man his father trusted to guard his map. Alex looked the chief's nephew over. Kyle

MacGregor appeared to be about a score years, perhaps a little younger, but he was every bit as arrogant as rumor claimed his kin to be.

He had no more time to contemplate the lad when the scent of wild heather and smoky peat filled his senses. He turned, remembering the fragrance of the archer who owed him a hat.

Caitrina.

"Bring them," she told Kyle, who, with a dozen or so men, rose from the table and escorted him, Samuel, and Andersen out of the Hall.

"Ye have Kyle to thank fer yer life," she slowed to tell Alex. "I thought we should have killed ye."

Seeing her face through the delicate mist was one thing, seeing it clear and drenched in firelight was another thing entirely. If she was an example of Highland women, then what the hell had he been doing in other parts of the world all these years? He wanted her instantly, even before he paused his steps to take in the even sway of her hips and the roundness of her rump as she charged on ahead of him. He wanted to stare into her glacial blue eyes and watch while he set her afire and conquered her like the beast he'd become at sea all these months.

Someone behind him gave him a harsh shove forward.

Alex was no fool. She was a prize he wouldn't win. In their fur-clad capes and long hair, the lot around him looked perfectly able, and, he'd go so far as to venture, a bit eager to cut him to pieces and question him later. The MacGregors. Every child growing up in the Lowlands heard of the MacGregors once or twice before bedtime, ensuring proper obedience to his parents.

Alex didn't give a damn about tall tales. The chief had somehow earned his father's trust. That said enough for him. But the map belonged to Alex and he would have it. His father had gone through much trouble to see that he got it and he intended on seeing his father's plan through. If it meant finding himself having to kiss the arse of a fine wench instead of dragging her to his bed, he'd be happy to do it.

He followed his escorts to the second landing and down a long corridor, then down another, lit by tall candle stands and flickering torches. He looked over his shoulder at Samuel and Andersen walking amid more of the tall, daunting-looking Highlanders who were escorting them. Were they being brought to the chief or to some far off room to be murdered?

They finally arrived at a heavy wooden door upon which Caitrina knocked.

Stepping inside the chief's private solar was like walking into the embrace of a loved one. Fire from the great hearth bathed the chamber in warmth and soft, golden light. Thick, colorful tapestries hung from three of the four walls, adding to its coziness. Two ornately carved tables stretched out beneath the windows, each hosting an array of books, vases of bunched heather and orchids, a flagon of beaten bronze, and a polished chess set. It was a good room, as far as rooms on land went. The best things about it were the women, four of whom sat in a half circle around the fire. Alex couldn't decide who was the most beautiful. The one in the third overstuffed chair, he told himself. With hair the same color of rich mahogany and eyes bluer than any charted body of water, she could only be Caitrina's mother.

Hell, he could be happy here.

These people weren't savages. He was glad. It would make getting his map easier.

"Captain."

He turned to the deep voice and rethought his initial assessment. The man rising from his chair where he'd been relaxing with a number of others in the farthest corner of the room looked quite able to take on all of England if he wanted to.

"I am Robert MacGregor, clan chief of the MacGregors of Skye. I have taken the men who came ashore with ye captive. They will be killed and dumped in the loch if I'm no' satisfied that ye are who ye claim to be. Yer ship also will be blown oot of the water."

Alex found Kyle by the window and offered him a confident grin before turning back to the chief. He would admit the lad's uncle could probably scare the piss from a man. Still, for Alex, that day hadn't arrived.

"Then 'tis fortunate that I can prove me claim." When he shoved his hand inside his coat, he found three daggers at his throat. He held up one hand to ward off the three men who had been sitting with the chief. "I mean to present a letter from me father."

They waited while he produced the parchment and handed it to the chief, who surprised him again by sitting back in his chair and reading the letter with no help from anyone else.

When he was done, the MacGregor handed him back his letter and shook his head. "Anyone could have written it."

"I bore witness to the penning of the letter by Captain Kidd."

Everyone turned to Andersen, who hadn't spoken a single word until then. The chief eyed him for a moment or two, then crooked his finger at him. Unruffled, Andersen stepped forward.

"I remember ye," the chief said. "Ye were with the captain when last he visited."

"I was," Andersen told him. "Just as I was with him before he was arrested. His wish was for his son to have the map. Now that I've found him, I will fulfill his father's wishes."

"And how d'ye know this man is the captain's son?"

Indeed, how did he?

"I have been searching for Alexander Kidd for some time and I've discovered much about him. For instance, he has many enemies in the Royal Navy and in many homes in New York City. If a man is going to live by a false name, surely he would choose one less notorious. Still, the best proof I can offer is Neptune's trident," Andersen said, then explained further when the chief quirked his dark brow. "A tattoo on his upper left arm. The trident is missing a point. His father told me of it..."

With nothing else to say while Andersen established his identity—and hell, but he knew a lot about Alex— Alex glanced around the solar. His gaze roved slowly over the faces staring back at him. He found Caitrina standing close to a pale-haired beauty of roughly the same age. He smiled at them. Neither smiled back.

"Captain Kidd," the chief called to him, breaking the spell Caitrina's gloriously big blue eyes had on him. "I would see the trident missing a point."

Alex obliged. He would have stripped naked if it meant gaining possession of the map. He removed his coat and handed it over to Andersen. His shirt followed—to a symphony of little female gasps—as he turned his muscled arm toward the flickering light.

The chief nodded. "I'm convinced that ye are whom ye say and therefore will turn over yer map. Yer faither was a good friend. Ye and yer companions here are welcome to stay and break fast with us. Fill yer bellies and then be on yer way."

Alex bowed, then replaced his shirt. Liking a room was one thing, but he'd wanted to leave an hour ago. He wasn't formed for land. His heart longed for the undulations of the bucking, surging beast beneath his bare feet, the spray of the ocean all over him. Someday though, if he lived long enough, he might want to settle down his feet. Camlochlin tempted.

But Alex didn't have time to make friends now. He had a treasure to find. "That's good of ya, my lord, but I wouldn't risk the Royal Navy followin' me here. We'll be leavin' once I have the map."

"Stay and break fast with us," one of the men seated with the chief said. He didn't ask. He rose from his chair directly before Alex and fixed his level gaze at him.

"My brother, Colin MacGregor," the chief introduced.

Kyle's father, Alex knew right away, if resemblances meant anything. But for a harder cut to his eyes and a dash of salt at his temples, he could have been Kyle's twin.

Colin tilted a corner of his mouth.

Only darker.

"The navy won't follow ye here."

"Why wouldn't they?" Alex wanted to know.

"Cannons," Colin told him, then stepped around Alex and moved toward the center of the chamber, arm extended.

One of the four women around the hearth rose and met her husband, a blush stealing across her nose like a newly married maiden, fresh from their bed.

"My sons and nephews," the chief continued, demanding the return of Alex's attention, "will escort ye back to the Hall. Adam, Edmund," he motioned to the two men appearing at Alex's shoulders. "Malcolm, Lucan, Patrick, take them back with the rest of ye. I'll be there shortly."

And just like that, Alex, Samuel, and Andersen were whisked away without another word.

"So what then?" Sam asked, eyeing the group encircling them. "Are ya all related? Married to each other?"

Alex tried to pay attention for as long as he could while they all explained who they were and what their relationship was. He lost track soon into the genealogy and turned while he walked to look Caitrina over.

Neptune take him, but she was beautiful. He let his gaze skim over her from head to foot. The milky mounds of her bosom drew his attention and ignited fire in his blood. The long column of her throat seduced his mind with thoughts of kissing it, biting it.

"Be there any hat makers here?" he asked her, lifting his eyes from her lips.

"Nae." She swept a cheeky, gloriously dimpled smile over him, dashing to pieces his resolve not to sweep her off her feet and kiss her, and to hell with the consequences. He'd leaped out windows before to escape hounds on his arse. Kissing her might be worth it.

"We have nae hat makers, but we have a few trusted physicians. And since 'twas either yer heart or yer hat I needed to remove from yer body, I thought ye'd prefer to lose yer hat." She stopped moving forward and set her cool gaze on him. "Was I mistaken?"

He shook his head, fired up by her saucy mouth.

"Good." She continued on, pushing past him. "Ye can thank me fer my thoughtfulness some other time."

"I will." And he meant it. He'd love to stay and thank

her long into the night, but a kiss or two before he left would have to do. "That's a promise."

"So," another voice said, as Kyle came to stand at Caitrina's back, his sudden appearance jarring her a bit—or was it the interruption of their not so cool smiles that made her glare at Kyle when she looked over her shoulder at him? "What kind of treasure did yer faither hide?" he asked.

"If I told ya," Alex said, swinging back to the forward direction, now at Caitrina's side, "I would have to kill ya."

"'Tis a ship," Caitrina told her cousin, then proceeded to completely ignore Alex's surprised gaze on her. "'Twas called *Quedagh Merchant* and later *Adventure Prize*." She finally met Alex's eyes and shrugged a shoulder. "I listened when yer faither visited and spoke of it."

Why? he wanted to ask her. Women weren't interested in the sea or in what pirates had to say about it. But what did it matter? He stopped himself from trying to work her out in his head. He'd be gone in a few hours and Miss Caitrina Grant would be forgotten.

Today, he would eat, drink, and enjoy the company of his hosts. After that, he would set sail for his treasure and make Camlochlin a memory.

※

Chapter Four

Trina thought she might go mad at the constant struggle she endured during breakfast. She found that keeping her eyes off Alex Kidd was the most challenging endeavor she'd ever had to perform. The worst part was that she failed—along with almost every unwed female in the Hall. How could anyone succeed when he smiled with the arrogance of a prince and the danger of a wolf? Och, how she wished they were still in the dark outdoors so she couldn't see the spark in his sultry dark eyes, the deep cleft that dimpled his strong chin. And Lord, she'd never seen a man wearing earrings before, but his thick golden hoops and shoulder-length hair somehow added to his dangerous appeal. Even if she never looked at him again, the memory of his bare torso when he removed his shirt for her uncle would haunt her for ten lifetimes. Cut to absolute perfection, his chest and upper arms were crafted in hard, twitching sinew that boasted power and lissome strength. His tanned, flat belly made her curious to touch him. She blushed, thinking of having never touched a man in such a way before. He strode like a conquering emperor across the Great Hall filled with deadly Highlanders. He didn't fear them, or, if he did, he masked it quite well. Virility oozed from his every nuance of movement, and even she, a virgin, felt the sexual pull of it.

Listening to the velvet pitch of his voice while he spoke of his adventures made her hate him...or fall in awe of him. She wasn't sure which, and she didn't like it.

"He's quite an unusual man, don't ye think?"

Trina turned to her cousin, Abigail, eyeing the pirate captain across the hall, where he stood speaking with Abby's older brother and the chief's heir, Adam. At Abby's side, Mailie and her younger sister Violet stood as if entranced by the sight of him. Until their mother walked past them and gave them each a smack on the rump.

"Turn yer eyes the other way," Isobel MacGregor warned her two daughters. "That one is trouble."

Trina agreed. The sooner he left, the happier she'd be.

Abby inched closer to her when Isobel left with the others. "Malcolm and Edmund were on the shore when the sun rose," she told her. "They said his boat was impressive."

His boat. Och, how she wished she could see it. Just a glimpse before he left. "Is it a sloop or a schooner?"

Abby shrugged her shoulders. "I've no idea what the difference is."

"A sloop is rigged with a single mainsail, whereas a schooner has two masts. Both are extremely fast. Then again he might have—"

"Honestly, Trina," her cousin cut her off gently. "Ye know more aboot boats and navigation than most of the men here. When I'm chief, I'll let ye sail my boats."

Trina smiled at her as Abby moved away to rejoin the

crowd. Everyone in Camlochlin and all throughout Skye adored the daughter of Rob and Davina for her beauty and steadfast loyalty to her kin. Abby was born to lead the clan more so than her older brother, who cared nothing for the title. If Abby were chief, Trina would happily follow her.

Alone, Trina returned her gaze to where Alex had stood earlier. He was no longer there. She looked around the Hall and was about to go look for him outside when his husky voice came from close behind her.

"'Tis a brigantine," he said, his warm breath against her ear making her spine tingle.

She'd never seen a brig before. They were larger than schooners, thereby slower in a chase. Cannons were set into the ship's sides, not in the front and back like smaller ships, positioned to fire when pursued. So, Captain Kidd didn't run much, but preferred battle?

"Tell me, what else do ya know about ships, Miss Grant?"

"Not a thing," she replied without turning.

"Navigation?"

"Nothing at all." He'd been eavesdropping. A very rude characteristic she made a mental note to hold against him.

She took a step forward, eager to be away from him. She didn't like how he made her skin feel clammy and her throat, dry.

"Ya didn't strike me as the kind of woman who ran away from men."

She stopped and turned to him. She did run away. All the time. She ran from the boredom of courting and the confines of marriage. "I run from nothing, Captain Kidd. I thought I proved that to ye already last eve when I took ye prisoner and held yer men at bay."

He laughed, a short, amused sound filled with deep baritones and a sensual cadence that curled Trina's toes and made her curse him silently. "I've heard that Highlanders were stubborn and prideful. I hadn't considered it to be true of Highland women, as well."

Trina thought she should look away in some modest, repentant gesture, but to hell with that. "That's quite all right, Captain. I dinna' imagine ye consider many things." Before he said another word, she whirled around on her heel and returned to her table, where Kyle was waiting for her.

Before she returned to her seat, three women encircled Alex where he stood, giggling at something he said.

"Why does he cause ye such ire?"

"Kyle," she said, severing her gaze from the licentious pirate and turning it on her cousin. "What makes ye assume I keep the captain in mind long enough to let him irritate me?"

The crook of Kyle's mouth said all he needed to say.

Trina sighed and shook her head. She hated not being able to keep her thoughts private around Kyle. Still, she wouldn't go so far as to admit anything more than the slightest interest in Alex Kidd. He was a pirate after all.

"He's quite full of himself."

Kyle looked in his direction. "He has reason to be. He moves with a certain kind of menace in his grace. Like a wolf."

"I hadna' noticed."

Her cousin laughed, but only for a moment, until she kicked him hard under the table.

"I dinna' care how he looks or how he sounds, or moves," she told him while he bent to rub his ankle under the table. "If I cared aboot the beauty of a man, I would have married Kevin MacKinnon last winter. The only thing I find of interest aboot Captain Kidd is his adventurous life."

"How d'ye know he leads an adventurous life, Trina?" Kyle put to her. "Mayhap the majority of his days are lonely and dull and coming ashore is like waking up again?"

This wasn't a guess. Kyle read expressions better than any book in their grandmere's vast library. She knew he'd want to study any new souls who turned up in Camlochlin, but had he gleaned this from the captain himself, one of his men? Trina turned to examine Alex with a new perspective. Did he spend months at a time at sea? Was setting foot on land with different faces to look at, fresh food to eat, and fragrant women to share a night with, better than hunting treasure? She could understand that. Aye, she could. She felt her dislike for him fading and when he glanced at her with the residue of a smile he was in the middle of offering to another, she smiled back, then turned away.

And looked straight into the cerulean gaze of her cousin.

"Yer faither would kill him."

She blinked as the fleeting realization of that truth sank in. She looked toward the table her parents shared with her aunts and uncles. Connor Grant was still the most handsome man in the Hall. Every woman in Camlochlin who wasn't his kin wished she were Mairi MacGregor. His smile was still as wide as the heavens and as bright as the sun. And it shone most on his wife and bairns. Because he loved her so, he would never let her leave Skye on a pirate ship.

"My faither would have no reason to kill him," she corrected Kyle when she realized it appeared—at least, to him, and he'd be correct—that she was considering it, "because I have no intention of doing anything so foolish as what ye're thinking."

"Good." He downed the cup set before him and rose to his feet. "Captain," he called out and beckoned Kidd to come closer. "Sit with us."

Trina stiffened in her chair as Kidd moved toward them, vowing to smash Kyle in the head with the flat of her blade later on. "There are things ye're bursting at the seams to know, but he makes ye a wee bit breathless," he explained to her gently, ignoring the blush across her nose. "I'll find oot fer ye."

Was she supposed to forgive him now? What the hell was the use not to? This was why Kyle was her dearest, most beloved friend. She barely had to tell him anything he didn't glean on his own. Sure, sometimes his ability was irritating, like when he knew things she didn't want him to know, but most of the time, it saved her from having to explain herself.

"Captain"—Kyle offered the pirate a seat opposite hers—"I wanted to steal a bit more time to chat with ye before the hour is up and ye leave."

"Another lesson on readin' lips?" The captain slipped his gaze to her while he accepted the invitation.

Trina cursed her traitorous nerve endings for tingling over the barest attention from him. She didn't dare look at Kyle to see if he was watching her. She prayed he wasn't.

"I think I've got the art down close," Kyle let him know. "I'm a quick learner. Nae, I had hoped to learn more aboot the life of a pirate."

"Oh?" The captain asked with the slightest upward quirk of his mouth—a quirk that sparked more flames in Trina's belly. "What would ya like to know?"

"What are some of the places ye've been to?" Kyle asked.

Trina settled into her chair, eagerly awaiting his answer. After listening to him for a little while she grew captivated by his tales of adventure on the high seas, from places as far away as Africa and as exotic as Barbados and Madagascar. Och, but she'd never heard such tales and doubted they were true.

"Captain," she said while he swigged a cup of whisky—and after the sound of his voice and the slow slant of his mouth didn't cause her heart to accelerate. "I know many noblemen keep servants, but surely the kind of slavery ye speak of in some of these places is an exaggerated rendition."

"The Indies and Africa are not Great Britain, Miss Grant. They are far more untamed and foreign than anythin' ya're acquainted with. Slavery is a harsh truth some people live with. But there be places where the natives live, unbound to master or law. They live free, and they live hard, plantin', fishin', dancin' to music beneath the stars, to music that saturates yar soul and tempts ya to do the most wicked things."

Trina wanted to blink, but she couldn't separate her gaze from the pirate's, even for that brief amount of time. Her insides seared and burned and made her skin damp. He conjured images in her head that quickened her breath and turned her bones to mud. She wanted to leap from her seat and run away from the confident crook of his mouth, the menace of his dark eyes. No man had ever attracted her so. She was correct not to like him. He was more than dangerous. He was perilous to her morals, her virtue.

She remained for as long as she could, imagining him wielding his cutlass against a horde of enemies, wondering how he looked without his shirt, or standing at the helm of his ship, guiding it toward the next adventure. Soon though, she could take no more and excused herself from the table and the Hall. She left the castle, looking over her shoulder every now and again to make certain she wasn't being followed.

It didn't take her long to reach the shore. She only wanted a glimpse of his ship in the first light of day. She knew she shouldn't look. Curiosity had never been her friend. She should be satisfied with her life, safe and content in Camlochlin. But she wasn't... because of curiosity.

Her breath caught in her breast at the sight of the magnificent beast heaving atop the waves, gleaming in the sun, its tall masts piercing the heavens. She'd seen a ship similar to this one many years ago, when the first Captain Kidd visited Skye. She'd never forgotten it, letting the memory of its wind-stretched sails and buoyancy, despite its mammoth size, fuel her dreams of leaving in search of adventure. Here was one even more breathtaking.

She so wanted to see it up close. Smell it. Touch it. Just for a moment or two. She'd been too young to get any closer to his father's ship. How often would opportunities like this come along for her? She looked toward the rocky incline. Did she dare board the ship and take advantage of this moment? It may never come again.

She bolted left and took off along the steep coastline. She knew the best way to reach the boat. She just wanted to feel the ship's planks beneath her feet, the water rocking her to and fro. What kind of adventures would its sails lead her to? Although the thought did cross her mind, she didn't plan on hiding aboard, stowing away and setting sail to some strange new land... perhaps in the Indies. She paused at the top of the cliffs and looked back at her home. What would her life be like away from here? Would leaving her family tear her heart to shreds and make her long for home? Och, Lord, she didn't want to marry Hugh, or anyone else. Not yet. She wanted an adventure. Just one. What would following a map across the ocean and searching for treasure be like?

She would never admit that what she did next had anything to do with the pirate. Or that the thought of him at her side while they sailed across the horizon made her heart jump in her chest. She stood poised above the ship and looked down at the waves slapping against it, the rope ladder dangling from the hull, inviting her aboard. Desire to spread her wings and be who she wanted to be coursed through her veins the same way it had in her mother's and her grandparents' before her.

Just a brief visit upon its decks, a moment to look around and sear the memory into her mind. She would board and then leave before discovery, and...

...secured her bow and arrows to her waist and dove into the depths.

Seagulls scattered and took to the sky above the cliffs; the only proof that she had been there. The earth went silent for a moment and then shattered when Kyle cursed the wind and jumped in after her.

Chapter Five

"Why the hell did ye follow me?" Caitrina demanded the instant Kyle climbed over the starboard rail, only seconds behind her.

"A better question," he countered while she wrung out her long hair, "is what the hell d'ye think ye're doing boarding this ship?"

"I wanted to have a closer look, Kyle. I may never get the chance again."

He looked as if he were going to say something but clenched his teeth instead. Heavens, she thought, watching him commanding control over his temper, his eyes certainly were a perfect blend of vivid blue and sparkling green, made even more dramatic by his emotions. He wasn't angry with her. He was simply worried. Insulting, but she had to love him for it.

"I'll leave before any of them come back." She took a step forward and patted his soaking sleeve. "And then—"

He could hold his tongue no longer. "Have ye forgotten that most of them are still on the ship, Trina?"

She stepped back. Why...aye, she had. Fool! Once

again her curiosity kept her from thinking her actions completely through. What would Captain Kidd's crew do if they found her and Kyle on board without an invitation? Her stomach sank. They were pirates. She'd read enough about them to know what they would do.

"I just wanted to see it, touch it—"

"Then be at it, Trina," Kyle offered somewhat tightly. "Turn and see it and then let's be away before they awaken."

Trina smiled at him. Drinking in a deep breath of cool air, she turned in her spot and then stopped breathing altogether.

She craned her neck, following the enormous trimmed sails of the mizzenmast to the mainmast in the center and the foremast at the far end, toward the bow. Breathless, she marveled at the height of the masts, square on the foremast with fore-and-aft rigging on the mainmast. She'd never seen a brigantine before and she relished every vision before her. Such a powerful beast to ride the turbulent ocean. It took a man just as untamed as the sea to steer her.

She felt Kyle tug on her arm, but she didn't want to leave yet. Her eye caught the crow's nest nearly at the top of the mast, a small net basket where one could look out over the sea. Och, she'd love to sail from such a height.

"We must go."

"What d'ye suppose is doun there?" she asked, ignoring her cousin. She stepped away from him and moved before he could stop her toward an open hatch. She heard Kyle whisper her name in urgent entreaty, but she just wanted a quick look.

She froze in her tracks at the sound of male voices stepping onto the deck from somewhere beyond the bow. The crew was beginning the day and any moment now they were going to spot her and her cousin. She spun around and looked at Kyle. There wasn't enough time for her to run back to him and for them both to jump overboard. But he could make it if he jumped now.

"Go!" she commanded quietly. Without waiting to see what he would do, she turned and disappeared down the hatch.

Of course, he followed her. As each second passed with more of them waking up, Trina felt more guilty for getting them into this. The deeper they went belowdecks to avoid being seen, the more it would look to everyone that they were stowing away.

"We've got to get our arses off this ship," Kyle worried as they slunk into the shadows.

"We'll wait here fer a wee bit and give the captain time to return," Trina suggested, shivering in the dark and swiping her hand across her nose. "He'll let us leave withoot a sword in the back."

She yawned when Kyle held her, offering warmth. She wasn't calm, but she was tired. None of them had slept all night after discovering pirates in Camlochlin and then breaking an early fast with them. She leaned her head against Kyle's arm and closed her eyes. Just for a moment.

Trina opened her eyes to the pitch-black and the smell of fish, rotten vegetables, and urine. She sat up. How long had they slept? She waited a moment, listening, feeling the floor beneath her. Then she moaned. They were moving. They were moving! Dear God, what had they done?

"Kyle?" she whispered, unable to make out if he was still lying near her. He didn't answer. He snored though. Trina opened her mouth to rouse him then stopped. They were stowaways, set out on a brig to parts unknown. The thought of it thrilled her and terrified her at the same time.

She doubted the captain would kill her or Kyle. Not after meeting her kin, at least. Kidd was no fool. He would turn his ship around and bring her home.

She sat there in the dark, holding her breath and contemplating her future. Marriage waited for her at home, a dull future of cooking and cleaning and sewing. After another hour though, an hour in which she weighed her desires against what disappearing would do to her and Kyle's parents, she rose up on her feet and climbed over a crate. Where were they? Suddenly she wanted to know. If she could get a look at the landscape she would recognize Scotland. But what if she was no longer near Scotland?

Without waking Kyle—no sense in causing him more hours of worry than he needed—she found the creaky stairs and climbed up to the next deck. She set her nose to the air and followed the scent of fresh, briny air. They were on the ocean. She found a stairwell and ascended slowly, cautiously. The vast twilight sky above her appeared close enough to reach up and touch. She looked around but couldn't tell where she was. She was sure, though, that they weren't anywhere near Scotland. She climbed no farther when the sound of men's voices suddenly frightened her. She had to find the captain. Surely, Kidd wouldn't let his crew have their way with her. If she was wrong, she would fight to the death. Preferably theirs.

"Well, what d' we 'ave 'ere?"

Trina froze as terror gripped her heart. She said a silent prayer, then turned to look behind her. At least half a dozen torch-carrying men stood leering at her. There may have been more in the shadows. She couldn't tell. She prayed to God to keep Kyle asleep.

"I came aboard to admire yer ship and I must have fallen asleep." She offered them a smile and two moved toward her. "Take me to yer captain!" she demanded, stepping back and drawing a dagger. "'Tis in yer best interest to do as I request," she warned sincerely. "My kin will hunt down yer vessel and slaughter the lot of ye if harm comes to me."

A man with a patch over his eye laughed and snatched her by the wrist. He released her an instant later when Trina slashed his fingers and set him yelping like a puppy.

"Leave her!" another voice commanded, stopping the rush of men coming upon her. "She speaks true," he said, coming forward. "Her family will come after us and delay us gettin' our hands on the treasure."

Trina recognized him as Mr. Pierce, Kidd's quartermaster. Beneath his bandanna and the light of the setting sun, his golden hair glimmered. He was tall and quite handsome, despite the effects of what a dozen or so breaks had done to his nose. Would she find help with him? Hope sparked and she dared a step toward him. "Thank ye. If ye would just—"

"I should let the lads have their way with ya, Miss Grant," he interrupted, his blue eyes frosty on her. "'Twould serve ya right fer stowin' away on our ship and puttin' our lives in danger, but 'tis against our code of conduct."

She opened her mouth to speak but he shoved her forward and she turned to glare at him instead. Giving him a tongue lashing for manhandling her wouldn't be in her best interest though, so she kept her mouth shut, glanced one last time at the hatch from which she ascended, and kept moving. On her way across the length of the long main deck and up a few sets of stairs, she prayed that the captain would show her kindness and bring her back to Camlochlin—or mayhap he would consider France. Spain was likely lovely this time of year. In truth, she'd come this far. She didn't want to go home yet. If there could be no adventure, then at least let there be Spain. She felt terrible about the worry she knew she was causing her kin right now. She'd just disappeared. What would they think? She suspected her mother might know what she'd done. She was, after all, heir to Mairi MacGregor's wild spirit. Her father would likely lock her in her chamber for a month when he discovered what she'd done. A month, and then marriage...

She was here now and she might as well enjoy what she could. It was the last and only opportunity she would ever get. But could she convince Kyle to remain aboard a little while longer?

With a slight spark of renewed hope, she waited while Mr. Pierce beat his palm over a carved wooden door.

A grunt sounded from inside and Pierce pushed open the door without waiting for a coherent invitation. "Ya have a guest, Captain."

"A what?" came that smooth, husky voice, sincerely surprised by the introduction.

Pierce stepped aside and swept his arm across the entrance. "Ya're in his hands now." He flashed her a polite smile, exposing a row of surprisingly bright teeth, and only one missing behind his cheek.

Trina didn't like the way his smirk made her feel like he was happily turning her over to a shark.

She wasn't certain she cared very much for the quartermaster and was glad to see him go, closing the door behind her.

She looked around the cabin, rather than at the man whose unharnessed virility charged the air and made her nerve endings burn.

His quarters were cozily lit against walls of rich, waxed wood, with furnishings to match. There was no clutter upon the table or cherry dresser, but instead, any jars and other breakable trinkets, including lanterns, hung on rope from the ceiling and walls.

"Miss Grant?"

Damn the lush cadence of his voice, which drew her gaze to where he stood shirtless and bathed in flickering candlelight.

Her kneecaps almost gave out when he tilted his head at her and took a step closer. "Ya don't strike me as the chasin' kind."

With his fur-lavished bed behind him, he moved toward her, untying the laces of his canvas breeches. She watched, unable to halt the direction of her gaze down his chest, which was corded with sinew and scars, to his tightly sculpted belly. Oh, she would chase him. Any woman would.

"Ye have made a correct assumption, Captain."

His gaze suddenly shifted and found hers from beneath the dark veil of his lashes, misgivings clearly evident. "And if ya're not chasin' me, then perhaps 'tis me map ya'd be wantin'."

She laughed, probably not an appropriate response to such a grievous accusation, judging by the deepening hue of his sable eyes.

"Be ya so arrogant that ya supposed ya could rob from me and leave me ship alive?"

She shouldn't have laughed. He was quite serious. Her thoughts turned immediately to Kyle. She fought every instinct not to turn and run to her cousin. No doubt the pirate would chase her. He could overpower her with little effort. Kyle would die trying to protect her and then she would most likely be thrown overboard.

"Have ya nothin' to say in yar defense, woman?" he asked on a deep-throated purr. "I would have thought more from the MacGregor chief's niece."

"I need no defense, Captain," she said, determined not to reveal her fear and give him the upper hand. "I came not to rob ye. But if it had been my intention to do so, 'twould not have been too difficult. I could have easily escaped the ship unnoticed had I not fallen asleep."

He came toward her, a flame formed from the hottest depths, sent to tempt her away from her dreams. Stopping close, he looked down at her, slowing her heart as quickly as he accelerated it. He crooked his mouth, coming to some conclusion about her that apparently pleased him. He laughed, a full, robust sound, like thunder on a summer night in Camlochlin. It frightened her to know that her good sense scattered to the four winds when she but looked at him; the play of muscle in his upper arms, the way shadows and light danced over his tanned skin. She trembled at his closeness and silently cursed her traitorous body. She tried not to let the sight of his long, golden physique addle her, or the sexy way he walked, oozing with confidence and fear-lessness, overtake her. Hell, she lived with men bigger and brawnier than he. She wouldn't let him affect her so.

"Well, then, Miss Grant, if not to rob me, why are ya here?"

"I simply wanted to see yer ship," she told him with only the slightest crack in her voice. Did she want to steal his map, or chase it with him?

He remained still and steady on his feet while the ship bucked beneath them. Trina, on the other hand, landed straight in his arms. She didn't break free and make a mad dash for the door the way she wanted to. She was determined to stay strong even pressed up against his warm, bare mus-cles. She faltered when he dragged his cheek over her fore-head, but she held strong. She might be utterly innocent to the sexual wiles of men, but she was no quivering fool.

"I would have happily given ya a tour while we were docked." He traced his fingers down both of her arms, keeping her poised just a hair's breath away from his body. "Stowin' away until we're hundreds of leagues out to sea and claimin' that ya fell asleep—"

"I did indeed fall asleep!" she argued, pulling away from him. "I know I need yer help at the moment, but I will not be accused of being a thief *and* a liar in the same day. I ask ye fer nothing but to bring me home." Should she tell him about Kyle? Could she keep her cousin hidden until they...

The captain chuckled in her face. "Ya think I'm goin' to turn me ship around and sail all the way back to Scotland?"

"Aye, and avoid a battle with my kin," she stated, hoping it would sway him.

He moved up against her again, sending hot fissures down her spine, and curled his arm around her waist. His grip was filled with strength and tension, yet gentle when he pulled her closer. "Miss Grant." His breath scorched across her lips, hypnotizing her, paralyzing her. "I've had the Royal Navy on me arse. I don't care about yar kin comin' after me. Still, I'd prefer not to battle me father's friend."

In an instant the gravity of what she had done became clear. Her kin would indeed come after her and he wasn't afraid. He was obviously mad, not in his right state of mind. Nevertheless, her kin could die in a battle on the sea. "Then..." She arched her back to get away from him. He moved in over her. What would a madman do with her? With Kyle? She needed to know. "What d'ye plan on doing with me?"

He gave her no time to think, to catch her breath, to pull away...if she had a mind and the strength to do so.

Caitrina had been kissed a few years back by young

John MacKinnon. But she knew, as the captain's beguiling mouth dipped down to hers, that this kiss was going to be very very different.

And hell, she was correct.

There was nothing gentle or curious about it. His mouth covered hers with dominance and scalding heat while he dragged her in against the rigid, flat lines of his body. His tongue teased against her lips, licking, tasting her, tempting her to join in his sweet madness. Like that flame, he swept over her, consuming her muscles, scorching her nerve endings. He kissed her until she began to believe he had every right to do so—until her knees went weak and a slight, pitiful gasp escaped her lips.

He finally broke away with a slow, seductive smile she wanted to gaze at for years to come.

She slapped him hard across his face, lest he think to take further liberties in the future—since she hadn't stopped him the first time.

For a moment, something dark and fully seductive moved across his features. She thought, trying to slow her heartbeat, that he might either strangle her or rip the gown from her body and have his way with her.

"Fergive me," he said roughly and without a trace of remorse. "I misjudged. I don't bed children."

Her mouth fell open and her eyes narrowed into slits. Here she thought he was being gallant, when he was simply being insulting. Children! How dare he imply that she wasn't yet a woman! "I should slap ye again fer yer insult," she seethed.

"Do it," he provoked her with a sinful, sinuous smile, "and the beast that I am at this moment keepin' at bay will more than likely haul ya up against that wall and take ya, despite yar protests."

She felt the color drain from her face. She couldn't breathe, or think, or speak, blushing and stammering about for something to say. The images he conjured for her frightened and thrilled her out of her skin at the same time. She didn't like being threatened but she wasn't a fool to test him.

"I shouldna' have put my hand to ye," she said softly, lowering her gaze. "'Twas wrong of me."

He took her hand, compelling her to look up again, into his eyes. He brought her hand to his face and spread her palm over his prickly cheek where she'd slapped him, letting her feel his smile. Was she forgiven that easily? Could he possibly be so easy to bend to her will . . . at least until she got the hell off the ship? She had no choice but to leave. Either that or lose herself, or worse, her kin to him. She would be kind to him and flirtatious if it would keep him from tossing her and Kyle overboard—if it gained her what she wanted, that is, getting back home and saving her family, she would do anything.

"May we please speak of my accommodations whilst . . ."

He tilted his head to laugh, like a wolf calling to the moon. She filled her vision with the beautiful sight of him and forgot what she'd said to cause his humor. While it was coming back to her, a knock sounded on the door.

"Aye?" the captain called out.

Once again, Mr. Pierce appeared at the entrance. "Ya have a guest."

The captain's eyes fell to her. "Another one?"

Trina's breath tore madly through her chest.

"Aye." Pierce shoved Kyle into the cabin. "I'm havin' the men sweep the ship fer any more of 'em."

Trina wanted to weep when her cousin marched toward her. He didn't look well. He appeared quite greenish in fact. This was all her fault. He was right. She was trouble. The crew would be even more likely to kill him than they were her.

"We agreed to remain together, Trina." It was a whisper, but she heard it.

"I didna' wish to wake ye," she explained softly as he passed her.

"Quite an interestin' day this is turnin' out to be, aye, Sam?" the captain said, reminding them that he was there. "Two outlaws, proscribed by kings, and who know about me map, stow away aboard me ship to rob me and both of them fall asleep."

Trina shook her head at him. "We hadna' slept in more than six and twenty hours. We were weary. And I told ye we didna' come here fer yer map."

"What ya told me," he corrected her, then eyed Kyle when he swayed on his feet, "was that *ya* did not come here to steal it. Ya did not tell me about him. As much as I'd like to believe ya, I don't."

Before she could reply, he returned to his bed and kicked off his boots. "Sam, put them in the hold until I decide what to do with them and hurry, this one looks like he's about to puke all over me floor."

Pierce produced a pistol from a fold in his coat. "Let's go then."

The hold? Nae! Trina whirled around to look the captain in the face. "Ye would chain us to the floor in a hold without enough room to stand?"

He nodded and met her murderous glare with a hard, unyielding one of his own. For the briefest of moments he turned his eyes away from her. She would have missed it if she blinked. But she didn't blink.

"Until I decide what to do with ya is what I said, Miss Grant."

She wanted to claw his eyes out. Take out her dagger and fling it into his chest. Och, why had she studied books on ships and learned enough to know what, besides piss and manure and rats and bars, the hold usually contained?

"Sam," he said to his quartermaster, "have the men remove the bones of me last prisoners and make room fer these two."

"Captain!" she appealed one more time.

"Ya stowed away on me ship, and after I came into possession of a map to a priceless treasure. Give me one reason to trust ya?"

She couldn't. She couldn't think. "Bastard!" she snarled at him while Pierce led her away. "I hope my faither kills ye!"

That was all she could say before her captor slammed the door in her face and pulled her down the stairs.

There was no light in the hold. But there was Kyle. He shouldn't have followed her. Now he was sick as a dog.

"Fergive me fer getting us into this," she whispered to him later that night while he emptied his belly into a basket close by.

"I do." He told her softly. "I understand why ye came here."

In the darkness Trina smiled. She stretched her shackled arm, trying to reach a pin in her hair.

Of course he understood. He knew her better than anyone in Camlochlin, anyone on Skye. And she knew him. Kyle's natural instincts yearned for the new and unfamiliar. What could be more scintillating to him than digging around the mind of Captain Kidd and his unlawful crew?

If they both wanted to stay, who the hell would stop her kin from coming?

❖

Chapter Six

*A*lex opened his eyes to his morning hangover and cursed the new day.

Until he remembered the treasure he'd come into possession of the day before. He sat up and, leaving the bed, he pushed aside a small trapdoor in the wall. With a quickening heart, he expelled an iron strong box from its hiding place. A gift from the daughter of a sultan, it was designed with three locks and hidden keyholes as well as being booby-trapped. He didn't need to open it to see the map his father left him. He knew it was inside. As long as the box was here, so was the map. He still couldn't believe his father had left it to him. But Andersen had told him that William Kidd had understood why his son hadn't returned to his ship when they'd docked in Lisbon those many years ago. He'd understood that Alex had fallen in love and had wanted to begin his life with his woman. His father had never known how the woman his son loved had betrayed him.

But none of that mattered now. He had the map to his father's last treasure. But it was more than that. It was his father's exoneration, his forgiveness, and that was more priceless than any ship loaded with riches.

He'd studied the map last night, learning which direction to take to the *Quedagh Merchant*. He knew the location well, having spent many years in the West Indies and the Caribbean. He thought about the tales Andersen had told him about his father and was happy that his life continued to be an adventure.

His good mood cooled when he remembered what else he'd come into possession of. He needed to get rid of his two thieving guests before they set sail for the Indies. He almost regretted leaving Andersen on Skye. His father's boatswain could have looked after the two Highlanders in France and gotten them home without incident. But the Dutchman had to be left behind. Alex didn't need him anymore and he certainly didn't trust him now that he had something so valuable on board. His father had always told him that a man would do anything for treasure, even turn against his captain, and thanks to Madalena Barros, he'd learned that a woman would do even more. He wanted Miss Grant off his boat.

"Come," Alex called out when a knock came at his door. He hoped it was Cooper with his breakfast.

He swore when Sam came inside.

"What are we goin' to do about Miss Grant and Mr. MacGregor?" his best friend asked him, throwing himself in Alex's chair. "I don't like chainin' women in the hold."

"I don't intend on keepin' them down there fer too long," Alex said, returning the box inside the wall. "I don't know what they're up to yet. What are they really doin' on me ship?" He turned to Sam while he began dressing for the day. His quartermaster offered him no answers. Reaching for his bandanna, Alex tied it around his head, then followed with two sashes of bright green and purple around his waist. He tucked his cutlass between the sashes and his breeches, secured a smaller dagger to a clip up his sleeve, and hid a pistol inside his boot.

Sam chuckled, watching him. "A bit overdone, aye?"

Alex shook his head. "Do ya ferget who those two are or where they come from? She shot an arrow straight through me favorite hat and tore it from me head." She beguiled him with a set of huge blue eyes and a mouth made for kissing. And hell, but he'd kissed her. He couldn't remember a more passionate response from any woman in a long time. When she'd slapped him a moment later, her strike snapped like a whip across his flesh... Hell, he could have taken her right there. She was temptation incarnate. If she had come for his map, she would likely get it if he continued kissing her. She was the most dangerous kind of woman: the kind to whom a man would eventually give anything... even his treasure.

Sam quirked his mouth to one side and gave Alex a knowing look. "Is that why she's in the hold and not in yar bed?"

He clenched his teeth at the thought of her in his bed, beneath him and astride him, thoughts that plagued him since the first night he saw her in the fog. "Aye. I don't want her tryin' to kill me whilst I—"

The cabin door flew open and Jack Hanson, Alex's hulking master gunner, towered in the frame, interrupting their talk. "The prisoners 'ave escaped."

Alex and Samuel rushed to the door. "What the hell do ya mean they've escaped?" Sam demanded.

Alex stormed past them both and stepped out onto the quarterdeck. The news didn't shock him. He should have expected it. It angered him that he'd allowed Caitrina Grant's beauty...her full, ripe mouth...to dull his wits. Even now, the memory of her in his arms, fearless but submissive, softened his resolve. He reined it back in. She'd lied to him. She'd wanted more than to simply see his ship. What did she want? He looked over his shoulder at his cabin door. "Jack," he called out. "Ya and two others guard me cabin. Sam, relieve the helm."

"Three of us fer a boy and a woman?" Jack asked him.

"They're resourceful," Alex told him. "Don't underestimate them. Remember their clan survived a three-hundred-year proscription."

Jack gaped at him like he'd just sprouted a second head. "A three-'undred-year what, Cap'n?"

Alex turned toward the bow while the winds picked up and snatched his hair from his shoulders. Where were they? Did they jump overboard? He stepped onto the main deck and barked orders to his mates, who were waiting there for instruction. "Don't kill them. Bring them to me when ya find them."

"Aye, aye, Cap'n."

He watched them head off to their work then pondered his unwanted guests. Where would they have gone? He returned to the aft and the galley at the far end. He doubted they'd jumped. They didn't strike him as imbeciles. They hadn't escaped the hold just to hide again. How the hell did they escape the hold? He shook his head and smiled just a little, impressed with their competence. They had to be hungry.

He moved, ears alerted to sounds coming from the darkness. He made his way along the narrow hall to the galley and was promptly struck on the head from behind. He didn't go down but it was only due to his excellent sense of balance. He saw stars...and a host of other odd things swimming about his head. He shook them away and ducked just in time to avoid another blow. Coming back up, he turned and sent his blackest glare at his attacker, caught in the light of the porthole. He didn't waste time talking but pulled his pistol free and aimed it at her. "Turn around and head fer the stairs, Miss Grant, and while ye're doin' it, tell me where Mr. MacGregor is."

He cocked the lock when she didn't move. She obeyed.

"My cousin is right behind ye."

Alex hoped she was bluffing but the tip of a blade in his back proved she was very serious. His grin was dagger sharp. He remained very still. These two were trained fairly well in the art of craftiness. "How did ya escape yar chains and the hold?"

"A hair clip." She quirked a corner of her mouth, enjoying her confession.

"Where do ya plan on goin' after this? Ya will both be killed the instant ya step on deck."

"Not if it means *yer* life with ours, Captain," said MacGregor behind him. "We just want off this ship. We want nothing from ye but a lifeboat."

Alex laughed. "We're at sea, pup. Ya'll last until the first giant swell and then ya'll both drown."

"What d'ye suggest then?" Miss Grant asked, her pretty voice trickling over Alex's spine. "I dinna' want my kin to have to fight at sea because of me, but I'm afraid if I am not returned, they will come."

"In truth," Alex admitted, "I don't want to fight them either. They were true friends of me father's. I dispatched one of me smaller boats to set course for shore and arrange to have a message delivered from me to Skye."

His stowaways looked remarkably relieved for a moment. Then Miss Grant spoke.

"We willna' be kept in the hold until ye deliver us somewhere safely."

"I gathered that much," Alex told her succinctly. "But pointin' daggers at me is a sure way of endin' up in one again. Or worse."

"We don't want to be yer enemy," said MacGregor, withdrawing his dagger and clutching his belly.

"Wise." Alex took a step toward the girl. She stepped back. "What is it ya want, then?"

"Not yer silly map." The husky thread in her voice mocked him and sent a scintillating fissure down his back. "If we wanted it we could have had it all these years."

"Oh?" he asked, stepping by her and leading the way out. "Yar uncle would have stolen from me by giving ya me map?" He smiled in front of them. "That's interestin' to know."

"Nae!" she stormed after him. "That is not what I meant! Our chief is not a thief!"

He shrugged and caught Samuel's eye when he stepped into the light. "Everyone is a thief."

"In yer world."

He turned to face her as they reached his men and was caught off guard, which seemed to happen to him every time he set his eyes on the beauty of her round, dimpled face. "Woman, what do ya know of me world?"

"Some of the nastiest, most traitorous men who were ever born live in yer world, Captain Kidd. Even yer own faither said so when he visited my home. Toss treasure into the pot and a few months too long at sea and those men begin to imagine yer demise."

Aye, she was absolutely correct, pirates cared about their captains and quartermasters as long as they provided booty and muscles. No booty, no crew. But he didn't want her to know he agreed with her about his own hands. His men respected him, and they feared him a little too. Anything less would lead to mutiny. They knew he would take their side and fight at their backs. He intended on keeping it that way. He couldn't let her insult them.

He looked over his shoulder at his mates. "Is this true? Do any of ya plan my demise?" They all answered with a resounding, insulted *nay*!

"Tell me"—he turned away from the sudden panic in her ice blue eyes and looked at her cousin next—"what do *ya* think of me crew?"

The Highlander didn't so much as flinch, impressing Alex, especially when he glanced longingly at the rail but managed to sound controlled when he spoke. "I dinna' know yer crew, but I'll tell ye this, I willna' let any one of ye bring harm to my cousin. I'll take the lot of ye down before ye know which way I'm coming."

Alex cocked his brow at Kyle's bold declaration. He liked that he saw no fear in the lad.

"We have articles on this ship, MacGregor," Sam told him. As quartermaster he had say in all decisions aboard ship. There was little Alex could do now. "Article nine decrees that any man threatening the captain or the crew should walk the plank. Kiss yer cousin farewell."

He drew his cutlass and poked MacGregor with it. Then so did the rest of the crew.

Someone clutched Alex's arm. He looked down to find her there, terror widening her eyes, shaking her fingers while they clung to him. "Please, Captain, stop this. He didn't mean—"

Sam poking her cousin along the keel drew her gaze. Her grip tightened. Her eyes came to rest on a length of timber protruding above the water. She released him, stepped back, and had an arrow nocked in her bow before Alex knew what she was doing. She spread her legs and aimed at Sam. "Let him go."

Alex watched her, his blood set aflame by her fearless, if not foolish actions. He reached out, quicker than she expected, and snatched the arrow from her hands. He grasped her wrist next and yanked her close. He closed his arms around her and relieved her of her quiver. "Sam," he called out while he plucked away her bow next, not letting her go or easing his hold on her. "Let him go. Let's not kill him fer his noble attempt at protectin' Miss Grant."

"But Cap'n, the articles."

"I know, old friend," Alex told him, hoping to convince him to release her cousin. Why? Why did he risk disagreement with his partner for her? "But we've looked away from our laws before. And these are, after all, family of the MacGregor chief."

Sam stared at him for a minute while the men mumbled their disappointment at not getting to toss someone overboard. "Fine." Sam sighed and shoved MacGregor away. "But I'll not let him take a dagger to ya."

Alex nodded, then turned to his men. "Bring him to the mate's quarters and remove any weapons he carries."

"What of her?" Samuel asked upon reaching them.

"She'll be stayin' with me." He turned to one of the sailors to his right. "Have Cooper bring our mornin' meals to me cabin."

"Captain," Kyle warned, despite his brush with death, "if ye put yer hands on her—"

Alex held up his palm to stop Sam from hitting the Highlander. "Ya have me word, MacGregor."

That seemed to mollify Kyle, at least while he leaned over the side of the boat and dry heaved into the ocean.

"Captain, ye have my thanks fer stopping yer brutes from tossing my cousin overboard, but I will not stay in yer cabin." Trina tried to pull away from him. He held her securely.

"Ya'll obey the captain and be safe from the men," Sam told her. "Yar cousin may believe he can take us all, but he will die if he's forced to try to protect ya again. Will ya live with his death well?"

She looked over at her sick cousin and shook her head, terrified and defeated.

Alex felt a twinge of pity for her but Sam was correct in warning her of the consequences of her actions.

"Come." He tugged her toward his cabin and didn't look back at Sam or anyone else before he shut the door behind them.

"I can sleep in the cargo hold tonight without the others knowing."

"Ya'll sleep in the bed," he corrected her, letting her go. He leaned against the door to watch her while she turned, pale, and had a long look at the bed.

"And where will ye be sleeping?" she asked, returning her attention to him, chin raised.

He had to grin at her resolve. Her inner strength wasn't something taught but rather it flowed through her veins from the blood of her kin. He found her damned sexy. So much more so than the whores he paid for. He thought she deserved his approval and his appreciation, but her fire tempted him to pillage her.

"I'll be sleepin' in my bed, as well."

Her eyes widened to delightful proportions, but when she spoke, her voice was steady. "I'll throw myself overboard first."

He considered her vow and remembered that she had

already escaped from his hold. "Can ya escape any lock then?" He clicked the lock on his door and took a step toward her. Perhaps it was her cousin who knew how to—

"Mostly any," she replied, taking a step back.

He quirked his mouth and tilted his head at her. She piqued his interest. What kind of life had she led in Skye? Did she break into rooms and rob other people's goods? Did the rest of her clan know? He wanted to learn more about her. "Yar aim with an arrow is quite remarkable." He caught the subtlest hint of pride squaring her shoulders. She liked compliments, like any woman did. When he reached her, it took all his strength to resist the urge to hold her, kiss her mouth... "Ya know how to pick locks and board ships." He circled her, closing his eyes while he breathed in the sweet fragrance of her hair. Her backside brushed against his groin, but it was her reaction that nearly did him in. He moved away, despite his desire to remain and feel her tremble against him. "What else can ya do that I should know about, Miss Grant?"

A sharp pinch in his abdomen made him look down. He was surprised to see not just any dagger pushed against him, but *his* personal dagger that she held.

"I can protect myself from wild beasts."

He threw back his head and laughed, sincerely delighted by her untamed spirit. He moved aside, stepping out of her reach, and held out his hand for his dagger. "I'm glad to hear that," he said with the residue of his amusement lingering in his smile. "I suppose lockin' ya in is senseless then."

"Aye. 'Twould be, Captain."

"Ya'll use caution around the men, aye?" He paused for a moment to let Cooper in with two bowls and bread in his hands. "Only use yar own blade if ya must," he continued when they were alone again. "I'll get ya home safely to Skye."

He invited her to sit and then strode to a thick covered jar swinging from a rope. He set it free and sat in the seat near hers. He was surprised to see that she had pushed away her bowl.

"Ye mentioned delivering a message to my kin?"

"Aye," he said and told her of it. "I explained to yar father that ya and MacGregor came aboard and fell asleep until 'twas too late to return ya. I vowed to bring ya both safely to France."

She looked relieved and completely grateful. She even smiled, until she looked at her gruel again.

"Ya don't like oat gruel?" He tossed a playful grin at the jar, then popped the cork. "I have the remedy." He dipped his spoon into the jar and gathered several drops of golden honey. "I use it sparingly." He moved to tilt his spoon over her bowl. She stopped him.

"Then, please, dinna' waste it on me. Fer I willna' eat those oats, sweetened or not. There are bugs in them."

"It happens, Miss Grant." He shrugged. "Bugs get into everything the longer ya have it. We haven't been fully stocked since we left New York."

She forgot her food and rested her chin in her hand like she was settling in for a good tale. "Tell me, what is New York like?"

She liked adventure, this one. He could see the light of anticipation in her eyes. Though she had tried to hide it, she wore the same breathless look in Camlochlin when he told her and Kyle about Madagascar. She yearned for it just as he did. "'Tis very proper," he told her, liking the effect his words had on her, "or so 'twould seem until ya move about in its darkened alleys. Where I was, there are no mountain ranges, not too many wide-open spaces at all. Everyone wears too many clothes; ruffles are fine in moderation."

Her laughter gave his heart pause. Soon, he found that he liked talking with her. He liked watching her face and the different play of emotion that danced over her features when she told him about her kin. He liked listening to her, as well, but his duties of the day called to him and he rose from his chair. He left his honey jar with her, on the table in case she changed her mind about the oats.

"I would like to hear more about Camlochlin," he told her while he moved toward the door. "Perhaps later."

When she nodded, he offered her a smile. "I'll return later and show ya around the ship."

"That would be nice, Captain," she replied. "Thank ye."

He severed his gaze from hers, but he didn't want to. Then he returned his dagger to his sash and left the cabin without another word. When he reached the helm, he relieved his sailing master of the wheel and took over the course to their destination.

Hell, it was going to be a hot day, Alex thought, thankful when Sam appeared at his side and handed him his hat, still damp and sporting two new holes. "Who retrieved it?"

"Gustaaf," his friend told him.

Alex eyed him from beneath the familiar brim after he fit his beloved hat onto his head. "Gustaaf can't swim." It was shocking really. Gustaaf was the only Dutchman he knew who'd never learned to swim.

"I know. He nearly drowned. He was in the infirmary until this mornin'. I didn't know he had it 'til now."

Six months on his ship and Gustaaf was already loyal enough to drown for him. Alex had the notion that if he was ever arrested and hanged for piracy, Sam and Gustaaf would be there to see him off. Such loyalty was rare on board a ship. Alex would see that he did not go by unnoticed. "I'll see to his deed."

Sam nodded. "What do ya think of our guests?"

He thought about it, about how he'd known Caitrina Grant for a day and he'd already given her his honey, an abundance of his smiles, and his time, if he kept his word and gave her the tour she wanted. What else would she get from him? "Thieves. They be thieves after me treasure, Sam."

"What shall we do with them?"

"Sail to France and toss them overboard, then continue on our quest."

"Aye," his quartermaster agreed. "The sooner they're gone, the better."

"Aye." Alex turned the wheel, setting course for France. No truer statement was spoken today. His reasoning had nothing to do with her kin. If they still came after him, he would handle it. No, he wanted to get rid of Caitrina Grant so badly because if he didn't, he would end up in her arms, in her body, and probably in her heart. He didn't want to be the one who tamed her heart and then broke it when he left her.

Since when did he care about such trivial matters as a woman's heart? He didn't. Caring led to heartbreak, and he would never put himself through it again.

Caitrina Grant needed to go. The sooner the better.

Chapter Seven

Trina didn't wait for the captain to return. She grew restless after a while and pulled open the door. Her first thought was to find her cousin. He wasn't taking to sailing very well and she felt terrible for him. How was the crew treating him? Would he truly try to take them all on if she was hurt? She knew he would, or he would try to. He'd likely kill many of them too before they killed him. She had noted his hands slipping into the folds of his plaid earlier today, when Mr. Pierce pushed him toward the plank. He was reaching for his pistols, or daggers, or whatever he had hidden there. Sick or not, when it came to battle skill, no one compared to Kyle. He began his training early and became one of Camlochlin's most fearsome swordsmen. Trina prayed he wasn't provoked and she also prayed that he wasn't still suspended over the railing growing weaker with each crashing wave.

The rest of her thoughts revolved around the captain. Wasn't it thoughtful of him to pen a letter to her kin reassuring them that she and Kyle were safe? It gave her such relief knowing they wouldn't come after her. Enough relief, in fact, to let her consider his easy laughter and the way it drizzled down her spine like warm honey. How did he manage to paralyze her with a mere slant of his mouth? Och, his mouth...She cursed him for kissing her because she was quite certain that no man on earth would ever kiss her that way again. None would make her feel all weak and willing the way he did. She wondered how many women he'd kissed in the past in order to become such an expert at it. His mouth was so hot and hungry, his body consumed her and made her feel small and delicate...and eager for something more from him. He didn't mind her drawing his dagger on him. Would she do it again if he tried to touch her while they shared the bed? Och, they couldn't share the bed! The thought terrified her to her core. She didn't worry about how to stop him, but about not wanting to stop him. It was as if he had some powerful hold over her senses. When he was in her vision, she couldn't take her eyes off him. His touch set her nerve endings on fire. The sound of his voice, his laughter, even to mock her, melted the fibers of her bones. He tasted of rum and danger when he kissed her, and she wanted more of him. His power over her frightened her a little but it excited her too. It was like setting sail to a distant, unknown territory. Her heart pounded for it.

The ship rose on a swell, twenty feet high, and then fell to the waves. Trina clutched her belly and prayed Kyle wasn't hurling into someone's shoes.

She made a face and looked across the deck for any sign of her cousin. She didn't see him and let her gaze drift to the crew attending to the running riggings. Odd, she hadn't noticed before but none of them wore shoes. They did, however, all wear the same close-fitting canvas pants that the captain wore, along with bandannas to keep the hot sun from burning their heads and their hair out of their eyes. They sang while they worked and twice she blushed at the use of their words to describe women's breasts.

She turned and looked behind her, upstairs at the helm. Was the captain there? Before she could stop them, her feet moved her forward. She climbed, passing the sterncastle deck to the poop deck.

She saw him, hands on the wheel, legs braced, guiding the behemoth beneath him over the thrashing sea while sea spray moistened his shirt and made it cling to him. He had the look about him like he could conquer the world...and her, if he so chose. He was a danger to her and she knew it. Still, she angled her head to see his profile beneath his rescued hat. His gaze was steady on the horizon, his mouth set to his course.

"I told ya to wait fer me."

"I grew bored," she told him, only slightly surprised that he sensed her presence. "I'd hoped to find Kyle."

He slipped her a brief glance. His sexy smirk weakened her kneecaps. "Ya thought he'd be sailin' the ship then?"

"Nae, of course not." Hell, he was infuriating; subtly insinuating that she was looking for him and not her cousin. "I came up here because I...I...well, I..." She wasn't any good at lying. Kyle never could get her to master the skill the way he had. Then again, she'd never wanted to be a spy but an adventurer...She glared at the grinning captain, balled her hands into fists, and stormed away, back toward the stairs.

"Best remove them—"

She slipped on the wet stairs and tumbled down the rest of them.

"—shoes."

"Cap'n's right," Mr. Pierce said, standing over her and lending her a hand. "Deck's slippery. Ya can balance better barefoot."

"Thank ye." She rose to her feet and wiped her palms down her skirts. "Where is my cousin?"

The quartermaster broke his gaze from her and motioned with his chin along the port side of the ship. "He's bein' pierced."

Trina nearly shouted. "Pierced? Why?" She shoved past him without waiting for his response—which he gave her anyway as she hurried off.

"He's been pukin' all afternoon, that's why."

Good lord, what were they doing to Kyle? Had they overpowered him? Taken him down while their captain sailed off into the sun, oblivious to the cruelty of his crew? Was the captain oblivious to anything? Nae, the bastard wasn't. He knew what they were doing to Kyle. She came to the hatch leading down to the mate's quarters and descended without hesitation. Almost immediately she was abducted by a pair of grimy, groping fingers. It was dark below deck, but she managed to smash the end of her palm into his throat, the way her mother had taught her. She didn't wait for him to fall but hurried onward, eager to find her cousin. Her attacker hadn't fallen but gave chase and grabbed her by a fistful of hair. She cried out as he dragged her to her knees and fire lanced her scalp. She had to think, not about her pain, but about his. Her heart raced, making her feel a little light-headed with fear. No man had ever attacked her before. This was real. There were no big, brawny Highlanders here to protect her. Would he kill her? She had to control her terror and think about what she had been taught.

Clenching her hands together, she swung her arms

back between her thighs and then hauled her double fist high into his groin.

He came down beside her, still holding her hair. For a moment, she couldn't see, or think, almost as helpless as he. He gave her locks a yank, proving his quick recovery. She realized with the prick of a knife at her throat just how close her head was to his wounded groin. He pulled, wanting her face there, ripping the hair from her flesh. Trina fumbled for her dagger, hidden beneath her skirts. Suddenly, his hold on her loosened and then he released her. His knife quickly followed and he raised his hands in defense of the arm coiled tightly around his throat.

Trina fell back, freed and relieved. She watched the captain hold fast while his mate struggled and then collapsed at his feet.

"Are ya injured?" His face appeared above her own, his brow knotted with concern, touching some deep cavern of her heart. She had to guard against him and his maddening allure. More now than ever, since she would be sharing a bed with him. She broke their gaze and looked around him at the seaman.

"Not enough to warrant his death."

"He isn't dead, just subdued," the captain assured with a smile in his voice. Trina wanted to look at him and see it. Finally, she did. His gaze on her softened as he reached out his hand to touch her.

"Yar head..." His pitch dipped and he glared over his shoulder at his fallen mate.

"My cousin." She bounded to her feet, winced at the scorching hot pain in her head, then hurried off. "I must find him."

"Mr. Bonnet!" The captain's booming command made her whirl around, holding her ears.

"Aye, Cap'n?" came a slightly muted reply from down the narrow hall.

The captain's mouth crooked into a barely visible half-grin that made Trina's belly flip. He motioned her forward and followed her to a door behind which men's voices and laughter could be heard.

Trina put her hand to the wood, but the captain covered her fingers with his rough palm, stopping her from pushing the door open.

Her heart accelerated and then stopped altogether when he leaned down behind her and said close to her ear, "Ya don't want to be molested again, do ya?"

His warm breath stirred tendrils of hair over her neck. His body brushed ever so briefly against her rump. "Nae," her voice quavered. "Of course not."

"Let me enter. I'll see that ya're satisfied."

Trina closed her eyes, unable to slow her shallow breath. What did he mean? It had to be the thick, sensual timbre of his voice that conjured such perverse images to fill her head. Mayhap it was his close proximity behind her . . . and his promise, laced with double meaning.

"The men aren't accustomed to havin' a woman aboard," he explained, moving away from her. "Most of them will follow the rules, but there are some . . ." He left her with the memory of her attacker. "I'll bring yar cousin to ya."

She nodded, too afraid to open her mouth and say something that might mortify her, like, *I'm in yer debt ferever. Just tell me how to repay ye.*

She watched him open the door and step inside. He erred in not closing it behind him. Peering inside, Trina spotted Kyle slumped in a chair, blood trickling down his neck. She could wait no longer and plunged into the quarters, oblivious to the gaping stares of the men she passed, and to the captain, who raked his eyes over each of them.

"Kyle!" she rushed to him. This was all her fault. If he was dead... "Saints have mercy, what have they done to ye?"

"We pierced his ear is all." A one-eyed man she'd seen before stepped forward and scowled at her. "What do ya think we did to him?"

"Trina, I'm fine."

No one paid any attention to Kyle's assurance. Trina was too busy glaring at the patched pirate. "Why on earth would ye pierce him? And what in God's name did ye pierce him with? A harpoon?"

"Hell, I didn't know he came with a nursemaid," the rude one-eyed man said. The others around him agreed. "No wonder he has such a weak constitution."

Kyle stood to his feet, a full head taller than most of the men there, save the captain. "Mr. Bonnet, if ye would care to have someone meet me above, I'll be happy to prove how determined my constitution is."

Mr. Bonnet threw back his head and laughed. "I don't need someone to stand in stead fer me, boy. Don't let the absence of me eye fool ya."

Kyle smiled, looking pleased to hear it. Trina knew the first mate had just earned her cousin's respect. There were men in Camlochlin who fought with less than two eyes.

"After supper then?" Kyle put to him.

"Will yar mother be with ya?" Bonnet asked him. "If I damage ya, will she come at me with her little dagger again?" He held his hand up to show her a small scratch and she remembered him reaching for her and her slicing at him. She realized that getting off on the wrong foot with these men wasn't her best course of action.

Especially if they were going to be traveling together to France.

"I apologize fer—"

"After supper then, MacGregor," Mr. Bonnet cut her off and winked his eye at Kyle. "Bring her."

Trina bristled in her spot but said nothing. Ruffians. Miscreants. Black-hearted—

"Mr. Bonnet," the captain interrupted her string of silent insults. "Have the men see to Jacques in the hall. He attacked Miss Grant on her way here. Prepare him fer me when he wakes, aye?"

Immediately, Kyle stepped forward and clutched her elbow. "Someone attacked ye? Are ye hurt?" Without giving her a chance to answer, he turned his attention and anger to the captain. "We haven't been here a full day and she has already been attacked? I wish to see the man who touched her."

The captain eyed him coolly and shook his head. "This is me ship, Highlander, and while ya're aboard ya'll obey me commands. I will deal with me men. If ya take issue with that, ya can leave today and swim back to Scotland."

"The Cap'n's fair, MacGregor," one of the men called on his way out the door with a few others to see to her attacker. "Jacques will be punished."

Kyle didn't look convinced, so Trina pinched him.

She caught the captain's brief glance beneath the brim of his hat. She was glad he'd gotten it back—glad that he was there to help her a moment ago.

"How do ya intend to pay fer the gold in yar ear?" he asked, returning his attention to Kyle.

"By swabbing the decks every day until ye bring us to . . . ?" Kyle waited for the captain's reply.

"France."

Her cousin looked at her and smiled, his good mood restored. She wanted to punch him. So what if it was where she had wanted to go in the first place? She didn't want to go there now. Her grandsire would probably lock her up for stowing away on a pirate ship.

"The hoop's a loan, Cap'n," Mr. Bonnet pointed out. "He's been pukin' since he got here. We thought it might help."

The captain nodded, then looked around and called out to a tall blond man in the back of the quarters. "Gustaaf, fer returnin' me hat, ya'll take a half of me next share."

"I know how ye fancy that hat, Captain," the hulking, leathery-skinned sailor pointed out. "But you're too generous."

"Nonsense." The captain snatched Trina's hand and pulled her toward the door. "Don't argue."

Trina wasn't sure if he was speaking to Gustaaf or to her.

"Where are ye taking me?" she asked, careful not to struggle, lest Kyle feel the need to come to her rescue. It seemed her cousin didn't care that he was aboard a ship filled with pirates. He would still be a knight.

"Away from hungry gazes. Really, Miss Grant, how do ya manage to remain ignorant to the dangers of men?"

"Men were no danger to me in Camlochlin."

He turned to look at her, reminding her by the way his eyes traced the contours of her face that he was the most dangerous man of all. "Well, ya're not in Camlochlin. And while ya're on me ship, ya'll use more caution."

He was correct. The men did peer at her like they had just seen a succulent doe traipsing into their den. But if he were going to dump them in France, she wouldn't have to use caution much longer. Now that her kin would know she was safe, she wished she could travel a bit more with the captain. Och, she could taste the adventure. For years she'd dreamed of sailing away from the safety of Camlochlin. She'd come aboard to see the ship, to imagine a different life. But actually being on *Poseidon's Adventure*, smelling the sea, feeling the roiling pitch of the vast ocean beneath her feet, and the powerful pull of sails above her, well, it was just too hard to give up. She wouldn't be a bother. She could cook, and clean, and if anyone came against them, she could lend her sword. She and Kyle had much to offer. If he would only let them stay until...say Spain. She would be in his debt.

"Ehm, Captain," she said while they came upon, and then passed, a small group of his men lifting Jacques off the wet floor. "Speaking of my time on yer ship..."

Chapter Eight

"I didn't know she was yars, Cap'n!"

Alex leaned over the deck and shook his head at the man dangling by his ankles from the foremast, high above the waves. "What matter of difference is there if she be mine or not, Jacques? We don't rape women on the ship. Ya broke Article Eighteen and now ya're bein' punished. Be a man about it and don't shame the crew."

He stepped away, leaving Jacques to face his sentence alone. Alex didn't care if the offense of actual rape had been committed or not. Now the others knew what they would face for laying a hand on her. She was a temptation to all, mostly him. Another reason she had to go.

Leading her to his cabin, he wondered if this possessive streak he felt for Caitrina Grant would get him into trouble. He understood why he might be suffering the madness of being attracted to a woman who wanted to steal from him. She was beautiful, with grace and innocence and fire all mixed together. Of course he wanted her, just looking at the tumble of her sable hair, the curve of her waist, the sway of her hips, made him ache to bed her in every way possible. But why he would be plagued with worry for her well-being, he didn't know. Hell, he'd even insisted she wear his tricorn to keep the sun off her wounded scalp. His tricorn! He must be going mad. He guessed one reason he might think he gave a damn about her was because he'd spent more hours with her already, talking and even sharing laughter, than any other woman he knew. And, if the damned truth be known, he liked her. Hell, he was in trouble.

"How long will he hang?" Kyle asked him, coming up behind.

Caitrina had invited her cousin to dine with them in his cabin. Alex had agreed because of all the prior requests she'd put to him that he'd refused. One of them being to let her and her cousin sail a se'nnight or two longer with him. She was mad. The last thing he wanted was a woman on his ship for a day longer than she needed to be there. He didn't need the skills she offered in the galley or with a sword. He might consider keeping her for a bit longer if she offered him a more pleasurable means of repayment. But he couldn't negotiate terms with her now with her cousin present.

"He'll be lowered in three turns of the sandglass." Alex turned to the Highlander. "Why do ya ask?" He didn't trust this young ruffian not to pull his dagger on his men, and his men not to subsequently kill him. His duty as captain, one he shared with Sam, was to keep fighting to a bare minimum. The crew, including MacGregor, had to respect his authority or mayhem and mutiny would ensue.

"If ya start trouble that I've already ended, I'll throw ya overboard meself. Savvy?"

The Highlander nodded, looking none too pleased

about the order. "Seeing his punishment, I trust ye to keep my cousin safe."

"I dinna' need either one of ye to keep me safe," Caitrina huffed over her shoulder, presenting her profile beneath the brim of his hat. "I'm perfectly capable of defending myself."

Behind her, Alex and Kyle exchanged knowing glances. They both knew she couldn't fight a group of men if she had to, but neither corrected her.

"I appreciate ye both trying to protect me, but—"

"I'm simply keepin' order on me ship," Alex was quick to let her know. "I don't want me men fightin' over ya."

She turned around to face him fully. He smiled at her, not giving a damn who saw or what they thought. "Pardon my initial assessment, Captain," she said. "I hope ye dinna' think me a foolish twit fer believing ye a man of honor."

His smile widened while his skin grew tight around his bones. The slight arch of her brow and subtle flare of her nostrils made him ache to tame the hellcat lurking beneath her practiced smiles. But he didn't want her tame for too long. He craved the fight she'd give him. He would never rape her. He simply wanted her surrender.

"I would not think ya a twit, Miss Grant. But why would ya ever think me a man of honor? If I gave ya that impression, I will do me best to correct it."

His quick eyes noted her hands balled at her sides but she smiled as easily as if she just saw a school of dolphins when she spoke. "Dinna' burden yerself with the needless task. I was being polite. I know what ye are."

"Do ya, then?" he asked, amused, though he really wasn't. A small part of him didn't like that she thought she knew him. An even smaller part didn't like the way she saw him. "Then ya know to expect little from me."

He stepped around her and opened the door to his cabin. Why the hell did he just say that? Because he didn't want to deceive her, though he was certain she was very masterfully deceiving him. She might be a thief or a spy but along with her fire she possessed an innocence the likes of which he'd never seen. Perhaps it was her huge blue eyes or the guileless curl of her dimpled smile that he thought innocent. He should be keeping his distance from her. But he found himself thinking of her after she'd left him at the helm, following her like a predator on the trail of its prey, but instead of devouring her, he attacked one of his own men...

That didn't mean, when she moved past him through the door, that he didn't want to kick out her cousin and devour her now.

He waited patiently for Kyle to enter and shut the door behind him. Alex was no good for her, not even for a night. He turned in time to watch her remove his hat. She winced and something inside him almost pulled him back to the deck to cut the ropes holding Jacques's ankles.

"Take rest," he told them both and crossed the room to a grand chest against the wall. He opened it and took out a jug of rum from Madagascar. "Robbie or Cooper will deliver our food soon. Hopefully, 'twill be free of bugs." He winked at her and clapped Kyle on the back when the lad clutched his belly. "We may have to pierce yar other ear," he said quietly, then, "Let's share a drink while we wait on our supper."

Caitrina let him pour the golden nectar into her cup but Kyle put his hand over it.

"None fer us, thank ye, Captain."

"Why not, MacGregor?"

"Because I dinna' want my cousin to be alone and

drunk with ye while I try to prove my skill against yer first mate—and fail because I, too, am drunk. If that's yer plan then I must confess I canna' trust ye to be fair and honorable between yer men and me." Kyle stared up at him from across the table, surveying him, watching his reaction. "I will have to remain defensive."

Alex wanted to laugh...or clap the lad on the back a second time for showing such bravery in his honesty. Finally, he gave in and laughed, softly. Men of honor, eh? Honorable men could be trusted. He sealed the jug after pouring himself a cup, and put the rest back from whence it came. Who the hell raised these two to be so confident, and rash, and fearless?

"If I wanted ya rendered helpless from a spirit, I'd be offerin' ya some of me special gunpowder rum." He smiled when both his guests' faces paled. "Tell me, Mac-Gregor, should I be concerned fer Mr. Bonnet?" He sat between them at the small candlelit table. "How well do ya fight, Highlander?"

"Verra' well, Captain. But this is only a show of skill to gain worth and trust among yer men. I dinna' wish to harm Mr. Bonnet."

The lad was a fool! Why would he give away his plan? Their plan? "Why do ya want to gain worth and trust among them, MacGregor?" So that when he stole the map, some of the crew might turn to his side?

"Because fer as long as I travel with ye, my sword is at yer service. 'Tis a good aid in battle."

Hell, Alex almost believed him. His candor was as fresh and convincingly honest as his cousin's. They were likable, these two. Dangerous, but likable. Alex downed his rum. "Have ya been to battle then?"

"Aye, my uncles and cousins made all their sons fight

every day. My faither, ye met him in Camlochlin, Colin MacGregor?"

Alex nodded.

"He was once a general in King James's army. He oversaw our mock battles, sometimes twenty lads on both sides. At first we practiced with wooden swords and then we moved on to metal. We all swung hard and with purpose, preparing for a day when true enemies came to Skye."

Alex listened, understanding a little more about the place where Caitrina grew up, and the people who shaped her. "Who be yar true enemies?"

The lad shrugged his plaid-draped shoulders. "The English, and those who persecute us."

"Aye." Alex remembered the proscription. He would like to hear about it, but not now. Now he wanted to learn more about Caitrina.

"Did ya fight in these mock battles, too?" he asked her.

"When other duties allowed me time," she told him. "We live in a peaceful vale in the midst of a cold, harsh world. I've never wanted to be helpless in it."

He nodded, smiling at her because he understood and appreciated her spirit.

"But archery is my specialty," she continued, emboldened by his smile. "Taught to me by my cousin, Will MacGregor, the most skilled archer in all of Skye, in all of Scotland, mayhap. And speaking of my skill, when may I have my bow and quiver returned to me?"

"When we get to France."

He winked at her, ignoring her obvious ire, then returned his attention to MacGregor. "I will have a word with Mr. Bonnet before the competition to let him know ya don't intend a fight to the death. If ya deceive me and he is harmed, I'll have a blade through yar heart before ya finish him off."

"Ye can trust me, Captain," Kyle countered with a wry smile. "But if it is I who is betrayed, I will not go down as easily as ye think. I promise, I will take as many as I can with me to the hereafter."

"Ya have balls," Alex told him, wondering if the Highlander had ever considered a pirate's life.

Robbie arrived with their food, which consisted mostly of overripe apples, dried figs, some dried fish, and water. No bugs.

"Food goes bad and grows scarce fast here, but we should have enough to get us to France," Alex told them.

While they ate, Alex questioned them some more about their home life. They told him about Camlochlin's history and how their grandfather Callum MacGregor had built his fortress after escaping Liam Campbell's dungeon and the war he declared on the Campbells after that.

"And yet he wed a Campbell?" Alex asked while he ate. "She must be an exceptional woman."

"She is," both Trina and Kyle answered.

"She was raised on tales of honor and glory," Kyle told him. "And she passed those ideals down to her grandchildren."

Alex arched a brow and turned the smirk curling the edges of his mouth toward Caitrina. "Was it honor or glory that night we met on the beach that made ya suggest to yar cousins that they shoot me or set the dogs on me after I surrendered?"

When she set her full attention on him and smiled, he sat back in his seat to enjoy the view and ready his head for what she was about to bring him. Here was the thing that attracted him to her more than any other: that wide-eyed cherubic look changing into something far more threatening with a subtle tightening of her lips, a challenging spark in her eyes that promised a blazing fire if further passions were exposed.

He'd never wanted to kiss a woman more than he wanted to kiss her right now.

"'Twas honor, Captain," she confessed with a hint of arrogance squaring her shoulders. "If ye knew anything aboot it, ye would understand that I was trying to protect my kin from an uninvited intruder. Ye would recognize what I did as loyalty, one of honor's many codes. But since ye are a man who robs from others—"

"Plunders," he corrected her. "I loot and pillage and plunder. Robbin' is more civilized. A bit like boardin' a ship to rob in secret and hopin' to escape unscathed."

Her smile cooled, proving she was trying to rile him and angry that she was failing. "There is nothing on this ship I want, Captain."

"That will help me sleep tonight, Miss Grant."

"Good. Now, as I was saying, since ye are a man who plunders, loots..."

She must have seen in his gaze his dark desire to do those things to her, for her words faded and a scarlet tinge crept across her cheeks.

She blinked her glorious eyes toward Kyle. Her cousin was busy eating and looking around the cabin and didn't notice the silent exchange. He did, however, pick up the conversation between them.

"So, Trina," Kyle teased, "ye did read a few of the books, then."

"A few."

"A few doesn't make ya an authority, lass," Alex pointed out to her.

"True." She returned her attention to him, recovered. "But the little I know would take years to teach *ye*, pirate."

"Neptune take me"—he laughed and rose from his seat when Sam entered the cabin—"if I ever find interest in learnin' such useless values."

"Cap'n?"

"Aye, Mr. Pierce?" Alex was reluctant to look away from her and miss the lightning shooting from her eyes.

She spoke about honor with some conviction, but judging from what he knew of her already, honor, with all its rigid codes—and he did know a few of them—had probably grown dull to her years ago. He doubted she cared one bit about propriety and custom.

Whatever she was doing on his ship, whether to rob him or to fulfill her sense of adventure, the fact remained that she had found a way to board in the middle of a loch. Once found, she never truly appeared overly frightened. And finally, the most telling thing of all that proved she wasn't looking for a man of high moral standards was that knowing they were pirates, she'd asked him to let her stay with them beyond France.

She was a mystery to him. A mystery Alex wanted to try to figure out. He liked her but liking her was dangerous. "Mr. Bonnet is waitin'."

Chapter Nine

Trina had watched Kyle practice and fight mock battles her whole life. But his opponent was never a pirate who wouldn't hesitate to run him through and toss him to the sharks.

Mr. Bonnet fought well for a man with one eye. His vicious determination to inflict pain on Kyle made Trina close her eyes twice. But she didn't think he would find victory against her cousin. The gold hoop in his ear seemed to help his seasickness, though she had no idea why it would. She worried about what the others would do when the pirate fell. The captain said he'd spoken to his first mate about not fighting to the death, but would Mr. Bonnet and the others obey?

"He parries and blocks well."

She glanced up at the captain, standing beside her on deck, watching the contest. "He knows more than defense," she countered, catching his meaning while his mate drove her cousin back. "Look. See how cleanly he jabs? Ye can almost see the air being sliced apart."

The captain agreed, folding his arms across his chest.

"Yar cousin deserves respect fer his fine precision with a blade, but his arm grows tired from wieldin' a heavy claymore."

She shook her head and crooked her mouth at him. He took enjoyment in trying to irk her. He was good at it, but she was learning to control the constant challenge and anger he sparked in her. "The weight of his blade strengthened his arm over the years. If ye pay closer attention to yer man, ye will see his gaping mouth, his puffing chest, the slower reflex to a blow. I fear if ye dinna' call an end to this soon, Kyle will take Mr. Bonnet to his knees."

The captain smiled and her lungs quit working. "Ya're sure about that?"

"I am."

She was stunned when he called an end to the contest, declaring it a draw. The crew booed and complained but Mr. Pierce reminded them that it was against the articles to hold contest aboard ship. They had allowed it because a guest and a stranger issued the challenge. If any had issue with the results they could take watch for the next five nights. None did.

With the contest over and feelings spared on both sides, the crew opened kegs of rum and sang songs to the setting sun in the western sky. Even Jacques was released and set on his feet to live another day. Trina watched while Kyle accepted a cup from Mr. Bonnet and they toasted in celebration of each other's skill. She felt a bit queasy and refused to drink, determined not to spend a moment hanging over the side of the ship. This was what she wanted, what she'd ached for for years. To sail across the ocean, to feel the sea spray in her hair, to breathe in the briny fragrance of a world unknown to her. To sail upon a ship beneath a full moon and the heavens bathed in stars. She longed for adventure and excitement. She wouldn't spend her time aboard the ship, too sick to enjoy it.

With that thought settled in her mind, her eyes found the captain across the lantern-lit deck, reclining on the stairs alongside his cabin, laughing with a group of his mates. He looked ridiculously sexy just sitting there with a cup clutched in his hand and one knee bent on the step below. She was tempted to go to him by the traitorous skip of her heart, compelled by nothing more than the eruption of his thick laughter and the sight of him beneath the stars. She should go over there and give him back his hat since the sun had set and its heat was no longer painful. But he looked so sinfully appealing in his bandanna, with his shoulder-length sun-streaked hair pushed away from his face and his golden loops dangling from his ears. She guessed countless other women thought the same thing when they saw him.

She knew of the desires of men and what woman did to please them, not from fulfilling any of them, but from banter spread around the table at Camlochlin, mostly about her brother Malcolm and some of her cousins. There were brothels and taverns, and even some stately halls where women flung themselves at virile men, tossing virtue to the four winds. Trina didn't judge them, but she certainly wasn't one of them.

The captain's piercing dark eyes caught and held her gaze across the deck. Heavens, but he was the epitome of masculinity, a mixture of darkness and golden light, smoldering smiles and infuriating grins. Perhaps it wasn't the best idea to stay aboard. Not with him. On another ship, mayhap, with a short, plump captain with one eye and no teeth. With a captain who didn't tempt her to think about kissing his full mouth or running her hands, perhaps even her tongue, down his whipcord-tight belly.

"Good thing the captain didn't fight your brother."

Trina turned to look up at the giant Gustaaf. "My cousin," she corrected. "Kyle is my cousin. And why is it a good thing that the captain didna' fight him?"

"Your cousin would not have gained a draw, but more likely enough bruises to set him abed for a day or two."

She smiled out of the corner of her mouth, about to set this man straight about how Highlanders fought.

"No one finds victory over the captain. He was taught to fight by the dark-skinned warriors of the West Indies. He's quicker on his feet than any man I've ever seen fight."

"Pity ye could not remain in Camlochlin longer to have seen our men practice. Yer mind would have been changed."

The tall Dutchman laughed and shrugged his shoulders, blocking out half the dark sky. "I'm not speaking about practice, lady. Just before we set sail to your land, we took a ship off the coast of Boston. It got bloody when we boarded. Their captain foolishly did not surrender and decided instead to battle us. Captain Kidd cut men down like an angel of death bringing the wrath of God down on them. On some, he didn't use a weapon."

"Gustaaf."

They both turned, startled to find the captain standing before them.

"First ya risk yar life to save me hat and now yar singin' praises about me fightin' skills." Alex looped his arm as high as he could get it around Gustaaf's shoulder. "Yar a true asset to me crew."

"It's the very least I can do after what you did for my family, Captain."

"Hell, that was nothin'. Let's not discuss it further."

"Aye aye."

Trina watched Gustaaf leave in favor of another cracked keg. When she stood alone with the captain, she turned to him. "What did ye do fer his family?"

"'Tis nothin' that would interest ya. Are ya ready fer bed?"

Her heart fluttered, making her cough. "It would interest me and nae, I'm not ready fer bed."

"If ya want to discuss things, then discussin' me prowess in battle is more pleasin' to me ears than me good deeds."

"Are there many then?"

"There are enough." He slid his gaze to her and smiled.

Trina knew she probably shouldn't, but she couldn't help it and smiled back. Mercy, but the man was as prideful as a Highlander. Was it dangerous to like him? Of course it was. She wasn't here for some tryst with a sexy, swashbuckling pirate. She didn't need a man to love in her life. Her poor father could attest to that by all the suitors he had to turn down on her behalf. She loved her father for considering her wishes for as long as he had. She longed for the thrill of the unknown rather than the thrill of a man's body. But Captain Alexander Kidd could change all that. She still wanted to dive into the unknown, but now the thrill of a man's body sparked a whole new interest in her.

"Let's discuss this ship ye took near Boston."

"Proceed."

He held out his arm, offering Trina an unobstructed path to the stairs.

"Why did ye attack it?"

"We were low on supplies."

"What kind of ship was it?"

He turned to smile at her as they reached the quarter-deck. "English schooner."

"Ah." She swept her gaze at him from beneath the spray of her lashes. "A smaller ship."

"But faster"—his grin grew all the more sexy as he held out his hand to escort her up the rest of the way to the poop deck—"as I'm certain ya already know."

She looked up at the stars, trying to keep her head clear of the warmth and firm strength of his hand. "Ye assume too much aboot me."

"Ya don't know what that is then?" He pointed to the wheel and drew in closer to her—to intoxicate her with his scent.

She could have pretended ignorance, but why the hell should she? She didn't care if he thought her odd in her affinity. "The helm."

Still close, his smile washed over her and made her feel drunk with rum, though she didn't touch any. "Want to steer?"

Her knees nearly buckled beneath her and she would have gone straight to the floor since he left her to take the wheel from the man steering.

"I'll take her fer now, Cooper."

Trina managed to stay upright while watching Cooper leave and the captain turn to her and offer her the wheel. The wheel! Did she dare? What if she steered them into a rock or another ship? It was dark. She shook her head, hating that she had never studied navigation. "I canna' read the stars."

He pressed his palm to the small of her back and drew her closer to the wheel. "I can." He stepped around her and from behind, he closed his arms over hers. He took her hands and placed them on the wheel, then covered them with his.

"We can return in the day and ya can use the compass to yar right. Fer now though, I'll lead, aye?"

She nodded, knowing she should run for her life. Jumping overboard was safer than standing with him at the helm in the middle of God knew where, his body pressed to her back, his breath warm and scintillating against her ear. Lead? Hell, she was beginning to feel powerless against her own thoughts and desires. It was adventure, excitement, something more than a life of cooking and cleaning and sewing for a husband she didn't even love. Alexander Kidd made her desire something more. She should have fled, but she didn't move. She never wanted to move again.

She wasn't sure which was more hypnotizing, the power beneath her fingers and at her back as the ship rocked and rose or the sound of his voice and the scent of his rum-sweetened breath while he told her about plundering *The Devil's Grin*, the English schooner, and having to kill most of her crew. He didn't sound repentant, but Trina didn't care. She grew up in a world where men killed one another over less than supplies. Last year in Torrin, for instance, when Lachlan MacDonald killed John Frazier over a sheep.

"Why did ya board me ship, Caitrina?"

Her name never sounded so good. "I wanted an adventure," she confessed. "I love Camlochlin with all my heart but I craved something more."

Perched behind her, he remained quiet and for a moment she thought he had fallen asleep. Then she heard him inhale a great breath, as if he were readying himself for something. "So," he said, his voice a husky whisper against her ear, "I don't tempt ya?"

"Ye?" Her heart pounded in her head.

She could hear the smile in his voice when he spoke. "Me treasure. It doesn't tempt ya?"

"Nae, well..."

"Cooper!" He shouted so suddenly that he startled her. "Take the helm," he ordered and pulled her away.

"Where are we going?" she asked, feeling panic settle over her. He either didn't believe she didn't want to steal his map and was going to toss her overboard or...

"We're goin' to bed."

...that.

Chapter Ten

Trina wanted to sleep and the thought of a soft, fur-covered bed after her first night on the damp hard floor belowdecks tempted her to hasten her steps. But the captain had promised to sleep in the bed with her. She couldn't let him! If her father ever found out, he would kill the captain first and question him later. And saints help her, what if the captain touched her, kissed her, in the bed? What would she do? She'd never slept with a man before, save for the one time when they visited her aunt Anne Stuart in her convent in France and Trina had to share a bed with her brother Cailean. He snored and she was awake all night. This was different. Captain Kidd was a man, a virile, irresistibly attractive man who oozed sensuality from every pore. He drove her to distraction just standing behind her. She couldn't climb into bed with him and expect an innocent night of slumber. Already her thoughts were drifting toward the primitive. His face above her, his hair, free and falling onto her cheek while he whispered how she felt beneath him.

She patted her cheek and shook her head to clear it.

She had to think of something before they stepped into the cabin. She searched the faces for Kyle. He had to help her. Perhaps there was another bed in the mate's quarters...Nae, Mr. Pierce already warned her of the dangers of being around the men with only Kyle as her escort. They would likely kill him and take her.

She found her cousin slumped beside a barrel beneath the main mast, passed out, either from rum or exhaustion. She bit her lip. No help there.

And then, just when all hope seemed lost, help came from Mr. Pierce in the form of a jug of gunpowder rum, which, according to the ship's quartermaster, could grow hair on a young lad's cheek and render a wolf helpless.

"Share a drink with me before ya retire to bed, Alex." Mr. Pierce looped his arm around his friend's shoulder and tried to lead him away from Trina.

"I've had me fill, Sam," the captain refused. "Besides, I have a guest."

Trina looked away from the slight provocative curl in his smile. It was clear that his intentions were not honorable.

"Yar guest will remain," Pierce insisted. "She can bolt the door from the inside to keep trouble out."

Alex laughed and set Trina's nerve endings aflame with the sound of it. If his intentions were to "plunder" or "pillage" her, how would she stop him? Would she even try?

"And what if she considers me the trouble and locks me out?"

He'd likely kick down the door. She needed a weapon, something better than a dagger. It wasn't easy but she managed a smile and moved closer to him. "I wouldna' do that, Captain. Not after yer kindness." She patted his arm and lifted his pistol out of his sash with the other hand, unbeknownst to him. She had the weapon, now she needed time. If he drank Mr. Pierce's gunpowder rum, chances were likely that he would come to bed as helpless as a puppy. "I hate thinking that I am such a burden that ye canna' share a drink with yer friends fer fear that I might—"

His smirk, lazy as the summer afternoon, settled on her and rattled her bones. Unable to help herself, her gaze took in the sight of him full on. Beneath the light of the low moon the nuance of strength and grace in his movements reminded Trina of a supremely lethal wolf.

"Ya have me wrong if ya think I fear anything, Miss Grant."

She didn't have him wrong. She smiled, familiar with his kind of pride and how to stroke it. "God ferbid I should suggest such a ridiculous possibility. Yer valiant heart is apparent. I meant nae offense."

Whatever her motive for offering her submission it fell apart at the seams when she raised her gaze to meet his and felt the intimacy of his smile like a tender touch. No! There was too much at stake! At the last instant she reined in her feelings and regained her wits. The struggle made her breathless. "Of course ye fear nothing. Not even the notion that I might be a thief come to steal yer treasure, and that is why ye are afra...er...cautious aboot letting me enter yer cabin withoot ye. Fergive me."

He stared at her for a moment, then, clearly coming to some conclusion that genuinely pleased him, his smirk softened on her.

Mr. Pierce tugged on his arm when Alex drew a step closer to her. "Ya would have me drink alone, brother?"

Trina saw the regret in the captain's expression when he turned to his friend. "Nay, old friend. Come, let's drink."

He flung his arm around Mr. Pierce's shoulder and turned to leave her. He paused after a step and turned back to her. "Nicely played, me lovely. Ya'll be safe fer tonight."

She couldn't help but be pleased that he knew her scheme and let her play it. His veiled threat about tomorrow night earned him a dark look, but she had until tomorrow to worry about it.

"Don't bolt the door from me, Caitrina," he called out as he left. "If I have to break it down, the cost will come out of yar cousin's hide, savvy?"

It took more strength of will than she knew she possessed not to pull out his pistol and shoot him.

Why did he have to go and threaten Kyle's hide? She should keep the pistol and shoot him while he slept just for saying it. Just when she decides she might like him, he threatens her kin, her dearest friend. She reached the quarterdeck on her own and stormed inside the cabin.

She bolted the door while she undressed, swearing to herself that she wouldn't shoot him if he began kicking. In her shift, she tossed her clothes over the back of a chair, unbolted the door, and leaped into bed. If not for Kyle's hide, she would have left it bolted and let Alex kick it down if he wanted in.

She pulled his fur blanket over her and sat up, waiting for him to return, his gun cocked and ready for him when she made her demands that he sleep on the floor.

When Alex began to see two of each of his mates sitting around him in the galley, he knew it was time to go to bed. If he were going to see double, at least let him be looking at Caitrina. He stood to his feet, surprisingly steady against the gentle sway of his ship. He'd been drinking gunpowder rum since he was a boy. Its potent effects on him had grown stale. That didn't mean he wouldn't suffer the drink's consequences in the morning...and tonight. He'd done it for her, because she'd molded refreshing sincerity into her clever manipulation to get rid of him for most of the night. He'd agreed to temporary impotency from gunpowder as a favor to her. He would worry about why he did it tomorrow. Now he wanted sleep and nothing more. He made it to his cabin without falling over the side or slipping on his arse.

He was somewhat surprised to find his door unlatched. He entered quietly and looked toward the bed, visible in the candles she'd left lit. He stepped inside, pulling off his bandanna as he went.

The curse of gunpowder rum was that while he was drunk he functioned with pure clarity but would forget everything come the morning. He had threatened her cousin's well-being to gain her obedience. Of course, he hadn't meant a word. He liked Kyle MacGregor and would kill him only if he had to.

Stepping toward the bed, he remembered how she had looked like she wanted to kill him just before she marched away. He remembered how she felt in his arms while she steered his ship. Tomorrow he would forget the thoughts of lifting her skirts and taking her at the helm. Tonight, though, he remembered.

He stood over the bed and her sleeping body and smiled at the sight of her and his gun in her limp hand.

How the hell had she gotten it? He had it on him, didn't he? Was she a pickpocket as well as lock picker? And he was supposed to believe she wasn't a thief? She tempted him to believe it. And therein lay the problem. He had to get rid of her. He was glad Sam had taken him away from her and got him drunk enough to fail at anything he attempted with her. When they reached France, he would bid her a fond farewell, just like he had to other women in the past.

But something was different about her, something deeper, something he wanted to explore. He was wary of his protectiveness of her, and of the way she tempted him to agree to every demand she made of him. She distracted him. Just like she distracted him while she stole his pistol, and his dagger before that. She was beautiful, fiery, and fearless, and he found his thoughts preoccupied with her, rather than on his voyage and the legacy of his father's greatest treasure. He looked at his wall and the trapdoor hiding his map.

The ship pitched and rolled over a giant swell and flung Alex forward, onto the bed; he was perched over her when she opened her eyes. He could feel her heart pounding against his chest. The feverish pitch played like a drum through his blood.

"Remove yerself!" she demanded and pressed the barrel of his pistol to his temple.

She looked afraid enough to pull the trigger, so he pushed himself off her, holding up his palms while he went.

"What d'ye think yer doing?"

She looked genuinely terrified, an expression he'd never seen on any woman in his bed. He'd never forced a woman's affections and he didn't like that Trina didn't know it. "The ship bucked and I lost me balance. Fergive me."

She sat up, bringing the pistol with her. "All right but now that ye woke me, there is something ye need to know."

"What's that?"

"I canna' let ye sleep in this bed with me."

"Is that so?" Hell, he was sleepy. He tugged at his belt

and let it drop to the floor. He peeled his shirt off next and tossed it on the bed. "Are ya going to shoot me then?"

"I...I will if I must." Her throat sounded dry while she watched him unfasten his pants.

By the size of her eyes while he undressed, he concluded that she must never have seen a naked man before. Rather than frighten her enough for her finger to click that trigger...

"Why don't ya put that pistol down and I'll turn around."

She blinked and then dropped the pistol onto the bed. He turned his back on her and dropped his pants. He stepped out of them and strode toward the chair. When he reached it, he snatched up her dress and flung it to the end of the bed with his shirt, then took up her plaid and covered himself with it after he settled into his chair.

"That is my earasaid ye have wrapped over yer... naked body," she pointed out to him.

He closed his eyes. "Well, ya have me blanket."

"I'm not naked."

"Pity."

He heard her mumble something but he was too sleepy to care what it was.

"And what aboot my clothes? Where can I wash them?"

"In France," he told her groggily. "We'll be there soon enough."

She mumbled again. This time she sounded angry. "Ye havena' thought aboot letting us stay aboard fer a wee bit longer then? Ye already penned a note to my kin..."

"Woman, if ya think I'm goin' to sleep in a chair fer another fortnight, renew yar thinkin' now."

"Fine," she retorted. "I'll sleep in the chair fer the remainder of the journey."

He opened his eyes and saw two of her. He couldn't help but smile. He couldn't let her stay. She would drive him mad.

"What d'ye mean I would drive ye mad?"

For a moment he thought she read his mind and almost leaped from the chair to leave the room lest he begin thinking about his treasure and where it was and she hear that as well. Then he realized that he must have spoken aloud. Damn rum. Well, since she heard him, he might as well tell her.

"Ya're drivin' me mad right now. Chattin' on endlessly about keepin' ya. And trust me, woman, I want to keep ya. 'Tis takin' all my resolve not to go over there, climb into me bed, and make ya ferget what ya came here fer."

Finally, she was silent. He closed his eyes again and let the gentle rocking of the ship put him to sleep.

"Ye certainly think highly of yerself, Captain Kidd." Her lilting voice pulled him awake again. "Nae man— not ye or any other could make me ferget or give up my dreams. I seek adventure and I dinna' care if ye believe me or not. But dinna' think fer one instant—"

"Caitrina." He cut her off. He wanted sleep and he wanted her. He was going to get one or the other. Since he'd likely be done with her in the space of five breaths, given his condition, he thought it better to wait. "If ya don't stop talkin' I'm goin' to make ya walk the plank."

Blessed silence again, and then, "I'm not afraid of ye."

He smiled, on his way to dreaming. "I shall make certain to remedy that in the mornin'."

✴
Chapter Eleven

*T*rina opened her eyes and, for a moment, forgot where she was. Then she remembered and stretched. She was on a ship…his ship, his bed. Turning over, she looked toward the chair to find him still in it, thankfully, still covered in her earasaid, but barely. She should get up, get dressed, and get the hell out of his room before he woke up. But goodness, it had taken her so long to fall asleep last night after him leaving her with images of his naked body to haunt her dreams. Thank God it was the back of him and not the front, although the back was wondrous and sinfully perfect. She blushed afresh as the memory of his firm, untanned buttocks and thick, muscular thighs assaulted her. Och, she'd looked. She'd taken her fill and almost sighed out loud at the splendid sight of his long, sculpted back, the broad flare of his shoulders tapering down to his narrow waist. Gustaaf had told her that no one found victory over the captain in a fight. Trina wanted to see him wield a blade, dodge a series of strikes. Last night, with his sinewy muscles dancing beneath his skin in the candlelight, she could imagine him fighting and the thought stirred fire in her veins.

Finally though, thankfully, she'd fallen asleep, and och, but this had to be the most comfortable bed on the sea and beyond. Mayhap it was the ship, rocking her like her mother rocked her as a babe, or the soothing sounds of creaking wood and waves slapping against the hull. Whatever it was, it was heaven and she never wanted to leave.

She sat up and eyed him a little more closely. A foolish thing to do since, stretched out on the chair, his legs sprawled out before him, his bare arm tossed over his head, and her plaid riding down his flat belly and barely covering his hips and groin, he looked more like a sleeping god than a mortal man.

She'd realized last night that she wasn't going to be able to stay on the ship a day after France. Not after what he'd said to her.

'Tis takin' all my resolve not to go over there, climb into me bed, and make ya ferget what ya came here fer.

Lord, he was already making her forget. She'd come for adventure, not for him, yet here she was lingering in a room while he slept, letting images of his body make her blush and burn. She needed to get a hold of herself. She needed to think about what to do when he kicked her off the ship. She would have to go to her grandparents and try to explain what she was doing there. Och hell, she dreaded it.

She combed her fingers through her hair and plaited it into a long single braid.

She would have to tell them the truth. That she'd stowed away aboard a pirate ship and Kyle followed her. She felt mildly ill thinking about it. She would prefer penning a dozen notes to her kin in Skye to explaining to her grandsires face-to-face and telling them how foolish she had been.

A sound from the chair startled her. She looked to find Alex shifting uncomfortably. Her plaid slipped down a little lower on his hip. She practically leaped for it and managed to grab an end of the soft wool before it slipped off him completely. Her victory left her in the position of staring at his chest, then lower, over the slight, tight hills to his taut, tanned belly, farther down to the tuft of dark hair between his hips.

She swallowed, a little breathless with the thought of how all those sculpted angles would feel beneath her hands. The sudden desire to touch him coursed through her and she almost missed the slight change in his breathing.

She lifted her gaze to his face and found him squinting at her, his fingers grasping his forehead.

"Lookin' fer something?"

She wished the floor would open beneath her and swallow her up. He caught her appraising him like a cat would look at a succulent mouse and she had no other recourse to take but honesty.

"Yer covering was about to—"

He held up his palm to stop her and closed his eyes. "Speak softer."

She smiled, glad that he was suffering a wee bit after what he put her through last night.

"Yer covering was about to fall off," she said more quietly. "I was stopping it."

He didn't move. He didn't speak. He just breathed. Then, after she thought he might have fallen asleep or become unconscious, he said in a low, groggy voice, "Be a love and fetch me a cup of watered-down rum."

"Rum?" She stepped back and laughed at him. "Fer the morning-after effects?"

"Caitrina." He opened his eyes and looked at her. "Don't argue."

Don't argue? Was his word the law? She wanted to argue with him but the set of his jaw told her not to. Without another word, she swiveled around, slipped into her clothes, and left the cabin.

Don't argue. She'd heard him speak the command before to his men. Well, he wasn't her captain.

And yet, here she was obeying him. She huffed down the steps to the main deck and looked for someone to help her fill his order. She didn't see Mr. Pierce, or even Mr. Bonnet. She did, however, run into two seamen on their way to the galley.

One of them deliberately stepped in her path and sneered in her face. "Ya have the captain to thank that my cock is not in ya right now."

What a disgusting threat to make to a woman, Trina thought and swept her hand over his belt.

"And ye have him to thank that this dagger is not through yer neck right now." She jerked her hand forward and nicked his flesh with the tip of the blade.

He looked down and swallowed audibly. "That's my dagger."

From the corner of her eye, she saw his friend move toward her. Her reflexes were lightning quick, thanks to her mother's careful instruction while the boys practiced with the men in Camlochlin's vast fields. She lifted her ankle and plucked the captain's pistol free of the silken binds she'd made last night. She readied the weapon and aimed, halting him in his steps.

"Robbie, Nicky, step away from her or I'll gut ya from stem to stern."

She heard Mr. Pierce's voice behind her and said

a silent prayer of relief. She wasn't certain she could take two men coming at her at once. These weren't her relatives.

"Did ya both ferget that she's the captain's guest?" Pierce asked them. "Ya want to be hung up by yar ankles?"

When they paled, Trina took pity on them. "Dinna' tell him."

"But—

"Please, Mr. Pierce."

When he nodded, giving in to her request, Robbie and Nicky stared at her for a moment and then ran off.

Mr. Pierce watched them go, then turned to her and waited while she returned the pistol to her calf. "What are ya doin' out here alone? Tryin' to prove something?"

Trina shook her head. "He sent me fer watered-down rum. He's in much pain."

The quartermaster looked her over as if weighing her in his thoughts, then said, "Go back to the cabin. I will get the remedy and bring it to him."

Would not one but two men on this ship order her about then? She glanced at another group of rowdy pirates passing her and saw the reasoning behind Pierce's request. That didn't mean she was all right with the fact that she couldn't walk around alone. But she appreciated the quartermaster's warning. Still, until they reached France, she was going to have to do something about protecting herself. For now, she huffed, but remained silent and walked away.

By the time she returned to the cabin, the captain had pulled himself out of his chair and into his pants. The cut fit snugly over his hips and thighs, hinting at his masculine attributes as much as her plaid hanging off him had.

She cleared her throat and he separated his straight razor from his jaw and turned to face her full on.

"Did ya bring me drink?"

Stepping inside, she shook her head and gaped outright at the long, sleek muscles of his bare arms and torso. "Mr. Pierce is bringing it."

"Why didn't ya? I could have had it already."

She glared at him, not caring how good looking he was, and sat in the chair he'd slept in. "Ye could have gone yerself and had it even quicker!"

"Lower yar voice," he warned. "My head is—"

"Go to hell."

The door opened and Mr. Pierce stepped inside. "He's already there, Miss Grant. But this will help." He held up a huge flagon and shoved it in Alex's outstretched hand.

Trina watched the captain down the entire contents in one long guzzle. If he was going to puke, he better have a bucket. He burped instead and then fell to his bed.

"Poseidon's balls, never again," he breathed. "Do ya hear me, Sam? Come to me with gunpowder again and I'll maroon ya on the next island we come to."

"Yar guest needed protectin'," Sam said, folding his hands behind his back.

The captain sat up on his bed. Trina guessed his watered-down rum remedy was working by the swiftness of his movements. "Protection from whom?"

"From ya, of course. 'Tis why I fed ya gunpowder rum."

Alex laughed. "Since when do ya concern yerself with who needs protectin' from me?"

"Since last eve," his quartermaster answered.

Trina tried to get Mr. Pierce to look at her so she could smile at him. He glanced her way briefly, saw her gratitude, nodded, looking a bit uncomfortable, and then returned his attention to Alex. She realized then just how many times Mr. Pierce had saved her since she'd arrived. Mayhap he didn't hate her after all.

"Miss Grant." The captain leaned over his bed and cradled his head in his hands. "Ya should thank Mr. Pierce. My intentions were probably very obvious and not in yar favor."

"Probably? Ye dinna' remember?" she asked him, wondering how much more insult she had to endure. "Ye didn't appear that drunk to me."

"My body has grown immune to some of its effects, but 'tis gunpowder, woman. I don't remember anything about last night." He rose from the bed, glanced at the wall in the corner by his bed, then tied his hair away from his face.

"Did we speak of me treasure?"

"Aye, Captain," she lied, loving the dramatic pallor that came over his face. "Ye told me all yer secrets. When ye drop me and Kyle off in France, we're going to hire a ship and a crew and steal yer treasure from ye."

Mr. Pierce finally smiled. So did the captain.

"Robbie Owens and his brother Nicky approached her earlier…"

The captain didn't take his eyes off her when Cooper entered the cabin with their breakfast.

"Mr. Pierce," she tried to cut him off. "I asked ye not to—"

"She disarmed Nick in the space of a breath and held his own knife to his throat."

She thought she saw the slight crook in the captain's mouth while he listened to the quartermaster. She was certain Cooper winked at her before he left the cabin.

"She stopped Robbie in his tracks with her free hand, in which she held a pistol she keeps tied to her leg."

Both men's eyes dipped to her skirts.

"I don't think 'tis safe to let her carry around a pistol. Do ya?"

"Not safe fer who?" the captain asked. "Her, or us?"

"Us."

The captain shook his head. "I won't let her go around unprotected."

"Och, here." Tired of being the topic of their conversation, she yanked her skirts over her ankle and pulled the pistol free. "'Tis yers anyway." She tossed it to the captain, who looked at it in disbelief. "I took it back from ye last night after ye took it back from me. I dinna' need my own weapons. I have an uncle who taught me how to take my opponent's."

The men exchanged a brief glance. One was amused. The other was not. "Finally, she admits to bein' a thief."

"Being skilled at defense doesna' make me a thief, Captain." This time, she smiled back at him. She wouldn't let him goad her. "From what I know of ye, ye're easy enough to seduce. If 'twas yer map I wanted, I could have had it last night."

His sexy grin remained unchanged, but a slight deepening in his dark eyes revealed that he found her more than amusing. He found her alluring, and he found her dangerous. He didn't have to speak a word for her to see it.

"Let us get this straight, Miss Grant. From now on, ya don't hide anything from me and ya don't ask me men to do so either. Secondly, I'm no stranger to the wiles of women." His voice dipped an octave and danced over her flesh, settling somewhere in her belly. She realized that he had to be this desirable to all women, not just to her.

"I'm not as easily seduced as ya might think." He was an expert at it. "It would take longer than a night to seduce me. And ya don't have more than a night left on me ship."

He was kicking her off in France. There was no doubting it. She wanted to believe she was relieved. But she wasn't.

"Lucky fer ye, Captain," she said, turning for the door.

His laughter rang out, almost melting her kneecaps. "Why is that, Miss Grant?"

She turned to cast her reply over her shoulder. "A few more nights with me and ye could lose all. 'Tis flattering, really . . . to know I befuddle the rake Captain Kidd."

She reached the door and stepped out into the day without hearing his response. Her heartbeat pounded with such ferocity, she feared she might faint. She refused, and straightened her shoulders, descending the quarterdeck.

What the hell had come over her? Was she so deeply committed to staying, even for a little while longer, that she would cast aside the fact that Captain Alexander Kidd was a knave who could and would seduce her completely and then cast her aside when he was done? She'd never seduced a man the way she just promised she could. What if he expected her to prove her words?

Suddenly, France didn't seem so bad.

❖ Chapter Twelve

For Alex, France couldn't come into view quick enough. He had to get Caitrina off his ship. He'd told her that it would take longer than a night to seduce him. He was lying. If taking in different nuances of her face and reveling in them every time he looked at her meant anything at all, then he was already becoming a little seduced—befuddled by her as she claimed. A part of him wanted to hide everything he valued from her. The other part wanted to dangle his treasures before her eyes and fight her for them. Befuddled? Aye, he was. She rattled him.

He didn't like being rattled.

He tried to blame it on the gunpowder rum and the pain of two hammers striking his brains. But, in truth, he would have found her as curious, beguiling, and challenging whether his head pained him or not.

He stayed away from her while they crossed the Celtic Sea. When she approached him, once on deck, and once in the galley, he skirted her path, avoiding any contact between them.

He enjoyed rum and women of ill repute. He didn't

want anything more than that. He'd loved a woman once and she cost him everything, his treasure, his heart, and ultimately his father. If he ever decided to settle on one woman, she wouldn't be someone he didn't trust one hundred percent.

He didn't trust Caitrina. What did she want? Adventure, as she claimed...or was she like Madalena and she wanted his treasure?

When nightfall approached, he didn't go with her to his cabin, but watched her cousin escort her. He waited almost 'til dawn broke over the horizon, when cups were empty and much of his crew was hunched over the tables. He walked to his quarters pleased with himself for avoiding her. The more time he spent with her, the more she tempted him to let her stay, at least until their next port of anchor in Lisbon. Nay. She had to go.

He entered his cabin planning on doing as little talking as possible until they reached France.

He looked at his bed. She slept.

He resisted the urge to stand over her and simply look at her. He didn't like to admit, even if only to himself, that Miss Grant could possibly tempt him to offer what he hadn't offered to a woman in eight years. What he swore he'd never give again. He was an adventurer. He wanted no woman at his heels.

But Caitrina didn't stay behind him. She faced him head-on with enough confidence to make lesser men rethink their position.

He would have laughed at himself if the thought of losing his heart didn't scare the hell out of him.

"Is it morning already?"

Hell, even her voice, dulcet and low, seduced him enough to make him look at her.

"Almost. Go back to sleep."

She sat up in his furs, her thick glossy locks draping her sleepy face. Temptation incarnate. "I would speak to ye, Captain."

He would do more than that. "I would not have ya speak at all, lady."

He watched her full lips pinch with indignation, but she said nothing. What would have been her retort, he wondered? Once he left her in France, he might miss her banter, but that was nothing good rum couldn't remedy. He suspected he might dream once or twice about the allure of her dimpled smile. It was possible that he might recall the fire in her eyes the next time he saw lightning flash across the sky.

"Do ya have someplace in France I can bring ya?"

"Aye, my—"

A knock sounded at the door before Sam plunged into the cabin. "Alex, we've spotted something on the horizon."

"A ship?"

"Perhaps."

"How close?"

"Close enough to take by mid afternoon if we begin the chase now. We could use their supplies but we're not in dire need yet."

Aye, Alex knew the condition of his ship well enough. Plundering was sometimes not a question of need but of pleasure. But taking a ship so close to France's coastline would keep his guest here longer. A lot longer, as his trusted quartermaster was about to point out.

"If we plunder it," Sam noted, "'twould be wise not to dock again until we reach Portugal."

Alex agreed. The best way to stay alive was to plunder and get the hell as far away as you could without being captured. He wanted to do it. His blood pulsed for the thrill of the hunt, the glory of the victory, the joy in the bounty. There was one problem. He looked at Trina. Portugal. Two actually. "We don't have enough supplies to make it to Lisbon. We needed to fill up in France."

"We'll have our loot," Sam said, as eager for the chase to begin as any good pirate would be. "We will drop anchor in Lisbon as planned and gather enough supplies from there."

Alex nodded, and with his eyes still on the woman who would likely become a living hell for him, he cast her a shadowy smile. "It looks as if ya'll be stayin' aboard *Poseidon's Adventure* until we reach Portugal."

He wasn't giving her a choice.

"Inspect and load cannons!" he shouted over Sam's shoulder to whoever was on deck. Ah, this was what he lived for. What they all lived for. He pulled back and turned to Caitrina. "Things are going to get messy. Stay here. I'll send yar cousin to ya."

Without waiting for her compliance, he left the cabin with Sam and began shouting orders to his men to rise out of their drunken stupors and get the hell to work.

"Captain at the wheel!"

"Cap'n at the wheel!" Two more announcements went out, one after the other. The hunt was his. It was his duty as captain to shadow the prey and determine whether or not victory was in their favor. Once victory has been established, they would raise the black flag and fire a warning shot of lead from their cannons. After that, it was up to the other ship to surrender. If they didn't... Alex smiled. If they didn't, then combat would ensue.

He accepted the spyglass from Sam and adjusted his bandanna to hold against the wind. Ah, it was a good day to fight.

· · ·

Trina watched the door close behind him and stood frozen in her spot. She and Kyle were staying. They would have to pen another letter to Skye. For now she thought, the captain was about to take a merchant ship...and he expected her to stay put? She tried. She truly did. She was going to be traveling with him for a while. Och, Lord, they'd have to find different sleeping arrangements if she was staying. She didn't think she could resist him much longer. Waking up to his beautiful face was just as bad as going to sleep staring at it. Alex Kidd and a bed in the same space wasn't working out well for her.

She paced before the door again, trying so hard to stay put. She didn't want to irritate him by disobeying his orders yet again but she was aboard a pirate ship and the pirates were about to do what they did best. She wanted to be part of the action, not hidden from it. She paced, then sat down in a chair then paced some more. In the end, she asked herself what good was staying if she missed the adventure?

She stepped outside and the wind caught her hair and whipped it across her face. She cleared her strands and looked up at the thick, ominous clouds rolling across the vast sky and blocking out the morning sun. It made her dizzy and she looked away, toward the thunderous sea instead. Waves crashed against the hull, rocking the ship and her belly. How could anyone fight in these conditions? Without balance and the solid earth beneath their feet?

She heard shouting and watched the barefoot, drenched crewmen climbing the ratlines up the masts and maneuvering the running rigging to the sails.

Where was Kyle? What if he fought? Visibility was poor, balance was worse. How would he get onto the other ship if the pirates took it? Her cousin wouldn't stand idly by if there was a fight. No MacGregor would. Now that they were staying with the pirates, Kyle would lend his skills to any service required.

Heaven help her, she still couldn't believe it. Just like that they were staying. Her heart raced, recalling her threats to seduce their host. She would have laughed at the notion of her seducing anyone if she didn't fear her words would come back to haunt her. She had no idea how long the trip would be, but she certainly couldn't remain in the captain's cabin the entire time.

The sound of men's voices spun her around. She looked at the small group staring back at her. She wished she hadn't given the captain back his pistol.

"She sure is fair," one of them sneered. "Worth hangin' by yar ankles if ya ask me."

Another one elbowed him in the ribs. Trina remembered him from earlier, Mr. Pierce had called him Robbie. "Leave her alone. She'd cut out yar heart with yar own cutlass." He pushed the others on their way and paused before he passed her. "Thank ya fer not tellin' the cap'n about what Nicky said."

She nodded and smiled, then asked him if he'd seen Kyle.

"Check the helm. I saw him talkin' to Mr. Pierce a little while ago."

Trina thanked him and looked toward the stern. If these pirates were truly taking another ship, the helm was the place to be. Kyle knew that and was likely up there. With her hair snapping against her face from the wind, she made her way to the highest point of the wondrous brig, to the helm.

She didn't find her cousin, but the captain was there,

looking like some fabled myth come to life, the wheel in his left hand, his chest to the storm. He looked through a spyglass and shouted into the wind, "Bearing port two meters!"

The shout rang out from stern to stem, one voice after the other until everyone heard.

The captain steered steadily while waves rose up over the ship like phantom dragons come to swallow them whole. Mr. Pierce appeared as if out of the wind and sea spray. He took her arm and set her close to the captain's side, then closed her fingers around a rope he pulled from somewhere behind her.

"Hold on," he warned her before stepping away as the waves crashed over the bow, splashing them in the rear.

With nowhere else to look after Pierce left, she set her eyes on the captain once again. "Are ye mad to do this in a storm?"

He grinned at her and winked. "Don't be afraid."

"I'm not afraid," she told him, expecting his laughter.

"Good." He didn't laugh, but his smile softened just enough to be indulgent. "It pleases me that ya trust me."

He *was* mad. She might have told him so if he didn't begin shouting orders. "Raise the black flag!"

They were going to plunder the merchant ship, which, Trina was stunned to discover, was much closer to them than she thought. The captain had chased it, and now he was about to catch it.

Was she dreaming? Was this truly about to happen with her in the midst of it all? Her blood scored her veins and blasted through her heart like thunderbolts. Bracing her legs, she watched the merchant ship grow closer.

"Fire cannon!" the captain's order echoed forth.

"Cover yar ears, beauty," he said more quietly to her.

She did as he gently commanded and let go of the rope just as the bow lifted on a massive swell. Cannon fire roared across the heavens, and Trina's descent overboard was halted by an arm as hard as steel around her.

Alex pulled her in close, as he had the last time they stood at the helm. His chest pressed to her back, his arms covering her down to their hands clutching the wheel. All at once, Trina felt like she'd arrived at the place she'd been longing for her whole life. At the helm of a ship being tossed about in a raging ocean, yet held steady by a silken steel embrace.

"I almost lost ya there, lass."

There was something about the way he spoke against her ear. His tone was flippant save for the deep fissure of something more meaningful. She had to keep herself from shaking in his arms, even though it would have been understandable after almost going overboard.

"Yer cannons missed," she said, keeping her mind off him and what almost just happened.

He smiled against her temple. "Nay, 'twas only a warnin'. We aren't all the blood-thirsty savages the noble folks would have ya believe. We give them a choice to raise their white flag."

She smiled at his logic. She wasn't here to judge him. She was here to live. And now, with the wind snapping at her hair and a warrior breathing down her neck and heating her in places where she never knew its power until now, she felt more alive than ever before.

He let go of her and stepped back, leaving her to steer on her own. She almost let go, but his voice soothed her.

"Feel the force of it in yar hands, Caitrina." He took hold of her hair and cleared it away from her face. "Like a bow," he whispered against her ear while he wrapped one of his sashes around her forehead and tied its ends into a knot on the side of her face, "as ya pull back on its line."

With her hair free from blocking her vision, she felt a bit more confident. They were gaining speed. They were almost upon the merchant ship.

"Fire muskets!"

Shots rang out and continued even as the captain ordered more cannon fire. Trina's hands shook as they gripped the wheel. This was real. The ship vibrated from the power of the deafening cannons. The power of the beast beneath her was too much.

Sensing her trepidation, the captain took the helm back and maneuvered his ship between the wind and his prey. "Fun's over, beauty." His voice covered her like a warm summer mist. "Go belowdecks. I would have ya safe."

"Would ye?" She turned to look up at him and smiled.

"Aye, I don't want yar savage kin comin' after me."

He didn't give a rat's arse about anyone coming after him. She laughed and nodded and turned to step into Mr. Pierce's waiting hands.

"Hurry back," the captain ordered his quartermaster. "I need ya to steer."

On the way back to the cabin, Trina looked up at Mr. Pierce's lightning-lit eyes and wondered where she stood with him. He did his best to keep her safe because the captain had ordered him to. He was as loyal as a well-loved dog...She blinked at him as a thought occurred to her. "D'ye have a brother in the Royal Army called David?"

"What?"

"Captain David Pierce?" she asked him, remembering the handsome captain who had helped her cousin Edmund and Amelia, his love, escape the Duke of Queensberry. "He came to Camlochlin several months ago to take one of Grendel's pups—"

"If I had a brother in the Royal anything"—the quartermaster curved the path of her thoughts—"I would cut his throat while he slept."

Trina forced a smile even though he reminded her constantly that she didn't like him. "My error. 'Twas silly of me to think that just because yer names were the same, ye were related. I am a result of a village, not a city."

She was relieved to see his misgivings about her vanish on the gale.

Continuing on their way, she heard the men begin to scream war cries and death threats while flailing and banging weapons against the gunwales of the ship. Simon the musician began to play a fiddle. The air snapped with anticipation. She didn't want to hide.

"Yar cousin awaits ya in the cabin," Pierce said, opening the door for her. "Ya're lucky I can't lock ya both in from the outside. I wouldn't see ya hurt."

Aye, Trina was thankful for that. She hated being locked up anywhere.

He waited until she entered and then left her, hurrying off to do the captain's bidding. Battle was the only time a captain had full authority, and every man on *Poseidon's Adventure* wanted it that way.

She stepped into her cousin on her way in and then out of the cabin and back on deck. "We're staying, Kyle."

"Colors hoisted!" Alex's voice boomed across the deck to his men. "Board with quarter!"

"Our faithers, Trina," Kyle warned, "our kin will come after him."

"'Tis only until Portugal," she told him, knowing he

was right. "We'll be home before our kin stock their boats fer their journey. Let us not think on it now."

The merchant ship had surrendered. There would be no fighting. She was glad, and apparently the only one on the ship who was. The crew's moans and groans were almost as loud as the canon fire. Their disappointment didn't last long, though. If they couldn't fight, at least they could loot.

She watched in awe while the crewmen swung through the air on rigging and leaped onto their prey's deck. The merchant ship was close enough for Trina to see its crew. The men looked frightened. She looked for Alex but didn't see him.

"Something's not right." Kyle moved away from her and squinted his eyes on the surrendering crew. "There's something…" He thought about it for a moment, then said, "Off about their fear."

Trina watched her cousin study what expressions he could make out on the crew. Kyle was a master at reading people, a skill taught to him and inherited from his father. She made a mental note to speak with him about Mr. Pierce.

"Och, hell," he cursed quietly, coming to an obviously troubling conclusion. "Captain!" he suddenly shouted as the captain came into their view, rope in hand, ready to fly.

He stopped and waited while Kyle ran to him. They shared words. The captain's expression grew darker and more menacing. What was Kyle telling him? Trina couldn't take the curiosity and had to stop herself from running over there to hear.

Soon, though, her curiosity would be satisfied. She watched Kyle hurry back to her, and the captain launch himself over the side, his foot wrapped securely enough around the rope to hold him up, using one hand while his other unleashed his cutlass. He cut through two men before any of the others realized what had happened.

The merchant ship had surrendered. Why was Alex killing their crew?

He shouted something to his men, but his voice blended with the wind—and Kyle's as her cousin reached her.

"Get inside the cabin and lock yerself inside!" he ordered.

"What? Why?" Even as she spoke, her eyes moved to the scene over Kyle's shoulder, a short distance away. Their victims multiplied by at least fifty men, each wielding swords, some loading pistols. Those were the ones Alex cut down first.

"'Tis a trap, Trina. Get inside!" Kyle pointed to the captain's quarters one last time, then he turned and ran, ready to lend his sword.

Her foot moved to follow him. She wanted to lend her skill as well. There were too many against the pirates. She searched the merchant ship's deck for Alex. She didn't see him again. If he was killed, who were these men who'd set a trap to catch him? What would they do to a woman?

She wasn't going to sit around waiting to find out. Her bow was in the captain's cabin. She kicked off her boots and ran to find it.

Chapter Thirteen

For at least a quarter of an hour the fight between ships wore on. Most of it, to Trina's relief, took place on the other ship. A few times, though, men from the opposing side came aboard.

Kyle wielded his sword alongside Mr. Pierce and some of the other men. Trina knew that while he practiced daily, Kyle had never actually killed anyone before. He was killing them now, though. He had no choice if he wanted to live. She had no time to retch or panic at the carnage and the danger around her. These men, privateers hired by the Royal Army as Robbie had called them, wouldn't kill her if they won. Her fate would be worse than a quick death. Suddenly the full impact of what was happening truly hit her. This was what it felt like to have to fight and pray for your life. Though it turned her blood cold in her veins, she had an arrow with bows and she knew how to use them. She took out a few, fearing she would be hanged for killing the queen's men, but when the next opportunity presented itself, she let her arrow fly. She didn't miss. She never did.

In between shots she searched the decks for the captain. As the number fell, she spotted him on the other ship and smiled, pleased that he still lived.

She didn't see the four men creeping up behind her but the instant arms came around her, she reacted and drove her heel into her attacker's foot. It wasn't enough to stop him or the rest from grabbing at her hair, her wrists, her skirts. She gouged at the closest captor's eyes and kneed another hard in the groin. One of them, a man with pale yellow hair and ice-colored eyes, hauled back his arm and backhanded her in the face.

Everything faded to black for a moment, and then another. Trina shook her head to hold on to consciousness. She wasn't going to let this lowborn son of a tavern whore knock her around.

He pushed her back against the rail and bent her over it, wedging himself between her legs. He groped for her skirts. Was this madman going to attempt to rape her here and now? Her heart pumped furiously in her chest. She fought a battle to keep from letting terror have its way.

She felt the hard hilt of his dagger digging into her hip and slipped her hand beneath his belt to set it free. He realized what she'd done and closed his fingers around her throat. She rammed the dagger deep into his belly. Stepping away from him as his hand and everything else went limp, she gave him room to double over, then grabbed a handful of his flaxen hair.

Lifting his head, she swiped his dagger across his throat and let him drop to the floor. She turned to the next man closest to her and came face-to-face with the barrel of his pistol.

Her family in Camlochlin raided her thoughts. She hoped they knew she loved them. She hoped Kyle lived through this day...and Alex. Nae, damn it, she didn't want to die. But...at least she died in an adventure. She also wouldn't close her eyes. If death was coming to her, she wouldn't be a coward about it.

Because her eyes were open, she saw Alex coming on the air like an angel of death, poised to kill with his rapier ready. If she had closed her eyes, she would have missed the single driven purpose in his course. He came at her from behind the gun-toting thug and swung, severing the man's head cleanly from his shoulders. Now Trina did look away, unprepared for such brutality directly in front of her.

Landing both boots on deck, the captain released his rope and brought a swift end to the two men remaining before they had time to do anything. He saved her in seconds. Gustaaf was correct. She doubted anyone could ever beat Alex in a fight.

When it was over and the four men lay scattered around her, she shook from the violence of the day. He came near her, his hands reaching for her as if to take her in his arms. His eye caught the blond head of the man who struck her and he turned to the man's fallen body instead. He muttered something that sounded like "Ya lily-livered scabby-arsed cockroach. Ya're not fit fer Fiddlers Green." He bent down and hoisted the dead man over his shoulder and then without another word walked to the rail and flung the body overboard. When he returned to her, she thought he might admonish her for disobeying him yet again, but he closed her in his arms and said softly against her ear while she shook, "We have their captain. The fight is over. Sam will do the rest now. Ya're safe now. Ya're safe. Come, let's retire to me cabin." He smiled and Trina nodded, then followed.

"Kyle." She stopped and looked up at him. She needed to make sure her cousin was all right, and that he stayed that way.

The captain sighed but thankfully he indulged her and called out over his shoulder, "Kyle! Come with us."

Trina turned to see her cousin approaching and smiled at him, proud to see him alive and looking so well after his first real battle. When he reached them, she looked him over for any injuries, then grinned at him. "Ye're well."

Kyle nodded and took her hand. "Never better. And ye? Were ye hurt?" After she shook her head and smiled at him, he turned to Alex. "Thank ye. I'm in yer debt fer saving her."

The captain flicked a light smile to Trina and made her light-headed. "'Tis bad luck fer a woman to die on a ship."

He couldn't rile her. Not now. She liked to think that she was strong and well skilled, able to take care of herself. The MacGregors and the Grants did not raise cowards. And yet she couldn't save herself from a steal ball to the head. He'd saved her and she wasn't too proud to admit it, and to want to thank him for it. She didn't care *why* he did it. Only that he did. She was in his debt.

She wasn't pleased about it, but if not for him, she'd be dead.

They entered the cabin and sat around the captain's table while he explained to them who the men were and what he intended to do with them. They were privateers, seamen who are authorized by the government to plunder enemy ships.

"What's the difference between pirates and privateers?" Trina asked him.

"Privateers turn over their booty to the governments who license them, while pirates keep what they've taken."

"Like mercenaries."

"Aye." He nodded and smiled at her. "I'm guessin' the purpose of these men was to find me and follow me to me father's treasure. The governors and investors in Boston and New York want the *Quedagh Merchant*. They hanged me father fer it."

"But how do they already know ye have the map?" Kyle put to him. "We havena' stopped anywhere. These privateers must have been following ye before Scotland."

Alex nodded. "They don't know about the map. They've been followin' me fer seven years on and off, believin' me father told me where the ship was before they killed him. But they've never tried a ruse like this before. If not fer ya," he told Kyle, "we would likely be dead right now. How did ya know 'twas a trap?"

She liked that although he did most of the killing and then saved her life, he thanked Kyle for saving them.

"They were counting moments until they could fight," Kyle told him. "I could see it in their eyes. I suspected something but when one of them lifted his hand to scratch his head, I spotted his pistol in his belt, an English flint-lock. A man who carries a pistol usually uses it. Why hadn't he?"

Alex shrugged.

"Because he was waiting fer his orders."

The captain grinned at him and tossed his arm over the back of his chair. "Ya figured all that out just by lookin' at them?"

"Not looking," Kyle corrected. "Watching. And if ye dinna' mind, I would like to be present while Mr. Pierce questions the prisoners."

"We don't usually take prisoners, MacGregor. Particularly not sneaky ones."

"With respect, Captain"—her cousin's tone proved his sentiment true—"prisoners should always be questioned."

Alex nodded. "Go. Interrogate, but ya'll find that here at sea, a man will sell his soul for a scrap of gold, nothing else."

Kyle stood up and thanked him, then kissed the top of Trina's head and left the cabin.

The quarters suddenly felt small and stifling with just her and the captain in it. Trina refused his offer of ale. She already felt muddleheaded. She didn't need help getting there. She looked around to avoid looking at him. Her eyes settled on the bed. How long was their journey? How long would he keep away from his bed?

"Captain, ye must find a room fer me to sleep in that is safe and away from ye."

"We're alone." He pointed out the torturously obvious. "Call me Alex and tell me why ya want to be away from me in particular."

"Ye know perfectly well why, Captain. 'Tis only a matter of time before ye can no longer control yer hungry appetite."

And I willingly succumb.

He raised his brows and smiled. "Me hungry appetite?"

"Aye," she said. She refused to think about all the ways he could devour her. She would not allow the memory of his kiss to addle her good senses. She could have had plenty of men. Many had offered. She'd refused them all, seeking freedom to discover what she truly wanted in life and needing clarity of thought not to let anything stop her.

"And what will happen when I can no longer control meself?"

She sighed and rolled her eyes heavenward. She didn't

want to play this game of coy blushes and feigned propriety. If they were going to sail the seas together, he needed to know that she wouldn't lie to him or pretend to be someone she wasn't. "Ye will have yer way with me. Force me to lie with ye and…" She paused and swallowed, sorry for opening her mouth when images, perverse and scintillating, overwhelmed her. Images of him pushing her down onto his bed, his hard, lithe body poised over hers…

"And?" he asked on a sorcerer's whisper.

As if the sight of him sitting there spread out over his chair like a lazy prince wasn't bad enough, visions of him fighting and flying toward her on a rope to rescue her invaded her thoughts and formed knots in her belly. And? he'd asked. And, she wanted to tell him, kiss every inch of his body.

She blinked at him. His smile deepened as if he were reading the thoughts that made her blush. She severed their gaze and rose to her feet. He followed.

"Caitrina." The sound of her name on his lips drew her to look at him. "I'm havin' fun with ya. I would never force meself on any woman, not even one as exquisite and entertainin' as ya."

Did he mock her? She couldn't tell. Och, why the hell did Kyle leave? He would know.

"But," he continued, his sable eyes growing even darker beneath his brows while wicked intentions passed through his thoughts, "ya're correct about me hungry appetite, fer I'd love to sample yar delectable fruit and discover if 'tis as sweet as yar mouth."

She should slap him. Shouldn't she? She might if she could breathe. Tiny beads of sweat formed on her forehead, her temples, and her upper lip. No man had ever dared speak to her in such a manner, so wickedly, not with her kin around. But they weren't around now. And she didn't want to slap him. She wanted to kiss him. Saints, what had come over her?

"But alas, we come from two different worlds," he was saying. "Ya have nothing to fear from me, Caitrina. I prefer my women less...innocent."

How did he manage to make her feel like he was denying what she ached for? Bastard. Why did she want to declare that she wasn't as innocent as he thought? She should have slapped him. Of course she wasn't innocent. She knew what men and women did in beds. She grew up hearing tales about sexual pursuits and satisfying victories from men who mastered the art of seduction. Her brother Malcolm and her cousin Adam never woke with the same woman twice. She knew plenty, but she didn't have to prove it to Captain Kidd.

She offered him a cheeky smile. "That's good to know. Now where can I sleep besides yer bed?"

He laughed, looking more intoxicating than a dozen ships all bound for lands unknown.

"I'll speak to Sam and Mr. Bonnet about finding ya someplace private. Hungry?"

"What?"

"Are ya hungry, Miss Grant?"

For an instant she feared that he'd stripped her of her thoughts and read them. Then she remembered she hadn't eaten. "Aye. I am."

"Do ya think 'tis safe to share a meal with me?" he asked on his way to the door. "Or might me hungry appetite take control and ravish ya?" He turned away from her and to the door. Opening it, he called out to someone to have Robbie bring them food, then shut the door again and turned back to her.

"If it does," she told him, following where they had left off, "let me assure ye, Captain, before ye're done, ye'll be dead."

He grinned, wide and inviting, sincerely amused. "How would ya do it?" he asked, offering her back her seat at the table. "Do ya think I would succumb as quickly as the man ya killed on deck?"

She had the urge to fan herself but she didn't want to let on that he had any effect on her. He was enjoying this as much as he believed she was. He was right.

"Quickly or not," she promised, unyielding in her pride, refusing to lose to him, "ye would eventually lose to me."

He leaned back in his chair and swung one leg over the arm. "I think ya would find me difficult to kill."

She shrugged her shoulders and offered him a slight, indulgent smile. "Think what ye will."

He arched his brows at her audacity. If he was trying to intimidate her, he might have succeeded if he wasn't grinning at her like some sexy halfwit. Och, how she wanted to just go over there and melt on top of him.

"I think I'd like a demonstration of yar skill."

She shook her head. The last thing she wanted was to get physical with him. "I dinna' need to defend myself against yer misgivings."

"Of course. By the confidence in yar voice, I thought ya knew some skill no woman before ya has ever tried on me."

He knew how to bait her. Thank God for Kyle and his endless, annoying lessons on dodging the hook. "How difficult is it to cut a man's throat while he sleeps?"

His eyes took her in like she was a long-awaited sunset, but his words dripped with desire. "The difficulty"— his voice dipped to a low growl—"at least fer ya, would be wonderin' how ya got into me bed in the first place."

Her smile remained intact, cool, and distant. Keeping calm was a challenge she enjoyed. "Ye waste yer seductions on me. I willna' be in yer bed, Captain. But I'll be in yer cabin if ye dinna' find me a new bed. And I can kill ye in yer sleep if I'm here."

She enjoyed the fullness of his smile, the different nuances of it, and that he was confident enough to laugh at her.

"In truth," she admitted, wanting his help in teaching her never to need it again, "I could use a few lessons in hand-to-hand battle. Mind ye, I'm not suggesting that I dinna' know how to kill ye—or any other man—if I had to. I just want to be able to take on more than one man at a time."

"Wise."

"Will ye help me?"

"Aye."

She tilted her head at him. "Dinna' hope these lessons will lead to anything more than learning combat."

He laughed softly at her. "Ya certainly think highly of yarself, woman. I agree because I might not reach ya in time if ya're attacked again. I won't have ya helpless to any number of men."

"Neither would I." She smiled more genuinely. She would never forget the sight of him coming for her on a rope. How far away was Portugal? She hoped it was months, years, a lifetime.

Chapter Fourteen

$\mathcal{A}$lex watched the last of the booty being carried from the privateer's ship to *Poseidon's Adventure*. He'd helped haul most of it back over planks connecting both ships while Sam took inventory. They'd collected fourteen barrels of water, five casks of rice, dried fish, live chickens, candles, thread, soap, sugar, spices, some bolts of cloth, kettles, and of course kegs of spirits.

After interrogating the captain of the ship, Kyle discovered that it was Captain Harris of the *Excellence* who hired the privateers. Alex wasn't sure what good that knowledge did them but he appreciated Kyle getting it. Alex and Sam decided to let the captain of the merchant ship live, and sent him on his way with a skeleton crew and limited supplies. If they killed every enemy they faced, there would be none for another day and the seas would become a dull place.

Although Alex doubted this journey would be a dull one, what with the beauty Caitrina and her landlubber cousin aboard. He thought about them both while they raised anchor and set sail for Portugal. If not for Kyle, his crew might very well be dead. As much as Alex hated to admit it, he would likely have boarded the ship and been taken by surprise when the privateers attacked. The Highlander's keen eye and ability to spot trouble could come in quite handy. Not to mention his skill with a sword. He was a tad clumsy, but that was due to the absence of solid ground beneath his feet. Alex was glad to have him aboard. For now. He couldn't say the same for Caitrina.

Aye, she was a skilled archer. She took down half a dozen men before trouble found her. But still it found her and he didn't like the way it made him feel. So, she managed to take down the bastard who struck her . . . and oh, what Alex would have done to him if she hadn't, but she couldn't fight four men. He closed his eyes, thinking of what would have happened if he hadn't made it to her in time. She wasn't his charge. He had plenty more important things to see to, than seeing to her. Now he had agreed to train her in combat. Blast him.

He turned, sensing her coming near.

Was it her?

What had she done to herself? Who gave her those clothes?

"How do I look?" she asked, reaching him and twirling in place.

His eyes devoured her in her canvas pants, cinched at the waist with a rose-colored sash. She wore a loose-fitting shirt, like his, but with more tantalizing curves. Her luminous dark tresses were secured beneath another sash of pale coral.

He thought his heart might have stopped a little at the sight of her. It would explain the sudden wave of light-headedness that usually only came upon him after several tankards of rum. *Never* when looking at a woman. He didn't know whether to smile at her or scowl at the way she so easily addled his soundness of mind.

He should have bypassed the merchant/privateer ship, dumped her in France, and moved the hell on, eager as he was to find his treasure.

He'd never cared much if he was rich or not. He enjoyed his life and the women in it. It wasn't that he couldn't give his heart to one. He had given it, long ago. It took him a long time to get it back. He wouldn't lose it again. He'd never considered giving up pirating and living somewhere on land with a wife and children. Not even with Madalena. Pirating flowed in his veins. The sea was his home, his crew was part of his family. He never thought to leave it.

And then he met her.

A fearless Highland lass who knew what she wanted and went after it.

"Ya look…ehm…" his voice faltered an instant when a soft blush stole across her cheeks. She was confident and strong, and yet there remained in her wide gaze, in her tenuous smile, an innocence that sparkled like a treasure rivaling any other.

"Who gave ya the garb?" he asked, trying to sound glib.

He noted the slight disappointment marring her brow, likely because he didn't tell her how maddeningly beguiling she looked.

"Mr. Pierce did after he showed me to my new quarters. A closet, I believe he called it. He said these clothes belonged to a dead sailor called John Gable. He said Mr. Gable was the smallest man he ever knew."

Alex laughed, remembering his crewman Gable. "Aye, he was. His slight size made it possible fer him to repair the masts at their highest point, without fallin'."

"Do ye think I could make it up to the crow's nest?"

The crow's nest? Was she mad to think he would allow her to climb to the highest point on the ship and nestle in a small box secured to a mast?

"Nay. Absolutely not."

"But ye just said that Mr. Gable did it."

"Aye, and it killed him one afternoon durin' a storm. Don't argue," he said when she opened her mouth.

He ignored her indignation. Rather her anger than her death.

He looked down at her bare feet and ankles. "Wise. Ya will do less fallin'."

"I fell only once." Well, all right she had to confess. "A few times. But I already have a splinter, and in truth, I dinna' know which is worse."

He liked the sound of her voice along with everything else. "Sit with me after supper and I'll pluck it out."

Instead of answering, she moved to the rail and drew her palm over it. "I have a theory," she told him as their ship moved past the other, "that once a boat stabs ye, ye're kin."

"Aye," he agreed. "But she wouldn't have ya die from an infection in yar foot. Splinters get taken out. Savvy?"

She nodded, then, when he looked away, across the sea, she moved closer to him. "Ye have my gratitude fer letting me and Kyle stay a little longer. But if I may be completely honest..." She waited until he nodded. "I don't think all this ordering me aboot will be in our best interest if we mean to get along."

He almost laughed right in her face. Neptune's arse, but he loved her honesty. She wasn't afraid of him in the least. Every sailor should fear his captain a little. It kept mutiny from happening. Still, he liked that she wasn't afraid of him.

But she couldn't be in earnest with these claims that she

truly wanted to stay. What woman would ever want this kind of life? She'd tried to convince him of her desire to remain, but he had to suspect that she had intended on staying from the beginning. To somehow find a way to beguile him until her first opportunity to rob him presented itself.

"Ya are goin' to have to bury yar feet in a bucket of warm sand every night so that yar soles don't get so soft they rot. Many of the men have lost their toes. Two weeks on any ship and ya're goin' to have to eat food that's goin' bad. The water goes warm and stagnant, but ya drink it if ya want to keep livin'. Some of the men begin to stink…Hell, everything begins to stink. Soon, ya will find yarself considerin' jumpin' overboard to end the misery of boredom. And if there's ever a fight, like today, most men will try to rape ya. Ya will have to fight and kill without remorse."

"But ye're free," she insisted. "Free to make yer own choices."

He smiled and shook his head. "If bein' trapped on a ship fer weeks, sometimes months, at a time is free to ya."

She considered his words for a moment, then shrugged her dainty shoulders. "'Tis temporary. Ye're moving forward, heading fer parts unknown. Keeping that in mind would aid in keeping ungrateful thoughts at bay."

He sized her up. Perhaps she truly did have a strong passion for adventure. Would it matter to him in the end if she were after his treasure, or after his ship?

He would give up neither.

But for an instant, he imagined her standing at his side at the helm, in his bed beneath him, atop him. He fought the urge to coil his arm around her waist and drag her in close to him. Nay, he didn't want a woman sailing the seas with him.

"Ya come from a wild, beautiful place," he said, taking

hold of the rigging and of her to keep her from falling. "Why would ya prefer this?"

"No place on earth will ever be more bonnie to me than Camlochlin," she said, looking out over the sea, "but though they are unseen, and despite the loving reasons they were placed there, I live with chains around my ankles. My kin are proscribed. Leaving Skye could get me arrested withoot trial and hanged withoot my kin even knowing. My father would never have let me leave."

She could be hanged? He pushed back at the anger boiling to the surface. He couldn't save his father years ago. But now he would massacre anyone who tried to put a noose around Caitrina Grant's sweet neck. "I've heard of this proscription," he told her. "While ya're a part of me crew, even if 'tis only until we reach Portugal, I won't let anyone hurt ya."

She smiled, keeping her eyes on the horizon. "And Kyle?"

He sighed inwardly. "Kyle can keep himself safe, but if he needs me help, he will have it." Bloody hell, would he promise her anything? When she turned her smile on him, he knew that he would.

"Ye're quite agreeable of late." She flashed her dimples at him. "What has changed?"

"I'm always agreeable, woman," he muttered, knowing she was damned correct. Why, he might as well take up dancing or poetry next. It wasn't that he wanted to please her. He didn't go around trying to make women happy... at least, not for more than a night. He simply didn't see any reason to constantly argue with her. *Poseidon's Adventure* might be a big ship, but it would get smaller over days, until it seemed cramped and crowded. Bickering could lead to tossing someone overboard. "Don't press me favor."

She shrugged again and returned her attention to the water. Alex took a moment or two to bask in the alluring curve of her nose, the sweet angles of her cheekbones and jaw against a backdrop of pewter skies. She was breathtaking.

"Why are ya not wed?"

She cut him a wry glance. "Were ye not listening just now when I explained aboot wanting my freedom? Why are *ye* not wed?"

"'Tis different. Ya're a woman."

She turned on him, her eyes blazing like twin blue flames. Her anger was palpable, sizzling around her and making Alex brace himself up to meet it straight on. He tried not to enjoy it too much but hell, he wanted to snatch her up and carry her to his cabin.

"Aye, and a woman is nothing withoot a man in front of her."

He shrugged his shoulders. "I prefer bein' behind a woman."

His lips curled ever so slightly as his reply settled over her and she paused at its effect, and then blushed. He regarded her with curiosity and desire. Such hellfire and innocence all packaged up in one so beautiful. It hardly seemed fair to other women.

"Why does being a woman mean I should want a husband and children, and if I dinna' want them there must be something wrong with me?"

"Who told ya that?" he asked, not liking that anyone should say such a thing about her. "I know plenty of women who don't want husbands or children."

She set her hand to her hip and narrowed her eyes on him.

Hell, he wanted to delight in ravishing her.

"Did something I said give ye the impression that I wanted to hear aboot the women ye've bedded?"

He hadn't considered it would bother her, until now. She looked about to open her mouth and shoot fire at him.

"I assume ye speak of whores since ye never spoke of anything more. Am I to be compared to whores then? Are they the only other women who seek something different from life?"

"They don't seek anything, Caitrina," he told her. He wouldn't give her insult by lying about the women he'd known. But he wanted her to know how different she was from them. "They are as stagnant as our drinkin' water will be. But ya, beauty, ya are vibrant and alive."

His words were spoken with genuine sincerity, and though she stiffened, he knew he'd triumphed over her anger.

"Thank ye."

She didn't smile. Prideful wench. Would one night be enough for him?

"But the question remains," she said. "Why do I have to marry, but a man can have a whore in every port?"

"Captain," a voice called out. Alex turned to see Kyle approaching. "A bit of free counsel," the young Mac-Gregor offered. "Nothing ye say will be correct. She's argued this topic fer years and has mastered it."

Alex grinned at them both, then let his gaze settle on hers. "There are laws, spoken and unspoken, and like us"—he stretched his arms out wide to signify the crew—"ya don't like them." He arched his back to get a better view of her, from her delicate ankles peeking out from beneath her pants to the sash around her head. His grin softened. "Seems ya have some pirate blood in ya, Miss Grant."

Chapter Fifteen

Trina thought she could ignore her surroundings and enjoy her adventure. She thought her mettle was strong enough. She was wrong.

Just a week into her journey and she began doubting every decision she'd made since jumping off the cliffs and boarding the ship.

She didn't mind being wet almost every day, or the splinters in her feet, or the constant rocking and having nothing more to look at than the horizon. Those things she could ignore. But she hadn't counted on Captain Kidd and his all-consuming presence day in and day out to drive her mad. She hadn't prepared herself for the way the husky dip of his voice when he said her name made her kneecaps melt. Or for the sight of him stepping out on deck in the morning, shirtless and slumberous and looking better than any man had the right to look fresh out of bed. How could she pretend to be unaffected by the sight of him standing firm at the wheel, guiding the beast beneath him over the roiling sea, or the thrill that singed her blood when she caught him watching her.

And och, how she missed his comfortable bed, which she'd insisted on changing into a mat stuffed with hay in a damned closet.

Her body ached from her cramped quarters, so when Alex called her to practice swordplay with him, she thought about refusing. She prayed he would be a little easier on her but five minutes in, she knew she was in trouble.

It wasn't that he struck her or hurt her in any way. On the contrary, he was patient and careful not to touch his blade to her flesh. Nae, he wasn't dangerous to her body, but to her good senses, to her heart, to her reasoning. She knew it was a bad idea to practice with him when he parried her jab, sidestepped her next blow, and wound up behind her. Before she could react, he looped his arm around her neck and pressed her back intimately against his hard angles.

He took her breath away and conjured images in her head that made her heart accelerate.

"Lass." His warm breath just beneath her ear sent quivers through her body. "I could jam me blade up into yar sternum from here. Try again."

He gave her a gentle shove and waited for her to begin again. She lifted her blade to strike, a cutlass he'd given her to use. It was lighter and smaller than the claymores at home and unfamiliar in her hand. He countered with an arced strike above her head and then another quick blow to her legs. She tried to block but he changed position suddenly and his blade twisted and danced in the air before sending her sword across the deck. He took a swift step forward and held the tip of his blade to her throat.

"Ye're showing off."

He smiled, swept his blade away from her, and bowed.

"What good is bein' so skilled if I can't show off once in a while?"

All right, she was done letting him win. He was damned good but she'd trained with the best and it was time he saw just how good she was. She hadn't realized that some of the crewmen had gathered around to watch. Kyle was there, as well, laughing and rooting her on. She wouldn't let him down.

Readying her blade, she braced her bare feet and smiled while he circled her. She could feel the heat from his body radiating off him. She listened close to the rhythm of his breathing. Hell, he made her blood boil, her palms moist. A small, secret part of her wanted to let him conquer her. But she came from men and women who never surrendered.

Just as he was about to strike a blow to her shoulder, she bent her knees and ducked. His blade whooshed over her head as her sword came around and whacked him across the backs of his knees. Unfortunately, his balance was superior, as was his defense...and offense. He could have taken her out at any time, but the wickedly seductive grin he wore the whole time was an indication that he was enjoying this game too much to end it.

She didn't want to stop either, though she was growing tired of the quick pace and even quicker thinking she had to do to keep up with him.

When she swiped her weapon close to his throat, he offered a stunned, yet pleased, look and then came at her with a bit more zest. It took every ounce of determination she possessed to keep him from disarming her. He was quick on his feet, quicker than any man she knew. He swung with one arm and reached for her with the other. Catching her, he dragged her in close and for a moment that seemed to last an eternity, he simply looked into her eyes, triumphant and sexy as hell.

"Do ya concede?" he asked her in a very low whisper that twisted her belly into knots. "Or do we continue until ya end up in me bed?"

In his bed? Saints, judging by the husky tone of his voice and the smoldering embers in his eyes, he wasn't threatening injury. It wasn't the first time she'd imagined him in bed with her, but it wouldn't do to think on it now with Kyle and the crew watching. She didn't want to concede. She hated having to do it. But she believed his promise and ending up in his bed scared the hell out of her.

Difficult as it was, for being near him weakened her, she slipped out of his grasp and backed away. "Ye leave me with nae choice but to concede then." She bowed to him and then stepped up close to him to hand him back his sword and to whisper, "When I give myself to a man, I willna' be fergotten the next day." She offered him a stiff smile, then turned on her heel to leave.

She tried her damnedest to ignore the shard of wood that pierced her heel upon making her exit. She didn't want to limp away like a wounded animal in front of Kyle and the men. Mostly, she didn't want the captain to think she couldn't take pain. She could... but truly, wearing her boots and falling was worth exchanging for the holes and pain in her feet. She'd never had a splinter before. They weren't excruciating, like, say, an arrow piercing flesh might be. But they poked and they itched and irritated until she thought she might go mad. This one felt different. Bigger. But she refused to limp.

"Yar flesh will adjust." The captain's deep voice just behind her, falling so intimately against her ear, vanquished pain and every other thought save one. That she wanted to fall back in his arms and rest on him, for just a moment.

"And until then?" she asked. When she felt his arms come around her, she let go.

"Until then," he told her, scooping her up off her feet, "I'll just have to carry ya around."

She smiled at him. He didn't deserve her scorn after giving her such rest. But if he meant to take her to his cabin, she would prefer to walk. After another moment or two.

"Where are ye taking her, Captain?" It seemed Kyle was thinking the same thing she was.

"To the infirmary."

She didn't know if she could trust her mettle to fight him if she was alone with him. She looked to her cousin for help, but it didn't come.

"Don't be afraid."

She blinked up at the captain, caught in her worry. "I'm not afraid," she promised. "Afraid of what? That ye're helping me." She laughed. "Dinna' be absurd."

He watched her from beneath his hat with eyes that didn't believe her, and didn't care. Amusement danced across his features and set her nerve endings aflame.

She noticed that he wasn't in any hurry to reach their destination. "Will ye be strolling slowly along the entire way?"

He laughed, a rich, robust, resonating sound that saturated her skin and seeped into her muscles, her bones, and finally her heart. "If I wasn't certain ya were a woman"— as if to convince her that he spoke the truth, he squeezed her buttock in his palm and hefted her closer to his chest—"I would think ya had balls to speak to me so."

She didn't know what possessed her. Mayhap it was

the way he always seemed to appear when she needed him, or the way his eyes betrayed the glib words of his mouth. Whatever it was made her loop her arms around his neck. "Ye're not accustomed to women standing up to ye then?"

"Ya're not standin', lass."

Goodness, he was infuriating. She tugged at his hair and when he laughed playfully, she wished she had the courage to keep her fingers curled around his locks.

"What are ye accustomed to then, Captain?"

"No one like ya, Caitrina."

She had the urge to press her palm to her forehead and check herself for fever. Her body felt hot enough to combust. She hoped he was complimenting her. She suspected he was from the warmth in his eyes while they took her in and the subtle hook of his mouth when his gaze settled on her lips.

He hadn't kissed her since that first day, but she could tell, on more occasions than one, that he wanted to. What was stopping him? She doubted it had anything to do with his morals. If he had any at all. He'd told her that he preferred his women more worldly. But how was one supposed to become more worldly if no one kissed her? And why the hell was she thinking in such ways? What did she care about kisses and innocence and coy smiles? That wasn't the life she wanted. Not yet, at least. That was why she'd refused her suitors.

They entered the temporary darkness of the stairwell below deck. She listened to the rhythm of his steady breath, was acutely aware of his hands on her while he carried her down the next stairwell. The only light came from lanterns scattered here and there. In the soft golden glow that reflected off the light streaks in his hair, he looked even more irresistible.

"Ya fought me well."

"I could have fought ye longer."

"But ya knew I would enjoy it all the more?"

Hell, was it the devilish quirk of his lips or the twinkle in his otherwise dark eyes that bubbled her blood and made her want to go toe-to-toe with him?

Damn him, why wouldn't he kiss her?

He brought her to the infirmary and set her down on a wooden table. She hopped off when she spotted bloodstains from some prior patient.

She looked around at a heavy cabinet and hooks drilled into the walls. Hanging from them were various knives, razors, head saws, forceps, cauterizing irons, syringes, and some horrifying apparatus that looked like it might be used for pulling teeth. In the cabinet were scissors, stitching quill and needles, splints, sponges, soft rags, cupping glasses, blood porringers, chafing dishes, a mortar and pestle, weights and scales, and plasters.

"Who is the physician on board?"

"Harry Hanes."

"Is he not the carpenter?" Trina asked, dreading the answer.

"Aye, but he's quite able," he told her. "Patchin' up a body is similar to patchin' up a ship. Or so I'm told. I'll go fetch him."

"Nae!" Trina grabbed for his arm. "I'll see to the splinter myself."

"Nonsense." He took her by the shoulders and sat her down in a wooden chair, probably carved by Mr. Hanes. "I'll see to it meself. I've removed plenty of these things." He pulled another chair close and sat opposite her. "Let's have me a look, then."

She wasn't sure she wanted him poking around in her

skin, but she supposed he was a better alternative than a carpenter . . . although a carpenter was likely very familiar with splinters.

"Did ya have many suitors in Scotland?" he asked, interrupting her reasoning to pull her foot out of his hand and wait for Hanes after all.

"A few," she told him, watching him place her foot in his lap and examine her wound. His fingers were warm and they tickled. "Dinna' ye need more light?"

He shook his head and unlatched a large medicine chest close to his feet. He looked inside. "What happened to them?"

"Who?"

"Yar suitors? Did ya refuse them all?"

"I did."

"Preferrin' adventure as yar husband." He smiled with her when she dropped all pretenses and nodded.

"Finally," she admitted, "verra' recently, in fact, my faither agreed to a betrothal fer me. He fears my dreams will get me killed, and if they do not, then I should have a husband to take care of me, protect and provide fer me while I live."

She jumped and hissed at him when he tugged on the splinter.

"Were ya runnin' away then?" he asked her.

"Mayhap . . . in a way." She smiled, feeling at ease enough to be perfectly honest with him. "'Twas selfish of me, I know. I didna' think my actions through and I fear fer my kin if they come after me."

"Don't fret over that," he told her. He poured something cool over her foot and picked up a tool.

"Did any of them kiss ya?"

She was about to answer when he plucked the shard

from her foot. She looked at it, feeling queasy by the size of it. She was grateful that he'd asked such a jarring, unexpected question to keep her mind off the splinter, but when he looked at her, expecting an answer, she blushed to her roots.

"One of them did."

He reached for a few jars inside the chest, uncorked them, and sprinkled a bit out from each. After producing a little pile, he spit into it and molded it in his fingers to make a paste.

"And what became of him, Miss Grant?" The thick cadence of his voice fell like an elixir over her, summoning her heart from its hiding place.

"He returned to his home and I never saw his face again."

"He was a fool."

He lit her blood with flames of desire. But she didn't want to be another notch on his cutlass. She'd meant what she said above deck. When she decided she wanted a man, and that wasn't coming anytime soon, she would choose one who was loyal to her.

"Have ye had many splinters, Captain?"

He smiled at her, letting her change the topic, and began rubbing the paste onto her sole. "I've had me share. If ya stayed after Portugal ya would get more before ya got less.

"Yar skin is soft." He pressed his index and middle finger into her sole and raced a path to her heel.

She laughed, watching, and liking his reaction to it. "Would ye let me stay if I asked?"

His smile faded. "Nay, don't ask."

"I know ye give up much to live this life, Captain."

He shook his head. "Ya would lose more than I did."

Aye, she knew what he meant, for the weight of it grew heavier with the passing of each night. "Ye had nae family, then?"

"I had two families. The people of the Islands and me father's crew…until I left them to find me own way. By the time I realized our ways were the same, 'twas too late. Me father had sailed away and I never saw him alive again. I tried to see him after he was arrested but they wouldn't let me near him. He was the hardest thing to give up," he told her. "The men I considered family, the ones who never came to his defense while he was on trial, were much easier."

He was right. She didn't realize how much she would miss her mother and father, Abby, Malcolm, and aye, even Cailean. Her heart ached for them on her mat at night. "I would not let them go completely," she said softly. "I would return to Camlochlin to visit my—"

"Ya wouldn't go anywhere near them after what ya've become out here. Ya will have changed too much to go back. Ya cannot truly want this life, Caitrina."

"I do!" she said, pushing forward in her chair. Then she sat back again, deflated. The problem was her kin and she didn't know what Kyle wanted. She couldn't make them stay if Kyle didn't want to, or if he wouldn't leave without her. "If I could, I would not change," she told him. "Ye dinna' know me. I'm a stubborn woman. I would visit my kin and I would not change."

"Ya want to find the *Quedagh Merchant* with me then," he finally said.

Lord, was he really asking her? It sounded more like an accusation. She shouldn't answer him. She couldn't answer him. The decision wasn't hers alone. "If you're asking, let me decide in Portugal. If I choose to go home,

I can board a ship to Scotland and be nae more trooble to ye."

His smile vanished in the space of a breath.

Trina tried to think of what she'd said to cause his ire. And his ire was evident when he moved her foot off his thighs and stood up.

"Ya will be able to walk back."

"How have I offended ye?" she asked, standing with him.

"Ya didn't," he told her. "I'm a fool. I should not have let ya stay past France." He looked away from her questioning gaze, then walked away, mumbling, "I am a damn fool."

❧❧❧

Chapter Sixteen

One of the most beautiful cities in Europe, Lisbon, capital city of Portugal, spread across steep hillsides that overlooked the Rio Tejo. The city retained some of its old Moorish influence, seen most dramatically in the design of the quarters surrounding Castelo de São Jorge and extending as far as Rossio Square, the central part of the city. Alex loved and hated Lisbon. It was here that he found out who he was and then lost everything he had. One thing he loved most about it was its wine. A coastal trading community more prosperous than any other, Lisbon was most well known for its fine port.

A treasure Alex longed to possess. They brought along goods to trade but no one would do business with them dressed in rags. Emulating gentleman merchants, they wore their best clothes, including footwear. Alex wore knee breeches and leather boots, an embroidered waistcoat with a lace-trimmed shirt, and a long coat. And, of course, a ring on every finger. Absent of his hat and his bandanna, his hair was tied neatly into a tail at the back of his neck and he'd removed the golden hoops from his lobes. He felt a bit out of place, as he always did on land, but it wouldn't do to look like a thieving pirate if he had to steal.

They would find a way to get all that they needed. They always did. They traveled like paupers, but they lived like kings.

Alex led the way up a long, winding road with his men and a woman behind him. He'd been here before a decade ago when he met Madalena and broke off from his father. His feet had brought him to the Caso do Alberte then and they brought him back now.

He looked over his shoulder at Caitrina, walking a few paces back between Gustaaf and Kyle. She looked damned beautiful dressed in her bodice and skirts, her hair flowing freely in the breeze. He cursed under his breath. How had he gotten himself into this? He couldn't get rid of her. He was stuck with her for the next month. When he had decided to take the privateer's ship, he wasn't thinking about how she would get back to Scotland from Portugal. But the day he pulled the splinter from her foot, when she assured him she could get back on her own, he realized what she meant. She would stow away again. How the hell was he supposed to let her do that?

He'd never planned on bringing her with him all the way to the West Indies. He'd told her about how bad things became on a ship after sailing for a long time in order to help her understand that a pirate's life was not at all what she imagined. Freedom came with a cost.

And he didn't want to help her pay it.

Hell, staying with her these last days was harder than the days before. He couldn't forget her words to him. She didn't want to be forgotten when she took a man. It was what strengthened him to stay his hand from touching her.

If he had his way with her, she would expect something in return, like his love. So he'd managed to successfully avoid her since the splinter two days ago, angry with himself for not thinking this through before he took the privateer ship.

Two weeks on a ship was nothing. Two more weeks with another on the horizon could drive her mad. What the hell would he do with her then? He couldn't lock her away with her damned knowledge of escaping. He sure as hell couldn't let her stow away on another ship. She would be discovered and the captain would not likely be as kind to her as Alex had been. And what about her kin?

"The men are talkin'."

Alex cut his hard gaze to Sam, walking up beside him. "What are they sayin'?"

"They're sayin' the cap'n fancies Miss Grant, and she gets larger portions of food than the rest."

Alex stopped walking and laughed. "Twice I gave her half of me portion, and 'twas only after I noticed she'd been given only scraps. Am I to let her starve?"

Sam shrugged and Alex grew angry. He turned to his crew and with a flourish, freed his cutlass from the many colorful sashes tied around his waist. "Who among ya accuses me of favorin' someone with rations that are not me own to give? Speak up!"

As he suspected, no one did.

"The rations were mine to feed to the seagulls had I chose to. If any one of ya scurvy-infested, bilge-drinkin' swabs takes issue with it, step forward and let yar blade do the talkin'!"

He raked his gaze over the sailors and then let his eyes settle on Caitrina. He didn't need a woman on his ship causing trouble among the men. Somehow he had to get her home. He'd have to pay her way aboard a ship bound for Scotland. Kyle should go with her. Letting Kyle go would pain Alex deeply. He could use a sailor who could fight better than a dozen of his men and sense trouble with uncanny ability. Hell. Nothing to be done about it now.

"If I hear tongues flappin' again," he continued speaking to his men, "I might just cut a few off. If ya have a grievance, ya come to me about it." He turned forward to continue leading, letting the matter go for now since no one was challenging him. Mutiny because of a woman. He had to laugh at himself for getting what he deserved for treating women frivolously in the past.

"I heard a trader speaking of an old church called Saint Domingo," he heard Caitrina say. "I would love to visit it."

"I know where it is," Gustaaf told her. "I can take you."

She spent much time with Gustaaf of late. Alex wasn't sure how he felt about it, or why he would feel anything at all, but he didn't want to find out.

"Gustaaf," he said, pivoting on his feet to face them again. "I fear I'll need ya to help Robbie carry the sacks we need to trade. I'll take Miss Grant to the church before we leave Lisbon. Ya don't mind, do ya, Miss Grant?"

She smiled stiffly. "In truth, Captain, I would much rather be in the company of someone who actually spoke to me."

He smiled, having missed her fire for the last forty-eight hours.

"How be yar foot?"

"Better," she said, stepping up to him, waiting for him to continue moving. "My skin is getting thicker every day."

She was angry with him. Understandable. He didn't explain to her why he avoided her. He wasn't used to explaining things to women. He was even less familiar with taking their delicate sensibilities into mind when decisions were being made. He guessed the best thing to do now was help her decide with whom to travel back to Scotland. First, he needed a cup of wine.

He continued on their path to the city square and the old Moorish palace now known as Caso do Alberte. He stepped inside first and breathed in the lush fragrance of sandalwood incense and rich spices like saffron and fennel, cinnamon and cloves. Little had changed since last he was here. He and his crew gathered in the enormous inner foyer ringed by six high arched entryways all covered in beautiful mosaic azulejo, a kind of Portuguese painted, tin-glazed ceramic. Alex knew where each archway led. If the rules of the caso hadn't changed, then they needed to wait for the arrival of Senhor Alberte Barros, the proprietor. Once their rooms were paid for—they would buy three, one for the captain and two to store their wares and any of the men who cared to sleep with it. The rest of the men would sleep on the ship.

"Welcome, honored guests." A woman appeared through the archway.

When Alex turned to her, he smiled, remembering why he'd come here so long ago and fell in love with the place. The women here were more beautiful than anywhere else in the world. Their modest form of dress, from their colorful skirts to their tight-fitting jackets, could not conceal their shapely curves. This one swept toward them across the tiled floor wearing a white muslin scarf over her head and shoulders, giving teasing glimpses of her long raven hair. Her large obsidian eyes looked familiar. Where was Alberte?

"Senhorita Jacinta Barros?" Sam stepped forward to get a better look at her.

Little Jacinta? Alberte's daughter? She was ten when he saw her last. She'd grown into a stunning beauty. He watched her study Sam, trying to place how the stranger knew her name.

"Sam?" She remembered soon enough. She stepped closer and smiled, then she turned to him. "Alexandre?"

No one had spoken his name like that in so long. Before he had time to answer, she threw herself into his arms. "I never thought I would see you again, Alex."

She smelled of coriander, with a hint of rose, but even as her succulent aroma went to his head his gaze found Caitrina among the men.

"Jacinta," he said, stepping out of her embrace to look at her. "Ya've grown. Where is yar father, Alberte?"

"He left this world four years ago, Alex," she told him, with glossy eyes as dark as midnight. "My mother and my sisters keep the house open now."

"Yar sisters?"

She shook her head. "Madalena never returned."

He smiled. He truly was relieved. He'd wanted to come here because it was the closest thing he had to a home so far north. Not because he hoped he would see Madalena Barros.

"My mother is taking her afternoon nap, but she will be so happy to see you both."

"We'll be here 'til tomorrow night," Alex told her. "Do ya have three rooms fer us, *anjinho*?" The youngest of the Barros family, he'd always called Jacinta "little angel."

She looked up at him and smiled, looping her arm through his. "Anything for you, Alex." She led him and his crew toward the archway on the western wall. "You are almost family. Tell me what you want and you will have it."

"Just the rooms fer now." He took her hand in his and brought it to his mouth. "What will be the cost?"

She shook her head, then tilted it up toward his. "My father never would have charged you for three rooms. Neither will his wife or daughters."

She was correct. Alberte would not have taken his coin. Another reason Alex wanted to come here. If they didn't have to spend their coin, they wouldn't...and not spending it was the key to a triumphant visit.

Jacinta led them past the old cavernous courtyard and then up the stone stairs to their rooms, the three largest in the house.

"Will the"—Jacinta looked at Caitrina and did not return her smile—"lady be needing her own room?"

"Nay," Alex told her. "She'll share." He didn't supply any further information when Jacinta cast him a questioning look. Finally, she gave them their keys and promised to have a feast prepared in Alex and Samuel's honor.

"Ye were here before?" Caitrina asked him when Jacinta left.

"I practically lived here once, long ago."

"Who is Madalena?" she asked, standing still while the men carried their wares into two of the rooms. "'Tis such a bonnie name."

He smiled, oddly pleased that she found such interest in that brief part of his and Jacinta's conversation. But the last thing he wanted to talk about with her was losing his heart to a viper. "She is Jacinta's sister. Ya will sleep in one of the rooms with Kyle."

She shook her head. "Kyle said he is going back to the ship tonight with Mr. Bonnet and some of the others. He has grown fond of the rocking and insists that it helps him sleep."

Hell. He wasn't about to make her sleep in a room with his men without someone to protect her. He wanted her in his bed. He ached for it. But he had to guard against his desires for her. He feared they went a bit deeper than mere lust. He had to get her home. Out of his sight and out of his thoughts. "I'll request another room from Jac—"

"Nae," she rejected softly, veiling her eyes behind the inky darkness of her lashes. "I'll go back to the ship with Kyle."

He nodded, then watched her turn to leave him. "Caitrina," he said, stopping her. "I'll find ya a way home. A safe way home."

The edges of her full mouth lifted slightly while the rest of her remained still. "Thank ye fer yer thoughtfulness, Captain."

She left. In truth, she marched away from him, clearly angry that he was making her decision for her. He didn't care. She couldn't stay. It was better for his men, better for him, if she went home. He thought about her too often, he worried about her. Hell, he never worried! She questioned him on every level. She made him think about his heart, or at least remember that he had one. And that could be deadly for a pirate captain.

He looked around his room, his empty bed. Bloody hell, he needed a woman in it. He patted the hidden breast pocket of his coat. His map was there, safe and sound. He'd keep it with him while on land. Keep your treasures close and your enemies even closer, his father always told him.

He thought about those words for another moment and then dumped his trading wares on his bed and left to seek Caitrina.

Chapter Seventeen

*T*rina stood off to the side listening while Alex spoke with Captain Batista Delgado of the ship *Santo Andre*. As it happened, Captain Delgado was sailing for Scotland in the morning and was willing to take her and Kyle along for a substantial fee. Alex agreed. He couldn't wait to be rid of her. She didn't know why it made her feel so miserable.

She shouldn't be surprised really. Of course she knew she couldn't stay, but since the day she'd mentioned it, he barely said another word to her. The few times he did, it was to dump his food onto her plate, tell her not to argue, then go back to his chair. She appreciated it, since the ship's cook, Eddie was his name, thought she could survive on what he scraped from the bottom of his pot. She would have thanked Alex but he'd made absolutely no effort to speak to her, so she left him alone.

She was stunned today when he offered to take her to the church. She thought he might even sound the slightest bit jealous of Gustaaf and was surprised and a little mortified that the notion made her belly flip.

He proved her a fool when he told her he wanted her to go home. He wasn't jealous. He likely wouldn't be taking her to the church either. He didn't want her alone with Gustaaf because he was afraid they would hurry back to the ship and steal his damned map. She was a fool, all right. A fool to think sailing around the world with him would be anything but torturous.

She knew she was being overly dramatic. She'd never intended to stay on the ship. It was time to go home. She should be thankful that Captain Kidd was taking the time to find her safe passage.

"Can we not find a ship that is leaving sooner than the morning?"

He paused in his conversation with Captain Delgado and flicked his dark gaze at her. Her knees almost buckled. She held fast against the power of his stare and the humor in the tilt of his mouth.

He finished up his talk with the Portuguese captain, then came toward her. "The morning," he said with a dark spark in his eyes, "can go to Hades. Tonight we're in Lisbon, far from the regrets of tomorrow." He smiled and scooped her hand up in his. "Tonight, we laugh."

He led her by the hand back to the Grand Hall in Caso do Alberte. By now, guests swarmed all around her, traders mostly, come to drink and spend the night in a warm bed. He brought her to a polished table, where sat a few of the men, including Kyle, and offered her a chair. When their cups arrived, he held his up in toast to her while the others raised theirs to various other beings and things.

"Ya're an interestin' woman, Miss Grant. Part of me shall be sorry to see ya off."

She arched her brow at him. "And the other part of ye, Captain?"

"The other part shall be sorry to see ya off before I've taken ya to me bed."

She wanted to laugh at his boldness. "I should slap yer face."

"If we were alone in me cabin I'd offer ya both sides."

Regretfully, Kyle interrupted him with an unrepentant look cast her way. "Gustaaf tells me ye've gotten us passage fer home in the morning."

Alex had the grace to take the hint and not rile her cousin any further. "Aye, 'tis what's best."

"Aye," Kyle agreed, then smiled and accepted Alex's cup.

The wine flowed endlessly thanks to the captain's efforts. Friendly and charming, he tossed back his head and filled the tiled halls with the rich luxury of his laugher and a tale or two about his past adventures. Every guest wanted a few moments with him and they were willing to pay for it. He provided free wine and ale for his friends without touching his pouch once.

He moved through his victims with the same lethal grace as the ribbons of tobacco smoke hovering in the air like the mists above the Cuillins. Every woman in attendance—and many, Trina was certain, were there for money—every woman in the place, including Senhora Theresa Barros, Jacinta's mother, secretly watched him behind fans and long lashes, willing to give him whatever his sorcerer's heart desired.

A friendly thief who didn't pick or pilfer the way some of the other sailors were doing, but whose victims offered him their money willingly.

He was so good at what he did that it was no wonder he didn't trust anyone.

He drank with them all, but once or twice, when his warm gaze met Trina's across the sea of heads, his eyes were clear and coherent. The strangers thought he was drinking with them but he wasn't. She wondered why.

When she wasn't taking in the sights and sounds of him, she watched Mr. Bonnet cheating at dice and Gustaaf lifting his fourth cup of wine that he hadn't paid for to his lips. Her eyes caught Mr. Bonnet lifting a pouch of coin from a man's pocket.

As if all the drink, the laughter, and the smoky seduction weren't enough to mesmerize her, music filled the halls, haunting, beguiling tempos played on guitarra and lute. It was all so foreign compared to home. She loved it. She loved the mystery and the newness of it. This was adventure, traveling to other lands and living, even for a night, the way different people lived.

This was what she wanted. She didn't want to go home. She wanted more nights like this one, where they laughed and lived and cheated and sang. More nights getting to know Alexander Kidd and what he was about. She didn't want to go home. She had to tell him. She would not get on Captain Delgado's ship tomorrow. No matter what, she would not. She would earn her way. Even steal if she had to. Somehow, she would make her kin understand that this was the life she chose. Anything else and she would die a slow death. She looked for Alex to tell him and saw that he had left the table but was just now returning to it. Her belly tied in a knot over the prospect of talking to him. Fool, she chastised herself. She was no child and he was no god. Still. Knots.

Jacinta Barros reached him first. She glided into his arms out of nowhere and Trina was close enough to watch his arm come up around her. She sat forward in her chair, hoping he couldn't see her with the other bodies in the way. She didn't want to see him kiss another woman and before she could stop herself, she left the table.

She hoped Kyle wouldn't follow her and looked around for him. It seemed he, too, had found the company of a woman and didn't notice her departure.

She should have left the Hall instead of returning to the archway and watching the captain against her will. She couldn't tear her eyes away from him while he laughed with Senhorita Barros, touched her and drank, or so it appeared, with her. Trina wanted to leave but Kyle was still engaged in his own private party with a woman...a woman who looked very much like Jacinta. A sister, no doubt. There seemed to be a dozen of them. Raven-haired, exotic beauties whom any man would offer his heart to.

Her eyes settled again on the captain, now being tugged along by the delicate Jacinta. Trina didn't blink while he mouthed his captor's name, stopping her and then reaching his beringed fingers to a lock of her hair escaping her veil.

Trina didn't want to see any more. Turning away, she left the Grand Hall and entered the courtyard. She couldn't go back to the ship by herself. She looked around at the tiled archways. Which one led to the rooms? She couldn't remember. She turned in a circle, looking at the six identical archways and feeling dizzy for the first time since leaving the ship.

Three quarters of the way around, she nearly toppled backward when she came face-to-face with Alex in front of her.

"Where are ya goin'?" he asked her.

Lord help her, but she felt faint. How many cups of that delicious wine had she had? No more than three. Or four. She fought it. Now was not the time to show weakness. "Anywhere that is away from ye, Captain. Now if ye will excuse me..."

She took a step forward and tumbled into his arms. "I seem to..." She patted her forehead. "I fear I've had..."

"Too much wine," he finished for her. She looked at him above her, and then went still while he hoisted her up with one arm curled about her back.

She grew weaker and his arm grew more secure.

"Come, ya need fresh air."

"Where is yer lady friend?"

He shrugged his shoulders, dismissing the topic of Jacinta Barros and setting her nerve endings on fire when his shirt stretched over his chest as he leaned down to her. He practically carried her out of the house and into the cool night, saturated with the fragrance of pine and rose. Her head felt light but her heart, heavy. Why did he want her to leave tomorrow? Did he like her at all? She liked him. Why had she drunk? She never drank at home. Then again, the MacGregors' homemade whisky tasted nothing like the delicious port of Caso do Alberte.

"Caitrina," he said softly, beguiling her senseless. He slipped his arm down hers and entwined their fingers. "Come, there's something I be wantin' to show ya."

For a moment, Trina couldn't move. She couldn't breathe. Had he refused a night of passion with a beautiful woman to stay with her? She would have taken a few more moments to mull it over in her mind, but his hand felt too big, too warm, and oh so intimate she nearly stumbled into him again. It had to be the wine.

He pulled her forward, hurrying them along the quiet roads. When he smiled at her over his shoulder, something pulled in her chest.

"Where are we going?" she asked breathlessly.

"Ya will see."

She trusted that he hadn't planned something nefarious for

her. He was a pirate, and a son of one, after all. Piracy flowed deep in his veins. He plundered ships, cities, and women with the same carefree abandon. But she trusted him.

"I like it here," she told him while he brought her across Rossio Square.

He smiled and she realized that his easy, casual humor was one of the things she liked best about him. Little fazed him. He always seemed confident that whatever the situation, the outcome would work in his favor.

"Lisbon is one of me favorite places," he told her while they strolled together. "Everyone is pleasant because their pockets are full."

She stayed quiet while he led her down more alleys and darkened roads. He slowed his pace as they turned a corner.

"While I was enjoyin' drinks with Senhor Morgado," he told her, releasing her hand and sweeping his arm across her path, "I remembered that ya wanted to see the church." He smiled while she gaped, breathless at the glorious church bathed in torchlight before her. "'Tis more beautiful at night."

She'd never seen anything so grand and majestic in her life. She wanted to get closer and feel the full effect of it. She took a step along the path he offered then paused, stilled by his confession of him remembering her while he worked. She didn't think he considered her at all. "But 'tis late," she pointed out on a quavering breath. "Can we enter?"

"'Tis what we came to do, beauty."

She smiled and led the way.

She wasn't prepared for what she saw when she stepped inside São Domingos Church. Thousands of candles lit the vaulted ceiling, casting gold and crimson shadows along the high altar and the red marble columns supporting the sculpture of the Holy Trinity. A feast for her eyes. She closed them and let the scent of candle wax fill her lungs.

She sensed he had come up beside her. She opened her eyes and took his hand in hers. "Thank ye fer bringing me here."

"Does it remind ya of home?" he asked quietly.

"We have no stone masterpiece like this on Skye. But God inhabits every church. 'Tis the feel of Him that's familiar."

He looked around, taking in the majesty of it, then returned his smile to her. "'Tis peaceful."

She nodded and slipped into one of the polished wooden pews. "Do ye pray?" When he shook his head, she folded her hands in front of her. "Do ye mind if I do?"

"Nay, lady," he told her softly. He remained quiet while she did.

"I dinna' want to go home, Alex." She shared her confession in the rosy light of the church. "I dinna' want to marry Hugh MacDonald. I want to stay on *Poseidon's Adventure*, with ye."

"Who is this Hugh MacDonald?" he asked, and she wasn't prepared for the urgency in his dark gaze. Amid thousands of candles, the sight of him stilled her heart. The beauty of the church paled in comparison to the man beside her. "Ya haven't spoken of him before."

She shrugged her shoulders. "Just a neighbor to whom my faither promised my hand. I didna' speak of him because I chose to ferget my destiny while on this adventure. But I know I cannot avoid it. Now that my head is cleared once again, I know that my kin would never stop looking fer me. I canna' cause them such sorrow."

"Aye" he said quietly. "'Tis best."

"Aye," she told him soberly, leaving the pew to head back to Caso do Alberte to meet up with Kyle. "Best fer everyone else."

Chapter Eighteen

Captain Delgado was a very agreeable man. When Trina explained to him early the next morning that she had just come to have a look at his ship before they set sail, he agreed to give her a tour.

She never expected him to attack her. Hell, she'd told him her cousin would be along any moment to join her. She'd told him Captain Kidd would see her off as he'd promised he would. Why would Delgado attack her when she had men coming? When he clasped his fingers tight around her wrist and dragged her toward one of the hatches on deck, she knew he was a fool and she was in trouble.

Taken by surprise, she had only a moment to react. She kicked him in the kneecap as hard as she could, and then elbowed him in the gut when he released her to grasp his knee. There was no time to reach for her dagger or his before he grabbed her by the hair and hauled off to backhand her in the face.

The blow never came. Instead Captain Delgado crumbled to the ground in a heap and Alex stood in his place, his face a mask of fury, dangerous and deadly—until he looked at her. He stepped over his fallen victim and scooped her up in his arms. He crushed her to him and then held her at arm's length to look her over again.

"Are ya hurt? Did he harm ya, Caitrina?"

She shook her head and gazed into his eyes at the concern there. "I'm unharmed." But her father was right about the world. She didn't mind danger. She just wanted to be able to protect herself in it. She didn't mind Alex saving her this time either. She wasn't a prideful fool. She was grateful to him. Out here in the world, fighting was very different when men fought to actually kill you. "How did ye know I was here?"

"I saw ya leavin' the house and followed ya."

She scowled at him, but he'd already bent to rifle through Captain Delgado's pockets. He came back up with a pouch of coins in his fingers. "Fergive me fer almost settin' ya to sail with this pig."

"Is he dead?"

"Not from a blow to the head, but we should go. His crew will be either wakin' up or returnin' to the boat."

He took her hand and hurried with her off the ship. When they were safely away, he paused, turned to her, and handed her the coin. "Keep it. Ya earned it."

She smiled at him and took in every inch of him, from the sensual nuance of his movements to the subtlest change in his expression. She wondered if reading him so easily was attributed to her lessons from Kyle, or if Captain Alex Kidd presented himself so openly to all, unconcerned with being unguarded. He allowed her to dive deep into his warm, dark gaze and feel him touching her before he actually did. And when would he touch her again?

She accepted the pouch and lifted her skirts to tie it to the band around her calf, which already housed a dagger.

She felt his eyes on her, on her leg, felt the heat coming from his gaze. He wanted her. She shared his sentiment. She wanted to feel the tightness of his muscles all around her, as if he were restraining some beast he feared setting free on her. She wanted him to kiss her again. Saints, she wanted to take him by the collar of his coat and pull him down to her waiting mouth.

"Stay with me fer a while longer, Caitrina." The shaky nuances of his voice revealed what it cost him to say those words.

Trina stared deep into his eyes. Did she just hear him right? Did he ask her to stay? Her heart skipped a beat, and then another, making her light-headed.

"As part of me crew," he continued. "I spoke to Kyle earlier this mornin' and he has agreed to it. I cannot trust any man but meself to bring ya home. But it will have to be after I find me treasure."

Her knees felt too weak to support her. They threatened to crumble and cast her into his arms. He wanted her to stay aboard his ship, as part of his crew, while he hunted for his treasure?

"Aye." She didn't need to think about it. She couldn't have refused him if she tried. She didn't want to try. She wanted to stay and sail off to... "Where is it we're heading?"

"To the Caicos Islands in the West Indies."

Och Lord, help her not to faint. She steadied her breath and kept herself from jumping up and down. "The Caicos Islands in the West Indies." Could she possibly get away with living this life? The answer, she knew with a shallow breath escaping her lips, was no. Her kin loved her too much to let her go without a trace. They would search for her and hunt for him until they found him and killed him.

She had to refuse. She had no other choice.

"As much as I want to stay," she said a bit broken-heartedly, "I could not live with the thought of losing... anyone. My kin will search fer me. They will come, Alex. My father and Kyle's, our uncles and the saints know who else, will find us. As skilled as ye are, ye will not defeat them all. I want no fighting."

"I will take care of that when the time comes."

He was a fool not to fear them. "I canna' go with ye." She felt like weeping. "I shall go home and figure oot a way to live my adventures with my kin's blessing. Thank ye fer a lovely pair of weeks. I shall never ferget... Why are ye laughing while I'm bidding ye farewell?"

"Ya're not goin' anywhere."

"I do it to save yer life!"

He looked up at Heaven again but grinned indulgently when he returned his gaze to her.

"Alex, ye dinna' understand. They'll come and if ye fight with them, someone will die, ye or one or more of them. I realize the danger I put ye in, and I'm so terribly—"

"If I don't lift my blade to them"—he cut her off—"will they fight me unarmed?"

"Of course not. They have been savage but they are not withoot honor."

"Then I won't fight them."

"Nae?" She stared at him, waiting for him to laugh in her face. He didn't. "This is yer chance to get rid of me, Captain. I'll let ye put me on another ship home. I'll go withoot word. But if ye promise not to fight them, I will trust ye with yer word and continue with ye."

He chuckled but looked away, as if he wanted her to

believe he didn't care if she stayed or left. After another moment, he seemed to come to some conclusion that didn't please him. Then he said, "I promise, I will not fight them."

Trina stood silent for a moment, just looking at him. She'd given him a choice, and he chose for her to stay.

Fearless.

Before she could think about what she was doing, she stepped toward him, grasped handfuls of his coat in her fists, and pulled his mouth to hers.

Her dominance was quickly answered with his body enveloping hers. He drew her in close to his hard angles and fit her face in his hands. He stroked her with his thumb along her cheekbone and with his tongue, devouring her mouth. When his arm slipped down her back and hauled her in closer, she felt faint and delirious with want.

"Captain." A man cleared his throat and then repeated himself again, harsher this time.

Trina pulled herself away from Alex's arms and looked up at Kyle.

"Take yer hands off my cousin."

"Kyle—"

He held up his palm to silence her without taking his eyes off Alex. "Heaven ferbid a woman should get away withoot ye seducing her first, aye, Captain?"

"Normally"—Alex nodded and stepped away from her—"ya would be correct, MacGregor. But yar cousin is not goin' anywhere. Ya're both stayin' with me."

Kyle laughed. "Ye think I would let her stay so ye could have yer way with her?"

Trina stepped between them and gave her cousin a stern look. "Kyle, no one is having his way with me. *I* wanted to kiss *him*."

"I cannot let her take all the blame," Alex told him. "I wanted to kiss her, too."

Trina's heart flipped in her chest and made her smile, despite her cousin's angry glare.

Bound to the honor instilled into all of Camlochlin's children by Kate Campbell, their grandmother, Kyle pulled his claymore free of its sheath. "Captain, I've heard many tales aboot what a scoundrel ye are. I willna' let ye seduce her. We are leaving yer company and if ye try to stop me I will draw yer blood."

Alex cast him a challenging smile but folded his hands behind his back. "I cannot lift my hand against ya, MacGregor."

"Why not?"

"Because I just promised yar cousin that I wouldn't hurt any of ya. I may be a scoundrel, but I keep me word." Alex smiled at her and then walked away, leaving her with Kyle.

Trina turned to her cousin. She didn't know what to say to him. She knew he meant well, but she wanted to punch him in the nose. She pinched his arm and gave it an extra twist instead, then stormed away.

"You will make certain he gets this letter?"

Senhor Moreno nodded his head and took the parchment in his hand. He didn't know this trader, but a closer look at him revealed that he was definitely a seaman. His boots were stained with salt. He carried a cutlass, and his clothes were a bit threadbare. His skin was heavily tanned from many hours in the sun and his fingernails could use a good scrubbing.

"And you say this Mr. de Gaulle in Brittany is expecting word from you?"

"Aye," the trader answered. "He awaits word in the port city of Saint-Malo."

"What is in the note?" Moreno asked boldly. He didn't want to be passing missives from spies against France or Portugal.

"You don't need to know what's in the note," the trader growled. "I paid you handsomely to deliver it. If you can't do it, I will take back my coin and find someone else. If the seal is broken upon delivery—" His lips rose into a snarl that changed his entire countenance and made him look deadly in an instant. "Well then, the recipient of the note will have no choice but to take the matter into his own hands."

Senhor Moreno almost handed the missive back to him. He didn't want to get involved in things or with people who threatened his life, but he needed the coin. His dear Lucinda was about to deliver his third child. What did he care what was written in the note? This was a quick way for him to make extra coin.

"No need to make threats, sailor," he said. "Your note will be delivered untouched and unread. I have enough troubles of my own to worry about more."

The man smiled, thanked him, and left.

Senhor Moreno watched him slink off, looking around covertly, as if he didn't want to be seen by others just yet. He was likely a spy but Senhor Moreno turned away and patted the pouch inside his jacket pocket.

Like he'd told the trader, he had his own troubles to see to.

Chapter Nineteen

"My family left the Netherlands eleven years ago and settled in the Colonies."

Trina listened to Gustaaf tell his story while *Poseidon's Adventure* sailed toward the North Equatorial Current. She still couldn't believe that she was on her way to the West Indies...on her way to a true adventure. Part of her exalted. This was what her heart had hungered for for so long. Her life spread before her like an open book, one she wanted to write, not read. Let other lasses, like her cousin Abby, dream about their knights in shining armor. Trina followed a different path, one she would carve for herself. One that found her in the company of a man who stole her breath and made her forget why the hell she was here other than to spend her moments with him, getting to know him, hoping he'd kiss her again.

The moments when she saw Captain Kidd were brief for the first few days after they left Lisbon. He saw to much business about the goods they'd picked up and the ship and the sailing of it. He saw to divvying up the shares of what his crew plundered in Lisbon. Whether a city, a town, or a ship, whether they all participated, or only some, they shared what they stole. After she and Kyle signed the ship's Articles, they both got one share of the booty. Or rather, they would be getting it after supper.

"We lived peaceful lives," Gustaaf told the small group of them sitting around the table in the captain's cabin. "Until my sister was captured and taken by the pirate captain Charlie Roberts. My mother almost died from the heartbreak of it. I swore to my father I would bring my sister home. To see to my word, I stole our neighbor's boat and set after the captain."

"Ye went alone?" Kyle asked across the table.

"My family left the Netherlands alone. I had no one else to go with me."

"Ye're verra' brave, Gustaaf," Trina told him and reached over to pat him on his giant hand.

He shook his head. "I was foolish. I could not take on a horde of pirates by myself. Soon, they captured me too. Aleida and I were to be put to death when Captain Roberts spotted *Poseidon's Adventure* on the horizon."

He looked toward Alex and smiled. In return, his captain groaned. "Cease with this dull tale."

"Nae." Trina slapped the table softly. "Let him speak." She wanted to hear what Alex had done that had earned him such loyalty. "Please," she added with a smile.

"Very well then." The captain swept his jeweled fingers across the air and sat back in his chair, trying to look uninterested in the rest of it. "Proceed, Gustaaf."

Trina was the only one who caught Mr. Pierce's quick glance toward Alex and watched while he gave in to her. Just before that, he was looking at her. It was three times now at the table that she felt his eyes on her.

"Our captain had visited my town often," Gustaaf continued. "He knew my father. He knew my sister and me, and he came for us."

Trina couldn't stop the smile curling her mouth, nor could she stop herself from looking at the captain.

"Ye saved them both?" Kyle asked Alex.

"Aye," Alex confessed. "'Tis nothin' worthy of accolades."

"Why not?" her cousin asked him. "Did ye receive coin fer it?"

"Nay. They were friends of mine."

"'Twas noble then." Kyle lifted his cup.

Trina was thankful that Kyle had come to grips with her liking the captain. He liked him too. Still, he'd insisted that she and the captain not engage in anything more than sharing words. Her virtue was in his care.

Alex finally returned her smile, thoroughly amused by Kyle and his whole idea of honor and integrity.

Alexander Kidd didn't concern himself with such notions. Or, at least, he didn't want anyone to know he did. How could he be known as a heartless pirate if words of his honorable deeds seeped out?

His secrets would be safe with her.

"In gratitude for saving my sister, I pledged him my service."

"All right, enough of this." Alex rose from his seat, snatched up his cup, and downed its contents. "Let's get back to matters at hand. Miss Grant." He handed over her share. "We have a lesson before the sun sets. Get yar cutlass and meet me on deck. Kyle, Gustaaf." He gave them their spoils next. "Keep yar ears open fer talks of me lettin' a woman remain aboard ship." When they nodded and left, he turned to Mr. Pierce. "Send in the men fer their shares."

When everyone had gone, Trina lingered about his door for a moment or two before he closed it.

"What does it mean that I've been at sea fer weeks now and I dinna' yet hate being here?"

He laughed, setting her nerve endings aflame. "It means ya're mad, and so am I fer bringin' ya on me hunt fer a treasure."

"I'm relieved that ye stopped believing that foolishness aboot me wanting to steal yer map."

His smile remained while he took a step toward her and traced his thumb along her cheekbone. "I should have sailed ya directly back to Scotland instead of bringing ya farther south. But I like yar company, Caitrina. I'm provin' me trust in ya by bringin' ya with me. I hope it isn't put to the test. But if I'm wrong, I'll let ya cut out me heart."

She gazed into his eyes, trying to see deeper into him, where the heart he spoke of lived. "Why would ye want me to do that?"

He smiled as if it didn't matter and gently pushed her out when Robbie Owens appeared at the door for his share.

On her way to the deck she wondered what his words meant. Cut out his heart if he was wrong about her? Was it a clever way to gain her loyalty or was it something more?

They met on deck a short while later for sword practice, one of the many ways she kept busy aboard, day after day. She was also learning how to navigate, as well as how to climb the ratlines to the masts. She wanted to reach the crow's nest at the top of the mast and look out, but so far, under Gustaaf's tutorage, she'd made it only a few feet up without tangling herself and almost falling. Gustaaf always caught her and usually they laughed. She made him promise not to tell the captain what she was up to—since when she'd asked him if she could be his new lookout, he nearly had a fit.

She studied him now, barefoot and suntanned, his white, loose-fitting cotton shirt open at his collar, puffy at his cuffs while he readied his cutlass. His bandanna was wrapped neatly around his head, gold hoops dangling from his ears. He looked every part the devil-may-care rake, dangerous to the rich, the ill defended, and women.

Trina couldn't deny that he was striking to behold but there was much more to him than good looks. "I enjoyed Gustaaf's story," she told him, gripping her blade. "It pleases me to know that ye are just as loyal to yer friends as they are to ye."

"Well, beauty, pleasin' ya is what I live to do." He crooked his mouth into a teasing grin and swung. "Remember," he said while she blocked, "to always strike at major organs—heart, lungs, brain—anything to end the fight the quickest way ya can." He feinted for her head then struck at her legs. She leaped back just in time to avoid getting cut.

Well then, she thought, smiling at him. He meant business.

"Slicin' off an extremity will work too. Wait until yar opponent lifts his blade, then take off his arm."

She nodded at his instruction. She already knew most of what he was teaching her, but fighting in the close quarters of a boat, unbalanced, against men who wanted to slice off her head, took more practice. She appreciated his aid. But she wasn't completely helpless and since he meant business...

She feigned a blow to his torso and struck low. She moved quickly, thanks to the lighter weight of her sword. Alex barely had time or position to block.

Alex smiled when she tapped his leg with her blade. "Good, Caitrina. Very good."

He fought hard against her but she forgave him because he didn't want her to be hurt or killed. She was thankful that it was his ship that docked in Loch Scavaig. She couldn't have chosen a better captain.

"And when ye can—"

She turned to her cousin, who had captured her eye a moment ago, and caught the axe he tossed her.

"—fight with two weapons."

She swung hard, clashing the edge of her axe along Alex's blade and hooking it so that he couldn't move it when she sliced her cutlass at his torso.

He sprang back on his feet, barely missing her blade. With his cutlass still locked in her axe, he yanked her upward and over. To keep herself from falling, she had to drop the axe. After disarming her of her second weapon, he wasted no time in disarming her of her first.

Trina watched her cutlass fly into the air and then fall, hilt-first, into Alex's hand. She stepped back when he moved forward, but he leaned over her and spoke softly against her ear.

"Me promise to ya pains me every time I want to take ya in my arms and kiss ya and I can't because yar cousin will wish to fight me. But how much longer can I avoid ya?"

He stepped back before she could reply and handed her back her sword. "Tomorrow, we will practice fighting at closer proximity. Steal someone's dagger to fight me with." He winked at her, then bent to pick up Kyle's axe. When he handed it to Kyle, Trina sighed, thankful that he didn't strike her cousin with it. Would he grow tired of Kyle's watchful eyes and finally do something about it? If he hurt

Kyle—and after his last skillful maneuver to avoid harm, she had no doubt he could hurt anyone he pleased—but if he hurt Kyle, her kin would bring a war to him.

She had to speak to her cousin. She wasn't angry with him for wanting to protect her. He'd protected her their whole lives. But the captain was no danger to her. Whatever happened between them, she wanted it to happen.

She didn't get the chance to talk to Kyle. He tucked his axe away and hurried to catch up with Alex, calling out for him. She paled as she watched her cousin hurry away. What the hell was Kyle doing? She thought to follow them but was stopped by Mr. Pierce stepping in her path.

"There's somethin' I wish to speak to ya about, Miss Grant."

Trina cursed under her breath and looked around his waist. Kyle and Alex were gone.

"'Twill take but a moment."

Trina closed her eyes, then nodded. "What is it, Mr. Pierce?"

"I wanted a chance to speak to ye aboot something, Captain."

Alex hoped it wasn't about Caitrina. He wasn't sure that he could keep his temper in check if the lad threatened him again.

"What is it, MacGregor?"

"D'ye trust Mr. Pierce?"

Alex stopped before they ascended the stairs to the quarterdeck and blinked at him. The Highlander's query was so unexpected that for a moment Alex didn't know what to say. Then he answered, "More than I trust anyone else."

MacGregor smiled and nodded his head. "Of course. Ferget I brought it up."

"Aye, I will." Alex continued up to the poop deck.

"This might help," the Highlander offered with sincerity, briefly straining his voice. "During our visit to Lisbon, I met the lovely Senhorita Rafaela Barros."

"Aye, I noticed."

"She told me of ye and her sister Madalena."

Why the hell would Rafaela do that? It was so long ago. Why must his past be dredged up when it deserved to be forgotten?

"Whatever she told ya, ferget it, as I have," he said. He relieved Cooper at the helm and untied his tricorn from his sash. He put his hat to his head and sailed his ship through the Sargasso Sea.

"What else, Kyle?" Alex asked after ten minutes passed and the lad hadn't left. Alex didn't want to know what else but if it would end this conversation about Madalena, he'd suffer through it. "Did ya discover who me real mother is while ye were at it?"

Unfazed by Alex's sarcasm, the Highlander continued on. "Senhorita Barros told me ye broke her sister's heart and drove her into the arms of a traveler so that their family never saw her again."

"He was a merchant from Porto," Alex corrected blandly, "and she left me after I gave her everything I had."

Alex prayed for the strength not to toss Kyle overboard. Caitrina would hate him, and damn him to Fiddler's Green, but he didn't want her to hate him, or even dislike him. Twice since they left Lisbon, he'd gone to Harry Hanes believing himself sick with delirium. He'd let her stay, risking much, especially from her kin when they came for her, and he knew they would. But he couldn't send her back not knowing if she was safe in the hands of another captain and crew.

"Ye speak the truth."

Alex looked at him, hoping that doing so might help him to remember that Kyle was Caitrina's kin. "I'm glad ya think so," he said wryly.

"Don't take offense where none was meant," the lad offered boldly. He wasn't afraid to keep going, despite Alex's glare. "'Tis simply an observation, Captain. Now may I offer my regrets that she broke yer heart."

Alex smiled. He wasn't about to admit to a lad that he'd been foolish enough to allow his heart to be broken. "She didn't break my heart."

"And at the same time," the Highlander continued as if Alex hadn't spoken at all, "express my gladness that it wasn't ye who did the breaking."

Alex laughed and turned the wheel starboard. What was the use in trying to argue the point of whose heart took longer to heal? "'Twas the past, lad. I don't live in the past."

Kyle shrugged his shoulders as if he didn't care about the past either. "My cousin is fond of ye," he said instead, leading Alex to believe this was what Kyle wanted to speak of all along.

"She has no reason not to be," Alex told him, almost relieved now that Kyle had brought it up. There were things that needed to be said between them. "Should I create a reason so that this journey is easier fer ya, even if it might be harder fer her?"

"Nae," her cousin answered quickly. "I would just ask ye to give her time to make certain that whatever decisions she makes will be the right ones and not lead her into a life of regret."

Alex tightened his jaw and nodded his head. How could he not give his word to such a request? He didn't want her to regret her life. Besides that, he liked Kyle. There was something about the lad's staunch belief in honor that Alex admired, though he sometimes scoffed at it.

"Thank ye, Captain."

He groaned as he made another promise he hoped he could keep.

"MacGregor?" He stopped the Highlander from leaving. "Did ya take Senhorita Barros to yar bed?"

The lad shook his head.

"Why the hell not?"

He shook his head again, but gave no reply—at least not one he could correctly utter. "I...We...I didna' think..."

"Have ya ever taken any woman to yar bed?" Alex asked him. Hell, with all those exquisite lasses in Camlochlin and Kyle's good looks, the lad couldn't be a virgin.

"Most of the lasses in Camlochlin are my kin, and the ones who are not, I've known since birth, so they might as well be."

Alex grimaced and set his gaze on the horizon. "Have ya never left home then?"

"I could have gone on raids and adventures with my cousins but I preferred to learn everything I could from the warriors who went before me."

Neptune take him, the lad probably didn't know what to do with a woman who wasn't a sister, cousin, or a cradle mate. He had much to learn and there was no one better to teach him than the brown beauties of the Islands.

"MacGregor?"

"Aye, Captain?"

Alex smiled. "Ya're goin' to like the Islands."

Chapter Twenty

Alex had been right. The days aboard the ship were getting more difficult. Trina's growing misery, though, had little to do with boredom or spoiled food. She missed her kin and worried what would happen when they came for her. But it was the captain's face, the glistening, golden slabs of muscle moving in his bare arms and even his belly when he practiced with her that kept her awake at night. He was crafted to fight, to move, to mesmerize. And mesmerized by him, she was. The skill with which he disarmed or potentially killed her every time they practiced impressed her. The way his arms felt coming around her, making her feel protected rather than captured, stilled her heart. The sound of his husky voice telling her he'd won again boiled her blood.

She wanted him to kiss her. She ached for it in places that made her blush and burn. She wanted to run her hands and her tongue all over his hard planes. Without truly understanding it, she wanted to lie beneath him, touching him, kissing him, while he slipped himself deep into her.

She feared she was growing overly attached to him. It had been difficult not to ever since the day he asked her to stay with him. She'd been happy that Captain Delgado was such a lech that she was able to stay with Alex, but she knew she couldn't remain with him forever. What would happen when he left her? She tried to think of it as little as possible.

Training with him was torturous and eating with him was no less challenging. He laughed with the crew at her or Kyle's tales of their kin back home. He watched her eat, mostly bug-free food. He watched her drink and speak with the others. She felt his eyes on her often and sometimes turned to catch him looking. His smile, across the span of his drunken crew, was sober, intimate, and longing for her as well.

But he hadn't kissed her since Lisbon. Save for their practice time, he barely touched her. It was driving her mad. She wished they could drop anchor at the nearest port and leave the ship, even for a few hours. She needed to be away from wherever Captain Kidd was.

They were three weeks in. She wasn't sure how much more she could take. To keep her mind and her eyes off him, she kept busy with other activities, one of them being how to climb the ratlines and finally make it to the crow's nest. At first, Gustaaf didn't go along with keeping his instruction a secret from the captain, but Trina didn't let up on him until he agreed.

That's why she felt so bad for him one day when Alex discovered her on her way down from the mast. She hadn't seen him on the forecastle deck and nearly slipped through a hole in the ropes when he shouted her name.

Her near fall didn't help in the argument that ensued between them. He ordered her never to climb again. She adamantly refused. She sincerely couldn't believe he was so pig-headed and primitive.

"Ye're being unreasonable and uncooperative!" she told him, following him around the mast and rigging and waiting while he ordered Gustaaf to come down. "And ye will not blame him!"

The captain shot her a look that proved she'd finally managed to irritate him enough to throw her overboard. "I be the captain of this ship, woman," he warned in a low voice. "I'll do what I damn well please. Gustaaf!" he shouted when the sailor's feet touched the deck. "Do ya carry ill will toward Miss Grant?"

"No, Captain, I'm fon—"

"Then why the hell would ya go along with this madness and agree to teach her how to climb the ratlines? If she fell—"

"I will not fall again," Trina promised, then backed up when he glared at her and then at poor Gustaaf. "He caught me every time!" she insisted, trying desperately to protect her friend.

Alex covered his face with his palm. "How many times did he catch ya?"

She knew her error immediately. He'd seen her almost fall only this one time. Knowing that it had happened more than once wasn't going to help her cause. "Today and yesterday. That is all."

The guilt on Gustaaf's tanned face told Alex she was lying. She sighed, tired of hiding. She hadn't come aboard to be told what she could and couldn't do. "Pretend I am a man," she seethed at him. "Pretend I am John Gable. Remember, ye told me yerself how well he repaired the masts."

"Ya don't know a damn thing about the masts, lass,

and I'll not have ya fall to yar death on me ship. As fer pretendin' ya're a man"—his eyes drifted over her like a tangible caress, warming her, devouring her—"that's quite impossible."

She hated doing it, but if using his desire for her was the only way to get him to go along with her schemes, then so be it. "Alex, please. I will be more careful. That is the only place on the ship I havena' been. Dinna' deny me. I need to be away from . . . things."

His expression didn't change—at least, nowhere but in his eyes. "Ya will call me Captain in the presence of others," he told her woodenly, unfazed by her plea. "If I find out that ya have disobeyed me again, ya and Gustaaf will careen the hull when next we dock. Savvy?"

"Nae, I dinna' savvy!" She folded her arms across her chest. "I dinna' know what careening the hull even means, *Captain*!" She wished there were something on deck to throw at his arrogant head. She wished she had the courage to kick him.

He cast her an infuriating smile and turned to her friend. "Tell her, Gustaaf."

"But, Captain," Gustaaf said quietly. "I cannot swim."

Trina blinked at him. What kind of sailor couldn't swim?

"Well then, Gustaaf, the next time ya see Miss Grant attemptin' to climb the ratlines, ya will come get me, won't ya."

This sounded like blackmail to her. "What is careening the hull?" She turned to Gustaaf. "Does he threaten ye?"

"'Tis cleanin' the barnacles off the hull," Alex said, saving the Dutchman from having to answer what, she realized a moment after she said it, was a demeaning question to put to a man. "Barnacles grow beneath—"

Trina nodded. "I know where they grow, Captain. And he cannot swim. Ye are despicable to use such tactics, and all to deny me what ye would deny no one else."

"Think of me what ya will, Miss Grant. I would have ya live."

"Living is more than just breathing, Captain."

"On me ship, livin' is what I say 'tis." He passed her and continued on his way to the quarterdeck.

Did he honestly think she would let that be the end of it? Poor fool, he was as guileless about women as she was about men. How dare he make light of her words when they meant so much to her?

"I didna' come here to live under yer rule," she said, following him.

"Then get off me ship and go get yar own."

Och, if she could just fling her dagger into his back, all her troubles would be over. When she saw him heading toward his cabin, she followed him. They were going to get this settled now.

"I will not be treated differently from the men here, Captain," she warned while he opened the door to his cabin.

A man stood on the other side. "There ya are," Mr. Pierce said to Alex, exiting the cabin. "I was lookin' fer ya."

Trina hadn't spoken to the quartermaster since he stopped her the other night to ask her more questions about David Pierce, who had traveled to Skye for a puppy a few months ago.

"Is it important?" Alex asked him.

Pierce eyed her from beneath his lids. "She's been climbin' the ratlines with Gustaaf."

Trina folded her arms across her chest and glared at

him. Had he sought Alex out just to tell him that she'd disobeyed orders? She wanted to give him a piece of her mind, but Pierce was, if nothing else, loyal to his captain.

"I already know about that," Alex told him, "but thank ya fer comin' to me with it."

"Aye, thank ye, Mr. Pierce," Trina said coolly. The quartermaster looked away. "Now if ye will excuse us, we were just in the middle of a fight about that very thing."

Pierce went quietly, leaving Alex at the entrance, half blocking it with his size.

"Well?" Trina continued as if there had been no interruption. "What do ye intend to do aboot treating me like one of the men?"

He stared at her for an instant, looking like he simply couldn't believe her audacity. It amused him. "Disobey me again," he smirked, "and find yarself marooned—just as I would do to one of me crew."

He moved to enter his cabin. He wasn't going to win by keeping her away. Not this time. She squeezed past him—hell, everywhere she went she had to squeeze past him and rub up against his solid planes and rigid muscles, thanks to the tight quarters on the ship. It was driving her mad. Now was no different. This time, she didn't slip away. This time she stopped in the center of him, pressed against him, unable to move, to breathe. She looked up into his dark eyes and felt his heart accelerate against her.

"Disengage yerself from me, Caitrina," he demanded quietly.

"Nae." She defied him yet again.

She felt every inch of him tense and tremble against her. She exhaled and felt the quickening of his breath and his shaft hardening against her hip.

She didn't want to move for the rest of her life, and

without thinking she reached her hands up to clasp his shoulders. "I dinna' mean to continue disobeying ye. 'Tis just that yer demands are impossible to—"

He reacted instantly, lifting her off the floor and into his arms while he slammed his door shut with his foot. He didn't give her a chance to speak but covered her mouth with complete mastery and barely leashed control. She opened to his curious tongue and cupped his face in one hand. The other traversed the sculpted lines of his shoulder, down his arm, curled tightly now around her back.

Coming up for a breath, she licked his lips. She bit them and he groaned like a beast she should fear. When he bent her back over the crook of his elbow and exposed her throat to his hungry mouth, she knew whatever he wanted to do to her, she would allow.

His large hand moved over her covered breast, cupping her, running his palm over her and dragging a deep groan from the back of her throat. Her nipple hardened instantly and he rubbed it with the pad of his thumb. Once. Twice, until she trembled and gasped in his arms, needing more. What was it she wanted? She didn't know. More of him. All of him. His hands, his mouth, all over her. To be devoured, or mayhap to devour him.

Just as he grasped the fabric of her shirt to tear it off her and kiss her where no man had ever been before, someone pounded on the door. Caitrina was grateful to be stopped. Hell, the passion he unleashed in her frightened her.

"Captain," Cooper shouted on the other side. "We've spotted a ship leaving the Sargasso."

Alex ignored him and continued kissing her neck.

"From here it looks poorly defended."

Alex disengaged and looked down at her. She smiled, knowing what he had to do. He was a pirate, after all.

Besides, she could use the break to examine this part of herself she didn't know, rein herself in before she made a fool of herself.

"Hell!" He closed his eyes and rested his forehead against hers. "We don't need more loot," he whispered into her hair, trying to talk himself out of leaving her. "We have everything we need from Lisbon."

She pushed him away, smiling. "Go," she told him regretfully. "I willna' have the men accuse me of stealing their captain away from his duties."

Her legs felt weak and her breath was shallow when he released her. Her body screamed for him. Would he discard her afterward? After he had what he wanted, would he run off with the next lass who offered herself to him?

Kyle had told her what he knew about Madalena and Trina understood a bit more clearly why he didn't trust her. She would prove to him that he could. She would never rob him, though she made light of it when he brought it up. She may not have read all her grandmother's books, but she knew enough about her kin's moral code. Her take on Madalena was that she wasn't in her right mind when she left him. Any woman who had gained his heart would be mad to toss it away. Kyle said she broke his heart. He said Alex had given her everything he had.

Now wasn't the time to ask about his past loves, not that she was sure she even wanted to know, or what Alex planned on doing after Trina gave herself to him.

She went with him to the door and blushed when Cooper and Mr. Pierce saw her, her bandanna askew on her head. Alex let out a long, nearly silent sigh, but thankfully, said nothing.

"Spyglass." Alex held out his hand to either man. Cooper hastily slapped the apparatus into his palm.

"Should I set a course to follow, Captain?" Cooper asked.

"Let me take a look." He stepped outside, then paused and turned to Trina. "Comin'?"

She wanted to, but she didn't want Kyle to see her so disheveled. As long as he didn't suspect her of being dishonored, he wouldn't try to defend her honor and get someone killed. She needed to sit and discuss with him the fact that she didn't need his blessing when it came to Alex, but she asked for it because he was her dearest, most treasured friend. "I'll follow ye in a moment," she told him quietly. "I want to freshen up."

He smiled, clearly not understanding the fairer sex at all. "Freshen up fer a fight?"

"Captain?" Cooper pressed from the stairs.

He bid her do as she would and then left her. Alone, Trina shut the door and adjusted her shirt so that it wasn't half loose at her waist and nearly tangled about her neck. What had come over her while he kissed her? She'd felt wild and dangerous in his arms, weak and willing. Did she love him? What if she did? How could she not? He offered her her dreams and so much more. She was in the middle of retying her bandanna neatly around her head when she noticed a small door in the wall by his bed. She'd never noticed it before. But it had never lain open before. There was something inside it, a box. She supposed she should close the latch and keep hidden whatever he was obviously hiding. She went to the wall and bent her knees. She'd meant to close the door, but the box called to her and she picked it up in her hands to examine it. It was beautiful, with several sides, all cut into ornate designs. She shook it. Something was inside. She looked for a latch with which to open it and...

"It has turned out to be an old friend...Caitrina?"

She spun around at the sound of Alex's voice. The instant she looked at him, saw all his uncertainties about her boiling to the surface, she knew she was in trouble.

His map. She looked down at the box in her hands. Och, dear saints. It had to be his map.

"What are ya doin'?" he demanded quietly. "Ya have five breaths to explain before I throw ya off m' ship."

Trina closed her eyes. He'd accused her of coming aboard to steal his map from the beginning. It was his greatest fear, that she could easily be as vile and merciless as Madalena Barros. Now here she was, clutching his treasure in her hands like she'd been scheming for it all along. Saints help her, this was bad.

"The small door swinging open drew my attention and I—"

He turned and walked away from her and, without listening to another word, shut the door in her face.

Chapter Twenty-One

*A*lex shut the door to his cabin, leaving Caitrina inside. He leaned his forehead against the cool wood. He should have trusted his instincts. He was the worst kind of fool. The kind who didn't learn from past mistakes. The kind who ignored what he suspected from the beginning. She was here for his map.

He closed his eyes as the cold truth of it hit him like a kick to the face. She was just like Madalena. How could he let this happen twice? How could he have let himself trust her? Care for her?

She was unable to give him an explanation for what she was doing with his box in her hands. Hell, he'd wanted to be wrong about her. She made him want it. If she wasn't there to rob him, then perhaps he could trust her. If he trusted her, he could love her.

He pounded the door and stormed away from it. "Robbie!" he shouted as his men hurried to their duties. "Guard the door," he ordered when Robbie reached him. "No one comes out or goes in, savvy?"

"Aye, aye, Cap'n."

He stormed toward the helm and bellowed orders to bring his ship around starboard. It was his good fortune that the ship in the distance belonged to a captain he knew well from New York.

He listened as his commands were repeated.

How the hell could she be so good at her thieving? She made him believe her. She made him doubt his misgivings and then forget them completely. He'd let her in. The pain in his chest was proof and he cursed it to the four winds. What did she think she was going to do with his map? How did she think she would get off his ship with it? Well, he knew how she was getting off it today—and Kyle with her.

He reached Cooper at the helm then passed him and came to stand at the wooden rail, looking out over his ship. He set his gaze to the sea and the sloop growing in the distance. A part of him wished he were chasing an enemy ship. He wanted to fight. He wanted to smash in some heads.

But Alex knew Captain John Henley of the *Colony's Lady*. There would only be favors today, no fighting.

He leaned over the rail and rotated his hand in the air above his head while he shouted to the men below. "Raise the flag!"

"I would have a word with ye, Captain."

If he didn't want to tie her to the highest mast and let the winds take her, he would have admired her unabashed boldness to come to him now.

"How did ya get by Robbie?"

"That doesna' matter. I need to speak with ye."

"Miss Grant, if ya want to see another sunset—"

"D'ye earnestly threaten me?"

He stared at her for a moment. He didn't know what to do next. No lass had ever defied him so bloody much. Should he just pick her up and bring her back to his room, or fling her into the waves? Hell, he didn't want to do that. He'd believed her. He'd let himself begin to trust her.

"Did ya finally think of an explanation then?"

"The same I would have given ye below. I was about to leave when something caught my eye. 'Twas the small door in the wall. 'Twas open. I—"

"I don't leave the door open, Miss Grant."

"But opened it was nonetheless, Captain."

He turned away from her and watched the other boat pull in its sails, slowing in the Caribbean breeze coming in from the south.

"Why would I want to steal yer map?" she put to him, giving his sleeve a tug. "I had years to steal it from my uncle! I didna' have to come all the way to the West Indies to get it! I admit that I was curious about the box and what might be in it, but I wasna' trying to steal it, Alex. Where would I go with it that ye wouldna' find me? D'ye think I'm a fool?"

She was convincing. "I might believe if not fer one thing," he pointed out. "I always check the door. 'Tis hard to see when 'tis closed. Ya had to have been lookin' fer it."

She looked like she wanted to slap him. He took a step back.

"But ye didna' check it when ye were busy kissing me," she accused him instead. "When we found Mr. Pierce in the cabin."

His eyes darkened beneath his brows. "Do ya dare accuse him? He knows where the map lies hidden. He doesn't need to steal it."

"I do like Mr. Pierce," she said. "He is kind to me and he always seems to be around when I need him, but 'tis the only explanation I have."

Was his father right all those years when he spoke of

Alex's mother and how easily she had abandoned him? Were all women heartless, merciless creatures? And when the hell would he learn? His heart wanted to believe her. He didn't want to think he'd been duped yet again. But his heart was untrustworthy. It was what had gotten him here for the second time. This time, he would escape with more than a shred of his heart intact. "Go find yar cousin, Miss Grant. Ya're both leavin'."

Returning to the helm, he relieved Cooper and ordered him to remove Miss Grant from the poop deck.

When she was gone, he thought about her accusations against Sam. Kyle, too, had asked him if he trusted his closest friend. Why were they both trying to turn him against his friend? Did they think to blame Sam when Alex found the map missing?

He laughed at the idea of it, but he felt miserable. He didn't remember feeling this bad since... Madalena. Hell, he shouldn't have trusted Caitrina. Why hadn't he learned his lesson? Of course she wanted his map. Many people wanted it. His father was killed because he wouldn't give up the whereabouts of the *Quedagh Merchant*.

"Why are we racin' fer *Colony's Lady*?"

Alex turned to look at Sam coming toward him. He wouldn't tell his friend about Caitrina's and Kyle's suspicions. They were unfounded and ridiculous. But he did tell Sam about finding Caitrina with his map.

"What explanation did she give?" Sam asked him.

"One I do not believe. I want her and her cousin off the ship and put to Scotland or France under Captain Henley's care."

Sam was silent for a bit. then sighed. "I must say in her defense, Alex, I don't believe either of them fool enough to think they could steal yar map."

"It doesn't matter. I won't sit around waiting for her to take more than me treasure. 'Tis time to send both of them off. We have serious business to get to."

They sailed close to *Colony's Lady* and boarded without exception. After being invited on deck, Alex shared a drink in Captain Henley's cabin. He wasted no time in procuring safe passage home for Caitrina and Kyle. Understandably, Henley wanted a barrel or two of water to compensate for the two additional mouths aboard his vessel. Alex threw in extra wax and ten crates of fruit, since it was the first thing to spoil.

"I heard from a trader in Spain that there was a man from the ship *Excellence* askin' questions about ya."

"What kinds of questions?" Alex asked him.

"If anyone had seen ya or heard anything about ya."

Excellence, the majestic man-o'-war sailed by Captain Harris of the Royal Navy, whom most pirates knew.

"D'ya know in which direction his ship sailed?"

Henley shook his head. "He'd already left by the time I reached Spain."

All right, so Harris was in fact on his trail. It stumped Alex how quickly the navy had picked up on him, but it was good to know just the same.

Caitrina boarded the ship like a queen going off to visit a neighboring country. She wore her skirts and carried her shoes in her hands. She didn't spare him even the briefest of glances beneath her thick chestnut tresses, nor did she offer him a last word in her defense.

It pricked Alex deep in the heart. He wanted to curse or tear a beam loose and cast it into the sea. He hated sending her away. He hated the thought that she hated him for doing this. But he hated even more that she'd tried to steal from him, that she'd been lying to him the entire time she was here.

Kyle had been informed of what was happening by his cousin and shook his head at Alex as he was taken past him.

"I thought ye wise," he said. "But ye're a fool, Captain Kidd."

"Aye," Alex agreed. He was indeed a fool to trust them, to take them in as part of his crew, to believe they were only after adventure. "But no more."

Finally he felt her eyes on him, hot with anger. He shouldn't have, but he looked at her. It was like looking at a priceless jewel, unattainable to all. But he'd wanted her. Hell, how could something so beautiful be so cunning?

Would she be safe with Henley? Aye, she would. Alex had known the scrawny captain for years and had never seen or heard of him being cruel to a woman. Still, he waited while they were taken belowdecks and then he stepped up beside his old mate. "There's one other thing. If any harm is brought to them ya'll make an enemy of me and I'll cut out yar heart. Savvy, John?"

The short captain gave his word, but Alex paused as he turned to leave and a thread of foreboding passed over him.

"Captain?" Gustaaf came up beside him after he crossed the planks connecting the decks. "Are you sure you want to leave her with those men?"

No. No, he wasn't sure. But he didn't want to be reminded of it. How could he let her back on his ship when she wanted to rob him?

"She'll be safe with Captain Henley and she has Kyle with her."

"With respect, Captain, you are wrong about her. She would not deceive you in the way you believe."

So, she'd found time to tell Gustaaf why she was leaving the ship. Alex looked at him blandly. "Did she not climb the ratlines against me orders and keep it from me?"

"She has a spirited nature, Captain, but she is not a thief."

Well, the first part of that statement was true, at least. She did indeed have a spirited nature. Before he could stop himself, Alex's guts wrenched at the thought of her disobeying his every bloody word and the way she stood up to him and pleaded on Gustaaf's behalf when he'd caught her on the ratlines. He thought of her smile, alluring beyond description. The passion in her temper and the fire in her kiss. He looked around the deck of the ship he loved and it seemed dull and lifeless.

"Captain—"

"Don't argue." Alex called out orders to his crew and immediately they continued on their course, leaving *Colony's Lady* behind them. "Let it go. She will be returned to her home and no harm will come to her."

"Captain."

Alex cast him a dark look.

The giant Dutchman backed away, but he wasn't gone for long. Within fifteen minutes he came banging on Alex's cabin door.

"His name sounded familiar to my ears but I couldn't place it, Captain," he said the instant Alex opened the door. "Did you say Captain Henley? John Henley from New York?"

Alex nodded, his expression changing from anger to terror when Gustaaf held on to the door frame and groaned from deep within his chest.

"Captain, we have to go back."

✺

Chapter Twenty-Two

"⟨T⟩his is my fault." Trina looked out the single porthole in the tiny cabin she occupied with Kyle. She watched *Poseidon's Adventure* sail away across the waves, taking with it her dreams and desires. Captain Kidd was one of those desires. She wished she could have convinced him of her innocence, so that her dreams of visiting faraway lands could be fulfilled. But she'd failed, and in so doing, robbed Kyle of his adventure, as well.

Going home wasn't what was breaking her heart though. She could live without seeing the West Indies or the Caribbean and tasting some of their flavorful life. She'd lived without it before—not entirely happily, but she'd lived.

No, it was him. He was leaving her, casting her away like the bones of old seagulls. She thought he felt the same for her as she felt for him. But what did she know of men, save what she told herself? Alex grew up as a pirate. He didn't have the loving kin she had. He cared for no one.

She would never see him again and he didn't care.

"Dinna' blame yerself fer this," her cousin said beside her. "But explain to me again about the door in his wall."

She swiped a tear from her cheek and turned from the porthole to look at him. "'Twas small and square in shape. It hung open." She described again for him how she went to it with the intent to close it, but temptation overcame her. She didn't realize it was his silly map until he arrived.

"I didna' open the door," she told him. "I dinna' know how it came to be open, save that Mr. Pierce was alone in the cabin when we arrived."

"Ye told the captain this?"

"Aye," she told him. "But he scoffed at my insinuation against his friend."

"As he did mine," Kyle agreed.

"I think Pierce is the brother or relative of Captain David Pierce, who took one of Gaza's pups. D'ye remember him?"

"Aye." Kyle nodded, listening to her. It reminded Trina of games they used to play of figuring out the secrets of others, before there remained no one new to play it on. "Do ye think the captain knows?" he asked.

"If he doesna' know," Trina replied, "that means he's been well deceived fer a decade. Is Samuel Pierce that good at hiding his true motivations, cousin?"

Kyle would know.

"He might be. He is difficult to read beyond his outward loyalty to the man he might be betraying."

"Ye admire his talent," Trina guessed. She knew Kyle, the son of a great spy, would appreciate someone of the clever caliber that Pierce would have to be in order to keep such an enormous truth hidden.

"That's not what's in question here." Kyle swayed her back to the topic. "The question is why the deception? It makes no sense."

"Is there always a reason fer it?"

"Always," he told her.

"Well." She sighed. "We will never know what it is."

The door opened and Captain Henley entered the cabin.

"If you would both follow me to the upper deck." He smiled, turned, and left as suddenly as he'd appeared.

Trina exchanged a glance with Kyle, then followed him out the door.

They'd barely exited the hatch when Kyle was hoisted up the rest of the way and snatched from Trina's reach. She tore her skirts getting up the stairs to the deck in time to watch six men lift her cousin off his feet and carry him to the railing.

Trina bolted forward and screamed as Captain Henley's order reached her ears and they tossed Kyle overboard.

Just like that. Just like that he was gone.

The first two men to reach her and put their hands on her were dispatched with swift kicks to the groins and fingers in the eyes. Possession of their daggers was easy once they were on their way down. Disarm. The first rule her mother taught her. Don't wait. Defeat. She sliced their blades across their throats and waited for the next two. One of them pulled out a pistol and aimed it at her. She flung a blade and without watching where it landed turned and jumped down the hatch.

She closed the door of the cabin and bolted it, then fell against it. Dear God, this was real. They threw Kyle overboard, to his most certain death. For what man could survive the sea? She swallowed a sorrowful groan. He was dead and it was her fault. If she had never gone aboard Alex's ship...This wasn't the time to fall apart, not if she wanted to kill the bastard who gave the order. And Alex knew this man?

She had one dagger. She looked around the room for any other weapon. She heard the rush of many footsteps on the stairs. Her heart thumped wildly in her chest. She had to ready herself. They were coming to her through a narrow doorway. She knew what to do when they broke in.

"Come out of there, Miss," Henley called down. "I promised my men the pleasure of your body when I'm done with you."

She had to kill him, and before anyone touched her, she would join Kyle in his watery grave.

She wiped her tears away. "Come get me, ye scurvy, flea-infected arse of a rat, whose own mother carved out her insides just to ensure she never spat out such vileness again!"

"Ah, you curse like a pirate." Henley laughed. "I hope Captain Kidd didn't have his way with you before I do. I'm hoping you're a virgin."

"I'm hoping ye value yer organ so that when I cut it from yer body—" Someone smashed his body against the door. Trina ran to it and waited against the wall beside it. But silence reigned. No one tried to get in. She listened. She waited, her muscles drawn tight and her heart pumping in her ears. Kyle was gone because of her. Her wonderful Kyle. She wanted to fall to her knees and weep for a month.

If only she could live long enough to kill another man. The one who put her here and cost her dear Kyle his life.

Alex cursed Caitrina for betraying him, and himself for not giving a damn and turning his ship around to go and save her. He had to. After what Gustaaf had told him, he didn't spare his decision a second thought. John Henley, a slave master?

Dear God, he grieved, what had he done?

Alex shouted the change in the direction of the sails that would bring him to Henley's ship the fastest.

According to Gustaaf, Henley's name was mentioned many times while he and his sister were held captive on Captain Charlie Roberts's slave ship.

Alex's heart rumbled in his chest with the thought that he had placed Caitrina into the hands of a slave master. By now, she may have been violated. Kyle was likely dead. No! He had to get to them. They weren't that far behind and they soon caught sight of *Colony's Lady* in the distance.

He thought of her under Henley's heel and groaned at the fire in his belly. "Me thoughts tell me I'm mad, Sam." He didn't know why he admitted such a thing to his friend, but he wanted someone to tell him he wasn't.

"I think ya have been racin' toward madness since the night ya met her." Sam didn't look up from sharpening the blade of his dagger. "I don't like her on that ship either. I must be mad as well, because I agree with yar decision to go back fer her."

Alex hoped it wasn't too late. "Race the wind, mates!" he bellowed.

"Thirteen port!" Sam shouted, giving the direction of the wind. They sailed hard over frothy waves. It would be only moments now.

His eye spotted something he'd been trained most of his life to look for. Arms flailing in the waves. His heart banged once then paused, stilling his breath. No! Alex's mind railed against his vision. He ran to the rail to get a closer look. "Man overboard!"

Alex didn't pause but dove into the water. He moved with expert precision and extra strength and urgency in the deadly current. But the figure had stopped flailing.

Alex wasn't one to ask anything of God, but he did now. *Let him be alive. Let him be alive. Please.*

Kyle! His heart battered against his chest while he swam. When Alex reached him, he took up the Highland lad against him and turned them both back toward *Poseidon's Adventure*. He saw Gustaaf lowering a rope ladder over the side, and swam toward it.

The Dutchman lowered himself over the edge to grab Kyle's lifeless body. He hoisted him into the boat and Alex followed right behind. Sam watched, pale and silent. When Alex reached the deck he left Kyle in Gustaaf's competent hands while he returned to the rails and searched the seas for Caitrina's body. Every instant grew more impossible to bear as the fear of finding her facedown in the waves gripped him.

"Kyle!" he demanded the half-revived man. "Did they throw her over?"

Her cousin cursed and tried to sit up. Gustaaf held him down as they caught up to Henley's ship. "I don't... I don't know." He fought against Gustaaf's strong arms. "We have to get to her."

"How does right this moment sound?" Alex asked and then sprinted to the quarterdeck. They were close enough to *Colony's Lady* that he could leap onto a long, dangling rope and swing himself over the waves and onto her deck without breaking stride. Kyle, Sam, and Gustaaf soon followed. Alex hoped the Highlander wouldn't get them all killed.

It didn't take him long to realize what a true benefit Kyle MacGregor's sword arm was to his side, despite his near drowning. They took down ten men on deck within minutes, but without finding her.

When Kyle turned toward one of the hatches, Alex

followed him. Slashing their way through a round of men on the stairs, they descended, leaving a trail of bodies behind them, and met Captain Henley standing at a cabin door. When he saw Alex, he paled. When he saw Kyle, he near fainted.

"I..." Henley began, then paused as his bleak future flashed before his vision. "She..."

Alex didn't wait but kicked the door in. Upon entering, he dodged the swipe of a blade to his neck and then another to his arm. He leaped away from the doorway and turned to her blade held high over her head.

"Caitrina!" He held up his palm to her. "'Tis Alex. We've come to get ya."

"She killed three of my crew from that doorway," he heard Henley tell Kyle.

Aye, his lass was courageous, and she was alive. The relief of it near made him dizzy.

"Alex?" She blinked in the low light as if she couldn't trust the good of her eyes. Tears gathered almost instantly beneath her lids. "Kyle is dead."

"I live, cousin."

Alex lost her to the Highlander's arms, but he didn't mind. She'd thought her cousin dead, and to discover he lived was a celebration to be relished. Besides, Alex had other matters on the ship that needed his attention. He would see to Caitrina when they boarded *Poseidon's Adventure*. She was alive and seemingly unharmed. That was all that mattered. He knew she had had to fight for her life. He would never forget the terror in her eyes when he broke through the door. She had obviously had to keep Henley and his mates at bay for as long as she could. Fighting them off, killing them as they entered. Threatened, afraid, and alone because of the position *he* had put her in. He'd understand perfectly well if she never spoke another word to him. If she didn't, he deserved the torment of it. He never thought he'd lose his heart again. He'd been careful not to. But it was clear to him now that he'd failed. It was hers and he didn't want it back.

He still wanted answers though. He wanted to know her intentions from the beginning. He wanted the truth. But later, after she was safe again. Nothing else mattered presently.

He handed her off to her cousin while Gustaaf cut down another three sailors in his path with one swing of his mighty axe. Sam waited on deck with a bloody-nosed Henley gripped in his fist. Alex wasted no time and showed Henley no mercy, cutting him down where he stood. "Let the rest live!" he called out to Gustaaf and the others. "Let them fight over who's to be the new captain. And let's get the hell out of here."

His men agreed and he hurried to meet them at the ropes.

"What happened to ye?" He heard her asking her cousin before Kyle carried her across the sea to *Poseidon's* deck.

Alex watched them return and was thankful, so thankful that they both lived.

When he landed on his deck, Caitrina lifted her icy blue gaze to Alex but severed it too fast to see what he feared he felt for her in his eyes. He dipped his gaze to her hands trembling at her sides. He noticed, too, that her bottom lip was quivering a little. He wanted to go to her and beg her forgiveness.

She turned back to her cousin. "I feared ye certainly dead."

"Thanks to the captain, I'm not." Kyle looked at Alex and smiled at him. "And neither are ye."

Her smile on Kyle faded and she shook her head. "If we had not been thrown off one ship we wouldna' have ended up on the other."

"I was wrong in my decision to leave ya with anyone else," Alex admitted, then glanced up at Gustaaf and scowled for all he was worth.

"Just a few more moments fer either of us and yer apology would mean nothing, Captain. As it means nothing now."

She was correct and he felt like hell over it. He hated that he felt like hell. He hated it even more when they reached the Caicos Islands the next day and she still hadn't said a word to him.

They docked on Parrot Cay, a small island off the western shores of North Caicos. It didn't matter if the navy found him here. According to his father's map, the *Quedagh Merchant* was hidden in Dominica. Besides, this was his home, or the closest thing he had to one, and he wanted to see his foster family.

Chapter Twenty-Three

Trina sank her teeth into the drumstick of a chicken prepared and served with mangos and ginger. She groaned with delight around an enormous bonfire burning below a low full moon and just a dozen or so feet away from the roaring ocean. Parrot Cay was the most enchanting island she'd ever been on. The landscape was so different from Skye's. Often inundated by the tide, the island was composed of mostly salt marshes and tidal flats, save for sheltered mangrove villages scattered throughout, like the one she was in now.

She'd wanted to discover other cultures and the island life was as different from living in the mountains as she could ever hope to find.

If she wasn't so miserable about Alex abandoning her and Kyle so quickly, she would be enjoying finally exploring her dreams. He'd asked for her forgiveness more than once since he'd retrieved them. But she hadn't given it. Could she ever forgive him?

One thing at a time, she cautioned herself and sampled jerk pork for the first time. She groaned again. Her aunt

Isobel was the best cook she knew, but island food was better than anything she'd ever tasted. Everything, from grits made from dried conches or peas to apple rum cake, cherry tarts, dishes prepared with dates and almonds and fruit called guava, drinks made with passion fruit and papaya, to their spicy ginger beer, was prepared to perfection with love and served with warm smiles.

As a matter of fact, most of the men were smiling at her...rather dreamily.

"Dinna' enjoy yer food so much, cousin." Kyle smiled into his beer.

Trina rolled her eyes and wiped her mouth. She grazed her eyes over the captain, barely giving him notice, but catching his gaze on her. So what if he was more beautiful than a beach lit in flames of gold and ruby left by the setting sun? Lucifer was beautiful and look where it landed the angels that followed him.

She turned her gaze on the women instead. They were exquisite, exotic beauties with dark brown skin and colorful sarongs wrapped tightly about their heads and voluptuous bodies.

Trina wondered how Captain Kidd hadn't settled here and wed one of them already. A thought occurred to her that made her find him where he sat around the huge bonfire, his arm tossed lightly over his bent knee while he laughed with his friends. She'd never asked him if he was wed. What if one of these sensual women was his wife?

Not that she cared. Not anymore. Not after he left them to die. It didn't matter that he'd come after them. He'd left them. He hadn't even given her a chance. He saw a thief and he tossed her away without mercy.

Let him have a wife. Trina would pray for the unfortunate lass tonight before she went to sleep.

"Ya be likin' heem, den, gal?"

"Pardon?" Trina looked up at the island girl draped in bright canary yellow and emerald cotton and smiled. "I dinna' understand."

The girl crinkled her brow beneath her ornately folded head wrap and slipped her huge coal-colored eyes to Gustaaf.

"She asks you if you like him?" Gustaaf supplied between bites of jerk pork.

"Who?" Trina asked.

"Dee captin."

Trina laughed but the sound fell like tin on her ears. "Nae. Nae, I dinna' like him."

"Why not?" the girl asked, seemingly astounded. Before Trina could reply, she brought her knuckles to her waist and called to Alex.

"Alex, why dis gal not like ya?"

Trina wanted to dig a hole in the sand and jump in. She didn't look at Alex while he heard the question.

"Because, Anjali," he called back, "I left her with evil men and she and her cousin nearly died."

"Dat's a good reasin," Anjali said to her. "Why did he leave ya wit dees evil men?"

"He thinks I wish to steal from him."

"Do ya?"

"Nae."

Anjali straightened her spine and gave Alex a hard look.

"I've apologized," Alex assured her, "but she hasn't forgiven me."

"Ya will work on it harder den."

Alex smiled and Anjali shone against the firelight like polished onyx. Did the native woman care for him? Did he care for her? Anjali likely knew if he had a wife—on this island or any other.

"Do ya think ya will ever share words with me again, Miss Grant?"

She looked up, surprised that he would show interest at all, and in front of the crew, in whether or not he ever spoke to her again. She remembered the stark fear in his eyes when he broke down Henley's door and saw her. It kept her awake all night. She told herself he was afraid she was about to stab him, but it wasn't that. He'd been afraid of what he'd find when he got there. For just an instant, her heart warmed with the memories of what she felt for him. What she *had* felt for him. Some of it remained, she would admit, but she was too angry, too hurt.

"Would sharing words with ye *now* suit ye, Captain?"

His smile widened and he gave her a slight nod, giving her leave amid the group.

Trina set her food down on the straw mat beneath her and folded her hands in her lap. "After I watched a group of men haul my cousin overboard, into the sea and out of my life, I found myself alone on a ship with men who either wanted to slit my throat or use my body fer sport." She was thankful, at least, that he wasn't trying to interrupt her to defend himself. He sat quietly while she spoke, as did the rest, as ghostly pale as the moon above him.

"Thankfully," she continued, "I had learned tactical defense from my kin." She lifted her chin, proud to claim such warriors as her family. "I killed some of them."

"I heard 'twas eight," called Mr. Bonnet, who was to Alex's left.

"I take no pride in what I was forced to do in order to stay alive." Her eyes slipped back to Alex. He was staring at her. She'd grown to womanhood among lots of men.

Not one of them ever looked more repentant in his life than Alex did now.

"The rest of the crew may disagree," she said, looking around the fire at the faces she knew. She returned her gaze to Alex. He deserved this. "But ye are an unjust captain. Ye didna' consider my argument. Ye offered me no defense but sentenced Kyle and me to death, had ye arrived just a few moments later. Fer that, I think ye are unfair and cruel, and I will be leaving yer presence as soon as I can."

"Miss Grant," he said, stopping her from turning away. "I agree that what I did was cruel. But unfair?" he asked, setting his drink in the sand. "Ya tried to steal from me. The evidence was in yar hand. What would—"

She didn't hear the rest. Och, she wanted to fling her bowl at his head! She couldn't, she'd already spoken mutinous words and was at risk of being hanged, so she stood and walked away into the darkness, rather than look at him...speak to him, without killing him.

He'd rescued her and Kyle. Why would he if he still believed her guilty? When would he cease with this foolish accusation of her wanting his map?

His strong fingers clamping around her wrist stopped her. She spun around and glared at him.

"We're goin' to get this settled between us once and fer all," he promised, his heavy voice playing over her ears like the waves dancing beyond the dunes when he moved past her. "Come with me."

She dug her heels into the sand. "Where?"

"The water's edge. I feel more at home with the sea beneath my feet."

When he tugged, she tightened and braced her legs. He merely slanted his mouth and his brow at her. "Truly?"

he asked, as if her not trusting him was the most preposterous thing imaginable. "Ya're not still afraid of me, are ya?"

"Why should I not be? Ye cast Kyle and me to the sharks already. How do I know ye dinna' have another shark waiting at the shore fer me?"

"Because I fergave ya fer tryin' to steal from me, Caitrina. I thought I proved that to ya when I came back fer ya."

She felt her blood boil. She didn't know what to say, so she took a step closer to him, pulled back her hand, and slapped him hard in the face. When he drew his palm to his stinging cheek, she stepped back, uncertain of what his reaction would be. He could stab her right now. Who would avenge her? Kyle? He would die. Gustaaf? He would die too. She rested her hand on the hilt of the cutlass he'd returned to her yesterday, and waited.

"Do ya feel better?"

"Nae," she lied. Striking him had helped ease her frustration a bit. "One or more might do it though."

"Later," he offered. "Right now, I would offer ya yar fair trial. I will listen and consider whatever ya tell me."

"That's it?" she asked, letting him lead her to the shoreline. "Ye're not going to hurl me into the sea fer slapping ye?"

"I've been slapped before."

"Och," she said, glaring at his back. "I dinna' doubt it with all yer merry adventures in brothels from Portugal to Paris. But I'm certain ye've never been slapped with such purpose before. I refrained from punching ye only because if I didna' knock ye oot, ye were more likely to stab me."

He laughed, then looked over his shoulder at her. He

drew her closer against his side and spoke softly close to her head. "Ya think I would stab ya, Caitrina?"

The rich cadence of his voice seeped deep into her nerves, her muscles, her bones, and coaxed her to lean into him for support. "Let us get back to the matter at hand." She separated herself from him by a hair. The size of him walking beside her on land felt too good, too right, to move too far away. The heat between them sizzled. "I was in the middle of retying my bandanna when I noticed the door in the wall swinging open." She told him the rest, realizing that she had told him all this before. He just hadn't listened then. He did now. "I never noticed it before. 'Twas well concealed."

"Aye, 'twas," he agreed. "And I know fer certain 'twas locked when I left the cabin."

She knew how bad it looked for her. She had no proof of her innocence. But she *was* innocent. She wanted him to know it. He was wrong to have punished her, and if he continued to mistrust her, staying with him would be foolish. Someone else knew where the map was hidden and had been looking at it. "If I didna' open the door, there is only one other person who was inside the cabin."

He smiled and she knew she was losing him. "Not him," he said, shaking his head slowly. "Someone else must have been there before him. Anyone, Caitrina, but not Samuel. He was with me when they hanged me father. When me father's entire crew, men we'd known fer decades, abandoned him when their support would have been most appreciated. 'Twas Sam who stood with me and watched with me while me father swung."

"I have no other explanation," she told him softly, realizing that it might be easier to convince him of her innocence, rather than his friend's guilt. She stopped walking and made him stop too. She looked up at him in the moonlight, knowing this was her last chance to make him believe her. She wouldn't fail. "If I knew what to say to help ye believe me, I would say it. I have only my word, and though I may have given ye the impression that I dinna' follow my cousin's..."—she paused then corrected herself—"my kin's standards of integrity, let me assure ye, my word means much to me. I dinna' want yer map, Alex. When ye made me a part of yer crew and gave me a share of the earnings, I admit, I considered the worth of the *Quedagh Merchant* and what a share of *that* booty would be. Also, would it not be more prudent to let ye find it, then kill ye afterward?"

He smiled, and damn her but she missed looking at his smile aimed straight at her. But whatever amusement he found faded rapidly as something dawned on him. She was telling the truth. His gaze deepened and darkened on her. "Fergive me fer almost gettin' ya and Kyle killed. I never would have fergiven meself if I'd been too late." He took a step closer to her and lifted his thumb and index to her chin and held it. "The thought of it sickens me. If I knew what to do to help ya fergive me, I would do it."

"D'ye believe me then?"

"Aye," he said, dipping his face to hers. "I believe ya. Will ya accept me most heartfelt vow that I will never treat ya cruelly again?"

"Aye," she whispered back, tilting her mouth up to meet his. Moving closer, taking her face in his hands, he covered her. He consumed her in white flames too hot to withstand. Her blood sizzled at the flick of his tongue over her lips, urging her open for him. She obeyed and relished the deluge of him, tasting her with searing, open kisses, branding her with long, lazy strokes of his tongue inside her mouth. When his hands swept down her shoulders, her back, settling over her buttocks and squeezing, she tugged at his hair, his shirt. Her wanton reaction was met with his gripping her rump and pressing and lifting her hips to his. She felt him grow stiffer while he guided her over his desire.

Trina had never been with a man, but she wanted to be with this one. She wanted him to strip her of her clothes, hoist her to his hips, spread her legs around his waist, and drive his manhood deep into her. She wanted to look into his eyes while he took her, run her hands over the tight plains of his body, and kiss him until she went mad in his arms.

She heard the sound of drums playing in the distance—or was it her heart? Music filled the air with celebration, joy, and something a bit more primitive.

When Alex picked her up and carried her away to a small private inlet, she didn't protest but coiled her arms around his neck.

"Be with me, lady." His breath seared her lobe when he bent to whisper to her. "If ya refuse me I'll go mad."

"I willna' refuse ye, Alex," she promised. Cupping his neck, she pulled him down until his lips hovered just above hers. Before he covered her mouth, she whispered, "I surrender myself to ye."

Chapter Twenty-Four

Normally, Alex wouldn't care where or how he took a woman, but Caitrina Grant wasn't just any woman. She was a woman he was falling in love with. How had it happened? Almost losing her didn't make it happen. His heart was already lost; almost losing her just made him admit it to himself. Him. Alex Kidd, in love... and not the love he had felt for Madalena. No, he'd been a boy when he let Madalena bewitch him. What he felt for Caitrina was what a man feels in his heart for a woman. A passion for her that cannot be quenched.

And he tried to quench it. He didn't want to be too rough with her, knowing, after she told him, that she'd never done this before. But she drove him mad with desire.

He kissed her while he carried her. When she tugged at his shirt, as eager for him as he was for her, he had to battle the urge to tear off her clothes and take her until he groaned at the moon.

He stopped kissing her to look down into her eyes. "Ya tempt me beyond reason, lass." Even as he spoke, she closed her eyes and parted her lips, proving his words true.

He set her down in the sand and untied her earasaid. She turned with him when he spread the plaid out before them, eager to be back to kissing him. He obliged, taking her in his arms and bringing her with him to the ground. They undressed each other, working frantic fingers through laces and buckles until they both lay naked beneath the moonlight.

Alex took in the sight of her body like a starving beast. How had so many men on Skye resisted this perfect being, when he could not? Did she not beguile the hearts of other men? They were fools. He smiled at her. And now she was his, pure, timid in her dimpled smile, yet fearlessly coiling her legs around his. He wanted to take her every way possible, even in her mouth. She made him hard, hot, and ready. He traced his tanned fingers over her pale, creamy skin, loving the fragility it added to the vision of her. He knew he was falling, or had already fallen, by the way his heart swelled with emotion for her.

"I'm not afraid," she whispered against him.

Somehow her admission sparked the flames scorching him. He cupped her ankle in his hand and raised her leg over his shoulder. He licked his way along her inner thigh until he reached the crease in her leg. When she realized what he meant to do, she tried to pull away. He held her still, cupping her hips in his hands. He dipped his face to the tuft of soft curls taunting him and spread his tongue over the hidden treasure. She groaned and arched her hips, inviting him to partake to his pleasure. And pleasure he took, drinking of her to the point of her release. Stopping short, he rose up over her, his heavy cock dangling between them. He looked down into her eyes and basked for an instant in the raw desire he saw looking back at him.

He wasted no more time but wedged his knees between her thighs and spread her wide beneath him.

He stopped when he felt the cold edge of his dagger against his throat.

"Do yer best not to hurt me," Caitrina warned with a sinister smile crossing over her lips.

He wanted to laugh at the notion of this woman needing him to rescue her. "I'll do me best," he promised and pushed his swollen head up against her opening. He moved slowly and with caution, at the end of his own blade. Each thrust he pushed a bit harder, broke further through her barrier. Sweet torture.

Twice, he almost drove himself into her, but he wanted her wetter. "Remove the dagger, love," he breathed. "I want to kiss ya."

She smiled, tempting him. Oh, tempting him. She moved the blade someplace else. Alex didn't care where. He covered her mouth and swept his tongue inside her.

Her legs spread wider.

He moved deeper inside her. He'd never been with a virgin before. He didn't realize how tight her sheath was until he felt the resistance of it against his cock. It burned like dipping into lava, but he dipped. He rode her slowly, inch by inch, until she clutched his chest and squeezed herself around him, pushing him out.

It was enough to set him over the edge. It was just what he needed.

Taking hold of himself, he guided his flow over her swollen nub and then his stiff shaft. When she was good and wet, he plucked his dagger out of her hand and tossed it away. He pushed deep, dipping his face against hers when she cried out. Every stroke grew deeper, slower, taking on the rhythm of the music on the wind. He kissed her mouth, her throat, while he rode her, feeling her moisten on her own. When he dipped his mouth to suckle her full breast, he finally broke through and almost came again.

But no. He could hold. He wanted to enjoy this with her for as long as it took.

It didn't take long.

When he rose up on his haunches and took her with him, curled over his elbow, connected at the hips, she cried his name. He knew she was close.

"Alex, I feel like I'm on fire!" she cried out.

Aye, he burned as well, his senses, his blood. "Shall I cease?" he asked.

"Nae! Nae." She opened her beautifully large eyes and smiled at him. "Never stop."

He thrust hard and deep, and deeper still when she dug her fingernails into his shoulders.

When she rose up and pressed her body against him, he filled his hands with her bottom and guided her up and down. She let out a long laborious moan. He looked at her and watched her climax. Another thrust and he burst deep inside her, riding with her over the crest of ecstasy.

When they were both done, they collapsed onto the plaid, breathless and spent. Alex rolled off her and smiled when she turned in his arms and snuggled into his chest. She fit. She belonged exactly where she was and Alex never wanted to be parted from her. The power of his feelings for her accelerated his heart.

She felt it against her ear. "What is it?" she asked, spreading her warm breath over his skin. "Why are ye racing? Are ye racing from me?"

He laughed and then yelped when she pinched his side.

"I'm being verra' serious, Alex," she told him, rising up on her elbow to look him in the eye. "Ye make light of many things where courage or yer heart is concerned. I would be more to ye than just another means to answer yer lustful desires."

He almost laughed again, then thought better of it. She was correct, after all, about him making light of certain things. At least, that's what he'd been told countless times by women. Sometimes he laughed because he didn't like thinking that assumptions about him were correct. But they usually were. He guarded his heart well but she'd broken through his barrier. He knew now that she was innocent of trying to steal his map. He believed her about finding the trapdoor open. He knew Sam had nothing to do with it, but he would ask him if he saw the door open.

"Me heart quickens because what I feel fer ya…"—he paused, trying to come up with the right words—"makes me uneasy."

"What d'ye feel fer me?" she asked softly, her huge sapphire eyes steady on him.

He let out a long, gusty exhalation of breath and cursed himself silently for bringing it up. "I feel…ehm…I care fer ya."

"Ye do?"

He cast her a dubious glance, not unfazed by how lovely she looked against the starry sky, aglow with the residue of their lovemaking. Did she truly not know that his heart had gone soft on her? That he feared losing his mind at the thought of losing her? He didn't want to love her. Not because of the pain her betrayal would inflict, but because if he took her on as a pirate, he could lose her to the sword or the noose. Hell, they were already likely being stalked. But if he sent her home, he would lose her for certain. "Of course, I do." He would train with her every day. He wouldn't let up until he knew she could defend herself. "I care fer ya . . . very much."

She raised her brow at him and looked as surprised as she confessed to being. "I never thought to hear ye speak such words." Her lips curled into a challenging smirk. "Or have ye spoken them to many?"

"I've spoken them to none. 'Tis why ya feel me heart race."

Her dimples deepened along with her voice when she asked, "Am I to believe that I have done what nae other women before me could do?" She shook her head, answering her own question, then she traced his nipple with her finger. "I hear how the men speak of yer prowess in the bedchamber. It takes a special lass to win the heart of a man like ye. My grandmother did it. So did my aunt Isobel. But I dinna' possess such power that binds ye to me."

He smiled. "I turned me ship around fer ya, lass. Ya possess something. If ya don't think that Gustaaf is bound to ya, then ya're a fool. He lied straight to me face about yar climbin' the masts."

Her smile went soft in the moonlight and she nodded her head. "Dear Gustaaf. He protects me like a brother." She gave him a curious look when he grunted at her.

"Och, I knew this would happen."

"What?" he asked. "Ya knew what would happen?"

"I tried to warn ye, if ye recall. I said that a few nights with me and ye could lose all."

"Aye." He remembered, smiling at her like some love-struck fool. She was right, she had warned him. "Ya spoke of befuddlin' the rake Captain Kidd."

"And have I befuddled ye, rake?" she asked, bending down to kiss him on the mouth.

"Aye, ya have." He tasted the sweet fragrance of her

lips, her tongue. He lifted his hands to her face and tunneled his fingers through her hair, drawing her down over him. When her soft breasts touched his flesh, he pulled her closer until she straddled him.

"I know ya are sore," he whispered, kissing her mouth, her cheek, her chin. "I will not take ya again so soon." He almost went back on his promise when she groaned. She wanted more but he knew it would pain her too much tomorrow. Her body was delightfully untried and pure and he felt honored to be the first to have her. He told her so amid kisses and realized with a sense of stunned disbelief that he wanted to be the last. He'd never cared before about whether or not other men shared the women he made love to. He'd never felt this way about any of them. Just looking at Caitrina, kissing her, touching her, smelling her sweet fragrance, was enough to drive him mad with the need to protect and possess her.

"I don't want to share ya," he confessed, cradling her cheek in his palm and gazing into her eyes.

"I dinna' want to share ye either," she told him, then dipped her mouth to his.

Could he give up the rest for this one? He smiled into her face, unable to conceal what she made him feel. "Ya're stayin' with me then? Would ya make a ship yar home, Caitrina?"

She nodded. "Try riddin' yerself of me again and I'll kill ye while ye sleep."

He laughed and scooped her thick tresses away from her neck to kiss her pulse. "Ya sound like a true pirate already. Soon ya will be spittin' in a bucket with the rest of the crew."

She bit his lobe in response to his nibbling her throat. "Gustaaf taught me how to aim fer the bucket a few nights ago."

He tried to get his mind off her by conjuring her image spitting over her shoulder like Gustaaf or Sam would. It didn't help, but it made him smile.

"What other bad habits have ya picked up on me ship besides spittin' and disobeyin' yar captain, Miss Grant?"

She left his ear alone to gaze down at him and flash him her dimples. "I've learned how to curse. Want to hear me?"

He shook his head, aching to fit his mouth around hers again. Had he ever wanted anyone this bad before? No. No one. Caitrina was more than satisfying a desire. All of him was involved. He wondered, briefly, if he might go mad with his need of her.

"When I found Kyle in the waves, I thought I'd lost ya, Caitrina." He turned her over on her back, then he rose up and brought her with him in his arms. "I feared ya dead and it near drove me mad. When I found ya alive, nothin' else mattered. I would accept travelin' with a woman who hated me, as long as she lived."

"I dinna' hate ye, Alex," she purred against his chest while he carried her to the shoreline and into the waves. "I was hurt. Now I am not."

"Good." He smiled against her mouth as he carried her into the shallows. He held her still when she shivered and tried to squirm out of his arms. "Because I want more of ya."

※≺

Chapter Twenty-Five

*T*rina loved Parrot Cay. She loved the Caicos, and its people, and its hot, balmy nights. She didn't blame the women for wearing so little. Camlochlin was never this hot.

She closed her eyes and felt her heart pick up the beat of the crashing waves and distant drums.

"It sounds like ye here, Alex." She looked up at the silhouette of his chin and jaw against the firelight. She wished it were daylight, so she could see his handsome face more clearly. But his voice was what had bewitched her from the first.

Lying nestled in his arms, she breathed in the scent of his skin beneath her nose and smiled. Kissing his chest, she tasted the sea and wondered if water flowed through his veins. Nae. Blood coursed through him, hot and potent. Only a fool would deny it. He drove her mad with desire so lurid she hardly recognized herself. She'd given herself to him with a kind of carefree abandon she'd dreamed about, but had never attained.

Now she understood more clearly why her brother

Malcolm had been caught so many times stumbling out of maidens' homes from Perth to Skye. Nothing in her life compared to making love. Not hunting game or sailing toward adventure on the high seas. Nothing would ever compare to Alex's body inside her, atop her, his breath mingling hot and short with hers, his hands traversing the shape of her body, cupping her breasts while he kissed them. Was it so marvelously enchanting for everyone, or was it better when love was involved?

There was one thing she missed about home. Having a woman to tell things to. She missed Abby.

"I grew up here and in places like it."

She closed her eyes, listening intently to his voice, lost in the sound of him, excited to get to know things about him.

"The islanders became me family. Most of the time me father left me with nurses. I was raised as one of them until me ninth year."

"Where was yer mother?"

"I don't know much about her save fer what me father told me, which was different dependin' on whether he was drunk or sober. She abandoned me when I was a babe."

A shiver crawled up her back and she shook in his embrace. She couldn't imagine her life without her mother in it.

He gathered her in closer. "If ya are cold, we can go back."

She shook her head. "Ye grew up without a mother. 'Tis terribly sad to me."

"Nay, 'twasn't sad," he assured her gently. "I had many mothers."

She still felt bad for him. "What about yer father?" she asked him. "Did ye ever see him?"

"He came back fer me when I was nine. I hardly knew

him but he put me on his boat and made me crew. He taught me about the sea and how to live on it. I came to love it and him. I stopped missin' me family on the Islands and remained with him fer nine years."

"He made ye a pirate then."

"Nay," he whispered against her forehead. "He gave me a love fer the sea. Wantin' to serve no man but meself made me a pirate."

Aye, she understood that sentiment. She didn't want to serve any man either. Well, not until now. Would she agree to finally becoming a wife...if Alex asked her? What would being married to him be like? She'd never thought of it before with other men. The thought of keeping a home and raising children had never appealed to her. But she could have a child now. Now that she and Alex...

She sat up and stared at him, alarmed by a storm of thoughts and questions filling her head.

"What if I have yer child? How many children d'ye already have? Dear Lord, I didna' even ask if ye were wed! Are ye wed, Alex?"

He gazed at her with a slow smile curling his sexy mouth. How could she resist him ever again after tonight? "Nay, I'm not wed, and if ya have me child, I'll be surprised since, as far as I know, I'm not able to father any babes."

"How d'ye know this?"

He shrugged his shoulders. "I would have had one by now, and I don't. At least, no one's ever come to me and called me father of her babe."

She stared at him and shook her head. "D'ye keep eyes on all the whores ye've slept with then?"

He laughed. "Nay, but I've seen them all more than once. I'd recognize if they had a babe strapped to their hip."

She looked away, not wanting to think of his past.

He touched his knuckles to her face, drawing her gaze back to him. "If ya give me a child I will love it, Caitrina. But is this the life ya want fer a babe?"

When she didn't answer he pulled her down into his arms again. "Anjali knows a medicine woman who will give ya some herbs to keep a babe from growin' in ya. 'Tis yar choice, beauty."

Did she want such an herb? She closed her eyes and let the rhythm of his heart calm her nerves.

"Does Anjali know yer body intimately?"

"Nay," he told her quietly, further soothing her anxious heart. "Her mother was one of those who helped raise me. Anjali is like a sister to me."

Relief flooded Trina's veins and she kissed his flat belly. How could she compete with these bonny island women who were crafted for moonlight and dancing?

She kissed him again. His belly tasted salty from their bath in the sea. He couldn't stay too far from the waves. Was he a merman, her lover? She looked down the length of his hips, over his thighs, and down his shapely legs to convince herself that he wasn't. He was all man, with a sword of steel and granite. When his flesh shuddered against her lips, it sent a trickle of red-hot heat someplace low beneath her belly. She thought about the passion of his thrusts and the way all that hard male body felt while he drove himself into her deeper, his hands possessively caressing her breasts. She wanted more of him, but if she wanted to walk tomorrow without announcing what she'd been doing all night to the entire crew, she would have to deny her body.

But she didn't have to deny his.

Leaning farther down, she spread her tongue over his hot flesh, kissing and relishing the flavor and feel of him. When her hunger traversed a path lower and more sinful, his slow groan of wicked delight prompted her to eat him alive and leave nothing left. Moving on instinct alone, on some base primal desire to take him in her mouth and suck him like she needed him to live, she cupped his scrotum in the palm of her hand.

"Gently, love," he whispered, or perhaps it was the wind.

Reaching out her tongue, she ran the tip of it up his shaft. She let him guide her with his hands, then crawled between his legs and swallowed him up without any assistance. He hardened instantly, muddling her reasons for not climbing aboard and riding him like a storm. She held on tighter, closing her lips around his full head, and bit down softly. He spread his arms out to his sides and gave his cock up to her. She took, sucking him, licking him, worshipping him until he rose toward the sky.

He leaned up on his elbows to watch her mouth moving over his desire. She descended once, and then again, when he yanked her up, pulling her body over his until his cock was poised just beneath her opening. He looked deep into her eyes, setting her insides aflame with passion. She spread her legs along his sides and let him slide deep inside her. It didn't hurt as much as she thought it might. In fact, he felt rather wonderful clutched within her tight grasp.

She cried out when he cupped her buns in his hands and drew her up and then down, against his body, atop his shaft. She moved her hips in unison with his and they rode the waves together.

When they were done, and quite tired, they lay coiled in each other's bare limbs and fell asleep.

Until the morning, when the fire died, and Mr. Pierce woke them with a loud cough.

Trina thought she might faint, despite Mr. Pierce's averted gaze. Who knew how long he'd already been looking?

"Her cousin is lookin' fer her, Alex. I'd prefer, fer the crew's safety, that he didn't find her like this."

Lord! Kyle! She moved to reach for her clothes, then stopped and waited until Alex thanked him and sent him to delay Kyle's arrival.

She stood, dressing, watching Alex do the same. Their night had been magical, a night that she would never forget and planned on repeating again and again.

"I'll see ya later today, love," he promised, and with a kiss he was gone.

Trina looked after him for a moment, wondering if what he called her meant something. Love? Lord help her. Why in blazes did she feel like singing?

Sam Pierce walked back to where he'd left Kyle Mac-Gregor with Anjali. He scowled at his feet as he walked in the sand. How would he ever get the sight of her, naked and asleep, out of his head?

No. Not now. He had to remain in control of his thoughts and his emotions. The same way he'd done it for the last eight years. He couldn't fail now. Why did Alex have to let Caitrina Grant remain aboard after Portugal? Sam had feared this would happen. Alex was a fool ruled by his heart. He knew Captain Harris of the *Excellence* could be close by and yet he had to stop here and visit people he hadn't seen in years. Now he deliberately disregarded the MacGregor threat and seduced one of their women to his bed. He was going to get them all killed.

Normally, Sam didn't care who Alex settled beneath him. The queen herself would likely bed him given the opportunity. Sam didn't care. It was no concern of his. Aye, some of the captain's women grew jealous of his roving eye and, more often than Sam cared to remember, Alex found himself at the end of a knife.

Sam liked Miss Grant, and for that reason he regretted everything when he heard of what Captain Henley tried to do to her. He wished he'd killed Henley himself. Besides all that though, Miss Grant posed a whole different set of problems. One of them being her cousin. Kyle was protective of the lass. He was also a MacGregor and therefore rash and dangerous. He would likely try to kill Alex if he suspected that the captain had deflowered his cousin. Sam couldn't let that happen, and it had little to do with any map or treasure. Another threat was her kin. They would come for her. Sam didn't doubt it, and when they did, they would massacre everyone in their way and ask questions later. He knew about the outlawed clan from his brother, David.

Aye, Miss Grant had been correct in her assumption that he was Captain Pierce's brother. A clever lass, she was. Of course, she knew nothing for certain and if Sam could fool Alex all these years, a pretty little woman would cause no threat. His task was almost done. Just a bit longer. He wouldn't be stopped in what he meant to do. After living with Alex and calling him friend for eight years, he no longer believed in his first allegiance. But it was too late for regrets.

Royal Admiralty wanted that ship. They still did. No one knew where it was, though many guessed it was hidden somewhere in the Caribbean. William Kidd had never given up its whereabouts. They'd enlisted Samuel, a soldier in the Royal Navy, to lead them to the treasure. David, in the army at the time, didn't want him to do it. Pirates were a deadly bunch and if they discovered that Sam was spying for the navy, they would kill him. He knew he would likely not see David again but he had wanted to do it. He had been young.

His duty had been to get to know Alex and discover if he knew the whereabouts of the *Quedagh Merchant*. Alex didn't, of course, but Sam remained with him, partially for duty's sake, and partially because Sam had become good friends with the young captain. Aye, he'd grown fond of Alex, even to the point of denying his duty and putting all his heart into being a pirate. Everything changed again a few months ago when David transferred to the navy and had been put in charge of procuring the stolen ship.

Too late for regrets.

"I didn't find them," he called out when Kyle and Anjali came into view. "They could have left the island."

"Left it?" MacGregor stepped forward, breaking contact with the island lass he was about to kiss. "Why would they have left it?"

Sam had to admit that he liked this MacGregor. He liked all of them really. The sheer size of their men was enough to evoke feelings of inadequacy and doubt about one's battle skills. But they laughed with the same deep passion that they wielded their swords. He and David were raised around tough men like Kyle's uncles. They were far less intimidating when they were your friends. He wondered if there was still a way to win their favor. He glanced over his shoulder, thinking of Miss Grant.

"He may have wanted to show her his home on Pine Cay," Sam said, reaching him. This was the one he had to watch. Intelligence and mistrust shone in the depths of MacGregor's cloudless aqua eyes. The key was gaining his friendship, not his mistrust. "But let's check their huts again, aye? I could be mistaken."

MacGregor agreed and promptly left. He knew. Sam could tell that Kyle knew he'd been deceived. He knew Sam was lying about Pine Cay. He knew Sam had just covered for them and was giving them time to get to their separate beds. Was Sam so poor at masking his expressions or was MacGregor that good at reading them? It didn't matter. Alex would be better off without the MacGregors out to kill him. That was more likely to happen if Kyle didn't see him and Miss Grant naked and entangled in each other's arms. Sam wished he hadn't seen it either. When Alex forgot about Miss Grant, which would likely be any night now, no one would be the wiser.

"He loves her."

Sam turned and looked down into Anjali's soft coal eyes. "What?"

"Dee captain. He loves Miss Blue Eyes." She looked after Kyle. "I understand why."

Sam sighed and Anjali looped her arm through his on the way back to the village. "So my little spitfire has been done in by a pair of eyes?"

"Now, Sam, have ya seen dee man's eyes?"

He shook his head at her and hoped MacGregor's eyes found his cousin safe and sound. If Kyle tried to kill Alex, Sam would have to kill him. And then, besides the Royal Navy coming down on Alex, thanks to Sam's work, the captain would have to fight off Kyle's clan, because of him, as well.

He looked out over the sea and prayed that David had received the letter he'd sent off in Portugal with Senhor Moreno. He hoped his brother found them before Captain Harris or the others did, and mostly, he prayed David would grant him his request. David was Sam's only hope. Even though Miss Grant could help tremendously, her kin could just as quickly jeopardize everything. Sam was going to have to watch the two of them more closely.

Chapter Twenty-Six

$\mathcal{A}$lex hadn't expected that practicing with Kyle would be so taxing. He blocked a slice to his throat with a jarring crash of metal that shook his arms. He fought, for the time, on the defense, letting Kyle's speed and strength push him back. The lad fought with impressive speed and power. Alex's experience in actual combat proved Kyle's undoing though, when an opportunity presented itself and Alex slashed with his blade, turning his position to offense and taking the weary combatant down almost instantly.

"I didn't see that coming," Kyle confessed, rising to his feet with the aid of Alex's hand.

"That's the point." Alex smiled at him.

"Show it to me again."

Alex's smiled faded. He may have experience over the lad, but he had about seven or eight years on him as well. He wanted to rest, go find Caitrina, and steal a few kisses from her, perhaps a bit more. Practicing always made him more passionate. And now, at least, he was practicing with someone who would keep him in shape.

"One more time," he agreed, then raised his cutlass to Kyle's.

Metal clashed over their heads and Alex thought about what happened when Kyle had found him in his hut the morning Sam had come upon him and Caitrina. Alex had told him the truth. Since that morning, he had told no one else, even putting it out of his own head, or he tried to. He loved her. It wouldn't go away despite his determination to ignore it. He didn't want to think overlong about what it meant. What loving her could do to him. Kyle seemed to forgive him after Alex confessed to him, and to him alone.

"My faither was once the most infamous spy in the three kingdoms."

Alex blocked the strike to his neck and struck back, rattling Kyle's bones.

"His blood flows through me."

"Are ya tellin' me ya're a spy then, Kyle?" Alex retreated a step, holding him back.

"Nae." Kyle smashed his blade against Alex's, sparking the metal. "But I know how to read people, Captain. Remember the privateers disguised as merchants and know I speak the truth."

Alex remembered and nodded. He parried two more massive blows and waited for the third.

"Someone on this ship works against ye."

Alex saw Kyle's predictable opening and turned this fight into a victory. "I've known him fer eight years," Alex growled, holding the edge of his cutlass against Kyle's throat. "If ya mean to make charges against him, ya better have proof."

Kyle swallowed, then, seeming to gather his courage around him like a cloak, he stared at Alex straight on. "I believe I know his brother. He is a friend of my brother."

Alex shook his head and backed away, removing the blade. "So? I don't see—"

"The man's name is Captain David Pierce of the Royal Army. He is—"

"Kyle, I'll hear no more of this." He sheathed his sword and yanked off his gloves.

"Trust me, Captain, please. Something doesna' sit well."

"Trust ya?" Alex couldn't help but laugh. "I don't know ya. Him, I know. Do ya understand that?"

Kyle nodded, looking repentant. Why the hell did they keep trying to bring it up? Caitrina had tried talking to him about it last night around the village fire. He didn't know what they had against Sam, and Alex hadn't had the chance to ask Caitrina, since no one in the entire village had left them alone for a moment.

"Don't bring it up again," Alex said, turning away from him. He didn't want his crewmen, especially possible future relatives, hating his best friend.

"Aye, aye, Captain."

Alex thought Kyle had left the small meadow and sighed when he heard Kyle's voice again. "May I ask just one thing, Captain?"

"What is it?"

"What did he do fer ya to make ya trust his loyalty so fiercely?"

Alex thought about it. Hell, there was a lot. "He has me back in any fight. He has never failed to be where I needed him to be. He brought me back from a heartbreak I wallowed in fer almost a month."

"Madalena?"

Alex turned finally and looked him over. "Are ya studyin' me, lad?"

"Why would I?"

Extraordinary, Alex thought. Kyle didn't bat an eyelash while lying straight to his face.

Could Sam do it too? Was that why he didn't tell Sam about his feelings for Caitrina? No! They were making him doubt the only man he'd ever trusted besides his father.

"Ya give me no reason to trust ya."

Kyle lowered his gaze and then exhaled. "Aye," he admitted. "I study everyone. I canna' help it. It doesn't make me untrustworthy though."

"Nay, it doesn't," Alex agreed. "But lyin' does."

He turned again and began to walk away from Caitrina's cousin.

"How many years ago did yer faither take the *Quedagh Merchant*?"

According to what Alex had heard in New York, it happened shortly after he left his father's ship. "About eight years ago."

"And when did ye meet Mr. Pierce?"

Alex laughed over his shoulder at the lad following him. Was Kyle trying to tell him that Sam had been duping him for close to a decade? He had to laugh. To give credit, even the tiniest morsel, to Caitrina's or her cousin's mad accusations would have to mean that the only man he trusted in his life, *with* his life, was betraying him. And he was too dense to know it.

"Ya think me a fool." He tried to sound flippant but he heard the dip in his cadence, and if Kyle was as good as he suggested at reading people, he heard it too.

"Nae, Captain," Kyle answered, meeting Alex's steady gaze when he turned to face him. "He's difficult to read. I think 'tis because he genuinely cares fer ye. I have yet to hear him utter a negative thing aboot ye. Nor does he allow the faintest whisper of complaint against ye. I don't know what he's up to, but he considers ye his valued friend."

"Then why would he want me map?" Alex put to him earnestly. "Yar own words bear the truth." He turned again and walked away. "Let this go with Samuel," he warned over his shoulder, "before I take offense."

"Fine," Kyle called out. "If ye're going off to see my cousin, ye might consider picking her some flowers."

Alex stopped and pivoted around, doubting his ears. "Pick her flowers?" What the hell kind of men picked flowers? If the crew happened to see there'd be mutiny for sure.

"All the men in Camlochlin do it, Captain. From lads to warriors, young and old. I'm told my grandsire started it by picking flowers for my grandmere, but the Grants insist it began with Jamie, who mended the tattered heart of a young Maggie MacGregor by showering her with flowers."

"What the hell kind of people am I entangling meself with?" he muttered to himself.

"What kind should I pick?" he called out a moment later. After he lost his mind.

Her cousin shrugged, deciding suddenly to be no longer helpful. "Whatever ye think she would like."

How was he supposed to know what she'd like? Why was he even entertaining the idea of picking her flowers? Wild orchids immediately came to mind. He thought of Caitrina on the way back to the village. It had been two nights since he'd touched her, kissed her. They sat around the bonfires with the others and pretended that their bodies weren't aching for each other's embrace.

They smiled respectfully when they met on a path, hooding their eyes from the temptation of glancing upon desire and coming away unscathed. But their need for each other was palpable. Alex knew the others could feel it. It made the balmy air thicker, hotter. The nights, longer and lonelier.

He'd never kept himself from a woman before. He'd never had to control his desires until now. He did it out of respect for her cousin, her kin. Hell, what was he going to do about her kin? If they didn't come for him, he'd have to bring Caitrina back to Skye after he found his treasure. He hoped her father was a reasonable man and didn't mind a pirate courting his daughter. He was going mad. He was sure of it. Only madness would have him pondering talking to a gel's father, risking a claymore in his gut. But the treasure he'd found, the one he'd attained, was well worth the risk.

He wanted Caitrina. He wanted to feel her quivering body in his hands again. But more than that, he wanted to win her heart, her affections. He didn't care why. He would do whatever he needed to do.

He smiled, looking over the thick bushes of pink and yellow jasmine swaying in the slight breeze. He moved toward the flowers, their fragrance reminding him of her. Releasing a dagger from his sash, he snipped a dozen of each color and held the bunch out before him like a torch.

He realized what he looked like when he saw Anjali and her dearest friend, Hester, staring at him from three huts away. He put down his arm as he passed them, but it was too late.

"I not be knowin' how I feel about dee tradition of killin' flowers to show regard."

Alex glanced down at the wilting bouquet and agreed

with her. "Terrifyingly, 'tis more than regard," he told her, hoping his admission would earn him forgiveness.

It did.

She granted him a wide smile that hadn't changed since she was two. "I knew eet!" she boasted. "I saw how ya look at her. She's out wit Samuel and Charlie by dee water."

"Thank ya, Anj, I'll leave ya somethin' pretty before I go."

"Not flowers!" she called out over her shoulder as she and Hester continued on their way. "Don't kill any more of doze!"

Alex's smile faded when he passed the last hut and the seashore came into view. His eyes searched the coastline until he found them walking this way. What did he know of courting? It was too late to leave. And he wouldn't have gone anyway. He'd killed the damned jasmine and he was going to make sure he gave it to her. He returned her smile while he picked up his steps to meet them.

"Are ye visiting a grave nearby?" Caitrina asked him when they met in the sand.

He raised his brow, not understanding her question right away. When she glanced at his bouquet, he shoved it toward her.

"Aye," he told her. "Mine."

"Alex?" Charlie, Anjali's brother, stepped forward, eyeing the bouquet. "Is she yars?"

Caitrina wasn't any man's possession, and to call her his before he wed her would dishonor her, according to Kyle. But that didn't make it any easier for Alex to deny her. He dropped his hand when she accepted his offering, then looked at Charlie when he spoke. "Nay. She's not."

"Nevertheless." Her voice stopped him when he turned to leave. "I would speak to ye alone."

He nodded, offering his hand to her and trying to ignore the flood of pathetic joy he felt that she liked his offering.

Hell. He loved her. She left him breathless, mindless, helpless. It scared the hell out of him.

"Thank ye fer the flowers," she said, turning up her chin so she could shine her radiant smile and set those large blue eyes on him. "They're verra' bonny."

He nodded, not really knowing what to say. When she dipped her face into the jasmine and inhaled, he watched like one stricken. He didn't like it. He felt weak, a bit queasy in the belly, a little soft in the knees. It was repulsive and needed to be stopped.

But not now. Now, he wanted to kiss her. Now, he didn't give a rat's arse about who might take issue with his feelings for her. Let her kin come. Let his crew mumble. Let Kyle disapprove of their passion.

"I've missed ya, lass."

She moved in closer, tilting her face up to meet his. "Prove it, Captain," she whispered.

He smiled, intending to do just that.

Chapter Twenty-Seven

Trina gazed at Alex poised above her. She smiled at him while he moved his hips to a rhythm as spellbinding as the sounds around her; water falling and crashing below her, the dulcet cries of many birds, the rustle of leaves all around her. His body filled her, slowly, deeply, each thrust a dance that led her to the edge of reason.

She wanted more. Like some succubus of fable, she hungered for every part of him. She would be mortified later, but now she curled her calves around his waist and lifted herself to him, accepting him, drawing him deeper. He was hard enough to wedge himself into the tightest crevice, and big enough to hurt going in, despite the days she'd had to recover from their first encounter. She groaned with the pain and with the pleasure of taking him from head to hilt.

She scored her fingers down his sides, his hips, finally stopping on his muscled thighs. He dipped his face to hers, his eyes closed, his jaw clenched. Ecstasy. Aye, she felt it too, drenching her, threatening to overtake her.

She didn't want it to be over, and neither did he. She

looked at him, loving the sight of him above her, his hair falling about his handsome face, his playful mouth transformed into a dark, sensual smile that quickened her pulse.

She was in love with him. Whatever else she wanted in her life faded in importance. She was losing her heart to a pirate. No, it was already lost. She didn't care. Not now, when his arm caught her up behind her back and he hefted her up off the grass. She tightened her thighs around him and arched her spine while he laved his tongue down her neck to her breast. Her tight nipple ached in his mouth as he sucked and teased her with his teeth.

Wrapping her arms around him, she clung to his neck while he sat up on his haunches. She wanted to tell him how she felt, but by his own admission, Alex Kidd had had many women. She was likely just another one. He didn't love her. He loved sailing, and the sea, and rutting tavern wenches.

She closed her eyes and rolled them up at the titillating size of him driving her ever higher. When he arched her back and drank more from her breasts, she thought she might burst in colors of gold and red. She wanted to cry out, to scream with pleasure. She could do so and no one would hear them but the birds.

Squeezing her rump in his hands, he guided her over the length of his long, sleek cock, back down and then up again, until he took her to the brink of utter surrender.

But he wasn't willing to end it just yet.

Lifting her off him as though she weighed nothing, he turned her around and then set her backward on his steel lance. For some reason, she remembered how he felt in her mouth. She grew wetter and his movements grew slicker. With her back pressed to his chest, he carried her on his thighs over waves of pleasure. She knew it wouldn't take much more to surrender, and when he cupped her breast in one hand and her opening with the other, she looped her arms high over her head and let him take her to oblivion.

Behind her, he swept her hair away from her nape and bit her neck while he filled her to overflowing.

When it was over, she lay in his arms beneath swaying palms and a cloudless sky. She was certain, as the breeze brought with it the scent of wild orchids and tropical dew, that no matter how many men she met in her life, none would compare to him. No matter what other lands she visited after this, nothing would ever compare to the Islands.

"Was it difficult to leave this place, Alex?" she asked against him.

"Aye. I didn't want to go, but me father had come fer me. I had no choice."

"Did ye return then as soon as ye were able?"

"I returned a few times, with Sam and some of the others, but after a while I stopped comin' back."

"Why?" She closed her eyes against his chest and listened to his heartbeat.

"Because I wasn't the lad who left."

She kissed his skin and sat up to scan the lush, green landscape below, the waterfall to her right. He'd set them high upon a cliff where no one would happen upon them. She could scream his name until her lungs burst, and no one would hear. "This is paradise, Alex. Did it break yer heart to leave?"

He didn't answer right away, and she looked down into his sable eyes. He smiled as if he couldn't help it.

"'Twas hard. If ya stay, 'twill be hard fer ya. Ya will

miss home so bad that at times ya'll think ya're goin' mad. If ya develop a love fer the sea like I did, yar choice, though it be hard, will be simple. Ya'll choose this life over them."

He'd warned of this before. Was she willing to not return home? Mayhap never return? How bad would she get out here? What might she do that was so bad she wouldn't be able to face her kin after doing it? She was raised in the faith. She didn't think she would sacrifice her soul fer any lifestyle. If she ever felt she might be close to crossing any line, she would return to her mountains. Other than that, she came from a line of men who'd done things they would have preferred not to have done. She'd suffer no disapproval upon her return to Camlochlin.

Still, she thought she should know what soul-snatching demons lurked on the sea.

"What have ye done, Alex?" she asked him softly, turning to look at him rather than the glorious tropical scenery around her. *He* made her heart throb. He and nothing else. "What have ye done that has kept ye away from yer home?"

He looked deep into her eyes and lifted his fingers to her cheek. He stroked her with the backs of his knuckles, poring over her as though she were a map to some priceless treasure. Did he love her? He looked at her as if he did.

"Ya and Kyle speak of honor, but out at sea, there's no place fer it. Ya have to find ways to survive, to live. I became a rogue. A dishonest, thievin' rogue. I've killed more men than I can number, stole their ships, their goods. I'm afraid I won't find equal measure against yar moral code."

Would she hold him to the codes by which she was

raised? Could she steal, kill for coin? Could she truly ever be a pirate?

She opened her mouth to tell him when she spotted a huge green lizard basking on a sunlit branch. "What in heavens is that thing?"

Alex looked up. "An iguana. 'Twill not harm ya."

She would never get close enough to find out.

When someone's shout boomed through the air behind the reptile, she nearly leaped out of Alex's arms.

"Dey've landed, Alex!" Charlie rushed out of the trees behind the cliff. The iguana raced away, its long tail swishing as it ran. "Dey are lookin' fer ya, brudda."

Who was "they"? Trina thought as she scrambled for her clothes to cover herself. Her kin? Had they found her already? Her heart raced until she felt faint. Would her father try to harm Alex?

"What ship do they sail?" Alex asked while he yanked his breeches over his legs.

"Dee warship *Excellence*," Charlie answered, his coal eyes flicking to Trina, then off her just as quickly.

"Captain Harris," Alex identified, relieving her of the fear that her kin had arrived. He helped her to her feet once she was dressed and tugged her along, down the back of the cliff and back to the village.

When they arrived, everyone was scurrying to and fro like frightened children.

"Alan, I found him!" Charlie called out to another islander, who barked an order at two of the men running.

"Ya should be on yar way to distributin' pistols. Move!"

Trina watched them fly away on bare feet. They weren't running in fear, but to prepare.

Prepare for what? If she understood Charlie correctly,

the Royal Navy had arrived. How were these peaceful islanders going to help Alex? Were they foolish enough to try to fight the queen's navy?

"Alex," Alan called out to him. "Yar crew is at dee ready."

"What are we going to do?" she asked, turning to Alex.

"Not us, lass. Ya will be remainin' with Charlie. I'll come fer ya when 'tis over."

"Nae!" she commanded. "Are ye mad to deny me to fight at yer side? My own brothers wouldna' ask me to wait with the children."

"Yar brothers don't want to spend every day with ya until their last. They don't see their brats in yar eyes and they haven't considered givin' up everything they ever thought made them happy fer ya."

What? Did he mean it or was he just trying to get her to obey him? Either way, how could she argue when he made such claims? He brought a smile to her face while bringing tears to her eyes and palpitations to her heart.

After a brief kiss, so brief, in fact, that she had no time to recover from his declaration, he left her standing there with Charlie. Just Charlie. Everyone else was gone.

"Ye dinna' truly mean to guard me, do ye, Charlie?" she asked with a playful smirk curling her lips and making her dimples flash.

He returned her smile with a curious one of his own. "Ya don't truly mean to disobey him after ya agreed?"

"I agreed to nothing and ye know it."

His downcast eyes proved her correct, but his gaze didn't remain lowered for long. "It don't matter if ya agreed or not. Ya're stayin' here wit me like he said."

In the end, Charlie proved a worthy opponent. He sang while she threatened him and laughed when she flirted. It took actual tears ... *tears* ... to make him cave.

She wasn't a fool. She didn't rush to the shore, ready to die for Alex. She clung close to the trees and hid.

The crew was there, including Kyle, standing at the ready behind Alex. "Didn't think I'd see ya again so soon, Captain Harris," she heard Alex call out. She kept her eye on him while he sauntered closer to the naval captain. She moved in, readying her arrow, until she stood at Kyle's side. "What do ya want this time?"

Captain Harris was a tall man, with long limbs and a pointy nose that twitched like a rat at the scents around him. His dark gray eyes flicked beneath his hat to Alan and a group of island men holding their tar-dipped arrows close to a small fire in the sand. "I'm here," he finally said, returning his gaze to Alex, "to collect the map to where your father hid the *Quedagh Merchant*."

"What makes ya think I have such a map?"

Indeed, Trina wondered the same thing. He'd gotten the map only after going to Camlochlin. Who else knew her kin had the map? Alex and his crew had arrived in Skye with that Mr. Andersen who claimed to be a friend. But Alex had left him behind in Camlochlin. Did Mr. Andersen know where the ship was hidden? If so, why hadn't he simply gone to the navy and told them himself? It didn't make any sense. She looked around at the men surrounding Alex on the beach. They were loyal to him, weren't they? Her eyes searched for Mr. Pierce. Why wasn't he here at Alex's side? He knew about the map. He knew where they were headed and could have corresponded their destination to the navy while they were in Portugal. But how could he do it if he loved Alex the way she genuinely believed he did?

"There is a spy among your men, Captain Kidd." Harris told him smugly.

"Aye," Alex admitted with a casual shrug. "So I've been told." He turned to the men behind him and found her instead. Trina saw his skin go pale. He masked it well an instant later when he returned his attention, seemingly unshaken, to Harris. "Ya're not a man of any values. Why don't ya tell me the spy's name?"

Harris laughed and then scrambled for his hat when the wind blew it off his head. "You will discover it soon enough. Surrender the map and I'll let you live. You have my word."

Alex grinned and spread his arms at his sides. "Ya'll have to kill me to get it."

"I'll sink your ship," Harris warned.

Alex shook his head. "Ya still won't get it."

When the English captain raked his gaze over the islanders, casting an unspoken threat, Alex moved toward him.

Weapons went up on both sides.

"Ya have an hour to leave this island," Alex told him ignoring the naval soldiers before him. "If ya're still here after that time, I will slaughter yar entire crew. I will leave *ya* alive to go back and bear witness to yar superiors of yar failure. Savvy, Captain Harris?"

Surprisingly, Harris nodded and turned back for his ship. Alex watched them go and then turned to her.

Trina knew he was angry with her for disobeying him again. Well, worse, she'd lied right to his face, promising to stay with Charlie. She thought she could speak with him about it later, but his eyes on her glinted with raw anger.

"Miss Grant, will ya continue to defy me at every turn?"

"That depends," she answered him. "Will ye continue to treat me like a helpless child? Ye know how well I can shoot an arrow. Ye need my arm."

He looked like he wanted to throttle her. She'd seen

the same look on her father's face many times when her mother frustrated him.

"When I need yar arm," he said, reaching down to lift her off her feet and over his shoulder, "I'll let ya know. Right now though, I want ya off this beach and ya will obey yar captain, savvy?"

She sighed against his back. Would he always be this pigheaded? "Savvy, Captain."

Chapter Twenty-Eight

$\mathcal{T}$rina sat around the fire that night, pondering what to do about Alex and his resistance to letting her do her duty as part of his crew. Her grandmere had fought alongside her grandsire. Her mother would have died at her father's side against the English. What the hell was wrong with a woman against a man, or even a few of them? It was sweet of Alex not to want to watch her die, but insulting that he thought so little of her fighting skills.

They were almost done with supper when Mr. Pierce finally returned from wherever it was that he'd been all day. She watched him take his usual place directly at Alex's right.

Alex stared at him for a moment that seemed to stretch on forever. "Where have ya been?"

"Can we discuss it in pri—"

"No!" Alex's booming voice startled her. She looked at him in time to see him rising to his feet, clutching a cup of rum. "Kyle!" he commanded. "Walk with me. Ya also." He crooked his index finger to Trina and she followed.

Pierce looked up at his friend, as surprised by his invitation as Kyle was. He said nothing as Alex left the circle, and went off with her and Kyle.

They walked along an overgrown path, lit by tall torches shoved into the ground. She knew where they were headed. The beach, where Alex was closest to the sea.

"So tell me again, MacGregor. What are yar suspicions about Sam? Yars too, Caitrina, if they be different from his."

Was he truly giving thought to the possibility that his friend...? She turned to his profile and studied him. She saw the pain etched into his face. Pierce was his friend. She'd been cold not to understand earlier how deeply this would hurt him.

She hoped Kyle would discern to move slowly, not bombard him with all their misgivings at once. He needed to hear the evidence presented and form his own judgments.

"First and foremost," Kyle began, "we believe him to be the brother of Captain David Pierce of the Royal Army."

As she'd hoped, Kyle paused and proceeded with the right amount of hesitancy. But Alex didn't wait for any further suspicions. He walked up to the rolling surf and looked out into the darkness.

"If he is, he never told me." Alex turned around and looked behind him at the two of them. "He was not on the island all day."

"I know, Captain," Kyle told him. "I looked fer him."

"I looked fer him too," Alex admitted. "I looked fer him everywhere on the island." He paused and turned back to the sea, his voice deepening with the pain of what he was saying. "If he wasn't on the island, he had to be on a boat, and he wasn't on ours."

Trina wanted to go to him, to throw herself into his arms and promise she would never betray him or break his heart. She knew he believed himself to be a monster, one that couldn't return home because of shame. But they didn't know the pirate captain here. They only knew Alex, the lad whose laughter had never changed.

She moved toward him, repentant of disobeying him in front of Charlie. He deserved more than that. She didn't fling herself into his arms when she reached him, but took his hand. "Whatever is true or not true aboot Mr. Pierce, one fact remains, Alex. Yer kin love ye and stand united with ye, and so do I."

"As do I," Kyle agreed, then added, "Stand with ye, that is."

Alex looked at him first and grinned, enveloping his true emotions in charm and likability. But if Trina could almost read them, Kyle would find no trouble at all in doing so. She was glad her cousin wasn't fooled by the captain's air of constant control. It made Alex human.

When he looked at her though, the veil fell away, even against his will. His gaze softened on her, sending heat everywhere his eyes settled. "Ya love me then?"

"What?" She smiled at him like he was mad. "What would possess ye to assume such a ridiculous—"

"Ya said me kin love me, as do *ya*."

She cast him a mocking side glance. Neither of them took notice of Kyle's leave. "Ye are wishful thinking, Captain. I've bewitched ye."

In an instant she found herself swept up in his arms, his mouth pressed hard to hers. He kissed her senseless, until she transcended earth and time and ceased to feel anything but love for him. She adored him, would give up all for him, even her home and her kin, even her life.

All at once her senses came flooding back to her, like a tumultuous, rushing wave. Her heart raced wildly against both their chests. The scent of him, briny, sandy with a hint of almond, brushed across her nostrils and went straight to her head. Her touch over the tight sinew of his arms made his muscles tremble and her wild for more of him.

She drew back just an inch from his mouth. "Before I give in to ye again and say something I may regret." *Like I love ye madly and will follow ye to the ends of the earth even if ye break my heart and tell me ye dinna' feel the same way.* She bit her bottom lip and inched up his body. His embrace tightened. "I would have ye know that I regret my disobedience and I intend never to disobey ye again."

He smiled at her, tempting her to tear his clothes from his body and to hell with it all. She breathed to clear her head.

"Of course, I will need yer help." She pressed her mouth to his again and kissed him softly, briefly.

"Anything I can do, beauty." He pulled her in closer.

"Ye can begin by never again telling me what I can and cannot do. I understand yer fears about me fighting, my sweet captain," she said breathlessly against his teeth. "I will not put myself in unnecessary danger, but ye will find yerself less angry with me if ye just cease ordering me aboot."

Trina expected a number of different reactions from Alex. He might have ignored her, since she did seem to be driving him mad with her mouth and her body pressed close to his. He might have become belligerent. What man didn't enjoy ordering his woman about? Even if his woman never obeyed his orders, he still liked giving them. She'd seen it enough in Camlochlin. But why agree to do what he says and then not do it? It formed mistrust and Alex didn't need any more of that in his life. She expected a grin when his pride swelled and compelled him to challenge and then deny her. Mayhap he'd smile, since he had, after all, made her the constant source of his amusement.

She didn't expect him to toss back his head and laugh at the heavens.

"What is so humorous?" she asked, insulted and a bit hurt.

"'Tisn't humorous, Caitrina. 'Tis refreshin' and bold and exactly what I've come to expect from ya."

She smiled, liking his answer and liking even more that she made him laugh tonight after so much heartbreak. She moved to kiss him again. Mr. Pierce's clearing his throat stopped her.

"Pardon me, Miss Grant," he interrupted them, twisting his cotton cap in his hands and avoiding her glance. "I need a word with the cap'n alone. 'Tis important."

Alex nodded and smiled at her when she stepped out of his embrace.

"Of course, Mr. Pierce," she granted easily. What they suspected about him was based on nothing solid. His affection for Alex was either genuine or he was an absolute master of masking his true inner motives. And damn it, but she liked the quartermaster. She didn't want to think he was betraying Alex and she didn't want to see Alex suffer if he was.

Before she left, she turned back to Alex. She hadn't gotten her answer. "D'ye agree to helping me then, Captain?"

Och, but his wide, dashing grin was devastating to her good senses. She tossed one of her own back at him.

"Aye, I agree," he promised, as undone by her as she was by him. "Miss Grant?"

"Aye, Captain?"

"What is it ya might regret tellin' me?"

She smiled and blushed, looking in Mr. Pierce's direction. "It can wait."

Reluctantly, she left their company and headed back in the direction of the village. She had no intentions of going too far, of course. She wanted to hear what Pierce had to tell him. She didn't feel bad about eavesdropping. In fact, she wished Kyle were there with her so they could compare opinions.

"What did ya just agree to?" she heard Pierce ask, a trace of humor blending with familiarity in his tone.

"To help her not to disobey me by not giving her any more orders."

Listening from a nearby stand of dense brush, Trina braced herself for Samuel's disapproval. She heard him laugh instead.

"Hell, ya're in trouble."

"Aye, I guessed that."

Even if she didn't know them, Trina would have known that they were longtime friends. There was an ease about the way they spoke together, laughed together. A camaraderie they shared with no one else.

She prayed they were all wrong about Pierce.

"There is something I need to discuss with ya, Alex." The quartermaster grew serious, coming, Trina suspected, to his point.

"I figured as much when ya left the island," Alex said softly, flatly. "I've been ponderin' where ya might have been."

"I was procurin' fer us a safe passage aboard another ship."

He was confessing? And so easily? Och, Kyle would

be sorry he missed this! She tilted her head and continued to listen.

"Another ship?" Alex asked, sounding surprised by his friend's reply. "What ship? To go where?"

"To the Bahamas," Sam told him. His voice sounded urgent, honest. But what did she know? "To speak with a man who believes the map ya possess is a fake. That it was—"

"Captain!" Gustaaf's voice boomed through Sam's, "another English ship has arrived on the eastern shore!"

"How many?" She heard Alex call back, already moving.

"One, a schooner," answered the Dutchman. "Dropped anchor and is still in the water."

Och, who the hell was it now? Was this his life, always trying to keep ahead of the law? She'd wanted adventure, and hell was she getting it. She thought, while Alex and Sam raced past her on their way to the opposite side of the island, she should stay where she was this time. She didn't want to, but for him she did it. She would obey him and not fight... at least for now.

Chapter Twenty-Nine

$\mathcal{A}$lex peered through his spyglass and watched the schooner floating on the black water. He didn't recognize it.

A ship docked at Parrot Cay was nothing out of the ordinary, but one that anchored at night and on the deserted side of the island meant trouble. The trouble was most likely for him, since Harris had already found them. The navy was on his arse. Alex still wondered how they had found him so quickly. He lowered the spyglass from his eye and cut a brief glace at Sam.

Nay. Harris spoke of someone else when he'd warned Alex of a traitor in his midst. Not Sam. But what of this brother Sam allegedly had? Why the hell did he want him to go to the Bahamas? And what was it he'd said about his map?

Movement on the water drew him back to his spyglass. A smaller boat disengaged from the schooner and set a course for the beach. They paddled slowly, leaving the faintest moonlit trail behind. He watched them come ashore, three men…and a dog. At least, Alex hoped it was a dog and not a lion or a bear. It was difficult to make the beast out in the shimmering pale light. He remembered Caitrina telling him about Sam's brother getting a pup from Edmund MacGregor last year and this one was certainly as ugly as the ones in Camlochlin.

His heart sank a little, but he refused...he simply refused to believe that Sam would betray him—that he could have been betraying him for the last eight years.

He looked to his left when Kyle appeared at his side behind the dense shrub, silent and breathless.

"Everyone is being alerted," the Highlander informed him. "Gustaaf and Charlie are getting them ready."

"Good."

"D'ye know who they are, Captain?"

"Nay, I don't." Alex turned to the man on his right. "Ya?"

Sam shook his head.

"From what I understand," Kyle continued, "there is just the one ship? A schooner?"

"'Tis all I see out there," Alex told him and handed Kyle his spyglass. "A faster ship able to cut our time in a little more than half."

"They are naval, fer certain," Kyle said, making a closer examination. He remained silent while he studied what he could make out. "I will guess the captain himself is among them..." his words paused while he squinted into the glass.

Sam rose to his feet and walked around Alex's back.

"Is that a...dog?" Kyle removed the glass from his eye and looked harder at what he was seeing. He turned in Sam's previous direction, but Alex could tell that he already knew the quartermaster had moved. Kyle wasn't looking for Sam. He was looking for Alex and met his eye straight on. Something like deep regret passed across his face before he said, "There's only one Englishman with a dog that ugly."

"That's what I told him." Sam smiled and drew his dagger at the same time. He caught Kyle around the neck and held him still with the tip. "But he swore it came from good stock."

Alex fought the dizziness spinning his head, the collapse of his bones to the ground. This wasn't happening. Not right before his eyes. Sam? "Sam?" He shook his head. Nay. He must be dreaming. This couldn't be his best friend holding a knife to the young MacGregor.

"Captain," the Highlander said, defying the pressure of Sam's blade against his throat to keep silent. "'Tis Captain David Pierce who approaches. His brother."

The dog barked and the sound echoed through the palm trees and through Alex's soul. "Sam," he said quietly. "What the hell are ya doin'? Get yar damned dagger away from his throat before I begin to believe all this and strike ya down where ya stand."

"Alex," the quartermaster began quickly, desperately. "I wanted to explain earlier. Whatever this looks like—"

"Whatever this looks like?" Alex asked, his laugher sounding shrill and forced. "It looks like ya are about to betray me to yar English brother!"

"I would explain—"

"Do ya mean to defend betrayal, Sam?" Alex's hard voice cut him off. "Ya above all else know how I feel about it. I would kill ya before I listened to it. Let him go now. He isn't part of this."

"First, I would have ya know this one thing," Sam pressed foolishly.

Alex was no longer listening but turned his attention to

the men approaching them, the hound's bark giving away their position.

The man and his two companions stopped when Alex cocked his flint.

"Don't!" Sam shouted at him, tightening his grip on Kyle as leverage to keep his brother alive. "Put the pistol down, Alex." To his brother, he said, "What are ya doin' here? I thought we were to meet in Guana."

"I grew impatient."

"If ya want to live," Alex warned the captain in a low voice, ignoring Sam and their conversation, "call off yar dogs . . . both of them."

"Damn ya, Alex," Sam pressed on. "Listen to what we say."

Alex laughed and turned to him, giving Sam's brother the perfect opportunity to knock the pistol from his hand. The intruder didn't stop there but struck Alex in the head with the hilt of his sword, rendering him unconscious.

He awoke sometime later aboard the *Expedition*, in the custody of Captain David Pierce of the damned Royal Navy. It appeared the army captain had transferred.

He was sitting up. He tried to move and discovered that his hands were bound behind him, his ankles, in front. He looked around and guessed, judging by the fine furnishings and spacious quarters, that he was inside the captain's cabin.

For now, he was the only one there. Had they taken Kyle? Worse, had they taken Caitrina? Anyone else from his crew or family on the island? Despite his throbbing head, he managed to keep Sam's betrayal fresh in his mind. He had to, else some foolish part of him continue to resist what was right before his eyes. He couldn't tell himself that it was impossible anymore, because it wasn't.

The ship was moving. How far had they gone? Were

they heading toward the Bahamas? It had been Sam's plan all along to get him there. He had to get loose. He had to make certain no one else was aboard.

How was he going to get the hell off this boat without killing Sam? He wanted to kill him now. He closed his eyes and ground his jaw. How many times had he and Sam spoken of his father's crew abandoning their captain? Men were loyal until there was nothing left for their loyalty to gain them. Women were the same. They all sought to elevate their status, whether they were daughters of good men or tavern whores.

He knew all this and yet he'd trusted Sam. This was worse than anything his father's crew had ever done, worse than what Madalena had done to him by the years the deception spanned alone. Hell, he felt like the most pathetic kind of fool. What a disgustingly trusting, sappy heart he possessed. What kind of crew would want to sail with a captain who couldn't see danger right before his eyes? For eight damn years! He wasn't fit to be their captain. Anyone's captain.

The cabin door opened and Sam entered, his gaze low, his steps reluctant to enter. What had he tried to say earlier? Alex didn't care. What defense could one have for betrayal?

"How long, Judas?"

Sam stopped in his tracks and looked up, finally meeting Alex's dark gaze. "From the beginning."

Almost a decade of deception. Alex closed his eyes. He wanted to be angry, to feel rage, but his wretched heart bled in his chest. He wondered why some souls never experienced this kind of gut-wrenching pain while for others it began with their mothers and continued on with almost every person who meant a damn.

"Why?" he demanded, his anger taking root within some chamber of his heart. He felt it grow and nourished it with memories of counting on Sam in battles and drinking with him after a night of passion with a woman. How clever Sam must have thought himself. How damned clever. "I ask why?"

Samuel looked away again, and ran his palm over his face. "They wanted the *Quedagh Merchant*, Alex."

"I know, Sam," he roared back at him. "They killed me father fer it! Is that why ya betrayed me, ya sorry black-hearted bastard? Fer the ship?"

When Sam didn't answer, Alex slumped forward in his chair. The treasure they killed his father for...it was the treasure Sam wanted. He felt rage well up behind his eyes and his muscles grow tense. He would kill Sam for this. What pirate worth his weight in salt would blame him? His quartermaster had stabbed him in the back for his treasure. It was so damn hard for him to believe it all. Not Sam. Anyone but Sam.

"Where's Kyle?" he growled, vowing silently that if they had killed the Highlander, Alex would make Sam watch his brother die.

"He's unharmed on the other side of the boat." His old friend walked closer to him. "Alex," his voice deepened. "I mean to help ya, to save yar life, not hand it over to the authorities. Ya must let me explain."

"Sam." Alex lifted his head to him. He gritted his teeth and forced himself to remain still. "Though ya have deceived me, I've always spoken the truth. Have I not?"

Sam nodded.

"Then believe me now when I tell ya that if ya speak another word in yar defense, I will kill ya. I'm fightin' back the desire to do it now. Ya led the navy to me. Ya—"

"Nay," Sam argued, "not Captain Harris."

"Caitrina was correct. 'Twas ya who left the trapdoor in me wall open. Ya were in me cabin before we got there. I didn't want to believe it. Ya were there with me fer me father, Sam," Alex reminded him, not giving a damn about Sam's excuses. "Ya know how I felt about his last days alone. Was it easy for ya to deceive me ... to hand me over to me enemies?"

Sam shook his head but Alex didn't see. He closed his eyes to damn Sam to Hades. He'd been warned. Caitrina and Kyle and even Captain Harris had told him.

"My brother is not yar enemy," Sam promised. "He knew yar father and Mr. Andersen when—"

Alex was through listening to this scurvy rat dung's lies. Tilting his chair onto its two front legs, he balanced himself and rose up as far as he could on his feet. His head reached the perfect angle to ram into his opponent's jaw.

Sam went down like a lightning-blasted tree. Alex stood over him with an option of two ways to inflict the most damage with the chair tied to his back. He hesitated, not wanting to hurt Sam as much as he thought he did.

His thoughts went black an instant later when something smashed into his head from behind.

❊❊❊

Chapter Thirty

What do ye mean we shouldna' go after them? Have ye gone completely daft, Mr. Bonnet?"

Alex's first mate didn't bother to look at her when he argued, but turned toward the men instead, infuriating Trina altogether. "I'm just sayin' that we ought to know which way to go before we set sail, lads."

"We do know," Trina insisted. "I already told ye they were heading fer the Bahamas. Hester said they sailed north. What more d'ye want?"

Hester was Anjali's closest friend. It was she who informed Trina and the others what had happened. A few hours ago, she had gone off alone to visit Anjali when she'd come upon four men carrying away an unconscious two. If not for Hester, the crew might not have known what became of their captain and their mate in time to save them. But they would be saved.

Trina would make certain of it, even if she had to beat Mr. Bonnet senseless while he slept to do it.

"We must go now," she said, scanning her gaze over all the men. "While there is still time to catch up with them. A schooner will move faster than us. Right now, they have only a three-hour lead. Let's not give them a wider distance. We—"

"Mr. Bonnet's correct!" Robbie Owens called out to the others. "We need to move with caution."

"That's right!" cried Jack, the master-gunner. "If we go the wrong way it'll set us back days, may'ap weeks, and 'ho knows what in 'ell will befall the captain by then?"

Trina had to get through to them. She had Gustaaf on her side, willing to go rescue the captain and Kyle. But one man wasn't enough to man a ship, or to fight if they had to. And Trina was sure they would have to.

She looked up when Charlie entered the hut. The frond and wooden structure was big enough to house the entire village. It was a place of celebration as well as a meeting hall to discuss concerns.

"Any news of Pierce?" she asked the islander.

Sam was also missing. Hester thought she saw him on the beach with the others, as one of the four men walking. When Hester told of a beast of a mongrel dog accompanying the strangers, Trina believed it had to be David Pierce, arrived with one of Grendel and Gaza's pups.

Gustaaf denounced the notion of Samuel betraying their captain, but Mr. Bonnet claimed to have suspected Pierce of being a spy for years now.

"Nothin'," Charlie told her. "No one has seen heem."

Aye, his disappearance that night had diminished Alex's trust in him.

"Well," she said, scanning her eyes over them all. "Now we know he stands on the opposing side. If he approaches ye, ye shouldn't hesitate to kill or maim him."

"Who said we was goin' with ya on yar blind voyage?"

"Mr. Bonnet." She turned and set her gaze on him.

"I didna' know the bunch of ye were cautious, fretful men who doubted what was right there before yer eyes. I thought ye were all more intelligent than that."

As she anticipated, he squared his shoulders and tilted his chin. "Ya thought correct, lass. I want to go, but what if 'tis the wrong direction? What makes ya so sure they are sailing toward the Bahamas?"

She focused all her attention on his unpatched eye, letting him feel the strength in her voice, the steel conviction of her words. "I heard Samuel Pierce tell the captain that he'd procured safe passage fer them to the Bahamas."

"What the hell fer?" Bonnet sneered.

"That's what the captain wanted to know," she told him. "Pierce never got the chance to tell him because news of the schooner reached them first. I told ye already that I believe Sam betrayed the captain. I tell ye I'm correct. Though I have no proof as yet, I ask ye to trust me. If ye decide not to, I'm still going. The captain's life and the life of my cousin mean too much to me to do nothing. Ye either come with me or wait here. The islanders will help me rescue them."

She stared him down for a moment or two, determined to set sail without him. "Make up yer mind, pirate. We're wasting precious time."

Admiration flashed across his single eye before he raked it over her body, from foot to crown. He looked away when she covered the hilt of her sword, ready to draw it against him. She was the only woman on their ship and she knew that at some point she was going to have to convince them that she could defend herself against any of the men here.

But it would not be today.

"Mr. Bonnet," she said, "are ye coming or not?"

He scanned his gaze at the others, some for the idea and some against. "Aye, we're comin'."

She smiled and turned to Cooper. "Take the helm. Take us toward the Sargasso Sea. Gustaaf, take Charlie with ye and quickly gather any islanders who wish to come with us. We will meet ye on the ship in a quarter hour, sooner if ye can."

She left Gustaaf and barked out orders to the boatswain, the master-gunner, the striker, and the surgeon before Mr. Bonnet stopped her.

"I'm first mate, deary. I give the orders."

"Of course," she repented and then smiled at the shrewd glint in his eye. He saw, with that one eye, better than some men could see with two. He knew he wouldn't be giving orders for long but he didn't seem to mind.

Four hours later, Cooper sailed *Poseidon's Adventure* toward the Sargasso Sea.

High upon the masts, in the crow's nest, Trina shielded her eyes from the sun and looked out over the vast ocean for any sign of the schooner that carried away the two men she loved most in the world. The wind snatched away her breath and her heart pounded like a drum.

She was beginning to worry that they'd come the wrong way. Just because Hester saw them sail north didn't mean they continued on that course for long.

She had to find them. If they had to sail this ship around the world, she wouldn't give up. Alex had come for her when Captain Henley would have used her for his pleasure and then sold her as a slave. He'd plucked Kyle from the waves and then rushed to save her, not truly knowing if she was after his map or not.

If it was indeed David Pierce who had them, their chances of remaining alive were good. She doubted Pierce would harm Kyle since he knew Kyle's family, and he most likely wanted the map. To get it, he needed Alex alive. For the most part, Alex and Kyle were safe. Still, it was better to find them before the schooner docked somewhere to possibly meet up with an entire naval fleet, which she was guessing was waiting in the Bahamas.

After another three hours with no sign of them on the horizon, Trina began to pray.

If they were on the right course, the schooner should be coming into view any time now.

The time came a bit sooner than she expected when she spotted a flash of light in the distance. She squinted, trying her hardest to make out any sign of a ship before shouting the visual. At first, she saw nothing but the residue of blinding light. She looked away and focused her vision on the deck far below. When she raised her gaze again, she saw a spot on the horizon.

She leaped from the nest and tangled her hands and feet in the ratlines. She hurried down and stopped midway. "Ship ahead!" she shouted, once, twice, then a third time with her hands cupped around her mouth. Gustaaf heard her and so did Cooper, shifting starboard.

Trina watched, captivated and frozen in terror by the sight of a thirty-foot swell rolling quickly in their direction. There wasn't enough time to make it back to the nest, where she might find some safety. She was going to have to hold on for her life. She heard Gustaaf scream her name below. She shoved her hands through the net and coiled her arms around the rope while lacing her legs through the line and locking her ankles. The roar of the water was deafening. Or was it the blood rushing to and from her heart? She braced herself. Alex and Kyle awaited her on the other side, damn it.

Her gaze followed the ascent of the wave rising over Alex's ship. She squeezed her eyes shut and held on for all she was worth.

Poseidon's Adventure didn't sink, or even go under. It did, however, ride the colossal wave, tilting the ship, and Trina dangling from it, into an almost vertical angle. If having her weight jerked backward didn't make her let go, nothing would. She kept her eyes closed and her breath held when thick walls of sea spray drenched her.

Her weight shifted again and she opened her eyes to find the ship on calmer waters once again...and Gustaaf scrambling, soaking wet, up the ratlines.

"I'm fine!" she called down to him. "Go back and get us to them, Gustaaf." Shockingly enough, the huge Dutchman obliged and left her alone to return to the nest.

The dot on the horizon had grown into the outline of a ship, a schooner to be precise. They were found! Now she could return to her cabin and gather her weapons. Alex and Kyle were found, and Samuel Pierce was going to explain his betrayal and then pay for it.

She made it down to the quarterdeck quickly, thankful that all her practicing was worth disobeying Alex. She would point this out to him after she rescued him.

She sprinted inside Alex's cabin and reappeared a short while later securing various daggers to her waistband and beneath her bandanna. She ran toward Gustaaf with her quiver strapped to her back. She'd learned to sprint across the deck without stabbing her soles with splinters.

"How long 'til we reach them?"

She still didn't know how to determine their distance in leagues.

"We don't know yet if it's them," Gustaaf pointed out while he looked through Alex's spyglass, the one they found strewn behind a thick purple-flowered shrub. "We don't know if we travel in the correct direction."

"'Tis them," she told him, convinced, and letting him hear it. "Tell Mr. Bonnet to stay his course."

Her friend set his pale deep-set eyes on her. "You were born for this, were you not?"

She nodded and took the spyglass to look through it while he called out to the first mate.

In turn, Mr. Bonnet shouted the order to Cooper at the helm.

Now that she'd found the ship, she needed to consider who it might carry. All she knew was that a huge mongrel had accompanied them. But that had told her much. The man who kidnapped Alex and Kyle was most likely David Pierce. And that meant that she and Kyle had been correct about not trusting Samuel. She stared off into the distance while the salt spray whipped her braid off her shoulders.

"If we discover Mr. Pierce behind this, what do we do, Gustaaf?"

"If Mr. Pierce is behind this," Alex's loyal Dutch friend told her, "Alex has likely killed him by now."

Trina shook her head and cut her gaze to him. "D'ye believe Alex could kill him?"

She didn't have to draw it out for Gustaaf. The doubt etching his face spoke his true answer. He turned to Cooper and shouted, almost bursting her eardrum.

"Faster then, Coop! Or do I have to go up there and fly this thing myself?"

Cooper hollered back a vile reply, having to do with shoving Gustaaf's nether parts up into his belly with the tip of his foot.

Trina blocked out their shouts and leaned forward into the forceful gale. She prayed her men were alive and asked for help in rescuing them. Could she board Pierce's ship? Could she fly on lines over the waves and land with death at the end of her sword?

Aye. She could.

She could do it for Alex and Kyle.

She was a pirate.

Chapter Thirty-One

$\mathcal{A}$ lex dreamed of sunshine skipping lazily over the glistening coral dunes, of bright green iguanas feasting on mangos, and of the ocean spraying him with her refreshment.

The spray smelled foul.

Slowly, he opened his eyes and looked into a nest of blond fur. The beast's cold, wet nose bumped him in the mouth as it turned its massive head and set its dark eyes on Alex.

Alex tried to push the beast away but remembered quickly enough, when he tried to move, that he was bound to a chair.

He cursed when the hound lapped its long tongue across his face.

"Risa! Down!"

Alex watched the mongrel retreat and sit at the left heel of a man who didn't resemble Sam in the least. This one was green around the edges. "Captain Pierce," he said, trusting what Kyle had told him the night they were captured.

"Captain Kidd."

"Where is Kyle MacGregor? Did ya harm anyone on the island?"

"No one even saw us, Alex," Sam spoke at his brother's right.

Alex didn't acknowledge him. "Where's Kyle?" he asked the captain again.

"He is safe," the captain assured him, then turned to Sam. "Bring Kyle to us, please, Sam." When Sam left, his brother returned his attention to Alex. "The MacGregors are friends, especially Edmund, Kyle's brother. I'm not fool enough to harm the lad. You also should use caution with the daughter of Connor Grant. His battle skills are still spoken of in the queen's army."

"Leave her out of this," Alex warned. There wasn't much he could do...yet. He almost had one hand free behind him. He needed a little more time.

"So then, it's true." David Pierce clutched his belly and went pale for a moment when the ship lurched upward. "You do care for her."

"Captain," Alex cut him off and brought him back to why Alex was here on his ship. "Did ya take me prisoner to discuss Captain Grant's daughter?"

Not letting himself be overcome by the sea, Pierce pulled himself together and set his bemused gaze on him. "No, I did not. And you are not my prisoner. I will set you free if you give your word not to do anything foolish. I promised my brother I wouldn't hurt you."

Alex spread his lips wide and his hands over his shoulders. He was free.

Pierce ceased smiling and drew his pistol.

"I've no intention on hurtin' ya." Alex kept his palms up, then slowly bent to untie his ankles. "It wouldn't take me long to overpower ya though. Ya're sick as a dog. Let me leave and take MacGregor with me and we'll ferget we ever met."

He kept his eyes on the captain, praying he didn't shoot.

"Then you will leave with the wrong map, Captain Kidd, and I promised your father that I would personally make certain that didn't happen."

The door opened and Sam entered with Kyle. Alex looked the lad over for any sign of mistreatment and breathed easier when he found none.

"Untie him," Alex ordered them, seeing Kyle's arms tied behind him.

"He nearly broke my jaw," Sam said, rolling his jaw to test it again. "I'd rather not."

"Kyle," Alex turned to him. "When ya're freed, don't take hand to them again. Not unless I say so."

"Aye, aye, Captain," Kyle answered without hesitation.

"Untie him," Alex ordered again. "If ya want me to listen to what ya wish to tell me, untie him."

With a sigh and a quick glance at his brother, Sam obeyed.

Free, Kyle stepped to Alex's side. "Do they have Trina?"

"Nay, I don't believe so."

"We couldn't find her actually," Captain Pierce told them. "I would prefer to bring you and Miss Grant home when our meeting here is done, Kyle."

"What ye prefer means nothing to me," Kyle replied.

Alex stepped forward, ending their conversation. "What is this about the wrong map and Sam's mad ravins' that me father was some kind of friend to ya, an English captain?"

"Let us begin at the beginning, shall we?" Pierce gathered up three more chairs, the same kind that Alex had been tied to, and invited all to sit.

Within minutes, Pierce's hellhound, Risa, crawled up into Kyle's lap as if it were the size of a kitten. It was as if the beast remembered Kyle and had missed him. The Highlander didn't seem to mind and scratched her neck.

"When I left England," Pierce began, stopping to swallow and rub his belly, "plans to have ships search you out and follow you were under way."

"Why?" Alex asked. "Do they believe the *Quedagh Merchant* is worth such effort?"

"They do," Pierce answered.

But how did they know what was aboard the stolen ship? There had been no naval men aboard his father's first ship, the *Adventure Galley*, or even afterward, when William Kidd renamed his treasure *Adventure Prize*. How did his enemies know the value of the treasure?

"How did they know I'd come into possession of the map?"

"Hendrik Andersen."

"Of course." Kyle looked up at him from Risa's fur. "If 'twasn't Sam who led the navy to ye, it had to be Andersen. The rest of yer men are loyal to ye."

Alex looked at him. This lad had proven himself right about people time and again. If he believed the men were loyal, then it was likely that they were. Alex almost smiled.

"Next question," he put to Pierce. "The MacGregors gave me the map ya claim is the wrong one. Are ya tellin' me they deceived me, as well?"

Kyle shook his head. "Nae, they had no part in this."

Pierce agreed. "They didn't know anything about the map save to give it to you after Mr. Andersen validated your identity."

"Why would me father let them give me a fake map?"

"He had no choice. Andersen was part of his crew and your father's friend. He knew about the *Quedagh Merchant* and the value of it. He knew your father fashioned a map and was going to leave it with the MacGregors for safekeeping. Your father used a fake map to distract him from the real one."

A clever plan, Alex mulled. But was any of this true? He still had many questions. "Why didn't Andersen already know the whereabouts of the prize if he was part of me father's crew?"

"Because your father hired a separate crew to sail the ship to its hidden destination."

"Wise," Kyle said and caught Alex's eye. He nodded his head as if trying to tell Alex this tale might indeed be true.

"Andersen found me in New York," Alex continued. He needed more if he was going to believe it. "He had a personal letter from me father."

"All part of the plan to expose the traitor after your father was dead, and to keep you alive."

"Me father did all this to keep me alive?"

"Of course. As your father, why wouldn't he?"

Alex shook his head. He didn't know. He didn't know if he should believe any of it.

"How do ya know all this?"

The Englishman opened his mouth and then covered it with his hand. He fought the sickness and held it in check.

"Ya haven't been sailin' long then," Alex surmised.

"Only six or so months now," the captain admitted.

Taking pity on him, Alex reached into his pocket and pinched his fingers around the cure to Pierce's malady.

"What is it?" Sam's brother eyed the tuft of herb he offered.

"An island remedy fer what ails ya."

"Why did ye not give that to me instead of piercing my ear?" Kyle asked him.

Alex glanced at him, then at his earring. "Ya're a pirate. He's not."

Satisfied, Kyle sat back in his chair while Pierce accepted the offering.

"Hold it under yar tongue."

They waited while Pierce followed Alex's instruction and tucked the herb under his tongue. After he swallowed a few times, his color returned.

"Thank you," he said, and then smiled with genuine relief.

Alex nodded. "Now tell me how ya know so much?"

"Your father told me while he was in prison," Pierce told him. "We were friends. I sailed with him for two years aboard *Adventure Galley*, before my service to the throne. We remained friends until he left this earth. While he was on trial, I was allowed into his cell to question him. During my visits, he told me about Andersen and the true map."

Alex wished he was telling the truth. It would mean that his father had a friend by his side before he died. It would also mean that Sam hadn't betrayed him. But just because he wanted it to be true didn't mean that it was.

"And ya are the only man on the earth who knows its true whereabouts?"

"I am," Pierce admitted.

This was getting harder and harder to take seriously. "Ya expect me to believe that me father trusted an English naval officer with the map he gave his life fer? Ya think me a fool?"

"That remains to be seen," Pierce said reaching for

something in his waistcoat. "I expected you to be somewhat like him. He was a hard man and there were very few he trusted."

"And, of course, ya were one of them?"

Pierce ignored his mocking grin and handed him the folded parchment he'd removed from his pocket. "One of two, just like this map. You were the other."

The cabin remained quiet while Alex looked at him, trying to see through any veneer. Finally, he unfolded the parchment and held it to the lantern.

"The real map to the *Quedagh Merchant*," Pierce told him while his eyes searched over it.

"Madagascar?" Alex looked up. "Ya're tellin' me the *Quedagh Merchant* is in Madagascar?" He didn't really care what the captain replied. Why was he listening to an English soldier and his traitorous brother anyway? They probably hoped Alex would fall for this clever tale and hand over his "fake" map for the authentic one. He almost laughed. But he was tired of listening. He was getting the hell off this boat.

"If ya had the real map all this time, why didn't ya give it to me sooner?"

Pierce shook his head. "The navy, Andersen, the governors in New York... You have many enemies, Captain Kidd. You are being watched at almost all times. I thought it best, as your father did, to distract them by letting you go to Skye and then sail here, to the Caribbean. Everyone suspects the ship is hidden here somewhere. Let them all search for you while we sail toward Africa."

Hmm, it sounded good. But—"Me father taught me one thing, Captain Pierce," he said, rising to his feet and handing the map back to Pierce. "Never trust a man. They only want yar treasure."

"The navy is comin', Alex." Sam stopped him. "Or they'll send privateers. 'Tis only a matter of time before they arrive after Harris. How long can the villages hold them off before they all die? Charlie, Anjali?"

Alex's murderous gaze silenced him.

"Captain Pierce," he said slowly, turning to look at him again. "If ya want me to believe ya, ya will have to prove to me that me father would trust ya with the treasure's true location."

"Laura Ann MacIntyre," Pierce said.

Alex stopped in his tracks. He hadn't heard that name in years. The last time was with his father, after they took a small ship called *Laura Ann* and shared rum over it later. The name was the same as that of a lass William Kidd loved and lost before he met Alex's mother. He'd never told a soul about her, save for his son and one other man, the only man his father ever trusted.

So then, David Pierce was that man.

"All right." Alex returned to his seat. His head was spinning. "What's next?"

"Andersen's plan," Captain Pierce continued, "was to travel with you to Dominica, likely try to kill you once you found the *Quedagh Merchant*. Since you stopped him, he set the navy on your arse. He's had you followed since you left Camlochlin. It was clever of you to strand Andersen on Skye, by the way."

"'Twas Sam's idea to leave him." Alex looked at his quartermaster. Sam hadn't betrayed him then. He'd done all this to help him. Alex felt like hell and was relieved at the same time over Sam's innocence.

"But 'twill do the navy nae good to follow us," Kyle surmised.

Pierce shook his head at Alex. "Because you will be

on your way to Madagascar, away from the Caribbean, where they will search you out for at least a pair of weeks, maybe longer. The rest of the navy now knows that you are indeed here since you sent Captain Harris back with his head up his arse on a near empty ship. Sam is correct. They are coming for you."

Alex nodded. "I'll sail out as soon as I return to me ship."

"I have more men and a bigger boat in the Bahamas."

"I don't need more men or a bigger boat," Alex told him.

"I'm sailing with you." Pierce held up his palm to ward off Alex's further refusal. "I promised your father I would see this through. You will not sway me."

The sound of cannon fire brought an abrupt end to whatever Alex was about to say. They all sprang to their feet as shouts could be heard from on deck as crewmen scrambled to prepare for an attack.

Pierce flew out of the cabin but Sam paused to share a word with Alex. "My greatest regret in all this was letting Miss Grant take the blame for what I had done, and it almost costing her and Kyle their lives. I needed to make certain the map hadn't been moved. I hope ya understand now, old friend."

Alex did. He'd trusted Sam. His friend hadn't let him down. He was more than happy about it. "I do understand. But I still have more questions. We'll speak later over some rum. Aye?"

Sam agreed, returning his smile and looking more at peace than he had for the past se'nnight.

When Alex climbed on deck, he was surprised to see his ship gaining upon the *Expedition*'s rear. How had his crew found him so quickly? They were coming to fight. Who led them? Mr. Bonnet? Gustaaf?

"Captain?" Kyle said, suddenly standing beside him.

Hell, the lad moved without a sound. "Ye need to do something. They're going to attack."

It was too late. *Poseidon's Adventure* was almost upon them; the Jolly Roger had been hoisted.

Alex looked around at Pierce's crew, soldiers in the royal navy. As captain of his ship, it was Alex's responsibility to weigh the odds of a possible attack and not engage at all if victory wasn't certain.

"Captain," he shouted to Pierce, then ran to join him on the sterncastle deck. "Raise yar white flag," he said, reaching him and looking out over the rail. "'Tis all that will keep them from shootin' more canons at yar ship. Ya're built fer speed. We're built fer fightin'."

Pierce studied him for a moment, then called out to his crew to raise the white flag. No one questioned him.

"What's next?" the captain asked. "I've spent most of my years on land in the army. Are the rules of engagement the same?"

Alex didn't know if they were or if they weren't, and he didn't care. "They'll be comin' aboard fer me and fer Kyle. Let me show them immediately that I am free to return to them and we will avoid bloodshed."

"Of course," the captain consented quickly. So quickly, in fact, that Alex looked at him.

"Ya don't know me and yet ya trust me word without quarrel?"

Pierce eyed him and Alex saw years of battle and bloodshed in his steel-colored gaze. "Your father's blood flows through your veins, Kidd. My brother wouldn't be so loyal to you if you weren't worthy of it. Nor, I imagine, would Mr. MacGregor or Miss Grant. But if I am wrong about you," he said calmly, "if you try to kill my brother or me, I'll kill you and your entire crew."

Alex liked David Pierce. One didn't come across his kind of confidence often. Alex wanted to find out if his bold words held any substance. "Let's agree then, not to lift a weapon against each other's crewmen."

They agreed and watched *Poseidon's Adventure* bear down on them, ropes swaying in the sea breeze as Alex's crew prepared to board ship.

Seeing Caitrina at the rail in her breeches and bandanna almost made him forget his agreement...and his reason for being. When she swung out wide over the ocean on a rope, he watched her, enthralled by her very being. Oh, God help his pitiful heart.

She was the first to jump.

She had led them.

"I'm no prisoner!" he called out, holding out his palms. "Quarter has been granted on both sides!" He wanted to run to Caitrina the instant her feet hit the deck. He wanted to take her in one arm and a rope in the other and fly them back to his ship, to his cabin, to his bed. But he remained beside Pierce, watchful of any sign of going back on their agreement. His father may have told the Englishman about Laura Ann, but now Caitrina was involved. "There will be nay fightin'!" he shouted, noting the withering disappointment on his crew's faces as they landed like a plague on a village, ready to cut down their victims.

Remarkably, Captain Pierce remained steady, his expression unchanging while pirates took over his ship.

Chapter Thirty-Two

Trina was so shocked and so relieved to see Alex and Kyle standing together on deck that she almost mislanded and went sprawling on her arse. Thankfully, she stopped herself in time. Keeping her feet from running to Alex was a much more difficult task. During their hours of searching, she feared she might never see him again. She couldn't take life without him in it. Now, here he was, and Kyle, too, looking well and unharmed. She wouldn't let anyone take them again.

What was it Alex had shouted? No fighting? Why in the world would he order such a thing about the men who'd kidnapped him? She had to keep her wits about her, do nothing foolish.

Giving David Pierce a good tongue-lashing wasn't foolish, was it? Turning to him, she laced her hands together in front of her.

"Captain Pierce, I hadn't expected to see ye on the ocean."

"I left the army six months ago, Miss Grant. Soon after I left Skye, as a matter of fact." He smiled while she set her gaze on his dog.

"Ye're fortunate. She looks more like her mother than her father." She raised her eyes to the dog's master. "Do ye have to be reminded of who Kyle's brother is? Who his faither is, his uncle?"

"No, I do not," Pierce assured her. "Edmund is a trusted friend. As you can see, Kyle is unharmed."

She eyed her cousin and nodded.

"D'ye make it yer duty to kidnap yer friend's brother?"

Pierce shook his head. "My intentions weren't to kidnap either of you, but now that I've found you, I will be bringing you home after I aid Captain Kidd."

She laughed and crossed her arms over the thick braid falling over her chest. "I'm not going anywhere with ye. If ye have intentions of forcing me, let me warn ye now, Captain, I will not be bullied and I will not go without a fight that will likely cost ye an eye. It willna' kill ye, but 'twill make it more difficult fer ye to fight in the future. Unless, of course, ye're Mr. Bonnet." She angled her head to catch the first mate's eye. "He could cut down a man with no eyes at all."

Mr. Bonnet beamed at her. As did Gustaaf, Charlie, and the others. They liked her. Finally. She was glad, because she liked them, too.

"When your kin eventually learn that I saw you," Captain Pierce pressed, "had you safe in my custody, and didn't return you, I will lose my allies in the north. I will not sacrifice that."

Alex had apparently heard enough and stepped directly in front of Pierce, blocking his view of her.

He was close. His scent of sea and forest covered her like a dream of balmy nights and passion's many embraces. Her eyes soaked in the sight of broad, supple shoulders tapering down into a long, muscular torso, the golden streaks in his chestnut hair spilling out from beneath his bandanna. She wanted to step closer, to caress him. She remained still when Alex spoke.

"'Twill be yar allies ya sacrifice, or yar life, Captain Pierce. Ya can all have me father's treasure. I would give up his legacy to me, my inheritance as Captain Kidd's only son, but if ya try to take *her* from me, ya will lose it all. I'll hand over anything else. But not her."

Did he just say what she thought he said? Her heart swelled within her breast until it brought tears to her eyes. She swiped them away. Would he give up his treasure for her?

"For your father's sake," Captain Pierce said after a few moments thinking about it, "I will agree."

Alex bent his head to him in thanks, believing more and more Pierce's story about his father.

"I will ask in return a supply of the herb you fed me to stave off nausea."

"Agreed," Alex said.

"Good." Pierce seemed sincerely happy about their deal. "I'll go inform my crew that it will just be us heading for Madagascar."

Trina waited while David Pierce left and Alex finally turned around to look at her. She wanted to return his smile, to gleam like a star when the moon shone on her.

"What do ye mean giving away yer treasure fer me? Have ye gone daft, Captain Ki—"

He swooped down like a hawk and gathered her into his arms before she could finish his name. He dipped his sexy mouth to hers and engulfed her in flames with the simple stroke of his tongue. She fell limp in his embrace, entranced by this sensual sorcerer. She wanted him to carry her to the nearest bed and take her to the edge of the world.

But all the men were watching. Kyle was watching.

She didn't know she possessed such strength until she managed to push out of his arms.

"I'm glad to see ye alive." She looked at his lips and almost lost the battle not to pull him down for another kiss. She patted her braid and turned to the eyes staring back at her. "I wasn't about to leave ye, love."

Och, but the fearless confidence in his grin, in the flash behind the smoky shadows of his eyes...he coursed like wildfire through her veins. She tossed her arms about his neck and kissed him one more time. Hard, possessive, and to hell with any opposition.

None came, but she broke away from him nonetheless and ran to her cousin. "Were ye hurt? Mistreated?" After a brief hug, she examined him.

"I was treated well," he assured. "How did ye find us?"

"Aye, how?" She felt Alex's arm coil around her, careless to who saw him. Her bones went soft.

She told him about eavesdropping on him and Sam the night they were kidnapped and hearing Sam mention the Bahamas. She looked across the deck now and found Sam standing with his brother. How could he betray Alex the way he had? What kind of cold, calculating man was he?

When Sam beckoned her over, she decided now was as good a time as any to find out. She went, leaving Alex to his men.

"Ya won't believe me," Sam said, holding up his palms when she reached him, "so I'll put yar accusation to yar cousin, whom ya will believe. Kyle," he called, beckoning to her cousin, "did I betray our captain?"

She was stunned when Kyle shook his head. "Nae, ye remain a loyal and trustworthy friend."

"What is this all about?" Trina asked them.

They both filled her in on the meat of the tale and the truth of it. When she remained unconvinced, Sam continued, after a pulled breath and well-concealed tenderness in his gaze. He was clever at hiding his true emotions, better at it than Kyle, and perhaps even Kyle's father. He'd have to be a master in order to fool his best friend for so long.

"My brother had the map fer eight years," he said, "more than enough time to sail to Madagascar and steal the ship. Bringing the *Quedagh Merchant* to England would have made me brother a hero, likely got him promoted. But here he is, ready to hand the true map over to his friend's son."

He made sense, and since Kyle and Alex believed him... "Are we truly going to Madagascar?" she couldn't help but ask him.

When he nodded his head she resisted the urge to shout and leap around like a palsied fool. Madagascar? How much better could this dream become?

Pierce returned to the deck and stopped and turned to his brother. "You were correct about him."

Sam turned to Trina for a moment. "As ya were correct about Highlanders, brother."

It was that moment when Trina realized exactly how skilled Samuel Pierce was at masking his heart. But one only had to look a wee bit closer to see that he was no Judas. To see that he was in love with her.

Alex watched Pierce leaving him for the second time and decided he liked Sam's brother. But like him or not, what the hell was he going to do with him for the six-hour sail back to Parrot Cay and then on to Madagascar?

One of the first things they were going to do, according

to Sam, was to practice a bit with the soldiers when they reached shore.

"Do ya think 'tis wise?" Alex asked him while they prepared the crew to return to their own ship. Sam had chosen to return with Alex, not his brother. The gesture went over well with Alex, but he didn't want his friend to continue seeking absolution for sins he didn't commit.

"The idea was hers." Sam pointed and Alex turned to see Caitrina moving toward him. She smiled at him. He smiled back and reached out his hand to her. He didn't want to stay on board another instant. He wanted to get her in his bed. When she'd arrived with his crew to save him, he thought he couldn't want any woman more than he wanted her. He would marry her, live a new adventure with her, and happily make her fat with his children. He looked at her gazing up at him. He wanted to kiss her. He could barely keep himself from doing it when her lips parted.

He caught her in his arm and pulled her close, his muscles pulsing to claim her.

"Captain," she said, slightly breathless. "Ye look a bit flushed. Let me see to ye."

"I'd like nothin' more, Miss Grant."

He couldn't wait to get her back to his ship, to his cabin, his bed. He wanted to tear away her clothes and take her hard against the rocking boat walls.

He looked around at his quartermaster, his first mate, and Kyle, a lad he was growing to trust perhaps even more than he trusted Sam. "Make sure everyone is accounted fer before we set sail. I'll see ya all later. Me lady means to see to me."

He reached for the end of a rope and wrapped his ankle

around it. Holding Caitrina fast, he pushed off and covered her mouth with his as they soared back to his deck.

Their landing was rough, a fitting start to the night he intended on having with her. It would take the night to reach Parrot Cay, and Alex didn't want to be disturbed until the morning. If any of the men, including her cousin, took issue with them being together, they would have to learn to live with it or leave the ship.

After a quick run to his cabin, they burst through the door laughing and basking in the pleasure of being together...alone. Alex locked them inside and began removing his garments while he turned to her.

When she began working the laces at her own breeches, the last of his restraint shattered and he moved to her and took hold of her shirt. Looking into her eyes and seeing the same passion he felt for her, he pressed his mouth to the delectable fruit of her lips. Her arms coiled around his neck and rather than tear away to relieve her of her shirt, he rid her of her breeches instead.

Half naked and suspended from his neck, Caitrina commanded all the attention of his cock. Hell, he throbbed until he thought he would burst with the need to be deep inside her. He made a quick end of his breeches and taking hold of her soft, bare arse, dragged her against his hard shaft. When she leaped up and wrapped her thighs around his waist, he gripped himself in both hands and almost erupted when she sank down on him.

He felt mad with desire, releasing himself to make room to take her deeper. He spread his lips over her throat, her chin, her mouth, guiding her over him with her tight arse in his hands. He held her up with the strength of his hips, the passion of his thrusts.

"What is this spell ya have cast over me and me crew?"

She smiled against his mouth and bit his full lower lip. "Ye're crew has warmed up to me, 'tis true. But I am unsure of how their captain feels." She tossed back her head, exposing her throat to his hungry mouth. When he closed his teeth around her flesh, she felt her strength leave her and wilted in his strong embrace.

He held her under her shoulders, her nape cupped in one palm, and slid into her over and over, slowly, taking his time to enjoy her deepest niches, rubbing her nub over the length of his thick shaft. Her eyes fluttered open and invited him to take more, all of her. He did, and then he pulled her up into his arms and carried her to the bed. He set her down gently and covered her with his body. He thought nothing could feel better than the thrill of fighting for his life, but he was wrong. Being with her, inside her, atop or behind her, fired his blood even more. She claimed his heart when he'd forgotten he even had one left. It stunned him how much of his heart was lost to her. It scared him to think what he would give up for her.

He looked deep into her eyes and sank into her inviting warmth.

"Do ya truly not know what I feel fer ya?" He groaned, blending his breath with hers.

She smiled and shook her head. An audacious, adorable liar. He didn't care and gave in and told her.

"I feel like ya are the answer to my deepest longings, the peace in the storms that sometimes ravage me soul. Ya hold me heart in yar hands and I trust it there." He kissed her softly, briefly. "Ya are me treasure, Caitrina." He kissed her again and drew himself out, then back in. "More precious than gold, gems, silks. I would give up me father's treasure fer ya." He grinned against her smile. "How do ya not know that I'm in love with ya?"

She clenched a fistful of his hair and coiled her legs around him tighter. "I wanted to hear ye say it."

Poseidon's balls, the way she laid claim to him made him drive into her harder, slower. He didn't take her. She gave herself up to him, moving beneath him like a sinuous dream, clutching him to her body, screaming out his name, and finding her perfect release with him.

❖❖❖

Chapter Thirty-Three

*I*n the morning, Trina woke to an empty bed. She sat up and remained still, knowing by the movement of the ship that they were docked. She didn't know why she smiled while she rose and dressed to begin the day. Perhaps her heart danced over the night she and Alex spent together. He told her that he loved her. Och, she knew it deep in her heart. She suspected it. But why her and not any of the other women he'd taken to his bed? It didn't matter why. He loved her. And today she would tell him her heart. She thought she might not be able to stop grinning like a fool over the prospect of seeing him this morning, of seeing Parrot Cay again. Mayhap her happiness stemmed from the thought of sailing to Madagascar. She didn't just smile; she twirled her way out the door. Och, Abby would think she'd gone mad if she saw Trina now.

She didn't care. She held her breath when she stepped out onto the quarterdeck and spread her shaded gaze over the tropical paradise. Alex's home was as beautiful as hers. She wanted to come back often. She wanted to go there now.

Leaving the ship, she followed the sounds of men's

cheers and jeers to the beach. She came upon the crew and Captain Pierce's men, finally enjoying their combat. From her vantage point, she determined Gustaaf the champion over his English opponent. She smiled at Kyle in the crowd of cheerers, then looked around for Alex.

"What do you think your family will do when they find you?"

She turned to look up into Captain Pierce's cool slate eyes. She didn't want to think about it. "Alex promised me he wouldn't lift a blade to them."

He looked away, toward Gustaaf's victory. "They've no doubt been fed lies by Mr. Andersen, about the reprehensible character of a pirate, of Captain Alex Kidd in particular. Andersen's plan, if he's as clever as Alex's father believed, will be to rile your family up against him, enough to kill him when they find you, leaving his hands clean to steal the map for himself."

Could she talk her father out of killing Alex? Could she stop her brother, her uncles, and her cousins from swinging at him? Would Alex honor his vow if someone tried to kill him? Who would die in a battle between her kin and the crew? She didn't want to think about these things and looked around again for Alex.

"I wouldn't have you deceive yourself into thinking Alex would hand you over without quarrel. Nor would I have you believe that your father would approve of this lifestyle for you. A stand down can only be settled with swords. One will win you and the other, you will leave behind, dead or alive."

She didn't realize that her eyes had filled with tears until the droplets fell to her cheeks. He was correct. Alex wouldn't give her over without quarrel. He loved her. He told her so. Captain Pierce's words struck like nails in her heart. His voice remained tender and merciful. He wasn't trying to hurt her or to trick her into going back to Skye with him. He was being sincere. He was right.

"What should I do?"

"Wipe your eyes. Your captain approaches."

She did as he said and waved at Alex and Sam returning from the direction of the village.

Before he left her side and moved forward to have a word with Sam, he dipped a tad closer and said, "After he has his treasure, send him off without you and Kyle. Give him a chance to live, Miss Grant. If you care for him, give him his life."

Alex shouted his approval of Kyle's subtle aggression. He parried, jabbed, and blocked while keeping his cool. Alex didn't know how the rest of them fought, but this one did it with grace and deadly precision. He realized suddenly that all the time he practiced with the Highlander, Kyle deliberately underexaggerated his skill. Alex smiled under the warm sun. Next time he wouldn't hold back and if Kyle wanted to live, he'd do the same.

When he spotted Caitrina standing in the crowd, his gut went soft. He'd hated leaving their bed and the warmth of her body earlier. The memory of her body heated his blood now and he labored to control it.

"It isn't over yet, Kidd," David Pierce assured him with a friendly greeting.

Alex watched Kyle pummel his fist into his opponent's face and then bring him to his knees with his claymore clutched in both hands. "It looks over to me, Pierce."

He laughed at the English captain's muttered curses while his man went down.

"Ah, the reason the sun rises in the morning." He

reached Caitrina, now standing alone, and took her hand to bring it to his mouth like Kyle told him to do. He kissed her knuckles once, twice. He never wanted to stop kissing her.

"When are we leaving fer Madagascar?" she asked him as a round of cheers went up for a triumphant Kyle.

"In a few hours," he told her. "We'll be dockin' in Costa da Pimenta in West Africa first fer supplies. We'll be needin' plenty. Are ya excited about goin'?"

She nodded but lowered her gaze. "Of course, I am. 'Tis the kind of adventure I've always wanted."

"Ya looked troubled, me love."

She smiled and reached her hand up to his face. She traced her fingertips along his jaw, his chin. "I'm a wee bit concerned aboot my kin finding us. Sooner or later they will."

"I will see to it when the time comes. Don't trouble yerself with these thoughts, Caitrina." He took her up in his arms and gazed into her eyes. "They will love me as much as ya do."

She laughed, setting his heart to ruin. "Who said I loved ye, rake? Ye're a mad fool."

He dipped his grin to her lips and took her mouth like a starving beast. He hungered for her, for every part of her, body, mind, and heart. He had all of her. She didn't need to tell him. He could see it in her smile, feel it in her kiss.

"Och, c'mon now," Kyle groaned behind them. "Stay oot of the cabin until tonight, at least, aye? We have things to discuss."

Alex broke their kiss and looked into her eyes. "He's runnin' out of times when bein' yar cousin keeps me from beatin' him senseless."

"Ye have my thanks fer yer patience, dear Captain."

His grin returned. He wouldn't harm the lad and she knew it. Hell, how he loved her confidence in so many things. Gustaaf had told him how she led the charge to find him, spying Pierce's ship from the crow's nest. Fearless.

He released her, reluctantly, and turned to Kyle. "What is it, MacGregor?"

Kyle threw up his hands. "Ye mean to tell me neither of ye saw my victory over Lieutenant Caruthers?"

"Of course we saw it!" Caitrina let him off the hook too easily. "In fact, Alex told Captain Pierce that the fight was over before 'twas."

Alex wasn't surprised when the Highlander showed no sign of pride at all. He hadn't forgotten the precision and mastery in Kyle's arm, and how Kyle had hidden that from him. "I confess I was quite stunned to see how skillful a warrior ya truly are."

"Alas," Kyle bowed his head. Alex couldn't tell if he was sincere or not. "Not as skilled as others, yerself among them." Finally, he raised his guileless gaze to Alex's. "Lieutenant Caruthers is English so I take less pride in defeating him."

Alex laughed, mostly to himself. Whether Kyle was telling the truth or not didn't matter. He wasn't hiding anything vital. He was simply being the son of a renowned spy. "Then we'll be continuing our practice?" he said, going along with the possible façade.

"If ye can spare the time between yer"—Kyle slid his sea-colored eyes to his cousin and let a shadow of a smile pass over his face"—endeavors, I could use the practice."

"If the two of ye could cease speaking aboot fighting fer a moment," Caitrina interrupted, "I'd like a word with ye, Kyle."

"I'll see ya both on board then," Alex said, granting them their privacy. "We have much packin' to do."

He left them and moved on toward Anjali's hut. He wanted to bid her farewell and leave the emerald brooch he'd pocketed from a woman in Lisbon. He would return to Parrot Cay with his wife and children, splitting their visits between the Caicos and Skye.

He smiled up at the heavens, eager to begin a new adventure.

❈

Chapter Thirty-Four

Never in his wildest imaginings had Hendrik Andersen ever entertained the idea of traveling the seas with Scottish Highlanders. But here he was, aboard *Stirling's Pride*, an enormous brigantine belonging to Captain Hamish MacKinnon, friend of the Mac-Gregors, searching for Connor Grant's daughter, who was kidnapped by Captain Kidd.

Hendrik laughed. It was amazing how it had all worked in his favor. When he woke up bound in the MacGregors' castle and it dawned on him that Kidd had set sail without him, he was angry. He'd intended to sail to the Caribbean on *Poseidon's Adventure*, but now he'd have to find a ship and a captain to sail it.

In a brilliant stroke of luck, it was soon discovered that Connor Grant's daughter and Colin MacGregor's son were missing. Hendrik had used every bit of information to move the MacGregors into action against Alexander Kidd. Of course the pirate had taken her, he'd told them. She was a pretty girl, after all, and the pirate certainly liked his girls pretty. Where did they think Andersen had found him? Aye, in a brothel, fresh out of a pretty girl's bed.

A few times, his plan almost backfired when his hosts set their murderous glances on him while he fed their worst fears. They didn't like him anymore, and as he sailed with them, they grew ever more dangerous. Any one of them could snap his neck or gut him in one clean swipe. They were brawny and brutal and he was thankful that he'd learned to conquer his fears. It was one thing he was grateful to William Kidd for teaching him.

"How far behind them d'ye think we are?"

Hendrik looked up into Colin MacGregor's dark features and diamond-blue eyes. Who in blazes wouldn't soil his breeches coming upon this one in a shadowy English alley? All the MacGregors were huge, strapping men with even bigger swords hanging from their plaids. They generally didn't like strangers but they needed him to help them find their children.

He had to work hard to conquer the smirk creeping over his lips, but oh, when the MacGregors found Captain Kidd they would surely kill him first and take back their family after. Hendrik didn't care if Kidd had Miss Grant and the lad or not. The chief had already given his word not to kill him if Andersen was wrong. Why would they kill him when he was only trying to help them? He had no proof that Kidd even had them. If they were missing for some other nefarious reason, let the MacGregors worry about it. He only wanted the map.

"We should reach the Sargasso Sea tomorrow," he told Colin. "From there, I don't know to which island Kidd will be sailing. I didn't see the map."

"Ye don't know much," Connor Grant said, joining them. "Ye were wrong aboot them docking in France.

How do we know he came this way at all? What if he sailed back to the Colonies?"

Of all the Highlanders, Hendrik liked Grant the least. It was probably due to the fact that Grant had threatened to kill him if he mentioned what Kidd may have done to his daughter one more time. Andersen didn't dare suggest that Miss Grant went with Kidd willingly. After searching for Alex for years, Hendrik had learned much about him. Alex, it turned out, was very much like his father when it came to women. He had many in every town, province, and village he visited. Except...He remembered something William had told him.

"His father hated the Colonies and would never have left his treasure there," Hendrik told them. "The pirate sailed here, I know it. He may have sailed to the Caicos Islands. If I remember correctly, he was born there. Dogs return to their vomit, you know."

Colin moved closer to him, his mouth slightly curled in a wry sneer. "Ye don't like the pirate much d'ye, Andersen?"

Hendrik shook his head. This one he had to watch. All the warriors were quicker than lightning when it came to their weapons, but Colin dueled with his mind first. He was clever and watchful, often making Andersen fidget under his vigilant scrutiny.

"Why would I like a man who kidnaps women?"

"Yet ye traveled with him to Camlochlin and spoke on his behalf."

Andersen softened his expression and smiled at more of the Highlanders moving in to hear his reply. Why did so many of them have to come? They were like their own little army of deadly men. Even the chief was on board, leaving Camlochlin in the care of one of his brothers.

"I had promised his father I would find him and get the map into his hands. I never said I knew him, only that I knew that the man before you was, indeed, Alexander Kidd."

"Will we face much opposition on these islands ye speak of?" Malcolm Grant, Caitrina's eldest brother, asked.

"Nothin' we canna' handle, Malcolm," said a man leaning against the rail while he tested the flexibility of his bow. Andersen knew him to be William MacGregor, son of one of the most bloodthirsty MacGregors to ever live. Their bards sang of one they called the Devil and how he slew hundreds in his own, personal war against the Campbells years ago. William's father, Brodie, rode with him and was the only one said to have enjoyed all the bloodshed. "If ye're vexed, ye should have stayed home wi' the women."

"I'm not vexed, Will," Malcolm told him with a baleful curl of his lips. "I merely wish to know how many of ye I'll have to protect, beginnin' with ye."

Andersen watched some of the others smile at the banter. They all loved to talk about weapons, bleeding, and battle. They never actually fought, at least not in the month he spent with them. They lived on their island at peace with their neighbors. Or perhaps their neighbors were afraid of them. They practiced often though. Every damned day. Andersen couldn't wait to be away from them.

"If we will reach these islands tomorrow," Connor told the rest, "we should discuss a plan of defense. Cailean," he called to his youngest son, "find yer uncle Rob and tell him to meet us in the galley."

Andersen watched the lad set off to his task. He was

thankful that the topic had veered away from him—even happier that they were going to plan a defense against Kidd. He had nothing against the pirate, or his father, truly. He just wanted to find the *Quedagh Merchant*. He knew its value, having seen the ship in person, even boarding it. Its cargo was priceless and Andersen would be damned if he sat by and did nothing while another pirate got rich from doing nothing. He felt little remorse at the thought of the MacGregors killing his captain's son. William Kidd hadn't been that bad really. A bit guarded, but not cruel. It was a pity that Alex would have to die in order for him to take possession of the map. With Alex dead who would contest him? He almost couldn't wait and stepped off to follow the Highlanders belowdecks.

Colin MacGregor's hand on his chest stopped him.

"Wait here."

Andersen smiled and consented easily. What else could he do? Fight them all himself? He wasn't a fool. He would wait until he was a wealthy man and then he would go back to Camlochlin with an army of his own. He wondered how skilled they were against pistols and smiled at the sunset.

Trina watched the majestic silhouette of *Poseidon's Adventure*'s double masts against the sunset backdrop. Soon the anchor would be raised and all hands would return to the deck.

Everyone but her and Kyle.

How would she tell Alex that she couldn't continue on with him? An even better question was, How was she going to live without him? But she had to. She had to send him away. She couldn't let him die because of her, and couldn't let any of her kin die either. They might not fight, but she couldn't take the chance. Kyle had agreed with her when she told him her concerns. Her father would never allow her to stay with Alex, pirating the seas. He would demand she return home and the instant Alex tried to stop him...

Nae. She had to stop the unthinkable from happening. She wouldn't be the first lass in history to sacrifice her heart for those she loved. She wouldn't wallow in her misery.

She wouldn't.

"Caitrina?"

At the sound of Alex's voice coming up behind her, she swiped her tears away and ran her sleeve across her nose.

He reached her and turned her around to face him. "What is it? Why are ya weepin'?"

He remained silent while she told him she couldn't go with him and why. She would never forget the haunted look in his eyes, the heartbreak in his expression. When he tried to argue with her, she found the strength to hold fast from her love for him. Finally, he left her, walking off in the sand toward to sea. Gone from her for good.

A quarter of an hour later, she watched the ship leave the bay and sail off in the moonlight.

As soon as she ceased crying she would concentrate on forgetting him. How difficult could it be? But even as she questioned it, she heard the sound of his laughter in the rushing waves. She saw the quirk of his rakish smile in the pale moonlight sprinkled over water. When a cool, floral-scented breeze caressed her skin, she felt his arms around her, his breath against her.

"Ye did the right thing sending him away."

She closed her eyes at Kyle's voice behind her. How

could he understand when he hadn't loved yet? "It doesna' feel right." She hated her voice for breaking on a sob.

Her cousin went to her and closed his arms around her. He didn't say anything. He just held her.

"D'ye remember the maps in yer books?" She lifted her head, wiped her eyes, and asked him. "Where is Madagascar?"

"It lies off the southeastern coast of Africa, in the Indian Ocean." He let her go and drew a map in the wet sand, showing her where they were and where Madagascar was.

She sniffed, looking at it. "I wanted to go. I wanted to go with him, Kyle. Grow old with him. I was selfish and put my own needs first... and put him in danger. If he were to be hurt..." She didn't finish. She couldn't.

"There now," her cousin comforted her. "He willna' be hurt. Whoever comes looking for him will be directed to Dominica."

She looked up at him through tear-stained eyes. "Ye wanted to go with him too, did ye not?"

"Aye, I did. 'Twould have been quite an adventure, but I would prefer to keep him safe from Mr. Andersen."

"How will ye do that?" She sniffed.

"Well, if the Dutchman does indeed sail with our kin, they likely dinna' know of his treachery. Of course, I aim to tell them, but if he realizes that Alex is on to him, he might also suspect that the captain isn't sailing to Dominica. We canna' let on right away that we know, or that David Pierce is involved."

Trina nodded. She would do whatever it took to keep Alex safe. "He was so angry and disappointed." She began to cry again. Och, would it ever stop? Would the pain ever stop? "He isna' afraid of our kin. He has no idea what they might do if they believe he kidnapped us and brought us harm. He doesna' believe my reasons fer staying behind. He thinks...He thinks...I've betrayed his heart. I could see it in his eyes, Kyle!" she sobbed pitifully against his chest, not bothering to hide her feelings from him. She was easy to read.

"Come," he prompted as the ship's outline disappeared with the setting sun. "Let us eat and take rest. There's nothing more to be done fer now."

Trina didn't want to eat and when she slept her dreams were filled with Alex. The next day was no better. It offered her no solace, save that she had no more tears to shed. She felt empty and drained of energy. Worse, she missed him more with every second that passed. Kyle tried to help but in the end, he left her alone. Charlie and Anjali walked behind her for most of the next day, as if they expected her to throw herself into the waves and end her life. They urged her to eat, to help with the day's chores. She did. But nothing helped.

"When his father took heem from us, me mother wept fer a month," Anjali told her while they ground wheat with stones. "He often led me into trubble, but me mother loved heem nonedeeless."

Trina didn't want to hear about how well Alex was loved because despite it, he'd stayed away. It reminded her that he would never ever return to her.

"When he came back dee first time wit Sam, 'twas like he'd been raised from dee dead. Dere was much celebration. He brought gifts, provin' he hadn't fergotten us. After dat, we didn't see him much, but he always came back. Dis is his home."

"Was he forgiven?" she asked softly.

"Fer what?"

Trina smiled for the first time since she told Alex she wasn't going with him. He'd stayed away from his home for so many years, but no one cared what he'd become. Just as she suspected, they loved him regardless, as her family would have loved her had she become a pirate.

"I wish he understood why I didn't go with him," she said on a withering sigh.

"He will. Soon as his heart mends. It might take a little time, but he will come to realize dat ya did what ya did because ya love heem."

She nodded, grateful to Anjali and Kyle for trying to help her feel better. But nothing would help.

Not even when she saw the brig sailing into the harbor or her father and brother rowing one of the lifeboats toward the shore.

Chapter Thirty-Five

Caitrina didn't realize how much she'd missed her father until she was in his arms. When he whispered into her hair, "I feared I'd lost ye, my daughter." The tears she thought were finished began again. Och, had she truly been so selfish, not just with Alex, but with her kin, also? How could she just leave them without so much as a farewell? She'd thought only about what she wanted, not how the folks who loved her would feel if she disappeared from their lives. What had she put her father through? Her mother? Aye, she was a woman with her own dreams and desires, and she still wanted to live them. But she'd grown up living in the real world this last month, and in the future, she would do things right.

"Fergive me fer putting ye through so much worry, Papa. I am unharmed."

He smiled, exposing twin dimples as deep as hers.

"Where is Captain Kidd?" Her uncle Rob came around her and kissed her head while she savored her reunion with her father. She smiled, glancing at Kyle, who was caught in his father's tight embrace.

"He left," she told them. She was glad to see them and relieved that Alex had gone just in time to miss them by a day. There definitely would have been blood had they found him here. Besides her uncles, Will and her brothers had come, and her cousins, as well. They'd come to fight.

"He didn't hurt me or Kyle," she said, looking at her cousin for confirmation. He gave it. "I wasna' kid—"

"Where did he go?" A man, who Trina recognized to be Mr. Andersen, stepped forward and interrupted her. "We've been to half a dozen islands already looking for him."

"Mayhap"—she turned her most practiced smile on the lanky Dutchman—"we can speak of him after my kin have filled their bellies and dried their boots by a fire." She didn't want to speak of him. What if she began to cry? She wouldn't. Now was the time to gather her strength and make certain her sacrifice wasn't all for naught.

"Papa? Uncles?" She turned to them and in earnest, said, "Please eat something warm and not crawling with weevils. After that we will discuss what has happened. It's been a trying ordeal fer me." She patted her palm against her forehead, knowing exactly how to get the men in her family to concede. Every woman in Camlochlin knew. "I would take rest and comfort in your presence before having to relive it all again." She wasn't being deceitful to them. She intended on telling her father how she felt about Alex and what she wanted in her life, but she wanted to give Alex more time to get farther away.

"My dear." Mr. Andersen held up a finger to stop her when she would have turned toward the village. "No one is asking you to relive anything. We all know what the pirate is capable of doing. Just tell me where he went so that I may personally see that you have justice."

Trina wanted to punch him in the jaw, but her uncle Colin did it for her. She thought she saw a tooth go flying before Andersen slumped to the ground, out cold. Her uncle glanced at his chief and older brother.

"I told ye I was going to do it, Rob. I told ye I could tolerate only so much of his lying tongue before I broke his jaw."

"Ye didna' break it," William pointed out after a quick examination of the victim.

"Then there's still opportunity," Colin muttered and picked up his steps toward the village.

Trina adored her uncle Colin, but something cold passed through her blood. He was a warrior, they all were. They would have hurt Alex, perhaps killed him. She wanted them to know the truth. Alex was a good man, regardless of being a pirate. She wondered if it would matter to them. What would they think when she told them she loved him? She needed to tell them, tell her father, at least. Even if she never saw Alex again, she wanted her family to know the truth.

"He's correct," she told them, looking over her shoulder at the abandoned heap in the sand. "Mr. Andersen betrayed his captain, and has set the navy after his captain's son."

Her father followed her gaze and then looked at her. "There is indeed much to discuss over a full belly."

"Papa, they season their pork in something called jerk. Ye will melt."

He smiled with her, it being one of the things she loved most about him, his easy smile. But just as easily as it appeared did it vanish. "Ye're certain ye're unharmed?"

"Papa, he was kind to me even after he found me stowed away on his ship."

He stopped walking, and so did the men in earshot. "Ye...stowed away?"

She nodded and forged on ahead while he still wore that stunned look. "He could have thrown me and Kyle overboard but kindly planned to drop us off in France, where I, thoroughly repentant, would have sought Uncle Connor Stuart's house and joined grand—"

"Caitrina?" her father cut her off. "Ye *chose* to go with him?"

"Not with him, nae. With his ship. But aye, I did want to leave Camlochlin."

"She's tried to speak to ye aboot it fer years now," her brother Malcolm said, being the first to pick up his steps.

Her poor father looked about to be sick. She felt terrible, but this had to be done. She handed him off to Charlie and asked that he seat him beside her place. She would join him in a few moments.

"Thank ye fer standing with me just now," she said, looping her arm through her brother's. Malcolm had always been her favorite, fearless and a bit reckless, like her.

Behind a lock of sun-burnished hair, his turquoise gaze fell on her. For a moment, Trina pitied any lass who wasn't his kin. "What have ye been up to, Caitie?"

"Living a great adventure with a pirate who has fallen in love with me."

Her brother raised his brows. "And yer heart? Is it so stricken?"

She couldn't help but smile at his description of love. "Aye," she told him quietly. "'Tis so stricken."

For the first time, she witnessed something fazing her brother. He looked as ill as her father had moments ago. "Hell." His eyes darted to their father. "He willna' take this well."

"Aye, I know, Cal. I sent Alex ... Captain Kidd away to keep him safe from all of ye. But my heart longs fer him. The thought of never seeing him again is agony. Och, ye dinna' understand."

He took her in his arms when her tears began again and kissed the top of her head. "There now, Caitie, dinna' weep."

Trina didn't care what lasses said about her rakish brother. He was wonderful to her.

Chapter Thirty-Six

*C*aptain Alexander Kidd sat on his bed in his cabin and stared at his map, the map his father had given to David Pierce. Alex had known that the *Quedagh Merchant* was worth much—namely, his father's life. Everyone was after it, the navy, the throne, the stately politicians in New York and probably Boston, and Hendrik Andersen.

Alex thought he wanted it, too. But he didn't care anymore about riches. He'd left his treasure on Parrot Cay.

He understood Caitrina's fears about her family but he could have handled them. He was certain of it. It was his beloved who had so little faith in him. She was a stubborn wench and would not change her mind no matter how hard he argued. He was stunned and speechless by her decision not to come with him to Madagascar. He still couldn't believe she wasn't here with him now. He shouldn't have left her. He should have fought harder. No. He'd done everything he could to change her mind. She wouldn't be moved. She didn't want her family to hurt him. The thing was, how long would it have taken for them to find him if she'd gone on with him? No one knew about Madagascar save Pierce.

The MacGregors and Grants didn't know. They wouldn't have followed. She could have stayed with him if she truly wanted to. Perhaps she didn't want to.

He tossed the map onto his bed and stood up. It didn't matter. He was better off without her. Why the hell was he feeling so down? He'd done well without her before. He'd be fine without her now. He ran his fingers through his hair, wanting to yank out every strand. Damn her. She wouldn't leave his thoughts. He'd push her out. He'd exorcize her the way he'd seen them do on Parrot Cay when someone was believed to be possessed of an evil spirit.

Someone knocked on the door.

Alex bid entry and turned toward the table when he saw Sam. "Where are we?"

"Come out and see," his friend said, and followed when Alex flung himself into a chair. "Ya've been in here since yesterday. Come out and let the salty air cleanse ya."

"Cleanse me of what?" Alex brooded.

"Of her."

"Sam—"

"Hear me, old friend." Sam cut him off before he could deny that he needed cleansing. "I know what she means to ya. I was there when ya offered me brother yar map rather than give her up. She's taken yar heart—the once believed unattainable heart of the rogue Captain Kidd."

Damn him, he made Alex think of her...the way her lustrous locks fell perfectly around her face. The delicate curve of her nose and the way her smiles always began in her eyes. Hell, he loved the musical lilt in her voice and the way she said certain words.

He leaned his head back on his chair and closed his eyes to see her more clearly. "I've grown accustomed to havin' her around, that's all."

"Aye," Sam agreed just as quietly. "As have we all. The crew misses her."

She'd won his damn crew. What other woman could ever achieve such a feat?

Alex opened his eyes. He poured himself some rum and downed it. "It may take me a day or two, to quit thinkin' about the world in her eyes, but soon enough she'll leave my head, just as the rest of them have."

This time, Sam remained silent. Then, glancing at the jug of rum on the table, asked, "Is that gunpowder rum?"

"Aye, 'tis." Alex reached for another cup and filled it. "Here, brother. Let's drink to something, shall we?"

"Aye." Sam held up his cup.

"To whores. They don't bother with pretense."

"Alex—" Sam tried, setting down his cup, still full.

Alex held up his finger to halt his friend's words until he could refill his cup. When he did, he forgot whose turn it was to toast. "To a brother who didn't betray me and who forgave me for thinking he did."

Sam picked up his cup and hit it against his friend's. "And to startin' over, no matter how many times ya must do it."

"Here here!" Alex put the cup to his lips and tossed back his head.

He suspected the sinking, sickening feeling in his gut meant that he didn't want to start over but go back. Go back and make things right with her. Convince her that once her family knew how much he loved her, they would no longer want his head. If they didn't want her with a pirate, then he would become a farmer, a tanner, a blacksmith. Whatever the hell they needed in Camlochlin. But he was drunk and he might not feel this way tomorrow. There was gunpowder in his rum. He wouldn't remember anything at all.

He smiled and stood up. "I think I will come out and see what the men be up to." He reached for his tricorn hat and fit it surprisingly neatly on his head. "Where did ya say we were?"

"About two hours off the West African coast," Sam told him while he followed him out. "The wind has been good."

Alex groaned when he stepped onto the quarterdeck and a warm breeze drifted over his face. "I fergot how dreadfully dank and hot 'tis here, even at night. She probably would have liked it. Sam?"

"Aye."

"She didn't complain much, did she? We all know the challenge of bein' on a ship fer the first time. Hell, yar brother still falls ill from the waves." If he was closer to the rail, he might have considered tossing himself over. Was this what it was going to be like for him now? Would even gunpowder rum not cure him of her for even a few hours? He wanted to forget her, not tomorrow or the day after that. But right now.

"Do ya know how many splinters I took out of her feet?" he asked Sam. "Yet she didn't falter in her determination to remain barefoot."

"She ate everything placed before her once she got used to the bugs," Sam joined in. "Even when weevils had burrowed into the biscuits and the fruit went bad."

"Aye." Alex smiled for the first time since he left her. He closed his eyes and swayed on his feet. "Let's ferget her, Sam. Aye?"

"'Tis not goin' to be easy, Alex."

If not for the effects of the rum, Alex might have taken notice of the wretched earnestness in his friend's eyes and in his voice. Alex might have considered a possibility that hadn't occurred to him before. Of course Sam loved

Caitrina. All the men did. She'd bewitched them with her sparkling sapphire eyes and her playful dimples. How could they resist her?

If he remembered any of this tomorrow, he might ask Sam exactly what he thought of Caitrina Grant.

"Who's at the helm?"

"Cooper," Sam informed him.

"Tell him we're goin' back to Parrot Cay fer her."

"Aye, Alex. I'll go tell him that while ya go to the galley. The natives prepared fer us tarts and pies fer our journey. Me brother boarded an hour ago with some of his men and I'd have ya eat some of the fresh desserts before they are all gone or spoil."

Alex smiled and nodded his head. "I like tarts and pies. Of course, I'll join yar brother. He's an excellent swordsman."

"He says the same about ya," Sam said over his shoulder as Alex headed for the galley.

Alex would like to remember *that* in the morning. He made it belowdecks without incident. When he reached the galley, he looked around for David Pierce.

The *Expedition* traveled with them, keeping just ahead on the starboard side. He wasn't surprised to see Pierce on board. Captains often boarded ships while they sailed. Alex would try to remember to be impressed that Pierce could do it after only six months at sea. It made up for his sensitive stomach.

"Ya know, Pierce," he said, slipping into a seat near Sam's older brother, "yar dog truly is the ugliest mongrel I've ever seen. What breed is it?"

"Hell if I know. But she isn't ugly. She's unique."

"All right," Alex said, reaching for a cup and a tart. "If that's what ya wish to call it."

"Risa's mother once saved Edmund MacGregor from death at the hands of Walter Hamilton, Lord Chancellor of Scotland."

Alex gave him half his attention. The other half he gave to his banana almond tart. He bit into it and closed his eyes. Now this, this could make him forget. "Put some pineapple in yar rum," he advised Pierce, "and ya will never go back to bitter wine."

The English captain looked around the table and shook his head at the oblong, prickly fruit. "I've seen pineapples before but have never tasted one. Is it like the mango?"

Alex took the fruit in his hand, drew his dagger, and skinned and sliced it. He handed a piece to his guest.

"Tell me why the Lord Chancellor sought to kill MacGregor."

"Edmund kidnapped the chancellor's betrothed and stole her heart. Damnation! This is good!"

Alex grinned. He didn't know anyone who thought differently. "Edmund is Kyle's brother, aye." When Pierce nodded, Alex thought about it all for a moment and forgot everything . . . save one thing.

"Did ya meet Caitrina . . . er Miss Grant when ya visited Camlochlin?"

"I did."

Alex eyed him from above his cup. "What did ya think of her?"

Pierce squeezed more pineapple juice into his rum and then ate the flesh and licked his fingers. "I thought she is the daughter of Captain Connor Grant, the niece and granddaughter of some of the most notoriously dangerous men on earth. And then I thought of her no more."

Alex laughed. "Ya were afraid of them then."

Pierce nodded and downed more rum—not the

gunpowder kind. "As you should be, Kidd. You would do well to forget her and move onward."

"I know I would," Alex admitted. "She's made her choice and I must leave her to it."

"She chose for you to live."

He smiled but he felt like smashing something. Many somethings. He slammed his cup on the table. "What a great service she's done me." He rose to his feet and turned to leave the galley. "Remember to thank her fer me if ya ever see her again."

He left and climbed out onto the deck and into the cool night air. He'd already forgotten his order to Sam to sail back to get her so he didn't notice that they hadn't turned around. They could reach their destination in a day if the winds held up. He prayed they would. He wanted off the ship, away from the tedium, away from the memories of her in his bed every time he tried to lay in it.

Tonight, he avoided it and slept on deck, rocked to sleep by the Atlantic and plagued with thoughts of a stubborn Highland lass who'd come to steal his heart.

As he expected, he awoke the next morning with a thunderous headache and no memory of the night before. At some point in the night he must have eaten a tart because half of it was stuck in his sash. But gunpowder rum didn't erase memories further back than that. Alex wished it did. His mood remained foul during the day, even after two rum concoctions to ease his throbbing head. He ordered the men about and threatened Cooper twice to make this pile of rat-eaten wood go faster.

He didn't dine with his crew but found a quiet place at the bow where he sat with Pierce's dog, Risa, and a jug of rum. He spent many hours telling the dog about Caitrina, unable to keep her from his thoughts or his lips. He spoke freely, confessing to Risa's pointed ears his deepest heart, hoping this might be a way to exorcize her.

The next day, when they docked in Costa da Pimenta, Alex felt hopeful when he greeted some of the female natives.

This was what he needed to forget her.

Chapter Thirty-Seven

his wasn't the first time Trina rallied men to move. She'd succeeded in getting Mr. Bonnet and the crew to go after Alex, hadn't she?

Unfortunately, the men in her family were a bit more stubborn. Still, she didn't give up. She could feel the walls cracking. They would give in with more time. But she didn't have time. If the navy arrived, her kin couldn't sail anywhere without them watching. They had to go now.

She had hoped to keep her heart out of it, but that hope was quickly fading. She had tried to convince them that Alex needed their help. But they argued that since the navy didn't know his whereabouts, he was relatively safe. She wanted to see him again. She had to see him again, and she had to make her father understand her heart.

"I tried not to feel this way, Papa," she told him, then looked at the others sitting around the table in the meeting hall. Her brother's wink when she met his gaze strengthened her, as did Kyle's smile. "I canna' stop my heart from feeling the way it does. I have tried and I have failed."

"He's an outlaw, Caitrina," her father argued, still

looking a bit sick and miserable from the last four hours of talking. "What kind of life d'ye expect with him?"

"One of adventure. Even if we settled down on two islands, he would fill my days with spark and challenge. A life filled with love. You have it." She spread her eyes over each face and, no longer needing support, forged on ahead. "Ye married women ye wanted, with or withoot anyone's permission and ye are all happy. Why d'ye deny me the same?"

"We dinna' bring our wives with us to rob and pilfer—" her uncle Rob said.

"While barely escapin' the navy," Colin agreed.

"There have been at least two battles in Camlochlin," Malcolm pointed out in her defense. "Were not yer wives in jeopardy then?"

"Hell," Colin muttered. "Connor, ye should bring yer son outside and show him why our wives were never in any danger."

"I'm simply sayin'," Malcolm repented with a flash of his dimples, "that love is sometimes worth the risk."

Every eye at the table turned and looked at Malcolm like he'd just sprouted another head. Malcolm loved his women and to hear him utter such a thing was shocking indeed. Trina knew that he did it for her.

"Aye, I want to take that risk," she told them all. "I have fallen in love with Captain Alex Kidd and I want to sail to Costa da Pimenta to find him."

"The Pepper Coast," Kyle corrected, then smiled nervously when all eyes turned to him. "'Tis in Africa. West Africa."

Her father laughed, but the sound chilled Trina to her bones. She knew his reaction would not be favorable but actually seeing disbelief and frustration, not to mention deep concern, marring his handsome features broke her heart.

"Ye're so much like yer mother."

She smiled. He didn't.

"Papa, he is a good man."

"He's a pirate, Caitie. How can he be a good man?" He held up his palm to silence her when she would have said more. "I'll hear no more talk of him." He stood up, angry and taller than everyone, save the chief. "I've given in to yer whims fer too long. Ye should be married with a bairn or two by now, not stowin' away on a bloody pirate ship! I've indulged ye so much that ye honestly think I would entertain yer suggestion of bringin' ye to him and then biddin' ye farewell and sailin' back to Scotland without ye!"

His voice rose against her like she'd never heard it before. But that wasn't why tears pooled above her rims and spilled down her cheeks. She wept because this was the reaction Captain Pierce had warned her of. What if Alex was here right now and she hadn't sent him away? What would her father have done when Alex tried to leave with her?

She'd done the right thing. Knowing it didn't make it any easier. She'd saved her captain's life. She should be thankful. But she wasn't. Thankful that her father would never let her go? Thankful that her life was not her own? She looked toward Malcolm. Her brother offered her a comforting smile but nothing else. Kyle, too, remained quiet out of respect for his uncle's reprimand.

She loved them. She loved her father. But she felt her anger rise up inside like lava beneath a mountain. "If ye will excuse me." She moved to pass the men and her father. What more was there to say?

"Caitrina," her father spoke softly now and reached for her arm.

She pulled it away. "I will be waiting on the ship. But when we return home, I will not wed, nor will I have any bairns. That is my condition."

"Condition?" her father asked, looking sincerely stunned. The others all looked equally astounded at her declaration.

She nodded, quite boldly. "If I canna' go to him, then I will go to no man. I will live oot my matronly days under yer watchful eye and nae harm will ever come to me and I will make yer life a happy one."

She stormed away from him and everyone else. She meant what she said. She would never marry. How could she settle for a life without Alex? When she stepped out of the hut her tears came harder. She ran the rest of the way toward the beach, her soft cries flowing out behind her.

Kyle watched her until she disappeared in the darkness and then he looked inside the hall, spotted her father looking miserable, and went back inside to have words with him.

Alex liked the Pepper Coast. Over the years, Portuguese, Dutch, and British traders formed posts here and it became a region rich in trade imports. Its most important commodity was the malagueta pepper, or, as the Dutch and British called it, Grains of Paradise. Spices, gold, and ivory were exchanged for textiles, alcoholic beverages, general merchandise, and slaves.

The best thing about Costa da Pimenta, though, was that Caitrina Grant wasn't there. She still plagued his every damn thought, but the rum was beginning to help. Thieving helped, too, of course. He and his mates had already procured enough coin and trinkets to buy all they needed to make it to Madagascar in one haul.

They needed grain, lots of it. So Alex enlisted David Pierce and six others, including Gustaaf and Cooper, to help him fetch some, while Sam and the others traded for poultry and spices. It was always wise to invest in live chickens and some geese. The fowl provided eggs and fresh meat after weeks at sea.

And anything, no matter how rotten it became, tasted better with the right spices.

Alex didn't mind the idea of more weeks aboard ship. The need he'd felt during the last couple of days to escape the boat and his memories of her was gone. He'd felt trapped with nowhere to run. But he was a pirate, seawater flowed through his veins, and now, on his second day ashore, all he wanted to do was run to his ship and find comfort in her rocking embrace.

He would have preferred a woman's embrace...Ah, but there was nothing better than forgetting the world and all its vast emptiness in the embrace of a warm, willing woman. But he had no desire for any woman.

Only for her.

It scared the hell right out of him. It was worse than he feared. He was lost to a Highland lass who he would likely never see again. And why? Because she feared for his life and for her kin's lives, instead of trusting him.

He should have tossed her over his shoulder and apologized on their way toward Africa. He would have convinced her that after they got wealthy from the *Quedagh Merchant* they would sail back to Scotland and speak with her kin.

"We're goin' back to get her."

Pierce stopped walking and looked at him. "We can't do that."

"I wasn't askin' fer yar permission," Alex said, and kept walking. "Nor did I ask ya to come. *Poseidon's Adventure* will return here in a week. We will meet up and continue on toward the treasure. A minor delay."

Pierce picked up his pace to reach him. "Use your wits, Captain. Her family might have arrived by now. Between her and Kyle, they might convince her father that you had no part in taking her, but if you show up to take her from them, they will kill you without question."

Alex didn't reply, but smiled as he walked.

"I mean no insult to you," Pierce offered. "When I arrived in Camlochlin to get my dog, I stayed for a month and came to know them more. No one takes from them and lives. The vow began with their land and continued to their name. They are everything terrifying you've heard spoken of around fires, and more. They took me in as friend, then ushered me out like a friend who'd overstayed his welcome. They don't care much for strangers. Did I tell you that already?"

"What's yar point, Pierce?" Alex glanced at him.

"My point is that if you try to take her, there will be fighting. Why would you put her through such things? Even if you emerge victorious, do you think she will feel the same way about you after you kill one of her uncles, or cousins...or her father?"

Alex slowed and turned to him. "You were a good friend to me father. I'm thankful fer it. But I hold ya to no bonds, Pierce. Yar loyalty to me father brings gratitude, but ya owe me no such allegiance."

"I know," Pierce assured him with an irresolute smile, "but I do owe it to my brother. He's fond of ya."

Alex almost laughed for the first time in days. "So's yar dog."

They reached the others and paid for a dozen sacks of grain. The men hefted two sacks on each shoulder and headed back to the ship.

"I'll pay ya whatever ya want fer her."

Pierce laughed. "How is it possible that such an ugly dog has become so prized?"

"She's a good listener."

"I won't argue that," said Pierce, shifting beneath the weight of the sacks on his shoulders, "but she stays with me. I risked much going to Skye for her. I'll not part with her."

"Ya make the men of Camlochlin sound like blood-lustin' hounds with horns and forked tails. I met them. They didn't seem so terrible. I wouldn't lift me sword to them. I promised her that."

"Then it will be you who she watches die. Sword or not, you're trying to take her from them and give her an out-law's life. Her father will never allow it. Think, I beg you."

He didn't want to think. He wanted to hold her and look at her and bite her mouth. But Pierce was right. He couldn't go back for her now. Her kin might have arrived. He would travel to Madagascar, get his treasure, sell it, and sail back to Camlochlin to make her his wife.

He could wait.

When two native lasses, wearing nothing but skirts, crossed their path, he looked, the same way every other man in attendance looked. But he continued on toward the docks. For not throwing down his sacks and chasing after them, he received a smile from Gustaaf. Alex wondered how the giant was taking Caitrina's absence.

He slept fitfully that night and woke up four times to finish off his rum.

The next morning, Sam found him asleep in the dirt outside the small inn where they were staying. Risa was asleep beside him. Sam almost walked away, letting them sleep, when he heard a loud shout in the distance.

The MacGregors had landed.

Chapter Thirty-Eight

*S*tirling's Pride dropped anchor off the western shore of the Pepper Coast three days after Alex arrived. The landscape was arid and the absence of lush vegetation and tall, shady trees made Trina's eyes burn. There may have been trees here once, but endless rows of stalls had replaced them. Traders lined the roads as far as the eye could see. As men passed her, Trina picked up dialects of Dutch, French, and Portuguese she recognized from Lisbon. She squinted against the glare and almost tripped over a scrawny chicken. She didn't like it here. Not the way she liked Parrot Cay and even Lisbon. There was no music to fill this parched air, only the suffocating hum of hundreds of voices and crying in the distance.

She blushed four shades of scarlet when a native woman, absent of any covering on her breasts, passed her and the men of her clan. She didn't dare look at her uncles and she didn't need to look at her brother or the others to know what they were doing.

She didn't like that Alex was here, somewhere within the thriving, pulsating hustle and bustle. When another dark beauty appeared at her father's side and offered him pleasure, Trina wondered with a sinking heart if Alex was lying in a bed somewhere with a naked native.

"He shouldna' be too difficult to find." Kyle tore his smile away from a pretty lass with skin like smooth onyx and humble breasts that pointed toward the heavens. "'Tis a busy city but our crew will stand oot."

She smiled, grateful that he still considered the crew *their* crew. She prayed they weren't too late. Convincing her kin to sail her to West Africa had been nearly impossible. Getting them to take her to Madagascar would be too much. And too much to ask them to stay away from their lives at home for so long.

"If they are still here. We didna' see *Poseidon's Adventure* docked anywhere."

"The coast is long, Trina. There were many ships. We could have quite easily missed it."

She walked with him along one of the roads leading to the village. Keeping her eyes on the warriors who escorted her while they broke up into groups of three to cover more ground, faster. She assumed Alex would be staying in the village, perhaps in a hut, as he had on their previous stop.

"How did ye do it, Kyle?"

"Do what, love?"

She turned up her face and smiled at him. She owed him so much. Malcolm, too. They'd fought for her, as did Cailean and Edmund.

"How did ye make them listen?"

"Yer father was already willing when ye left the hut. It didna' take too much to get him to realize that yer unhappiness would soon break yer spirit. 'Twas ye who changed his mind, not any of us."

"I'll never ferget what any of ye did fer me. No matter how unimportant ye try to make it, my father has brought me to Africa to reunite me with the man I love. A pirate, Kyle. This was no small feat."

"Yer father loves ye beyond reason," a deep voice said, as her father came up beside her. "And would do anything in his power to make ye happy, though I must be honest, I am quite miserable."

She turned and smiled up at her father and took his hand. "I dinna' mean to make ya unhappy, Papa. I will be safe and I will come home to visit ye and..."

Her words trailed off as a man broke through a group of traders bickering over the price of a sack of barley. She watched him appear and come skidding to a halt when he laid eyes on her. She felt the same way. Everything stopped. Her feet. Her heart. Her breath. How was it possible to love the sight of a man so much that it made her want to race into his arms in front of thirteen Highland warriors? She held her place while she followed Alex's gaze to her father, standing beside her.

"Papa," she said softly, looking up at him.

She didn't wait for him to acknowledge her. Her father knew who he was looking at. She didn't need to tell him, so she turned back to her pirate.

She realized that her kin recognized him as well and were closing in on him slowly, from every position.

Her heart beat madly in her chest. *Dinna' draw yer weapon. Dinna' draw yer weapon*, she begged Alex silently.

He moved slowly toward her, his arms outstretched at his sides. She dared smile. He looked wretched. Like he hadn't slept in days. Her gaze darted to Sam, ever at Alex's side. He offered her a smile and then looked away.

She would make no apologies for smiling at Alex like a love-struck fool when he stepped up to her father and bowed.

"Captain Grant. 'Tis good to see ya again."

"It is?" her father asked incredulously.

"Aye. I'd planned on comin' to Camlochlin to speak with ya."

Her father cut her a glance. It wasn't a deadly one. A good sign.

"We'll speak of it later."

Alex nodded and turned to her. "Miss Grant," he said with his whole heart in his eyes.

"Captain."

He seemed to exhale a long breath and then smiled at her. "I've missed yar voice and have so wanted to hear it again."

Her uncle Colin stepped between them and looked straight into Alex's eyes, halting his interaction with Trina. "We're tired and would like a roof over our heads. Where are ye stayin'?"

"'Tis a small inn just up the road a ways," Alex told them. "Come, I'll see that ya're all fed."

Trina accepted Malcolm's arm when he offered it and let him lead her away. It was better this way. She and Alex needed to keep their hands off each other for just a wee bit longer. Her father would appreciate her thoughtfulness in knowing that he would want time alone with the man for whom she intended to leave Camlochlin. She looked over her shoulder, and sure enough, Alex walked with her father, the latter doing most of the talking. Kyle was with them as well, petting Risa's head as they walked.

"Dinna' fret. They willna' kill him." Malcolm urged her along.

She sighed with both relief and longing to run into his arms. "They have a tendency to gang up on a person."

Her brother looked back. "He seems to be holdin' his own with them. If Faither hasn't run his sword through him yet, he likely willna' do it at all."

"Och, just the thought of it, Cal." She turned around again. This time, Alex winked at her. He would be all right. He wasn't going to make demands or threats. He was no fool. "When d'ye think 'twill be safe fer me to speak with him?"

Her brother shrugged his shoulders. "Later. Mayhap tonight. I will help ye if opposition remains."

She thanked him, then pushed in closer to him. "I hope Cailean is more like ye when he grows up."

Malcolm laughed, a rich, vibrant sound that turned a few female heads. "Cailean is a troublesome pain in the arse at times, but nae more than Darach and Kyle, I suppose."

"Kyle is not troublesome," she defended.

"He stowed away on a pirate ship with ye."

"To protect me."

He smiled, and Trina thought if she hadn't met Alex, Malcolm would be the most striking man she'd ever seen. "Ye defend love, Cal. Is there a lass in yer life the rest of us dinna' know aboot?"

"Hell, nae. I defend my sister. Nothing more."

She smiled up at him and he tweaked her nose the way he used to when she was little.

Even though she found the Pepper Coast somewhat oppressive, it was turning out to be a very good day.

❖

Chapter Thirty-Nine

Alex sat at one of the three tables the innkeeper had butted together in order to house some of his men and the Highlanders while they ate. He liked her family. Aye, he was aware of their more savage nature. He respected who they were and the battles they'd won. If the only way to gain their respect was to compete with them in some friendly rounds with a sword, he was perfectly willing to do it. He would do anything that would get Caitrina into his arms faster.

During the talk he had with her father, Alex did his best to reassure him that he would always do what was best for Caitrina. Soon, he would be rich and providing a good life for her would not be a concern. He would do his best to keep her safe until she decided to live a quieter life and start a family with him in Camlochlin. Aye, he'd promised Connor Grant that one of their homes would be in Camlochlin.

Alex couldn't wait to get started.

His eyes found his love now across the length of the tables. He still feared he might be dreaming. He'd never expected her to come. But why hadn't he? Hadn't she come for him before? How the hell had she convinced her father to bring her back to him? Was there nothing his Highland lass couldn't do? He smiled at her when their eyes met. He couldn't wait to touch her. To kiss her full, pink, saucy mouth. Hell, if this woman had set out all along to win him and get his map, she'd succeeded. He'd give her the map and the world if she wanted it. Wherever she wanted to go, he would take her. Whatever she wanted to do, he would do it with her. He wanted to begin his new adventure with her and he couldn't do that with her kin guarding her.

Risa barreling into the inn first and bounding for him alerted him to David Pierce's approach. Damn it, he liked this dog. He greeted her with a rub behind the ears and a kiss to her head.

"Well, that isn't a good sign."

Alex looked up from his chair at the tall, golden-haired, only living English Highlander known in Scotland, Edmund MacGregor. At his side stood Gaza, Risa's mother.

"What's not a good sign?"

"Risa's reaction to ye, since she's his dog." He hooked his thumb over his shoulder and pointed it at Pierce. "I've seen it happen with both Risa's sire and her dam. Fickleness runs in her blood. Grendel, who was mine, became loyal to my wife. Gaza, who belonged to my wife, became loyal to me, and Goliath, the only male pup, which I wanted fer myself, chose my cousin."

Alex followed Pierce's descent into his chair and ran his palm down Risa's head and throat. "Will she switch her loyalty back to Captain Pierce?"

"It isn't likely."

Only a hint of amusement passed across Alex's eyes when the English captain met his gaze. "Then ya would agree that the dog belongs with me?"

Pierce laughed and Alex wondered if they would ever meet again after Madagascar. He hoped they would.

"Your attempts to relieve me of my dog remain feeble," Pierce said and waved to his brother, who was entering the hut with Malcolm. "Risa has four more sisters at Camlochlin. Perhaps MacGregor here will sell you one."

Alex looked at Edmund. "Do ya think ya can persuade Captain Pierce to part with Risa fer another dog? I would purchase it fer him. Whatever ya ask in coin, I will give ya."

Edmund shook his head. "I would not rob ye by asking fer more than a dog is worth."

"I never had one," Alex confessed. "But how do ya measure a good friend's worth? What was Grendel worth to ya?"

Edmund's cup paused at his lips. He smiled at the red liquid inside. "Caitrina told ye of him then." He drank, then put the cup down and grinned, remembering his faithful friend. "Grendel was unrivaled by anything on this earth."

Alex nodded and put his hand on Risa's head. "Something tells me she has her father's potential."

Edmund was quiet for a moment or two while Alex turned his attention to Caitrina. His heart burned for her across the chasm when he found her already looking at him. His blood felt ablaze in his veins, coursing through him. He wanted to speak to her, hear her voice, touch her—

"Ye understand the value in a friend," Edmund cut through his thoughts. "But what is my cousin worth to ye?"

Alex didn't hesitate in telling him. He knew the tale of Edmund and the Duke of Queensberry's niece. Edmund would agree there was no shame in speaking the words of your heart. "What I once considered priceless fades and dims in the light of the rarest jewel. She's worth me life."

Edmund smiled at him and patted him on the back. "All the dogs in Camlochlin are spoken fer, but I'll see what I can do about Risa."

Alex and his crew laughed and shared their supper and some good drink with the Highlanders of Camlochlin until the sun began to set. It was time for Trina's kin to leave. If the wind was good, they would sail up the North Atlantic and reach the area closest to where any naval ships lurked at about the same time tomorrow night.

They all walked to the docks together, preparing their farewells. Kyle was staying as well. He would be an asset for as long as he wished to stay, as he proved presently when he elbowed Alex and motioned toward the docks.

"Who is that?"

Alex studied the ship docked close to *Poseidon's Adventure*. It hadn't been there this morning. It was not a naval man-o'-war, which was a good thing, since it would have been difficult for David Pierce to explain what he was doing, docked and trying to escape the Pepper Coast with pirates and MacGregors.

A shot rang out and everyone scattered for cover. There was still enough light to see the smoky cloud from the pistol. Enough light to see the Highlanders go into action immediately. A signal from the chief sent Malcolm and Edmund around a row of trader's stalls to capture the shooter unawares, but they would be too late. Colin Mac-Gregor appeared from the shadows and drew his flint-lock pistol, aimed with one eye, cocked it, and fired. He waited, standing in the open until the shooter fell out into the open, clutching his chest.

Kyle raced past his father, and then waited for him behind stacks of hay, carefully concealed with Alex, Caitrina, and some of the others.

"How did they find us so quickly?" Sam asked, "Did Charlie tell them?"

"No. Never." He looked over Sam's shoulder at Caitrina's father. "I heard Captain Pierce askin' what became of Hendrik Andersen."

Colin looked toward the ships and cursed under his breath. "I knew we shoulda' killed him."

Alex was glad they hadn't. He wanted to take care of the man who had betrayed his father personally. "He must have overheard where ya were headed and bought a ride when the ship arrived."

"Who does he sail with?" her father asked. "Navy?"

"Privateers, licensed by law to pillage and plunder. They are sometimes as skilled as soldiers, and they always sail with more men aboard then the navy."

"So we'll likely have a descent fight at least."

Alex smiled at Trina's uncle Colin. He would have made a fearsome pirate. But he'd likely want to be captain.

"I don't like hiding," her father said.

"Nor do I," her uncle replied.

Before both men left the cover of the haystacks, Connor turned to his daughter. "Stay here."

Alex almost smiled at the reaction painting her cheeks scarlet. He didn't smile though. She didn't like orders and sometimes she was going to need to obey them.

"I beg ya," he said to her when she swore under her breath, "obey him. And if not him, then me, yar captain. Stay here."

He didn't wait for her reply but drew his pistol and disappeared with Kyle behind a small stage set up to show slaves.

"Well?" Trina looked at Sam, the only man who hadn't run off on her yet. "What are ye waiting fer? I'm not a child who needs someone to sit with me."

Sam smiled at her. She wasn't sure if he ever had before. She was certain she would have remembered if he had. He was quite striking when he smiled, when he let his guard down, like he was doing now.

"I stay behind because I want ya to know something."

She didn't know what it was or if she wanted to hear it. He gave her no choice when he began speaking.

"Alex is me closest friend. I've spent more time with him than me own brother. I would give me life for him, and never would I betray him."

Trina nodded. She knew he spoke the truth. "I no longer believe that ye would, Mr. Pierce. I was mistaken and I sincerely apologize."

"There's no need fer that. I just wanted to make certain ya knew. 'Tis important to me."

"Why?"

"Because when we leave Madagascar, I'm goin' back to the navy with me brother. Alex won't understand me decision."

Nae, he wouldn't. He would be devastated. Why would Sam do this to him?

"But ya will understand."

She quirked her brow. "I will?"

He nodded and inhaled a breath that expanded his chest. "I will never betray him, and bein' around ya tempts me to do that."

She blinked, too stunned to say a word for a few moments. He cared for her. That was why he'd saved her so many times. She was thankful to him and saddened that she was the cause of Alex's losing his best friend. When she looked away, his voice grew softer.

"I tell ya this because when I go, I don't want ya to think poorly of me."

How could she think poorly of a man who would give up his lifestyle and the friend he loved rather than hurt that friend? She looked up to tell him, but he was gone.

She fully intended to obey her captain and her father, this one last time. She would stay where she was and wait it out, even if it killed her. But then someone called her name, softly, as if they were in pain. It was a man's voice. Alex? Kyle? Her father? She left her hiding place and ran straight into the arms of Hendrik Andersen.

"Miss Grant, lovely to see you again." He took her by the arm and yanked her closer, pointing the tip of his dagger to her throat. "Give a shout to your father, will you? Tell him to gather his men and return to their ship else I will slice your pretty throat."

"Rot in hell."

He returned his dagger to his belt and pulled out a pistol in its stead. "Do it," he said, lifting the barrel to her temple, "or die. My fight is not with them. I merely want the map."

"The instant either one of us alerts my kin to yer position," she snarled at him and reached for his dagger, "they will slaughter ye. Look what they are doing to the men ye arrived with. Ye dinna' have a chance, traitor. Even if ye kill me, ye canna' fight them all. Are ye a fool?"

"I want that map."

"More than yer life?" It was Sam. He met Trina's gaze

for a moment, a cutlass in one hand and a dagger in the other. "If ya shoot her, I'll kill ya before ya draw yar next breath."

Andersen laughed, a cold sound that chilled Trina's bones. "Then perhaps I should kill you first." He turned the pistol on Sam and fired. Trina screamed and tried to break free of him, but he held fast to her wrist. She swiped his dagger across his face, cutting his cheek, and for an instant he let her go. She watched Sam go down. No! No! He couldn't die! Her cries didn't end even when Andersen tossed his used pistol aside and produced another one from his cloak.

"Call your chief now, or I'll blow off your head." He cocked the lock again and Trina closed her eyes.

A shot rang out and she waited to feel something. Pain. Blackness. The end. But nothing came. She opened her eyes to find Andersen clutching a smoking hole in his chest, looking quite stunned before he fell to a heap on the ground.

She looked across his body at Alex standing there, looking like he just saw the end of his own life. He'd saved her. Again. She had much to thank him for. But it would wait. Now she just needed to be in his arms.

✳✳✳

Chapter Forty

The Highlanders gathered around Caitrina and Alex for their final farewells, and for the first time Alex felt a bit intimidated next to them. But it was only because they were trusting him with a treasure more precious than gold and he felt the weight of what it was costing her father.

"Take care of her."

"I will," Alex promised him.

Captain Grant turned to his daughter. "Don't ferget us" was all he seemed to be able to say.

"Papa, I willna' ferget ye." Caitrina flung her arms around his neck and wept softly. "I . . . We will visit soon, and one day, when I am ready to be a mother, we will come home fer good."

"If I'm not there," Connor Grant said with a lighter tone in his voice, which made Alex feel better and Caitrina, as well, when she looked up at him, "'tis because yer mother has killed me fer not bringing ye home straightaway."

Stepping back enough to look him straight in the eyes, Caitrina curled one side of her lips, making her left dimple flash without the right. "Mother willna' kill ye when ye tell her that her favored brother, Uncle Colin, told me all aboot the both of ye in England when James was the king, before Malcolm was born. I know she was a spy fer the militia, that she raided the homes of Presbyterians, and that she made an enemy of her future king, William. I know she followed her own path and didna' let anyone stop her, woman or not. Tell her that her blood flows in the veins of her only daughter. I want to follow my own path, wherever it my lead. I've decided it, and I'm determined to see it through."

Hell, Alex thought, hearing her, she was his. This wondrously strong woman was his. He was proud of her for standing up for what was important to her. So many men he knew wouldn't. He couldn't wait to start his life with her at his side.

After more brief farewells, the MacGregors and the Grants left the West African coast and *Poseidon's Adventure* set sail for Madagascar.

Andersen was finally dead, along with almost all the men he had arrived with. Alex disliked privateers almost as much as he disliked the navy, excluding David Pierce and his soldiers, of course.

Sam had sustained a minor wound to his shoulder from Andersen's pistol and would live to see many other days. Alex was glad for it. He and his friend still had many adventures left. He was eager to get started.

Alex and Caitrina stood together on the poop deck and watched the light of *Stirling's Pride* grow smaller and dimmer in the distance. Alex closed his arms around her from his place behind her and smiled into her neck. "I want to take ya to me bed and stay there with ya until we drop anchor in Madagascar."

She slipped around in his embrace and faced him, her breasts pressed against him. "Alas, it canna' be so."

He leaned down and bit her bottom lip softly. "Why can't it?"

"We have nae herb to prevent a child between us just yet."

Just yet? She wanted his children then. He imagined her heavy with his babe and it made him hard and ready to begin. He prayed he could father them.

"We fergot to procure some on Parrot Cay."

"Nay, we didn't ferget, me love." He pulled a small pouch from his sashes and held it up. "I obtained it before ya refused to come with me."

"Well then, Captain Kidd." She looped her arms more tightly about his neck. "What are we waiting fer?"

They endured one more interruption before they made it to Alex's cabin. This time though, Alex didn't mind.

The sound of a dog barking was what had stopped him on his way to the quarterdeck. Pierce had left the ship. Sam was seeing him off, even now. They would sail together up the coast and meet again at their journey's end.

Why was Risa still here?

He turned, hearing her, and looked at Sam behind her as she cantered toward him, tail wagging.

"She travelin' with us, then?" he asked his friend, hoping she was.

"'Twould seem so," Sam told him, alive and well save for his bandaged shoulder. "She wouldn't leave the ship when David called to her. He tried, too, trust me."

Alex laughed and called Risa to follow him and Caitrina, but a moment after closing the cabin door, it opened again and Alex pushed Risa out.

• • •

Trina opened her eyes again, as the need to look at him overwhelmed her yet again. Alexander Kidd was the most beautiful man she'd ever encountered. Poised above her, he smiled when she looked. He was looking, too. She ran her fingers through his hair, clearing the sun-beaten locks from his eyes. She loved staring into his eyes while he made love to her. It made her feel a bit more wild inside. Like now, the way she groaned and closed her legs around him even higher. Looking at him made her want to run her palms down his strong shoulders and corded belly. He was so hard and tight everywhere.

She arched her back, trembling at the flame scorching her core. Alex held her with one arm and ran his rough palms over her breasts while he kissed her and thrust into her as deep as she would take him.

She watched his release and almost wept at the intimacy of it. She almost wished his seed had a purpose. She took him close and held him while he tossed back his head and clenched his jaw.

When he collapsed beside her, she didn't mind waiting. She loved lying with him and talking with him afterward. She would take him again later and show him little mercy. But now, she wanted to talk to him.

"What did ye think of my kin?"

He smiled, looking into her eyes. "Yar father loves ya, so fer that alone, I like him. Colin MacGregor seems a bit harder around the edges. Kyle told me he was a general, aye?"

Trina nodded and played with his hair. "He's the fiercest of my uncles fer certain, but not with us, not with his kin, and never with his wife and bairns. With them, he is a verra' different man."

"I like him."

Trina smiled and leaned up to kiss his chin. She loved his chin; strong, tapering into a shadowed square, darker in the center from his cleft. Mercy, how she loved him.

"Wait until ye meet the women."

He gazed into her eyes, filling himself with her, her with him. "I've met whom they've reared, Caitrina. I already know they are extraordinary."

"Ye know," she told him, running her hands over the tight, hard planes of his chest and belly, "if ye continue to sweep my heart up in hands with yer pretty words, ye'll leave me nothing but my body, raw and ready to take what I want from ye."

His eyes grew darker on her. "Ya want to take from me, then?"

She nodded and bit one end of her smile. "Aye, I want every inch."

He licked his lips, wanting to give them to her, growing hard and powerful before her. She went after it, lifting herself up and straddling him between her thighs.

"I want to impale myself upon yer sleek lance and have my gyrations guided by my arse in yer hands."

He obliged by cupping her buns and leading her over his tip, then down, upon him. She smiled at his deep groanings and his trembling hands, wanting to push her down hard on all of him, but resisting. Driving him a bit more mad—at least, that was her intention—she leaned down, covering him with her hair, and ran her tongue along his jaw.

"I want to show ye…"—she closed her eyes and buried her face in his neck as she slid down his length, resisting as he grew wider toward the base; he was big and hard and he might always hurt, but she loved it—"that ye've been wasting all yer gifts…"—she bore down, tossing back her head—"wasting all yer gifts on the unworthy. I am what ye truly want and all ye'll ever need."

She rode him like she meant to possess him, like an untamed creature, wild with desire. He held her by her hips, rolling her over him, up and down until he could no longer stop himself from letting go and leaning up to snatch her nipple into his mouth.

With one hand on her arse and the other on the small of her back, he guided her over his length with long, languid strokes until her flame burst into colors she'd never seen before. She thought she was dying. Still, he moved into her, out of her, over and over, stoking the fire, making her scream out in ecstasy while she found sweet, exhilarating, blissful release.

Chapter Forty-One

$\mathcal{H}$is map turned out to be of little help in finding the *Quedagh Merchant*, but, rather, the locations of twenty or so villages. Each village, David Pierce told him, held a clue as to the whereabouts of the treasure. If found in the correct order, the clues would lead to the ship. His father had made certain that if the map had fallen into the wrong hands it would still be near impossible to understand.

But the search to find it was worth it. With a unique blend of African and Asian landscapes, Madagascar was still the most beautiful place on the earth in Alex's estimation. The enormous island boasted more types of palm trees than anyplace else, along with baobab trees, orchids, and herbs. Thankfully they'd arrived in the dry season, otherwise they would have to contend with overbearing heat, monsoons, and tropical cyclones. Trina and Kyle enjoyed watching ring-tailed lemurs leaping through trees and hanging on branches from their tails and chameleons of every size, shape, and color.

The Malagasy people were friendly and quite beautiful and very sympathetic to the pirate way of life. Such sympathy, along with fresh water, an abundance of food, the absence of any type of military, and no rules, made it a particularly popular pirate hideaway. On this trip, Alex avoided the most popular spots, like St. Mary's Island and Ranter Bay, in an effort to keep attention off him and his hunt.

It took almost a month of searching through mangrove swamps and villages, living with the locals, and learning about the rumors surrounding the famous ship *Adventure's Prize*, as they knew it. One family remembered William Kidd and the crew that brought the coveted ship to the island. They directed him to another family, and then to another, each family knowing a different fact about a certain man from the crew.

In the second-to-last village on the map, they found Josoa. Josoa had never met David Pierce or Hendrik Andersen, or any of William Kidd's crew. He'd sailed across the waters with his brothers, his father, and his uncles. They were paid handsomely in gold to leave the ship in the cove and that was what they did. But the gold became a curse and their neighbors robbed them and forced his family to leave their village with nothing. But Josoa knew Captain Kidd had a son. William had spoken highly of him and told them Alexander would be coming for the ship. Josoa had remained in the village, waiting for him to come. He wanted gold to help his family. He wanted it, or he wouldn't give Alex the location.

Alex promised him all the gold he wanted.

Josoa brought them to a secluded cove, one among hundreds of coves along the coast. There, hidden quite well within the dense mangroves, noisy birds, and mosquitoes was the five-hundred-ton ship. She stood tall and, despite the overgrowth of vines along her masts and her sails stripped, the *Quedagh Merchant* was beautiful. His father's prize. He would have liked to keep the Armenian brigantine. But it was impossible. She was too recognizable. He'd have to leave her after he took the treasure she carried. Alex could live a good life and leave enough for his children. His crew need never pillage again. They would be rich for two lifetimes.

But that wouldn't stop them from seeking more adventures on the high seas. Pirating was in their blood.

But with every treasure comes the worry that someone can take it from you. So, after dividing their shares, Alex decided to bring his back to Camlochlin.

"We'll stay fer as long as ya want," he told Caitrina while they sat around a fire after a delicious meal of fresh meat and fruit. "A year, perhaps. Long enough to wed ya."

She smiled and at least four of the men around the fire beamed at her even as she clasped her hand in Alex's.

"Will ya be stayin' with us then, Gustaaf?" Alex asked him, grinning at the Dutchman's obvious fondness for his beloved.

"If the captain would have me, Captain."

"Of course, he will have ye, Gustaaf," Caitrina promised him. "We love ye. Dinna' we, Alex?"

His smile didn't falter. Besides Sam and Kyle, Gustaaf was the only man whose loyalty Alex completely trusted. "We do."

"I'll be sailin', too," Mr. Bonnet announced. "I have no family but this."

Alex raised his cup to that and pulled Caitrina closer. She smelled good, like lavender with a hint of salt underneath. He caught Sam watching them and raised his cup again.

"Where should we sail next, Quartermaster?" he asked his friend.

Sam smiled and then looked at Caitrina in a way he never had before, with adoration. "I won't be sailin' with ya again, Captain."

Alex lowered his cup and his smile faded. Sam loved her. Did he love her enough to leave everything he'd known for eight years?

"How long has this been decided, Sam?"

His friend shrugged. "Fer a time now. I need to go."

Alex couldn't believe what he was hearing with his ears. Sam was in love with Caitrina and had to leave because of it? Once they parted and... "What do ya plan on doin' then?"

"David," Sam told him. "I'm goin' with David to take me place among his men."

"As a naval soldier?" Hell, no, this wasn't what he was hearing. "Don't be a fool, Sam. I can live with yar feelins' fer me wife. Ya're not the only one who feels them."

"I can't live with them," Sam told him. "I'll be yar ally in the navy, Alex, watchin' yar back from another angle."

He was serious. He was sailing back with his brother. Alex wanted to be angry with him for choosing the life of a soldier over being a pirate. But he loved and admired Sam for his steadfast allegiance, even over his own heart. This was the man he'd come to trust after his father was hanged.

"'Twas an honor to sail with ya, Sam. I'll miss ya, brother."

"Aye." Sam nodded. "I'll miss ya, too. I suggest we elect Kyle MacGregor to succeed me."

Everyone nodded. No one smiled.

• • •

Trina knew Alex's heart was heavy because of Sam's leaving. She certainly wouldn't rush his mourning over the loss of his friend. But she could help ease his pain by offering him comfort. He found it each night in her arms, and in return he gave her his passion, unrestrained and a bit wicked. He showered her with jewels and the finest skeins of silk and she showered him with love and with praise for the man in full that he was. By the time they sailed for Camlochlin, his heaviness had lifted and at night, sometimes at the helm, he thanked her for it.

She didn't care anymore about living a risky, adventurous life. She just wanted a life with Alex.

She woke on the third day of the journey home to a wet tongue and foul breath.

A life with Alex and his dog.

On a mission to escort a Scottish lass to the royal court, General Daniel Marlow unexpectedly falls for his beautiful, spirited charge. But when he learns her shocking secret, Marlow must choose between love—or betrayal of queen and country...

Please see the next page for a preview of

The Scandalous Secret of Abigail MacGregor.

Chapter One

*F*aither! A letter was waitin' fer us in Broadford. 'Tis from London!"

Abigail MacGregor looked up from her embroidery and watched her twin brothers, Tamhas and Braigh, cut across her father's private solar and hand him the folded parchment.

"Who is it from, Faither?" She set her embroidery down and rose up out of her chair. She smiled at her mother, convalescing in her settee by the window, and pulled her blanket up to her chin.

"Lads," he said to his sons instead of answering her. "Go fetch yer brother and yer uncles."

"Which ones?" Braigh asked.

"All of 'em."

"Robbie, who is it from?" his wife asked softly when the boys were gone.

"'Tis from...the queen."

Abby turned to her father. Her mother sat straight up. Very few people in England knew Davina MacGregor was the true firstborn daughter of King James and Ann Hyde. She'd been secluded in an abbey her whole life, unknown to her sisters or anyone else, to ensure a Catholic successor should James die without a son. Those who suspected her existence didn't know she lived with the MacGregors somewhere on Skye. So why was the queen, her mother's sister, penning them a letter?

"What does she say?" her mother asked, her voice shaken.

Her father read the letter. She hadn't seen his face drain of so much color since his beloved wife came down with the fever three months ago.

"She says..." He stopped and looked up from the parchment, his blue eyes startlingly vivid. "She says she knows of ye and she commands yer attendance in London. She wants assurances that ye have nae plans to challenge her for the throne."

Abby shook her head. Her mother couldn't leave Camlochlin. The exceptionally longer winter had struck her sleight body like a plague. She was just beginning to recover and it was still brisk outside.

Her father shared her thoughts, proving it when he held up his palm to stop her mother from speaking. "Ye're not goin', Davina. My mind is set."

Thank God. Abby gave a soft sigh of relief. When her father set his mind one way, he rarely moved it again.

"Robbie, my love, how do ye know I was going to suggest anything of the sort?"

He looked at the letter clutched in his hands and then at her. "Ye will when ye hear the rest. But wait a moment fer the others. 'Tis something everyone should hear."

Abby swallowed and sat down beside her mother. What was it? What was so important that everyone needed to hear? She worried that life here would change now that the monarchy knew of her mother's existence.

She and her mother didn't have to wait too long before her uncles arrived. Her brother wasn't with them.

"Where's Adam?" her father asked the twins.

"He was with Murron MacDonald," Tamhas said.

"He said he'd be here shortly," Braigh added.

Her father didn't wait. When he told them who'd penned the letter, Abby's uncle Tristan poured them all whisky from her father's decanter.

"She threatens to send her full army to Skye to come get her if Davina refuses to go to England." He stopped when his wife gasped. He looked around at his brothers and his brother-in-law to gauge their reactions. He'd already decided Davina wasn't going. That meant the army would come. Their lives and their family's lives were at risk. Robert MacGregor was chief to his clan but he still discussed his decisions with them. If they all didn't agree with this one, what would he do? "She also commands," he continued without looking at the parchment again, "that my wife go with no Highlander to accompany her, but with the queen's personal guards only."

Everyone remained silent and still while his words settled on them.

"I must go." Her mother broke the silence and swept her blanket off. Abby held it in place in her lap.

"Are ye mad to think we'd let ye go, Davina?" her uncle Colin asked.

"Mayhap the fever has returned," said her uncle Connor Grant.

"Should I get Isobel?" her uncle Tristan asked, bringing more relief to Abby, knowing that they agreed with her father.

"I can't let people I love die because of me. Not again."

"We need to alert the other clans."

"Aye, Tristan," her father agreed. "I dinna' think the queen knows where in Skye we are. She'll send her army throughout."

"Robbie," her mother pleaded woefully. "Please. I can make it to London and stop any fighting from taking place. Let me do it."

Abby had heard tales of St. Christopher's Abbey, where her mother grew up, and how her royal family was responsible for hiring a madman to burn it down with the more than twenty nuns who raised her inside. She would have died as well if Abby's father hadn't rescued her from the flames. Her mother didn't want to be responsible for more deaths.

How had Anne found out about her? Had she always known? Did she really just want assurances that the first-born heir to England's throne didn't want the seat?

"Davina," her father said softly. "My mind is set, my love."

"What of our kin?" her mother insisted. "Our bairns, Rob. What if they are killed?"

"I will go in her stead, Faither!"

Hell, Abby wasn't afraid to go to England. Her mother was happy just where she was. Abby would make her aunt see that. She would win her favor for her mother's sake and try to guarantee some kind of protection for the clan. Protection against the loss of their name and their beliefs. She wasn't afraid. What was the worst that could happen? It wasn't like her pistol-swinging brothers were coming with her. Mayhap she might even meet a handsome knight like the ones from her grandmother's books. She'd be escorted by the queen's personal guards, so nothing . . . She blinked at her father, who was staring at her like she'd just sprouted a second head.

"Abigail, d'ye sincerely think I'd let ye go to England alone?"

Her eyes glittered like the frost on the mountaintops outside the castle, but there was nothing cold about her. Like her mother, everyone at Camlochlin loved Abby. She fit in with everyone—whether in the kitchen, in the sewing chamber, or on the practice field. The chief's only daughter won every heart, especially her father's.

"Ye dinna' have a choice, Faither. Our clan depends on it. I will do whatever I must to keep us safe. The royal army would do much damage and eventually they would find us. I'm not going to sit back while my beloved faither and uncles fight and possibly die in a battle. I'm going. My mind is set."

Colin was the only uncle who smiled. It was slight, but Abby caught it.

"Ye will go over my dead body, Abby," her mother told her sternly.

"And 'twill be dead indeed if *ye* try to go, Mother." She shook her head and turned to the men again. "Ye all know that one day I want to be the chief. Though I'm a woman, I want to prove to ye that I'm worthy of the title."

Colin raised his cup to her and smiled. "Ye're braw, lass. Ye'll have my 'aye' when the times comes fer the next chief to be chosen." He turned to her father and winked at him. "Not that I want that day to come any time soon, brother. I just think she's a better choice than Adam—"

"I dinna' give a damn about that," her father shouted. "Ye think my only daughter should go to meet our enemy alone?"

"Nae, of course not," Colin insisted. "Why the hell would ye think that? We'll stay a day behind her."

Tristan smiled. So did Connor. Abby loved them all.

Looking at them, she understood why she waited for a certain kind of man.

"I canna' let her go." Her father turned to her. "Ye ask the impossible."

She smiled softly and went to him, taking his arm in hers. "Faither, I love ye with all my heart, but I didna' ask."

Abby penned her reply to the queen herself and without waiting for her father's approval, she rode to Broadford and made arrangements to have the letter delivered to St. James's Palace. Upon her return to Camlochlin, she met up with her brother, who was returning from Torrin.

"Where were ye today, Adam?" she asked her eldest brother, riding her surefooted mount around his appropriately named dog, Goliath. "Faither sent fer ye and ye didna' come."

Adam exhaled a long breath and turned his eyes toward Camas Fhionnairigh. Abby knew where he'd been and what he'd been doing instead of seeing to his duty. She didn't blame Murron MacDonald. Adam was striking, with raven hair, pale skin like their mother's, and even lighter blue-gray eyes. He was a spectacular blend of both her parents.

"Aye, a letter from London. The twins told me." He swung his cool gaze to her. "Ye know I have nae interest in anything English."

"It seems ye have nae interest in anything that doesna' come in a skirt."

He smiled and Abby thought it a pity that he was so arrogant and flippant about his life.

"Ye are practically handing me yer birthright, Adam."

He shrugged. "Who says I want it?"

He didn't. He'd made it clear on more occasions than

one. He didn't want to rule. He wanted to raid, women mostly. That was fine with her. Less opposition later. She smiled.

"Give it to me then." She waited for his answer. If he handed his birthright over to her, no one would contest it. "Why wait?"

He laughed, infuriating her that he found his birthright a matter of jest.

"Why d'ye want the weight of our clan's survival on yer shoulders?" he asked her. "Find a husband and have babies, sister."

Oh, she wanted to punch him in the face. She never wanted to punch anyone so badly. "Adam, ye—"

"I say that because I love ye," he cut her off. "I dinna' want to see ye carry such responsibility on yer back. Ye dinna' understand how crushing being chief will be."

"And ye do?"

"I've been groomed fer it my whole life. I have a better idea than ye have aboot it."

She didn't care. It didn't matter how hard it was to be chief. It was all she wanted. And she almost always got what she wanted. She was strong, independent, and loyal to her clan. Her father knew she was as stubborn as him, and that was why she remained unwed. She wasn't opposed to marriage. She was opposed to marriage to a man who wasn't right for her. She would know her future husband when she met him, and until then she would remain unwed.

"'Twas a letter from the queen," she told her brother, wanting him to hear her decision from her own lips. "She knows of Mother's existence." Ah, finally, a reaction other than a glib smile. "Queen Anne has commanded Mother to travel to London with English guards."

"She canna' go."

"She isna' going. I am."

He laughed again and she smiled with him but there was no humor in her eyes. Let them all think she was mad or foolish. This was her clan and she wasn't going to let harm come to them because of a queen's command.

"And Faither has agreed to this?" her brother asked.

"He will. If I dinna' go, the queen has promised to send an army here."

They discussed it more, with Adam finally taking the matter more seriously. The thought of him leading the clan someday riled her. Thank God that she came from a line of strong, fearless women who knew what they wanted and took it. They would support her. They had to.

She was going to England with or without her father's permission, and one day she was going to be chief.

✦✦

Chapter Two

General Daniel Marlow of the Order of the Garter remained still while his valet dressed him. Hell, he hated formal attire, with all its pomposity and lace. His thick embroidered brocade waistcoat and justacorps made him feel heavier on his feet. He could barely move his damn head around the magnitude of heavy lace at his throat. His wrists, too, were shackled in it. And who in damnation decided to make shoes with high heels for feet the size of his? His squashed toes only added to his increasingly foul mood. He'd rather be wearing his uniform, though even that was a bit stiff and overdone.

"Think the queen would take offense to me arriving in my coat, breeches, and boots?"

His valet patted the creases in his turned-out lapels and shook his head. "No, my lord. Her Majesty takes no offense in anything you do. But it's always to your benefit to please her."

Aye, the queen had bestowed many gracious gifts upon him. She made him the Duke of Darlington, granted him the rank of captain-general of her entire army, and made him a knight of the Order of the Garter, the highest order of chivalry. She didn't have to grant him such honor. He had pledged his loyalty to the throne, as his father and grandfather had done before him. Regardless of who sat there or what they gave or didn't give him, he would serve them. Presently, he served Anne Stuart.

"She is so madly in love with you, I doubt she would care if you arrived in a moth-eaten sack."

Daniel flashed a glare at the old man but didn't admonish him for speaking so of the queen. Albert Carlisle had been in his service for fifteen years and Daniel was quite fond of him. What they spoke of in private was no one's damn concern.

Besides, Albert was correct. It was obvious to all that the queen loved him. Her husband either knew or he was a fool. Of course, Daniel didn't share her feelings, and up to a few weeks ago, she hadn't overly pursued him. But that changed; when last he saw her, she had commanded his body to her bed. Adultery was not part of chivalry, but instead of outright refusing her, he agreed to attend one of her indulgent balls and to meeting her somewhere alone after that.

"If you intend on giving her her way tonight," his valet pressed on boldly, "I wouldn't suggest a bed where you have to undress. Dropping your hose and—"

"I don't," Daniel cut him off, "intend on giving her her way tonight."

"A command was given, Sir Daniel," Albert reminded him, leaving his side to reach for the powdered wig on Daniel's dresser.

"No." Daniel halted him from lifting it to his head. "I'll not wear that ridiculous thing. And I won't disobey her. I know how to speak to her."

He hooked his finger under the layers of lace at his neck and tugged. "She'll see my way of thinking is best."

Albert shrugged his frail shoulders and bent to tie the bows on Daniel's shoes. "I hope you're correct, my lord."

Daniel took him by the shoulders and straightened him. "I'll tie them. I'm not an invalid."

Albert nodded, as stone-faced as he had been the day Daniel met him. Only now his skin was more weathered, his eyes, wiser. "If you're incorrect, though, shall I have the cooks prepare breakfast?"

Daniel smiled at him, then ushered him out the door.

Alone, he tied his ridiculous shoes, then combed his fingers through his short hair. On the way out the door to his dressing chamber, he untied the colossal bow around his neck and let it hang open in lacy waves down his coat. He ignored Albert's disapproval at his less than formal appearance when he descended the stairs and passed him on the way to the foyer.

"Is the carriage ready?" he asked while the butler pulled open the front door to allow his exit.

"It is, my lord," Albert answered him, hurrying forward.

"Good. I'll be home by midnight."

"Very good, sir," his faithful valet called out just before the door closed.

Daniel stepped out into the brisk night air, put on his feathered tricorn hat, and stepped up into his carriage.

He was a decorated warrior, honored in battle on three separate continents. He'd fought for many causes over the last fifteen of his thirty-one years of life. He'd never lost a battle or a brother on the field. Whatever he faced, he faced with firm conviction and without fear.

But tonight his heart beat harder and his nerves grew as stiff as his justacorps.

Tonight he was going to refuse his queen.

The palace was brimming with every haughty nobleman in the kingdom. When Daniel stepped into the queen's ballroom and swept his tricorn from his head, their daughters and some of their wives turned their heads to watch him. Almost all of them smiled. He set his eyes on the woman at the end of the long chamber, seated on an elaborate throne, her expression harder to read.

"Sir Daniel?" She grazed her dark eyes down the length of him then back up to his neck and bare head. "You appear before me in undress?"

"Hardly, Your Majesty." He smiled, bowing to her and then straightening again. "I merely prefer comfort to propriety. Besides"—he lowered his voice and looked into her eyes while he stepped boldly closer—"I thought you might like this." He pulled the lace from around his neck and handed the pile to her. "The lace is imported from Spain. It would better serve you."

"You presume to know what I like, Sir Daniel?" She kept her eyes on his while she raised the fabric to her nose.

"It's my duty to know everything about you, my lady."

Finally, she smiled at him, handing her lace over to a handmaiden at her side. "And your wig? Did you think I might like that, as well?"

He shook his head and returned her smile. "Not the wig but the true fire beneath."

Her gaze rose to his deep auburn hair and she sighed with delight. Aye, he knew her well. He hated himself for it sometimes, but taking advantage of her affection was sometimes the only way to escape her. He gave her what she wanted; the assurance of his devotion. And in return, she granted him freedom to mingle.

His smile broadened on Lady Anabelle Saunders, the Duke of Hanover's daughter. But he didn't go to her. Instead, he cut a path to Jeremy Embry, Viscount of Stockton, and his wife, Amanda. He'd known them both for years and sought their friendship among his enemies.

"Tonight they'll dream of hacking off your bare head."

Daniel pivoted on his damn high-heeled shoes and raked his eyes over every eye that looked at him unkindly because of jealousy and resentment. He didn't give a rat's arse what they thought of him. The only opinion that mattered was the queen's. And he kept it favorable with a few well-timed words and a gift now and then.

"Why must you provoke them to dislike you more?" Stockton asked him, handing him a drink.

"I don't provoke them. Their inadequacies do."

Amanda laughed and slipped her arm through his. "When are you coming to dinner at our home? We've missed you at the last two gatherings."

"You know how much I dislike all this, Manda."

"How am I supposed to find you a wife if you never attend any gatherings?"

"I've no time for a wife."

"Oh nonsense, Daniel." She slapped his arm softly and looked up at him. "You protect women from her."

"What's wrong with that?" he asked and smiled at her husband.

"It leaves you with an empty bed and empty arms."

She might be correct, but there was little he could do about it presently.

"His bed isn't always empty," Stockton told his wife quietly. "He's simply discreet about his affairs."

Daniel cut him a quick glare before offering a pretty raven-haired woman a slight smile. "As I wish you were, Stockton."

"Whom have you been with?"

Daniel laughed, moving his gaze to Stockton's wife. "Amanda, that's not a proper question to—"

"Lady Eleanor Hollister, for one," her husband confided.

Daniel stared at him while Amanda gasped and opened her eyes wider.

"She's pretty enough," Amanda decided, still holding on to his arm. "But her father is a heavy gambler. He's known at all the tables and is slowly losing the family fortune."

"I don't plan on wedding her, Manda."

"That's wise, dear." Stockton's wife smiled at him and then scowled at the man coming toward them with the queen on his arm.

Richard Montagu, Duke of Manchester and the queen's cousin, quirked his thin lips into a sneer when he reached Daniel and his friends. His salutation was brief but his eyes lingered on Daniel long enough to make Amanda squirm beside him. Daniel's body, on the other hand, went stiff with the authority of his rank and confidence of his skill.

"What is this wise thing you've done, Darlington?" Montagu asked. "Tell us"—he glanced at Anne, then continued—"so that we may believe in the impossible."

The queen deserted her escort, much to Montagu's indignation, and took Daniel's arm from Amanda's grasp. "Pay him no heed," she offered her favored knight and ignored her cousin. "He is jealous of the favor I show you. Are you not, Richard?"

Montagu turned two different shades of crimson and glowered at Daniel's ill-concealed smile. They were enemies. Daniel didn't care who knew it. "Nay, ma'am, I am merely . . ."

"Riddled with resentment, Richard. Do not deny it."

"Of course, Your Majesty." Montagu gave in with no further quarrel.

Daniel had offered him friendship over the years. Montagu had refused, choosing instead to let his covetous heart rule him. He constantly brought his false accusations against Daniel before the queen, trying diligently to discredit him in her eyes. Daniel had no use for him and preferred being away from his company.

"You are dismissed." The queen waved her hand at him, then turned to Daniel, dismissing her cousin from her thoughts as well.

Her cousin didn't want to go and remained in his spot, casting his murderous glare on Daniel.

Daniel showed him no mercy and smiled in return. "That will be all then, Montagu."

Standing to his right, Stockton snickered.

"You're nothing but a guardsman's son," Montagu accused through clenched teeth. "You may have my dear cousin fooled, but I see right through you."

"What is it you see, Montagu?" Daniel challenged him, with a dangerous curl of his mouth.

Before the queen's cousin replied, she held up her palm to stop him. Daniel wished she wouldn't defend him. It always denied him the privilege of taking Montagu to the lists. "In case you have forgotten, Richard, Sir Daniel quelled a planned invasion by my stepbrother, James, last year, ending a Jacobite uprising. Since then, he has subdued three other rebellions started by James's supporters. He fought in Spain and in the Colonies in the War of Spanish Succession, and he is the most loyal among all my men. If you insist on continuing to insult him, I will have no other choice but to have you removed from my presence."

She didn't wait for her cousin to agree, but tugged Daniel toward the entrance, dismissing the rest of her escorts. "I wish to have words with you in private, General Marlow." Her powdered face glowed against her periwig. Her rosy lips pursed as if she already imagined kissing him.

He went with her, as eager to get this over with as she was to begin. He let her lead him to her private gardens.

"I'm going to Somerset in a se'nnight," she began while they strolled. "I want you to escort me."

"And your husband?"

"He will remain here."

Her affections had indeed grown then, as did her boldness. She wanted an affair with him. Every man in the palace tonight would have leaped at the chance to bed Her Majesty, the Queen. But she was wed and his duty was to protect her from harm, not lead her into it.

"You risk the scorn of every nobleman inside your palace," he said, his voice blending in with the darkness. "Bedding me will give your enemies more reason to depose you."

"My enemies are those nasty Jacobites. I have a plan to keep them away. But I'm not concerned with that now. I don't care about what my subjects think. I want you inside me."

He closed his eyes. She wasn't used to being told no. Was he a fool to let morality guide him? He always did. He couldn't help it. Some called it a flaw. Some called it honor.

"My lady—"

She pushed him back against a tree and pressed herself to him. "Anne."

"Anne," he whispered against the mouth she tilted toward his. It wasn't that he didn't desire her at this moment, her breasts crushed to his chest, her hips pressed to his. She was his for the taking. A queen, offering herself up like a sacrifice. How easy to just . . .

"Please, Daniel. I know from whence your reservations flow. You see, I know much about you as well. You grew up under the tutelage of the kingdom's most learned master of the Arthurian legend, Geoffrey Hollister. I know you are a man of value and it is one of the virtues I love most about you. You must think me a terrible harlot, but I love you and I wish to have you."

Daniel didn't fully understand how dangerous this was for him until this very moment. If he broke her heart, she would hate him and God only knew what she'd do. He'd seen what she had done to a woman who showed him her favor openly, kissed him in front of the queen. She wouldn't think twice about hanging him or tossing him into some prison if he refused her. She didn't need to prove her charges. She was the damned queen. He could take what she offered and make her yield in a dozen different ways, but in the end, that too could end badly for him.

He had to use caution and do his best to spare his feelings. Ideally, he wanted her to continue to hold him in high affection without forcing him to abandon his values.

"You say I am a man of value and you love that the most about me."

She nodded, her breath growing heavier, her hands more urgent upon him. She tore at his justacorps but the brocade was too thick to rip.

"My lady, if I do what you want, I won't be the man

you lost your heart to." He captured her wrists and looked into her eyes. He recognized the fury brewing in their dark depths.

"Is it the Viscount of Stockton's wife? What is her name? Amanda? Is she the reason you don't want me?"

Damn. This was precisely what he feared when he took a woman to his bed, which, contrary to what his friend claimed, didn't happen often. He sacrificed much to please the throne and keep the queen's wrath off perfectly innocent women. But it angered him that this jealousy could bring harm to his dear friend. She should be careful, lest she get what she wanted. His expression darkened on her, and, still holding her wrists, he pushed them behind her back.

"Who said I didn't want you?" He leaned over her, enjoying the frantic beat of her heart against him. If she wanted him, then he would let her know what she was getting. He was no knight in the bedchamber, but a merciless bastard who took long to satisfy and who didn't stop until he was. He liked it hard and rough, passionate and possessive. "But know this, if I have you, I will take until there is little left. Do you understand, my lady? I will take your heart. You will never deny me from taking what I want, and I will rule over you."

Her anger over Amanda faded into indignation tinged in fear. "How dare you—"

He took her mouth with raw possession and kissed her until he felt her knees grow weak. He withdrew and stared into her eyes. "The first thing you will need to do is get rid of your husband."

She pushed away from him, her eyes wide with fear and self-restraint. "I will need time to think over my decision."

"Of course." He bowed.

She watched him and smiled while he straightened. "I mentioned my plan for the Jacobites earlier."

He nodded, thankful for having succeeded in getting her off him without insulting her.

"Captain Lewis is set to leave in the morning with a small number of his men," she told him. "They're going to the Highlands to escort a high-ranking Jacobite chief's daughter back here to be my handmaiden."

Why the hell would she want a Jacobite in her castle? "What's your plan?"

She shrugged her shoulders and waved away his question. "Peace. If I keep one of their daughters here with me, they won't attack."

Not necessarily, Daniel thought. But still a dreadful undertaking. He was thankful that it wasn't him that had to do it. The only thing he hated more than the Highlands were Jacobites. He'd fought enough of them to know they were among the most fearsome men who lived. He also knew they hated Anne, and William and Mary before her. They were rebels with no loyalty to the throne or obedience to any law. They were everything he was trained up to despise. Traitors to their king, or in this case, queen. Such people deserved the noose.

"But I think you should go fetch her instead."

Daniel smiled, sure that he'd heard her incorrectly. "Me?"

"You." She confirmed with a nod. "I think it best you take a few weeks away to curb this ravishing desire you have for me and to put from your mind these mad notions of ruling over me."

She turned away and raised her palm over her shoulder in case he thought to follow her. He didn't.

"You will leave at dawn. Travel sparsely and out of

uniform when you reach the Highlands. You know how Highlanders despise the English. See Captain Lewis about the rest of the details. And Daniel? I will miss you."

He stared after her. Disgusted and angry. Damn morality. Damn it to hell.

Fall in Love with Forever Romance

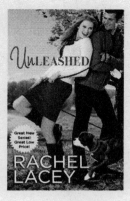

UNLEASHED
by Rachel Lacey

Cara has one rule: Don't get attached. It's served her well with the dogs she's fostered and the children she's nannied. But one smile from her sexy neighbor has her thinking some rules are made to be broken. Fans of Jill Shalvis will fall in love with this sassy, sexy debut!

MADE FOR YOU
by Lauren Layne

She's met her match... she just doesn't know it yet. Fans of Jennifer Probst and Rachel Van Dyken will fall head over heels for the second book in the Best Mistake series.

Fall in Love with Forever Romance

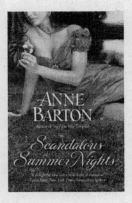

SCANDALOUS SUMMER NIGHTS
by Anne Barton

Fans of Tessa Dare, Julia Quinn, and Sarah MacLean will love this charming and wickedly witty new book in the Honeycote series about the passion—and peril—of falling in love with your brother's best friend.

HE'S NO PRINCE CHARMING
by Elle Daniels

A delightful retelling of the classic tale of *Beauty and the Beast* with a wonderful, sensual, and playful twist that fans of Elizabeth Hoyt won't want to miss!

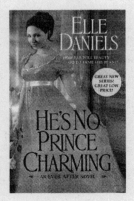

Fall in Love with Forever Romance

THE BURIED
by Shelley Coriell

"It's cold. And dark. I can't breathe."

Grace and "Hatch" thought they'd buried the past, but a killer on a grisly crime spree is about to unearth their deepest fears. Don't miss the next gripping thriller in the Apostles series.

SHOOTING SCARS
by Karina Halle

Ellie Watt has been kidnapped by her thuggish ex-boyfriend, leaving her current lover, Camden McQueen, to save the day. And there's nothing he won't do to rescue Ellie from this criminal and his entourage of killers in this fast-paced, sexy *USA Today* bestseller!

Fall in Love with Forever Romance

THE WICKED WAYS OF ALEXANDER KIDD
by Paula Quinn

The newest sinfully sexy Scottish romance in *New York Times* bestselling author Paula Quinn's Highland Heirs series, about the niece of a Highland chief who stows away on a pirate ship, desperate for adventure, and the pirate captain whose wicked ways inflame an irresistible desire...